The Proper Place

O. Douglas

Must Have Books
503 Deerfield Place
Victoria, BC
V9B 6G5
Canada

ISBN 9781773239033

Copyright 2023 – Must Have Books

TO ISABELLA CREE,

MY FRIEND

It was a wonderful flute! A note was heard all over the mansion, in the garden, and in the forest, for many miles into the country, and with the sound came a storm that roared, "Everything in its proper place!" And then the baron flew, just as if he were carried by the wind, right out of the mansion and straight into the herdsman's cottage. But in the dining-room the young baroness flew to the upper end of the table, and the tutor got the seat next to her, and there the two sat as if they were a newly-married couple. An old count, one of the oldest families in the county, remained undisturbed in his seat of honour . . . a rich merchant and his family who were driving in a coach and four were blown right out of the coach, and could not even find a place behind it, two rich farmers who had grown too rich to look after their fields were blown into the ditch. It was a dangerous flute!

Fortunately it burst at the first note, and that was a good thing; it was put back in the player's pocket again, and everything was in its proper place.

HANS ANDERSEN.

CHAPTER I

"This young gentlewoman had a father
—O, that 'had' how sad a passage 'tis."

All's Well that Ends Well.

"How many bedrooms does that make?"

Mrs. Jackson asked the question in a somewhat weary tone. Since her husband had decided, two months ago, that what they wanted was a country-house, she had inspected nine, and was frankly sick of her task.

The girl she addressed, Nicole Rutherfurd, was standing looking out of the window. She turned at the question and "I beg your pardon," she said, "how many bedrooms? There are twelve quite large ones, and eight smaller ones."

They were standing in one of the bedrooms, and Nicole felt that never had she realised how shabby it was until she saw Mrs. Jackson glance round it. That lady said nothing, but Nicole believed that in her mind's eye she was seeing it richly furnished in rose-pink. Gone the faded carpet and washed-out chintzes; instead there would be a thick velvet carpet, pink silk curtains, the newest and best of bedroom suites, a rose-pink satin quilt on the bed. In one of Hans Andersen's tales he tells how, at a dinner-party, one of the guests blew on a flute made from a willow in the ditch, and behold, every one was immediately wafted to his or her proper place. "Everything in its proper place," sang the flute, and the bumptious host flew into the herdsman's cottage—you know the story? Nicole thought of it now as she looked at the lady, who might reign in her mother's stead at Rutherfurd.

She was a stout woman, with a broad kind face under an expensive hat, and she stood solidly beside the old wash-stand and looked consideringly before her.

"We have the twelve rooms where we are," she told Nicole. "Deneholm's the name of our house in Pollokshields—but, of course, that's including maids' rooms. Four public rooms, a conservatory off the library, and central heating. Oh, Deneholm's a good house and easy worked for its size: I'll be sorry to leave it."

"And must you?" Nicole asked.

Mrs. Jackson laid a fat hand on the towel rail, shaking it slightly, as if to test its soundness, and said:

"Well, you see, it's Mr. Jackson. He's making money fast—you know how it is, once you get started, money makes money, you can't help yourself—and he thinks we've been long enough in a villa, he wants a country-house. It's not me, mind you, I'd rather stay on at Deneholm. . . . D'you know Glasgow at all?"

"Hardly at all," Nicole said, and added, smiling, "but I've often wanted to see more of it."

Mrs. Jackson beamed at her. "You'd like it. Sauchiehall Street on a spring morning with all the windows full of light pretty things! or Buchanan Street on a winter afternoon before Christmas! I've had many a happy hour, I can tell you, going in and out of the shops. It'll be an awful change for me if Mr. Jackson carries out his plan of living always in the country. Shop windows are what I like, and this"—she waved her hand towards the window with its view of lawn and running water, and golden bracken on the hillside—"this gives me no pleasure to speak of. I haven't the kind of figure for the country, nor the kind of feet either. Fancy me in a short tweed skirt and those kind of shoes—brogues, d'you call them? A nice fright I'd be. I need dressing."

She looked complacently down at her tight form in its heavily embroidered coat-frock—her fur coat had been left in the hall—and said solemnly, "What I'd be like if I didn't corset myself I know not."

Nicole had a momentary vision of the figure of Mrs. Jackson unfettered, and said hurriedly, "It's—it's comfortable to be plump."

Mrs. Jackson chuckled. "I doubt I'm more than 'plump'—that's just your polite way of putting it—but what I say is I repay dressing. I'm not the kind that looks their best in deshabille. See me in the morning with a jumper and a skirt and easy slippers—I'm a fright. But when I get on a dress like this over a good pair of corsets, and a hat with ospreys, and my pearls, I'm not bad, am I?"

Nicole assured her that the result left nothing to be desired, and then, anxious to break away from such a personal subject, she said, "I do hope you will begin to like the country if you have to live in it. I think you'll find there are points about it."

Mrs. Jackson moved towards the door shaking her head dubiously.

"Not me. I like to have neighbours and to hear the sound of the electric cars, and the telephone always ringing, and the men folk going out to business and coming back at night with all the news. You need to be born in the country to put up with it. I fair shiver when I think of the dullness. Getting up in the morning and not a sound except, mebbe, hens and cows. One post a day and no evening papers unless you send for them. Nothing to do except to take a walk in the forenoon and go out in the car in the afternoon."

"There's always gardening," Nicole reminded her.

"Not for me," said Mrs. Jackson firmly. "I like to see a place well kept, but touch it I wouldn't. For one thing I couldn't stoop. Now, I suppose you garden by the hour and like it? Ucha? And tramp about the hills and take an interest in all the cottages? Well, as I say, it's all in the way you're brought up, but it's not my idea of pleasure."

Nicole laughed as they left the room together. She began to feel more kindly towards this talkative and outspoken lady.

"Now I wonder if there is anything more you ought to see. You took the servants' quarters on trust, you've seen all the living-rooms and most of the bedrooms. There is another room, my mother's own room, which you haven't seen. Would you care——?"

"Oh, I'll not bother, thanks, just now. I've enough to keep in my head as it is, and the time's getting on."

6

"Tea will be in the drawing-room now," Nicole told her. "We ordered it early that you might have some before you start on your long drive home."

"Oh, well—thanks. A cup of tea would be nice. And I'd like to see the drawing-room again to be able to tell Mr. Jackson right about it. I must say I like the hall. It's mebbe a wee thing dreary with all that dark oak, but there's something noble-looking about it too. I've seen pictures——"

She stopped on the staircase for a minute, studying the hall with her head on one side, then went on. "Of course, if we bought it we would need to have central heating put in at once. Mr. Jackson's great for all his comforts. I see you've got the electric light. Yes—That's the library to the left, isn't it? Then the dining-room, and the billiard-room. I'm quite getting the hang of the house now, and I must say I like it. For all it's so big there's a feeling of comfort about it—grand but homely, if you know what I mean? . . . Deneholm, now, is comfortable right enough, always a nice smell about it of good cooking, and hot-water pipes, and furniture kept well rubbed with polish, but when all's said and done it's only a villa like all the other villas in the road. In our road nobody would ever think to have a stair like this without a carpet. This'll take some living up to."

Nicole was standing a few steps lower down, looking back at Mrs. Jackson, and she surprised on the face of that lady an expression half-proud, half-deprecating. Her bearing, too, had subtly altered; her head was held almost arrogantly, it was as if she saw herself cut from her moorings in Pollokshields, sailing as mistress of Rutherfurd in stately fashion over the calm waters of county society.

Opening the door of the drawing-room, Nicole said, "Is tea ready, Mother? Mrs. Jackson, my mother. My cousin, Miss Burt."

Lady Jane Rutherfurd rose from her chair by the fire and smiled at the newcomer, as she held out her hand in greeting.

Nicole knew what it meant to her mother to receive Mrs. Jackson smiling. It was necessary that Rutherfurd should be sold, and Lady Jane was brave about it and uncomplaining, but she found the preliminaries trying. She disliked exceedingly—how could she help it?—the thought of unknown people going through the house, appraising the furniture, raising eyebrows at the shabbiness, casting calculating glances round rooms that were to her sacred. Ronnie's room with the book-shelves made by himself—they always stood a little crooked—and the cricket-bats and fishing-rods and tennis-racquets stacked in one corner, the school and college groups on the walls, everything just as he had left it. And next door Archie's room—waiting too. And her own room, the big, airy, sunny room with its windows opening on the view she loved best; and next it the oddly-shaped Corner Room that had been a sort of sanctuary to the whole family. When the house was full of people she and her husband had, with a sort of guilty joy, escaped at times from their guests and crept to the Corner Room to play with the children and refresh their souls. In that room had been kept all the precious picture-books that were looked at only when hands were clean and records unblemished, and the toys, too good for the nursery—the lovely Manchu doll which had been sent to Nicole from China; the brass animals from India, the gaily painted wooden figures from Russia, kings and queens with robes and crowns, priests with long white beards. The pictures on the walls were all family portraits, faded water-colours of children long since grown up and gone away, many of them now finished with their pilgrimage. Four little pictures hung in a line over the fire-place, the three Rutherfurd children, each painted at the age of five—Ronnie with his serious eyes and beautiful mouth, Archie, blue-eyed and obstinate, Nicole, bright-tinted, a fire-fly of a creature. The fourth was the cousin, Barbara Burt, who now sat beside Lady Jane and poured out tea.

Barbara's mother had been a Rutherfurd and had married foolishly. Norman Burt had been tutor to the Rutherfurd boys, a handsome young man with brains and ambition, but unstable as water. His wife after two years of misery and anxiety had died, leaving a baby daughter which the father had been only too thankful to get rid of, so Lady Jane had taken the child and had never let her feel that she was not as much to her as her own.

Barbara had only a dim recollection of her father, when he came to Rutherfurd for yet another loan. He died when she was ten. Her uncle Walter took her into the Corner Room and told her. He called her "poor child," and she wondered why. She felt no grief, and was too young to realise that in that lay the tragedy.

At that time nothing had seemed less likely than that the Rutherfurds should ever have to leave their home, but the years passed, and the War came and took Ronnie and Archie and the light from the eyes of their mother. Lean years came, bringing the need for retrenchment to people who did not know how to retrench, and now Sir Walter Rutherfurd had been in his grave three months, and Rutherfurd was in the market.

The most casual visitor, entering the Rutherfurd drawing-room, was certain to break off any conversation in which he might be engaged, and let his eyes wander round the place in silence. It was an involuntary tribute to the spell of the old chamber, a spell compounded of homeliness and strangeness. Once it may have been part of the great hall of the fortalice, which was encased in the modern structure like a stone quern built into a dyke. But about the time when Mary of Scots came to her uneasy throne, a Rutherfurd clothed the walls with little square Tudor panels, now dark as ebony with age, and his grandson had imported some English craftsman— perhaps a pupil of Inigo Jones—who, in place of the oak rafters, had designed a plaster ceiling, with deep medallions and a heavy enrichment of flowers and foliage. That was nearly three hundred years ago, and the plaster to-day had mellowed to a fine ivory. Later, the Adam brothers had contributed an ornate classical mantelpiece, whose marble nymphs and cornucopias had, like the ceiling, a dull ivory sheen. By some queer trick of perspective, the room seemed to slope down towards each end as if the roof were a shallow arch, so that the fire-place became the centre and shrine of it.

But it was not the room itself, or even the faded Mortlake brocades of the old chairs and settees, which most enthralled the stranger. There was a window on each side the hearth of a more modern pattern, which served the purposes of light, but the window at the west end was of the small sunken type of Scottish architecture, and it was in itself a picture, for in its deep embrasure it framed a landscape. Not the shorn lawns and the clipped yews of a Tudor garden, which might have consorted with the panelling, but a long vista of rushy parks and wild thorn trees, with, at the end, the top of the Lammerlaw, which in August, when the heather flowered, hung like an amethyst in the pale heavens. That window was the choicest of the Rutherfurd pictures, but others hung on the dim panels. All but one were portraits of men. There was a Rutherfurd by Jameson, in black armour and a gorgeous scarlet sash; another by Allan Ramsay, in a purple coat, a sprigged waistcoat and a steenkirk cravat, pointing with an accusing forefinger to a paper, while a violent thunderstorm seemed to be gathering in the background. A lean warrior in shako and coatee held a red Kathiawar stallion by the bridle, oblivious of the battle that was raging round him. There was a Raeburn, too, of a Lord of Session, in which plump hands were folded over scarlet robes, and rosy cheeks were puckered as if at the memory of some professional jest.

All the pictures but one were of men. That one was framed in the panelling above the fire-place and gave the room its peculiar character, as a famous altar-piece makes the atmosphere of the chapel where it hangs. It was a woman, no longer in her first youth, with a mouth narrowed a little by pain and disappointment, but with great brown eyes still full of the hunger of life. It was a replica of the Miereveldt of the "Queen of Hearts," Elizabeth of Bohemia, and, as sometimes happens in copies, there was a smoothing away of the cruder idiosyncrasies of the original, so that what it may have lost as a portrait it gained as a picture. One saw a woman who had known the whole range of mortal joys and sorrows. Her eyes did not command, but beguiled, for her kingdom was not of this world. Her beauty had in it something so rare and secret, so far from common loveliness, that the thing seemed in very truth an altar-piece, belonging not to this epoch or to that land, but to the eternity of the human soul. Looking down with her wistful small face above the ivory of the mantelpiece, she seemed to make the marble nymphs fussy and ill at ease. She herself, was profoundly at ease among the grim Rutherfurd soldiers and sailors. She had always been at ease among men, for they must needs follow where she beckoned.

Into the dim beauty of this room came Mrs. Jackson, stepping delicately over the polished floor on her high heels. She seated herself in the chair that her hostess suggested as comfortable, and said:

"Well, I'm sure this is very nice, but they'll be wondering at home where I am! Yes, thanks, I take both sugar and cream and I like it strong. Servants' tea, they tell me I take, when I laugh at the weak washy stuff people drink nowadays! But I'll be home before it's dark, anyway. The extra hour's a blessing when the days begin to draw in."

Mrs. Jackson beamed at her hostess as she accepted a cup of strong, sugary tea, and Lady Jane said, "I do hope you won't be too tired after your long afternoon. It is such hard work looking at houses. Other people's belongings are so fatiguing, don't you think?"

"Not to me," said Mrs. Jackson firmly. She was sitting forward on the very edge of her chair, her tight figure very erect, a piece of bread and butter held elegantly. "I'm getting a wee bit tired of it now, but as a rule there's nothing I like better than a chance to get into somebody's house and take a good look. Mind, you learn a lot, for everybody has a different way of arranging furniture and ornaments, and all that. Just look at this room." She put the last bite of bread and butter into her mouth and twisted herself round to look. "That cabinet there . . . and the screen and that mirror." Her eyes wandered to the fire-place. "That's a new idea, isn't it, to have a picture put in like that? Who's the lady?"

"That," said Nicole, "is my Lovely Lady, the 'Queen of Hearts.' "

Mrs. Jackson looked utterly at sea, and Barbara said, "That is a portrait of Elizabeth of Bohemia."

"Is that so?" said Mrs. Jackson.

Nicole said, "Don't you know the poem about her?" and kneeling on the fender-stool, looking up into the pictured face, she repeated:

"You meaner beauties of the night,
  That poorly satisfy our eyes,
  More by your number than your light,
  You common people of the skies;
  What are you when the moon shall rise?"

Mrs. Jackson stared at the girl. The light from the dancing flames caught the ruddy tints in her hair, and her upturned face in the rosy glow was like a flower of fire.

The two cousins, Barbara and Nicole, were like each other, yet oddly unlike. Nicole once said, "Babs is consistently handsome. I've only got moments of 'looks.' " Barbara had very good features, but there was something buttoned-up about her face, something prim and cold. Her cousin had no features worth the mentioning, but her eyes laughed and sparkled and darkened with every passing mood, and she would suddenly flush into a loveliness which was far beyond the neat good looks of Barbara.

Barbara was inclined to be heavy, Nicole was light and supple, a "fairy's child." Nicole was four-and-twenty, Barbara was four years older. Nicole was all Rutherfurd, Barbara was half a Burt.

If Barbara had knelt on the fender-stool and addressed a picture in verse, she would have looked affected and felt a fool. Nicole made it seem a most natural thing to do.

Mrs. Jackson, as I have said, stared, her cup half-way to her mouth. "Elizabeth of Bohemia," she murmured. "Wasn't she assassinated?" The way she said "assassinated," with a lilt in the middle of the word, was delicious, and Barbara, who saw that Nicole, whose sense of the ridiculous could "afflict her like an illness," was giving way to laughter, rushed in with:

"That was the Empress of Austria, wasn't it? An Elizabeth too."

"Uch, yes, so it was. . . Well, I must say I admire your room. Not that we haven't old furniture, too, we have; Mr. Jackson's great on it, but I sometimes think our room's more like a museum than a room to be comfortable in. For one thing,

10

Father doesn't like photos in it. I used to try and make it more homely, you know, with a photo here and an ornament there, but he said I spoiled the effect. It's what the man who arranged it for us called a 'period' room, but what period I never can mind. I'm never in it except to see that it's kept well dusted, and when we have people to dinner. I've got a wee room of my own"—she nodded happily to Nicole—"the morning-room it should be called, but I like to call it 'the parlour.' "

"I expect," said Nicole, "it's a delightful room. Do have one of these hot scones."

"Thanks. I don't know if you'd call it a delightful room, but it seems delightful to me for I've all my things round me, my wee ornaments that I buy for souvenirs when I visit new places, and photos of old friends—I've got Andy (that's my boy) at every year of his life—and the plush suite that we began life with in the drawing-room. Andy says I like the room because I can come off my perch in it! In a way he's right. It's not natural for me to be stiff and starched in my manner. I like a laugh, and I'm inclined to be jokesome, but, of course, I've got to be on my dignity when we're entertaining people. Such swells as we get sometimes! That's because Father's connected with all sorts of public things, and I can tell you I've to be careful what I say."

Mrs. Jackson laughed aloud, and Lady Jane said in her gentle voice:

"You must lead a very interesting life. So varied. I always think Glasgow seems such an alive place. Babs and Nicole and I once helped at a bazaar there and we loved it." She turned to her niece. "You remember, dear, that big bazaar for a woman's hospital? Mary Carstairs had a stall."

"Oh," said Mrs. Jackson, "*that* bazaar. I was there! I had the Pottery stall—along with others, of course. . . . So you know Lady Carstairs? I've met her here and there, of course, but I'm not awfully fond of her. A frozen kind of woman she seemed to me, but I daresay she's all right when you know her."

"Oh, she is," Nicole assured her. "She's a cousin of ours, so we've had opportunities of judging. But I know what you mean about the frozenness. It's a sort of protective barrier she has raised between herself and the host of casual acquaintances that she is compelled to have. She says they would overrun her otherwise. The wife of a public man—and such a very public man as Ted Carstairs—has a sorry time. You must feel that yourself sometimes."

Mrs. Jackson gave Nicole an understanding push with her disengaged hand. "Be quiet!" she said feelingly. "Do I not know what it means at big receptions and things to have people come up and say, 'How d'you do, Mrs. Jackson?' shaking me by the hand as friendly as you like, and me with no earthly notion who they are. Of course I just smile away and never let on, but, as you say, it's wearing, and then there's the pushing kind that you've got to keep in their places—uch yes. . . . You'll not have been troubled much with that sort of thing, Lady Ruth—Lady Jane, I mean."

That gentle lady shook her head. "Indeed no. I've often been so thankful for my quiet life. With my wretched memory for faces I would be worse than useless."

Mrs. Jackson leant forward and said earnestly, "Oh, I wouldn't say *that*.

You'd be a great success, I'm sure, in *any* sphere of life." She paused, and added, "If Mr. Jackson buys this place—of course, I don't know whether he will or not—but if he does, I'm just wondering how I'm to come after you. It'll be an awful drop, you know, from Lady Jane Rutherfurd to Mrs. Jackson."

She laughed happily, evidently in no way depressed at the prospect, while Lady Jane, flushing pink at such unusual frankness, hastily suggested that she might have more tea.

Mrs. Jackson waved away the suggestion, too much interested in what she wanted to say to trouble about tea. Looking confidentially into the face of her hostess, she said, "How many servants d'you run this house with, if it's a fair question?"

"How many? Let me see. There's Johnson, the butler, he has always been with us, and . . ." She turned to her niece. "Barbara is our housekeeper. Barbara will tell you."

"Johnson," began Barbara, counting on her fingers, "and Alexander, the footman, that's two. And the cook and kitchen-maid, and an under kitchen-maid, five: three housemaids, eight. Then there's our maid, Aunt Jane, and Harris. That makes ten in the house, doesn't it?"

"My!" ejaculated Mrs. Jackson. "Ten's a lot. At Deneholm we've just the three—cook, housemaid, and tablemaid. I don't know if I could bear to launch out into menservants. For all the time we've had a gardener I've never so much as given him an order, and I'm not a bit at home with the chauffeur. . . . I must say I liked the look of the butler when he let me in—a fatherly sort of man he looked. D'you think he would stay on with us and keep us right—you know what I mean?—and the footman, too, of course."

She looked at Barbara, who said, "Well—I hardly know. As my aunt says, he has been at Rutherfurd a long time and he may feel himself too old to begin with new people. Alexander might——"

"Alexander," said Nicole, "is like his namesake, 'hopelessly volatile.' "

"I see," Mrs. Jackson murmured, looking puzzled. "Have you a large family, Lady Jane?"

Before her mother could reply Nicole broke in, "There are only we three now."

"Is that so? Well, well. I've only the one son, Andy. . . . I can't tell you what I came through when he was away at the War. Father had his business to keep him occupied, and I couldn't stay in the house. I made bandages and picked sphagnum moss like a fury, and did every mortal thing I could to keep myself from thinking. . . . But he came back none the worse. It would have killed Mr. Jackson and me to lose Andy."

Mrs. Jackson laid down her cup, arranged her veil, and prepared to depart.

"Well," she said, standing solidly on the rug before Lady Jane, "I don't know, of course—Mr. Jackson'll have to see the place himself—but I've a kind of feeling that it's here we'll settle." She looked round the room again. "I mebbe shouldn't ask, but will you be taking all the furniture away with you? That picture above the fire-place, now? You see, I could never get the room to look the same, and I know Mr. Jackson would like it like this."

She held out her hand, saying rather wistfully, "He has such high ideals, you know what I mean. . . . Well, thank you for that nice tea. It's been a treat to me seeing you. D'you know what it all reminds me of? One of Stephen McKenna's novels. He's an awful high-class writer, isn't he? There's hardly one of his characters but what has a title and a butler."

CHAPTER II

"The last sad squires ride slowly towards the sea,
And a new people take the land. . . ."

G. K. Chesterton.

Nicole went out to the hall to see the visitor depart. When she came back to the drawing-room, "Well?" she said.

"Well," said Barbara, and added, "*I must say!*"

Her cousin laughed. "Yes, 'smooth Jacob still robs homely Esau' or words to that effect. All the same I like Mrs. Jackson, though I admit at first I was appalled. The tight figure, the large red face crowned by the ospreyed hat! I thought '*That* woman at Rutherfurd!' But in a little I realised that she wasn't 'that woman' at all. She's a dear, and simple, and above all a comic. I do love a comic."

Nicole put a log on the fire.

"Wasn't she funny about Mary Carstairs? 'A frozen sort of woman' so exactly describes her when she is standing at bay, so to speak, before the advances of the populace. I think myself that it's silly of her. Her life would be enormously more interesting if, instead of standing aloof and looking 'frozen,' she would try to like and understand these kindly people. After all, it's a case of Canute and the waves. They're coming in like a tide, the new people, and the most dignified thing for us is to pretend we like it, and to get out of the way as quickly as possible. Anyway, I'm enormously cheered by Mrs. Jackson. I had a nightmare fear that Rutherfurd would be bought by horrible 'smart' people. I don't grudge it a bit to that comic."

Lady Jane laid her hand on her daughter's.

"That's so like you, Nikky," she said. "You never expect to receive evil things, but if they come you immediately discover in them some lurking good. That's why you're such a comfortable person to live with."

"I don't believe," said Barbara, "that we'll hear any more of this Mrs. Jackson. It seems most improbable that people like that could even think of buying a place like Rutherfurd."

Nicole wagged her head wisely. "Mark my words, in a few days Mr. Jackson will arrive. I'm not sure that I shall like him, I distrust his high ideals—wasn't it pathetic the way his wife said, 'He has such high *ideels*, you know what I mean'?— and he evidently has a correct mind and knows what to admire, which is so tiresome. Still, he may be a very nice man, and willing to deal justly and be decent about things. Yes, I feel it in my bones that the Jacksons are to be our successors."

"It's a mercy you can take it so light-heartedly," Barbara observed drily, but Nicole did not reply.

Lady Jane sat looking at the fire, not listening to what the girls were saying.

It hurt Barbara to see her. . . . She looked so wan in her black dress, so desolate. Barbara thought of her as she used to be, looking almost a girl in her pretty clothes, with her husband and Ronnie and Archie always hanging round her. Now she sat there having lost everything, her husband, her boys, her home, her position. And the worst of it was no one could do anything to help her. One could not even think, "Oh, well, in time she will begin to feel quite bright again. In time she will cease to mourn, and will become one of those contented, healthy widows that one meets everywhere." She was not like that. It sometimes struck Barbara with a sharp pang that her aunt was merely living from habit, that the mainspring of her life was broken. She wondered if the same thing had struck Nicole.

"Mums," said Nicole, "don't look at nothing. Turn your head round and try to look interested in my bright conversation."

Lady Jane smiled up at her daughter's down-bent face.

"Why, yes, darling. I'm so sorry I was dreaming when pearls were falling from your lips. Will you repeat your valuable remarks?"

Nicole bowed with mock gravity. "My words of wisdom are so numerous that it seems almost a pity to repeat. I was only philosophising. . . . You may not realise it, you and Barbara, but we are in rather a romantic position. Mr. Chesterton would describe us as 'the last sad squires riding slowly to the sea.' Why to the sea, exactly? I don't know. But, anyway, novels have been written about such as we."

"Very dull novels they must be," said Barbara. "I don't know how you can laugh, Nik. It's the most tragic thing that ever happened, that the Rutherfurds should have to leave Rutherfurd."

"Of course it is," Nicole agreed, "so tragic that the only thing to do is to try and laugh. Mr. Haynes says we can't afford to live in it, and our lawyer ought to know. It's the Jacksons' turn now, and we must go down with the lights up and the flags flying. A Rutherfurd fell at Flodden, and the name has been respected all down the years, and not the least honourable were the three Rutherfurds that we knew best —— We've nothing to be ashamed of. Simply, there is no room any more for our sort. We are hustled out. We can't compete. Rutherfurd must go to the successful man who can cope with life as it is now! We must find some other place to pass our days in. Well, *I* don't mind."

Nicole got up and went to the fire, her head held high, a certain swagger in her walk, such as one sometimes sees in small boys who are shy and homesick and wish to conceal it. Lady Jane was again looking at nothing, and did not notice the piteous touch in her daughter's attitude, or she would have replied to that and not to the brave words she had uttered.

She said, "Youth, my dear, never minds anything, really. It's all part of the adventure of life. Youth bounds through changes and troubles like an india-rubber ball, but middle age has ceased to bounce; middle age collapses like a pricked balloon. I'm fifty-five—more than middle-aged, getting old—and I don't feel that there is any bounce left in me at all."

"Oh, my poor little mother," Nicole cried, kneeling beside her to stroke her hands, "quite deflated, are you? And I don't wonder. Much as Babs and I love

15

Rutherfurd, leaving it can't be to us what it is to you."

Lady Jane looked at the two girls in a withdrawn way and said, "I leave everything when I leave Rutherfurd. I don't want to pity myself, or, as you would say, make a song about it, but Rutherfurd is my life. The house your father brought me to thirty-two years ago! The house in which my children were born—where Ronnie and Archie played. . . . I was always utterly content in my home, I never wanted to go away. I never felt it dull even in the dead of winter. In fact, I think I loved winter best, because nearly all the neighbours went away to Egypt or the Riviera, and we could draw in together and hug our delicious solitude. We often laughed, your father and I, at our own unsociableness, and then our consciences would prick us and we would invite a lot of people to stay, and ask people to meet them, and work hard to entertain them and enjoy it all quite immensely. But when the last guest departed what thankful sighs we heaved! Once more the place was our own. It wasn't that we were inhospitable so much as that we were so happy alone we couldn't bear to spoil it."

The very thinking of past happiness, the telling of it, had changed Lady Jane. Her blue eyes, that looked as if the colour had been washed out with much weeping, deepened and brightened, a flush that was almost girlish came into her thin cheeks; she smiled tenderly.

"But, Aunt Jane, you did sometimes go away from home," her niece reminded her. "I can remember you and Uncle Walter setting off, rather like two victims mounting the tumbril, to pay visits. We children were quite pleased to be without you for a little, for we had always a lot of nefarious schemes in our heads that needed your absence for accomplishment, but we soon got tired of it and welcomed you back with joy. Nicole, do you remember when Ronnie locked Johnson into his own pantry and lost the key? And the day when Mrs. Asprey said Archie might have one bun out of the batch she was baking if he would go out of the kitchen, and instead, he took a *bite out of each*!"

"And the strawberry-wine we made," said Nicole, "and the feasts. I don't think they ever told of us when you came home, did they, Mums?—about all our ill-done deeds?"

Lady Jane shook her head. "They wouldn't have done anything to spoil my home-coming. . . . When we went away on a visit I always looked up the train we would come home by before we left, and that somehow seemed to make the time shorter, and anchor me to you all. Of course it was quite different when we took you all with us, our glorious holidays in Switzerland . . . and when we had the fishing in Norway. . . . Don't let me grumble. For more than twenty years my life was altogether lovely. I've had far more than most people. Why, I've no right to complain though I should never have another happy minute. It's as you say, Nikky, we must plan what we are to do. The sight of Mrs. Jackson has made me realise things. Do you think, Barbara dear, you could make me understand just where we stand? You have got such a much tidier mind than I have, and I get so confused when Mr. Haynes explains things, though I'm sure the poor man is most lucid."

Barbara settled herself at her aunt's feet and tried to make her see the situation so far as the lawyer had made it plain to her, and Lady Jane fixed her eyes on her instructor like a child anxious to please, but when Barbara stopped, she sighed.

"It sounds very complicated," she said, "though you do explain very nicely, Babs dear. Then, what exactly have we got to live on?"

"That depends," said Barbara, "on how things go—on Mrs. Jackson, perhaps. But you will have quite a good income, and Nicole, of course, has her own money from Grandfather. What does it bring you in, Nik? about £500 a year? And I have about the same, so we aren't exactly penniless, dearest."

"Yes—but—if we have a good income, why need we leave Rutherfurd? If we lived very simply and spent almost nothing. . . ."

Nicole took her mother's hand and kissed it. "You want both to have your cake and eat it, my dear. Your income will come largely from the sale of it. We can't run Rutherfurd on a few hundreds a year. Think of servants' wages alone! No, I'm afraid there is nothing for it but to leave our Eden, and the question is, where are we to go? The whole wide world is before us. What are your ideas on the subject, Babs?"

"I haven't any. So long as I am with you two I don't much care where it is. What about a flat in London? . . ."

"A flat?" said Nicole. "Somewhere in Kensington, I suppose? I've got very little idea of how much money one needs to do things well, but I fear our combined incomes wouldn't go far in the way of a fashionable flat. Besides—would Mother like being cooped up in town? I doubt it. For myself I couldn't stand more than a month or two of London at a time, and it's not a place to be poor in."

"We might travel for a bit," Barbara suggested.

"We might!" Nicole agreed. She had perched herself on the arm of her mother's chair. "What about going round the world? I read in the 'personal' column of the *Times* the other day that a General, a K.C.B., was offering to take a party round the world at £950 a head, or something like that. Can't you see us staggering about Japan with the K.C.B.!—Babs, Mother smiled. Did you see? Well, you made a very good impression on Mrs. Jackson, anyway, Mums."

"Nonsense, Nicole."

"Oh, I assure you, as she left she said to me, 'It's been a pleasure to meet you, and I just love your mother.' After all my unwearied efforts to be nice to her and show her everything, it was galling to see you romp in and win her approval with no trouble at all. Why are mothers *always* nicer than their daughters? If this deterioration goes on, if every daughter is inferior in every way to her mother, what of the future of the British Race? I confess it weighs on me a good deal. But, seriously, Mums, what would you like to do? Now, don't say you don't care, you're bound to have some preference."

"I haven't, my dear, you must believe me when I say it. I shall be happy if you are happy. We must see to it that we go to a place where you and Babs can have a good time. Nancy Gordon—did you read her letter?—suggests that we go to them in Somerset. She says the dower-house is empty, and Tom would gladly let us have it. Nancy lives in a constant whirl of entertaining, so you wouldn't be dull. Then, Aunt

Constance wants us to go to her at once. She says Ormhurst feels so large and empty now, that it would be a real kindness to go and help to fill it. Constance was always my favourite sister. . . . But, perhaps—d'you think—we'd better have a place of our own?"

"Yes," said Nicole. "I doubt if it would be wise to plant ourselves on friends or relations, no matter how willing they are. They might easily tire of us or we of them. We must make our own niche. I've been thinking"—she looked from her mother to her cousin with a quick laughing glance—"I've been thinking that since Mrs. Jackson and her kind are all rising in the world, they must be leaving vacant places. Well, why shouldn't we, ousted from our own place, take theirs? Why shouldn't we become dwellers in a suburban villa, and taste the pleasures of suburban society? I think myself it would be highly interesting."

"Interesting!" Barbara ejaculated, but Nicole hurried on. "I don't mean, of course, that we should go making a fuss about ourselves. The time for that is past. Pooh-Bah could no longer dance at middle-class parties—for a consideration. There are none so low now as do us reverence! You and I, Mums, would get on all right, but Barbara"—she glanced affectionately at her cousin—"is so hopelessly aristocratic."

Barbara flushed, for she knew that what her cousin said was true. Social distinctions meant almost nothing to Nicole; to Barbara they stood for much. Nicole never thought of her position; Barbara gloried in belonging to Rutherfurd. When they were all children together they had played with other children about the place. There had been quite a colony of large families belonging to servants on the estate, and they had had splendid games. But Barbara had always been the Little Lady from the Big House, had held herself aloof, allowed no familiarities. Her cousins were different, their whole hearts were in the play, they had no thought of themselves. Barbara often felt that Nicole should have been the Burt, and she the daughter of a hundred earls. To see Nicole playing at "houses" with a shawl wrapped round her supporting a doll, as she saw cottage-women carrying their babies, making believe to stir porridge in a pot while she addressed her playmates in broadest Border Scots! It had been the summit of her ambition to live in a cottage—a but and ben—and carry a real baby in a shawl. She startled her mother one day by handing her a doll and saying, "Hey, wumman, haud ma bairn." The boys were as bad. Ronnie was found one snowy morning on the roof of the house—he had climbed out of a skylight—putting out crumbs for sea-gulls. When remonstrated with by his governess, he replied, "Wumman, d'ye want them to be fund deid wi' their nebs in the snaw, seekin' meat?"

Sir Walter said Border Scots was a fine foundation for Eton, and so it proved. The boys came home from school speaking correct English, but always able, at a moment's notice, to drop into the speech of their childhood.

"Well," said Nicole, "what d'you say to my suggestion?" Barbara merely shrugged her shoulders, but Lady Jane was unusually firm.

"Darling, I said I didn't mind where I went; but I do draw the line here. I'm afraid I can't fill the vacant place left by Mrs. Jackson. Suburbs are for people who have business in cities: we have none. Why not a small house in, or near, a country town? I think I should like that, only—not too near Rutherfurd, please."

18

"That," said her daughter, "is the correct idea. A country town. A rambling cottage covered with roses. Delightful Cranford-ish neighbours, quiet-eyed spinsters and gallant old men who tell good stories. I see it all."

Barbara wore a most discouraging expression as she said, "I never saw a cottage that 'rambled.' What you will probably find in any country town is a number of new semi-detached villas occupied by retired haberdashers. Cranford doesn't exist any longer—the housing problem killed it. You're a most unpractical creature, Nik. You don't know how horrible such a life as you want to try would be. Imagine living always with people like Mrs. Jackson! Just think how you would miss your friends— Jean Douglas, the Langlands . . ."

Nicole shook her head impatiently. "My dear, why will you insist on saying things that jump to the eye? Don't you suppose I am *full* of thoughts about having to leave the old friends? I never loved Mistress Jean as I do to-night, and the thought of Kingshouse makes me want to howl like a wolf. The jollities we've had there! And Daddy Langlands, and Miss Lockhart, and even Tillie Kilpatrick, though, poor dear, she does paint her face more unconvincingly than any one I ever saw. But Mistress Jean will be the great loss. To know that there is no chance of suddenly hearing Johnson announce 'Mrs. Douglas,' and to hear her say '*Well*,' and then, 'This *is* nice,' as she settled down beside us."

"Then why not stay where we are known? There are lots of small places that would suit us, and people would be glad to have us stay, and would make things pleasant for us."

Nicole turned to her mother. "What do you say, Mums?"

"My dears, I don't think I could remain near Rutherfurd. Let us try Nicole's plan for a year and see how it works. . . ."

"You mean," said her daughter, "that we should go to a new place and make a niche for ourselves? *Let's*, Barbara. I'm sure there are places without semi-detached villas, where we shall be able to cultivate 'high ideels' like Mr. Jackson. . . . But you must promise to make the best of everything—it would be terribly unsporting of you to grumble."

"Oh, very well," said Barbara. "Let's try it for a year. A lot can happen in twelve months."

CHAPTER III

"It is a sedate people that you see."

Glasgow in 1901.

While the Rutherfurds made plans for the future, Mrs. Jackson regaled her family circle with an account of her expedition to the Borders. They sat, Mr. and Mrs. Jackson and their son Andrew, in the dining-room of Deneholm. It was a fairly large room, elaborately decorated, with two bow windows and a conservatory.

Mr. Jackson and his wife sat at either end of the long oval table, while Andrew faced the fire-place. There was a reason for that. Behind him was a picture which his mother did not consider quite delicate. When it had been first bought and hung, and Andrew was expected home from school, she had arranged that he must change his seat and sit where he could not see it. Now he was thirty-two, and unlikely to be affected by any picture, but he still kept his back to it.

A long shining damask cloth covered the table, and the only decoration was a tall vase of rather packed-looking chrysanthemums. One felt had there been a daughter things would probably have been different. No large white table-cloth for one thing, but a polished table with embroidered mats: no bleak, tall vase, but a wide bowl with flowers.

Wherever Mrs. Jackson went, though it were only into town in the car to shop, she gave her men-folk on her return a circumstantial account of everything that had happened to her. Accustomed to her ways, they were apt to pay but a cursory attention to her talk.

To-night she was still somewhat breathless from the late home-coming and her hurried dive into the gown which she described as "a semi-evening," but between spoonfuls of celery soup she bravely panted out details.

"Oh, it was a lovely drive," she began. "Not at first, of course, for there was all that coal district to go through—Hamilton and those places. But afterwards, the Clyde valley, and round Lanark, and down the Tweed. . . ." She turned to the parlour-maid, "Another bit of bread, Mary. Thanks." Then, ". . . I got an awful fright as we left Lanark; we very nearly ran over a wee dog."

Mr. Jackson laid down his spoon and wiped his mouth with his napkin. He was a small man with sandy hair turning grey, and a scrubby moustache.

"What kind of place is Rutherfurd?" he asked.

But his wife was not to be hurried. "I haven't got that length yet," she said placidly. "We went away down past Peebles—d'you remember, Father, we stayed at the Hydro there one Easter? Was that before the War, I wonder? I think so, for Andy was with us, and we met yon people from Manchester—d'you mind their names? They stayed with us afterwards at Innellan; the man had asthma. . . . I don't care much for Galashiels, it's awful steep about the station yonder, but it's lovely all round about it. We seemed to go a long way down the Tweed, and, of course, I had no idea whereabouts Rutherfurd was. In the end we had to ask. We came to a cluster of cottages—mebbe they called it a village, for there was a post office—and a man told us it was the first gate-house we came to, about two miles farther along the road. Sure enough we came to it, white-washed, with creepers, and an old woman who curtseyed as we passed. The drive winds, and crosses a stream with bridges about three times, and there are parks with deer. Deer—fancy! I wondered if we were ever coming anywhere, then we turned a corner and there was the house."

She stopped dramatically.

"A good house?" asked her son.

"Beautiful. How many houses have I looked at, Father? Nine, is it? and not one of them was just what we wanted. Two were only big villas—we've plenty of them in Pollokshields. The old ones were awfully damp and decrepit. One was built in a hollow and got no sun, and the oldest of all was nothing to look at—it would have been a waste of money to buy it. . . . But Rutherfurd's a place you'd be proud of."

Mary removed the soup plates and presently they were engaged on the fish course.

"It's a big house," Mrs. Jackson continued as she ate her sole, "but not overpowering, if you know what I mean. A butler let me in—quite the old family servant—and I left my coat in the outer hall. Then he took me through the hall, a place just like a big room, with tables and chairs, and papers lying, and into the drawing-room. My word!"

"Was it very splendid, Mother?" Andrew asked.

"No, Andy, I don't think you'd call it splendid; because everything in it seemed to be about as old as the Flood, but it was beautiful in a queer way. I think you'd like it awfully. And it was all panelled in squares, and above the fire-place there was a picture let in, a picture of—well, I declare if I haven't forgotten who it was, Somebody of Somewhere. . . . Are you better pleased with these potatoes, Father? I tried another shop. Not any mutton for me, please, I'll just take some vegetables. They're quite your way of thinking about furnishing a room, Father, not a photo anywhere, and I don't think I saw a single ornament. . . . Well, I stepped very gingerly over the polished floor till I found a good high chair, and presently the door opened and in came a girl. A young thing she looked, not more than two-and-twenty, with reddy-brown hair. I couldn't tell you whether she was pretty or not, for her eyes fair beguiled me. She stood for a second and looked at me and an expression passed over her face that made me feel I had no business to be sitting there. But it was gone in a flash, and she came up and took my hand so kind like, and said, 'Mrs. Jackson?' Like that. D'you know, I never knew Jackson was a bonnie name until she said it. My! I'd give a lot to speak like yon. . . . Then she said, 'You've come to see the house, haven't you? Will you let me show you over?' and off we went together. She took me everywhere and talked away as if she'd known me all her life. Sensible talk, too, considering who she is, for those kind of people are always queer. Just once, when we were looking at a long row of portraits, I asked who the handsome man was, and she said, 'That's my great-grandfather. He was mad.'"

Andrew Jackson laughed suddenly, and asked, "What did you say, Mother?"

"What could I say? I just said, 'Fancy!' Like that, 'Fancy!' But imagine anybody saying a thing like that about a relation."

"Probably she only meant that he was known to be eccentric, a character."

Mrs. Jackson nodded, willing to think the best of her new friend. "Mebbe that was it, Andy. . . . There are twelve large bedrooms and eight smaller ones—all very shabby; I don't think they can have had anything papered and painted for ages. I got my tea, too. When we'd seen pretty well everything, this girl—I didn't know who she was till later—took me back to the drawing-room. Tea was all ready, as cosy as you like before a fine fire, and two ladies sitting. One was Lady Jane Rutherfurd, the mother of the girl—*my* girl; and the other girl was a niece—Miss Burt."

"And what," asked her son, "was the name of 'your' girl?"

"Well, Andy, I can't tell you, but it sounded to me like Nee-coal, and that's a daft-like name. The other was plain Barbara. I didn't like her much. I knew fine what she was thinking of me. Common. She handed me my tea as if I was a school treat. . . . But Lady Jane's a fair delight. I saw in a minute where the daughter got her pretty ways. But, oh, poor soul, she did look sad! Of course, I made no remark, but I saw by the deep mourning that they had had a loss, and I talked away to make it easier for them. My girl's *awful* cheery. It would take a lot to daunton her, but she's young, of course; it's hard for older folk. . . . I asked them if they'd be taking away all the furniture, but they didn't say. It would be nice if we could keep it just as they have it, then we'd be sure it was right. . . . And, Father, I'd like if you could arrange to keep on the butler, he gives such a tone to the house. Some butlers are just like U.F. elders, but he's more like an Episcopal clergyman, tall and clean-shaved and dignified. There's a footman, too."

Mr. Jackson stared at his wife.

"Good gracious, woman, what are you talking about? You'd think the whole thing was settled. D'you suppose I'd have any use for a place like that? A barracks of a place evidently, unsuitable in every way, far too far from Glasgow. . . ."

"Well," said his wife, calmly stirring the sugar in her coffee, "you're determined to buy a place in the country and there's no good in swallowing the cow and choking on the rump. If we're to have a place it may as well be a place we can be proud of, and we must keep it up in proper style, butlers and all. Rutherfurd's the sort of place you'd like, Father, I know that. You might try and arrange to go with me mebbe the day after to-morrow. I didn't commit myself in any way, I said you'd have to see it first. . . . Will we say Thursday?"

Mr. Jackson grunted, and, rising from the table, went off without a word to his study.

Andrew followed his mother out of the room, but instead of crossing the hall to the parlour, which was her favourite sitting-room, she began to mount the stairs.

"Why, Mother, is it not to be the parlour to-night?"

Mrs. Jackson gave a sigh. "No, Andy, I told them to light the fire in the drawing-room and we'll sit there. If I'm to take up my position at Rutherfurd, the sooner I begin to practise the better."

CHAPTER IV

". . . In a kingdom by the sea."

Edgar Allan Poe.

When Mr. Jackson went with his wife to see Rutherfurd the place conquered him. It was not, he complained, the sort of place he wanted at all; it was far too big, too far from Glasgow, too expensive to keep up, in fact, all wrong in every way. Nevertheless he entered into negotiation with the lawyer, and before October was well begun Rutherfurd had passed from the family who had held it through centuries into the hands of the hard-headed little business man from Glasgow.

"Mind you," Mrs. Jackson said to Lady Jane, "there's not the slightest hurry about your leaving the house. Though you stay here over Christmas we won't mind. Indeed, I'd like fine to have another Christmas at Deneholm, and there is so much to arrange before we leave Pollokshields that I don't believe we'll flit till spring. It's a nice heartsome time to flit anyway—so mind you take things easy."

This was the more unselfish of Mrs. Jackson as she was secretly longing to get the workmen into Rutherfurd to start operations for central heating, and to see the paper-hangers make the bedrooms as she wanted them. But, as she told her husband, she had "both her manners and her mense," for the Rutherfurds, realising that when a thing has to be done it were better it were done quickly, decided to leave as soon as they could find a roof to cover themselves and their belongings.

What they wanted to find was a smallish house in a pleasant village or country town, which they could furnish with the things they did not wish to part from, and keep as a *pied-à-terre*. They might decide to travel for a time, or pay visits, but there would always be this place of their own to come back to.

It seemed in the abstract a very simple thing, but when they set out to find the house the difficulties began. To begin with, they wanted to go somewhere quite out of reach of their present home. As Nicole pointed out, "We don't want to decline into a small house in our own neighbourhood and have all sorts of casual acquaintances feeling that they have to be kind to us. 'These poor dear Rutherfurds, we *must* ask them to dinner'—can't you hear them? Of course, our own friends wouldn't be like that, but we'd better go where we'll be on nobody's conscience."

But there seemed to be some insuperable objection to every place they tried. If they liked a little town, there was no suitable house; if a suitable house was found, the locality was disappointing, and the house-agents' advertisements were so misleading. An attractive description of a house—old-fashioned, well-built, with good rooms, and garden—suppressed the fact that a railway line ran not many yards from the drawing-room window, and that a row of jerry-built villas obtruded themselves almost into the rose-garden.

Day after day the two girls came home discouraged from their house-hunting. "If ever," said Barbara, "I valued Rutherfurd it is now. Let's give up this quixotic search for a habitable house, store our furniture, and set off on our travels. Thank goodness, there are still hotels!"

They had almost decided to do this when one day by the evening post came a letter from the helpful Mr. Haynes, enclosing a card to see a house which he thought they might consider worth looking at. It was in the town of Kirkmeikle, in Fife, and was called the Harbour House.

"Far enough away, anyway," was Barbara's comment.

"Fife," said Nicole, and, wrinkling her nose, she quoted: "*I never lik'it the Kingdom o'Fife.*"

"Still," Barbara said, "we might go and see the place. What d'you think, Aunt Jane? Have you any objection to Fife?"

Lady Jane looked up from the book of old photographs she was poring over.

"Fife," she said. "Your uncle and I once paid a very pleasant visit to people who lived, I think, near Falkland. . . . Oh no, dear, I've no objection. . . . There are no hills to speak of in Fife, and I seem to remember that it smelt rather oddly—linoleum, is it? But otherwise, I'm sure it would be a pleasant place to live."

"Dear contented one," said Nicole, "the smell is confined to big towns with factories. Kirkmeikle is a little town in the East Neuk, wherever that may be. I grant the lack of hills, but if we find we can't live without them I daresay we could always let the house. People love to spend their holidays near golf-links. I must say the name rather appeals to me—the Harbour House."

Barbara was studying the lawyer's letter.

"We may have a chance of it," she said, "for evidently Mr. Haynes thinks it's a house that will not appeal to every one. It belonged to an old Mrs. Swinton who died in it a few months ago. Swinton's a good name: probably she was connected with the Berwickshire Swintons. . . . Well, shall we start off to-morrow morning? It'll mean leaving by the first train, and we may have to stay the night in Edinburgh. . . . I'll see how the trains go from the Waverley——"

It was a bright autumn morning with a touch of frost when Barbara and Nicole crossed the Forth Bridge and looked down at the ships, and saw the sun on the red-tiled houses, the woods, the cleaned harvest-fields, and the long stretch of shining water.

"It's pretty," said Barbara, almost grudgingly "Living inland I had forgotten the magic of the sea. There's such a feeling of space, and a sort of breath-taking freshness!"

"Oh yes," Nicole agreed, gazing down into the sparkling depths, "the East Coast is fresh and caller, and beautiful in its way. The funny thing is, I never have been fond of the sea, perhaps because I'm such a wretched sailor. But, anyway, I prefer the East Coast sea to the West Highland lochs." She leaned back in her seat and smiled at her cousin. "Shall I ever forget going out with Morag MacLeod on that awful loch of theirs? The old boatman warned us not to go for the weather was most uncertain, and it's a dangerous place, full of currents and things, and Morag is one of the most reckless of God's creatures. I felt perfectly certain I was going to be drowned, and the thought filled me with fury, for I can't imagine a less desirable death than to go down in a horrible black West Highland loch, with sea-birds calling drearily above one. Morag, I knew, would save herself, and I could see her bearing my death so nobly, quoting a lot of stuff with a sob in it. I almost wept with self-pity as I clutched my coat round me with one hand, and held on with the other to some part of that frail craft. How I sighed for my own solid Border glens with no wretched lochs!"

"What about St. Mary's? And the Loch o' the Lowes?"

"Oh, but they're clear and sunny and comparatively shallow, with no towering black mountains round them."

"Loch Skene is dark enough."

"Yes, but small. You wouldn't think of yachting on it. . . . I've never stayed again with Morag, she's too comfortless. I like being in the open air as well as any one, and there's nothing nicer than a whole day tramping or fishing or climbing, but in the house I expect comfort. When I come home I want great fires, and abundance of hot water, and large soft chairs, and the best of food. One day—have I told you this before?—No. Well, one day she made me start off with her at nine in the morning, after a wretched breakfast, half cold, eaten in the summer-house. It was a chilly, misty morning, inclined to rain, and we plunged along through bogs and wet heather until we came to a loch where a keeper was waiting for us with a boat. We fished for hours, then ate some sodden sandwiches, and bits of chocolate. All the time Morag was chanting about the joys of the Open Road till I was sick of her. We didn't catch any fish either. About four o'clock we started for home, very stiff and wet about the legs, and I thought I could just manage to live till five o'clock, and tea and a fire. A mile from home Morag suddenly had an idea—a thoroughly vicious one, I thought. 'We've got some sandwiches left,' she said, 'let's sit here and eat them. You don't want to go home and eat hot scones stuffily by a fire, do you?' *Didn't I?* I positively ached to, but I'm such a naturally polite creature that, though I could have felled her where she stood, I only murmured resignation. Happily I was saved by her father. We met him at that moment of crisis, and he laughed to scorn the thought of mouldy sandwiches, and insisted on us going back to tea."

"I should think so," said Barbara. "Morag was always a posing donkey, and, I should think, no use as a housekeeper."

Nicole shook her head. "None in the world. A comfortless mistress makes careless servants, and the fires were always on the point of going out, and the hot water never more than tepid. The only time I was comfortable and warm all that week was when I was in bed hugging a hot-water bottle. I was sorry for Morag's father. It's wretched for a man to live in a badly run house."

She stopped and looked at her cousin. "My word, Babs, you'd be a godsend to any man as a housekeeper."

"Only as a housekeeper?"

"My dear, no. As *everything*, companion, friend, counsellor, sweetheart—wife."

They changed at Thornton, and in due course reached their destination. Kirkmeikle, they found, was a little grey town huddled on green braes, overhanging the harbour. There was one long street with shops, which meandered downhill from the station; some rows of cottages and a few large villas made up the rest of it. The villas were conspicuous and wonderfully ugly, and the two girls looked at them in dismay. Was one of those atrocities the house they had come to look at?

Barbara settled the question by stopping a small boy and demanding to know where the Harbour House was.

"Ye gang doon to the harbour an' it's the hoose that's lookin' at ye."

"Quite so," said Nicole, heaving a sigh of relief, and turning her back with alacrity on the red villas.

Proceeding down the winding street they came at last to the sea-front. A low wall, flat on the top, ran along the side of the road, and beyond that was the sea. At high tide the water came up to the wall, at other times there was a stretch of firm sandy beach.

A tall, white-washed house stood at the end of the street leading down to the sea. The front door was in the street, and to the harbour it presented a long front punctuated with nine small paned windows; the roof was high and pointed, and there were crow-step gables.

"What a wise child that was," said Nicole. "It is 'lookin' at ye' with nine unblinking eyes."

"It smells very fishy down here," was Barbara's comment.

"Fishy, yes, but salt and clean. . . . Have you the card?"

The door was opened by a stout, middle-aged woman with a rosy face and a very white apron on which she wiped her fingers before she took the card Barbara held out to her.

"Ay, come in, please, mem. Certainly, ye can see the hoose. I'll tak' ye through. . . . No, it's no been empty that lang. Ma mistress dee'd last July. There's been a gey wheen folk lookin' at it—kinna artist folk the maist o' them—but I dinna think it's let yet."

As she spoke she led them through rather a dark hall and opened a door. "The dining-room," she said, and stood aside to let them pass.

Nicole at once went to one of the windows to look out, but Barbara studied the room, measuring spaces with her eyes.

"Not a bad room," she said. "The sideboard along this wall . . ."

Nicole turned from the window. "Oh, Babs, do come and look. Isn't that low wall jolly? Fishermen will sit on it in the evenings, and talk and smoke their pipes. And the harbour! I like to think of ships coming in and unloading and setting off."

"Yes, yes," Barbara said absently. "I wonder if that fire-place throws out any heat. I distrust that kind."

"Let's see the drawing-room," said Nicole.

"Upstairs, mem. Mebbe I'd better go first."

The stair was stone with shallow steps, the bannisters delicate wrought iron with a thin mahogany handrail. The woman with the snowy apron pattered briskly across the landing and threw open a door.

"Ye see," she said proudly. "It's bigger than the dinin'-room by a' the width o' the lobby. Ay, an' fower windows nae less."

"How jolly," sighed Nicole, "oh, *how* jolly!"

It was a long room, rather narrow. Each of the four deep windows looked out to the sea, and was fitted with a window seat. The fire-place at the far end of the room had a perfect Adam mantelpiece: the doors were mahogany.

"Curious shape of room," Barbara said. "I'm not sure that I——"

"Say no more," interrupted her cousin. "This is where I'm going to live. As soon as I saw it I knew, as you might say, that it was my spiritual home. I'll sit curled up on one of those window seats every evening and watch the sun set over the sea. What? No, perhaps I'm not looking west, but it doesn't matter. Don't carp . . . I'm sure mother will love this room. She'll hang her beloved little portraits in a line above that fire-place; the bureau will stand just here, with the miniatures above it, and her very own arm-chair beside the table. . . . We'll be able to make it exactly like home for her."

"My dear girl, we haven't got it yet."

"Sensible always, Babs dear: that's quite true, we haven't. But I'm absolutely sure this is to be our home. I knew the house when I saw it. It seemed to give me a nod as I came over the doorstep. There's no doubt about it we were meant to come here, and that's why poor Mrs. Jackson was uprooted from Pollokshields. I'm going off now to wire to Mr. Haynes to take it at once. It would be too ghastly if those 'artist folk' got before us—come on, Babs."

"Nonsense," said Barbara. "Don't be so childish. We haven't seen the bedrooms—much the most important part of a house to my mind. And we don't know if there is a decent kitchen range and a good supply of hot water. It's so like you, Nicole, to look out of a window and immediately determine to take a house."

Nicole, instead of looking crushed, smiled into the eyes of the caretaker, who, evidently liking her enthusiasm, came to her help.

"Ay, my auld mistress aye sat in this room and lookit oot on the water. When the tide's in if ye sit ower here ye canna see onything but water, juist as if ye were on a ship. An' it's a warm room; grand thick walls; nane o' yer new rubbish, wan-brick thick. I'm vex't that ye've no' seen the room wi' the furniture in't. The next o' kin took it awa' to Edinboro' and hed it sell't. It was auld, ye ken, terrible ancient, and brocht a heap o' siller. . . . The bedrooms? Ay, fine rooms. There's two on this landin'—the mistress's room an' the dressin'-room aff, that the ain maid sleepit in."

They went with her to the room. "Ye see," she pointed out, "it hesna the sea view, it looks up the brae, but it's a nice quait room, for the gairden's round it. . . . An' there's a bathroom next the dressin'-room."

"It's all in beautiful order," Barbara said. "The paint and paper seem quite fresh—— What rooms are upstairs?"

"I'll show ye. There's fower bedrooms an' a wee ane made into a bathroom. That was dune no' mair nor seeven year syne (an' its never been used, so it's as guid as new), when the mistress's grandson, wha should ha' heired it, was hame frae the

War. We wanted to hae things rale nice for him, an' the mistress was aye readin' aboot the dirt in the trenches, an' she was determined that he wud hae a grand bath o' his ain the wee while he was hame. Ay, but he only got the use o't the wance. He was awfu' high aboot it, the laddie, but he never cam' hame again; an' the property ga'ed to a far-awa' freend that the mistress kent naething aboot." She opened a door.

"This is the new bathroom."

The two girls looked at the white-tiled walls, the gleaming hot-water rails, the glass shelves, the large luxurious bath, all spotlessly kept, then Nicole turned away with a slight shiver. "Poor little boy who liked his comforts," she said. . . . "May we see the bedrooms?"

Two of them looked to the sea, two to the brae: all good rooms.

"Now for the kitchen," cried Nicole, "and pray heaven that's as perfect as the rest." She turned to her friend the caretaker. "You don't mind, do you? It seems we've simply got to see the kitchen and inquire into the hot-water supply."

" 'Deed ye can see onything in the hoose. I'm prood o' ma kitchen. I've cooked in't for near thirty years."

"Oh!" said Barbara. "So you were Mrs. Swinton's cook? That explains why everything is so well kept," and she said it again with more fervour when she saw the kitchen premises. There was little left except necessities, but the tables were scrubbed white, the stone floors in the scullery and laundry sanded in elaborate patterns, everything showing that there was some one in charge who loved to work.

"It's awfu' bare: ye should hae seen it wi' a' the braw covers and copper pans, but everything's been sold." She shook her head sadly. "A body's little hert to wark—but still . . ."

"And when the house is let," Barbara began, and stopped.

"When the hoose is let, I'll tak a cook's place in Edinboro'. Ye get awfu' big wages noo-a-days, but I dinna ken hoo I'll like the toon." She answered Barbara, but she looked at Nicole.

"You'll hate it," said that young woman briskly. "Besides, think how lonely this old house would be without you. Thirty years, did you say you'd been here? Why, you must love every stone of it. I don't believe you could sleep now away from the sound of the sea. . . . Won't you stay on and take care of us? I want to hear all about old Mrs. Swinton and the boy who liked his comforts. You see, we're leaving our home and coming to a new place, and it'll make all the difference if we feel that it isn't a stranger in the kitchen, but some one who belongs. By the way, what is your name?"

"Agnes Martin, mem. I'm no married nor naething o' that kind, but ma mistress aye ca'ed me 'Mistress Martin': she said it was better for the young lasses, ye ken."

Nicole held out her hand, and after a moment's hesitation the old servant took it and shook it awkwardly.

"Then that's settled, Mrs. Martin. You stay with us in your own old place and I promise you will be happy. There's only my mother and my cousin and myself. Bar the door, please, to all further seekers; tell them the house is taken. We're going

29

straight now to the post office to wire to our lawyer." And seizing the hand of Barbara, who was regarding coldly her precipitate cousin, and smiling at the old servant, who seemed bewildered but rather pleased, Nicole left the Harbour House.

Later in the day, Agnes Martin took off her white apron, wrapped a grey woollen shawl round her shoulders, locked the back door of the Harbour House, and went to visit, as was her custom of an evening, her old friend Mrs. Curle. It was only a little way, a step or two round the corner into the Watery Wynd where stood the outside stair that led to Betsy Curle's one-roomed house. Agnes Martin turned the handle. "Are ye in?" she asked.

"When am I ever oot?" was the reply from the woman sitting by the fire.

Betsy Curle was not a very old woman, but for years she had been getting gradually crippled with rheumatism, and now could do little more than crawl round her kitchen. Yet everything was spotlessly clean. With her twisted hands she scrubbed and polished, remarking irritably when well-meaning people wondered how it was done, that there was no wonder about it, if a body had the whole day to clean a room it would be a shame to see it dirty.

"It's you, Agnes," she said to her visitor. "C'wa in to the fire: it's surely cauld the nicht?"

"Ay, I wadna wonder to see a guid touch o' frost. How are ye?"

"Fine."

It was odd the difference in the speech of the two women. Agnes's sharp intonation, rising high at the end of each sentence, seemed to have something of the east wind and the sea in it; Betsy's broad Border tones, slow and grave, made one think of solemn round-backed hills and miles of moorland. Betsy had come to Kirkmeikle as a young wife, but the thirty-five years she had spent there had done nothing to reconcile her to the place. Home to her was still the village by the water of Tweed.

Agnes took out a grey stocking and began to knit while she recounted the small doings of the day, which were eagerly listened to, for Betsy took an almost passionate interest in her neighbours, though she was now, by reason of her infirmities, unable to keep them under personal observation.

When various small bits of gossip had been recorded and savoured with relish, the important news was brought out.

"I'm thinkin' the Harbour Hoose is let then, Betsy."

"D'ye tell me that? Whae tae?"

"Weel—the day, juist aboot denner-time, the bell rang, and there was twa young leddies standin' on the doorstep wi' a caird to see the hoose. I saw they werena juist daein't for a ploy like some o' the folk that comes, they were terrible tae'n up wi' the hoose, specially the youngest ane. The ither ane was aye for haudin' her back, but she juist gaed a lauch tae me and never heeded her. A bonnie young thing she was, I fair took a notion o' her! D'ye ken, she shook haunds wi' me! Ma auld mistress never did that a' the years I was wi' her."

"Mistress Swinton was a proud body," said Betsy. "She couldna see that her servants were flesh and blood like hersel'; but she's dust noo, so we needna remember it against her."

"She was a just mistress to me, and I'd like fine to stay on in the auld hoose."

"Will the new folk want a cook?"

"Ay, did I no' say that? The young leddy askit me to bide. She said it wud mak a' the difference if I was there. She says, 'There's only my mother and my cousin and myself.' It would suit me fine. I like to serve the gentry, an' I dinna want to leave Kirkmeikle. If I took a place here wi' Miss Symington they'd ca' me a 'plain cook,' an' ye ken fine what that means—juist stewed steak wan day and chops the next—but I could see that thae folk were used wi' a'thing braw aboot them."

"But whae were they?" Betsy asked. "Did they no' tell ye whauraboots they cam' frae?"

Agnes laid down her stocking and fumbled in her pocket.

"Here, see," she said, handing her friend an envelope. "They left me that address. Did ye ever hear tell o' that place?"

Betsy, bending down to the red glow from the ribs, read the words on the envelope, and her poor disabled hands shook.

"Never i' the warld" . . . she muttered, then turning to Agnes, "Rutherfurds!" she cried excitedly. "I've kent the Rutherfurds a' ma days. Rutherfurd wasna faur frae Langhope. It's a *terrible* braw place; I used to gang as a bairn to Sabbath-schule trips there, and I mind when Lady Jane Rutherfurd cam' as a bride. . . . Ye're mista'en, Agnes, ma wumman, if ye think the Rutherfurds wud want a hoose in Kirkmeikle."

Agnes knitted placidly. "I d'na ken. Twa leddies cam', in deep black they were, an' that was the name they gae me, and they said they were ga'en straucht to the post office to wire to their lawyer to tak' the hoose. That's a' I ken—mak' a kirk or a mill oot o't, Betsy."

Betsy shook her head. "There maun be something far wrang, but I get nae news frae Langhope noo that I canna hand a pen. . . . I maun get Tam to write. I'll no rest till I ken if it's true. Rutherfurds awa frae Rutherfurd and livin' cheek by jowl wi' Betsy Curle! The thing's no canny."

CHAPTER V

"Oh, but her beauty gone, how lonely
Then will seem all reverie,
How black to me."

Walter de la Mare.

It was late in the evening before Nicole and her cousin reached home after their day in Kirkmeikle.

Mrs. Douglas from Kingshouse had been dining with Lady Jane, and was still there when the girls came in. She was a woman frankly middle-aged, slim, upright, with white hair rolled back in a style of her own from a small, high-coloured face. Her eyes were intensely blue, shrewd, kind eyes, quickly kindled in anger, easily melted to tears. One of the most striking things about Jean Douglas was her instinct for dress. Her clothes were perfect in every detail, and whether she was on the top of a hill with her dogs, or at a Point-to-Point meeting, at a country-house luncheon party (this is a great test), or in a London ballroom, she always looked exactly right.

She kissed the two girls with affection, but her words were severe. "You two stupid creatures, coming home at this time of night! Why didn't you stay in Edinburgh? I've been scolding your mother, Nicole, for not insisting, but well I know you're the real culprit. Your mother and Barbara are dragged at your chariot wheels."

Nicole smiled forgivingly at her friend. "Don't be nasty, Mistress Jean, when Babs and I are perishing with hunger. We had only a snatched cup of tea in Edinburgh, and we kept falling asleep in the train, and got so cold. Johnson," to that dignitary, who had come into the room, "is our ham-and-egg tea ready? Good. I ordered that as a great treat after our long day. Come with us, my dears, and watch us eat. We've got heaps to tell you."

At first they talked of other things. Nicole wanted to know how her mother had spent the day, asked for all the news from Kingshouse. She seemed completely to have forgotten the weariness of her long day, and ate her meal with relish.

"Babs," she said, "don't you think this is the perfectest sort of meal? . . . If I had my will I'd always have high tea. We got such a horrid luncheon at Kirkmeikle—very late, when we had ceased to feel hungry. It was in a pot-house of sorts, and we got soup out of a tin (I think), and roast beef that had been hot about an hour before, so couldn't be described exactly as cold. I felt like St. Paul and the Laodiceans! The room smelt like a channel steamer, and the table-cloth was damp to the touch. Kirkmeikle doesn't shine in the way of inns; we would need to warn people of that. Which brings us to the point—we hope we've got a house there."

Lady Jane said "Oh!" and gave a faint gasp.

32

Her daughter caught her hand. "I know. Doesn't it seem to make things horribly final somehow? I don't think I really believed we were leaving Rutherfurd until we sent the wire to Mr. Haynes asking him to take the Harbour House if possible."

"And where is this house?" Mrs. Douglas asked crossly. "I can't tell you how disgusting I consider your conduct. It's a poor compliment to your friends that you should want to put the sea—or at least the Firth of Forth—between us, I mean between them and you."

Nicole spread some jam on a piece of bread and butter.

"Blame me, my dear, me only."

"It's you I am blaming. What's your idea in rushing to Fife?"

"Can't find a house anywhere nearer."

"Nonsense."

"Oh, all right."

"You know very well," Mrs. Douglas went on, "that the Langlands are most anxious that you should take the Cottage. You couldn't find a more charming little place, suitable in every way, and you would have all your friends round you."

Nicole looked at her friend. "Why, Mistress Jean, I never knew you lacking in imagination before. Can't you see that it wouldn't be exactly pleasant for us to stay on here and see strangers in Rutherfurd? We must go to some place where we won't always be reminded. . . . The Jacksons——"

"The *wretched* creatures!" broke in Jean Douglas, so bitterly that the inmates of comfortable Deneholm might well have wilted. . . . "But I flattered myself that the fact of having all your friends round might weigh against the other. I was mistaken, it seems."

"Now don't be *sneisty*, my dear. You don't suppose we leave you willingly, do you? . . . Babs, we must tell about the house. You begin with the plain facts and I'll add the embroideries later."

Barbara poured herself out a cup of tea and declined to do her cousin's bidding. "Go on yourself," she said. "When you get too exaggerated I'll interrupt."

"Starting from the Waverley," Nicole began, rather in the style of a guide-book, "it is quite a pretty run—I had forgotten how pretty—and not very long. Kirkmeikle we found to be a funny little steep town of red-tiled houses tumbling down into the Harbour. I won't disguise from you that there is a row of atrocious new red villas standing in a line above the town, and we quailed when we saw them, fearing that our quest would lead us to them. But no; we were directed down the long winding street, and at the foot we found a tall white-washed house with crow-step gables and a pointed roof, and nine windows looking out to the sea."

"Surrounded," broke in Barbara, "with ordinary fishermen's cottages, and a strong smell of tar and fish, and small dirty children."

"Why not?" asked Nicole. "I've always wanted to rub shoulders more with my fellow-men, and now I'll get the chance. . . . And mother won't mind, will you, Mums? To my mind it's infinitely preferable to villadom."

"I think it sounds nice and unusual," Lady Jane said; "but I hope you asked if the drains were all right."

"We forgot," said Nicole, "but I expect they're all right, for there are two excellent bathrooms fitted up with every sort of contrivance. And Barbara *insisted* on hearing about the hot-water supply. . . . Would you rather have a bedroom looking to the sea or up the brae, Mums? The *best* room, the largest, that is, is on the land side, but we'll decide that later. The drawing-room is a pet of a room, I know you'll love it . . ., and the furniture from the Corner Room will be exactly right for it. . . . I planned it all the moment I saw it. The Russian figures will stand on the mantelshelf just as they do here, and your little portraits will hang in a row above them. And the old French clock that plays a tune must be there, and the Ming figures in their own cabinet. They will be quite in keeping with the Harbour House: all seaport towns are full of china brought from far places. . . . Of course, the dining-room furniture is hopeless, but I was thinking coming out in the train that the things in the Summer Parlour would be perfect in that sea-looking room. The Chippendale sideboard and table and chairs, the striped silk curtains and the Aubusson carpet will make it a thing of beauty."

Mrs. Douglas turned to Barbara. "Nicole's as pleased as a child with a doll's house."

Barbara shrugged her shoulders. "It *is* a doll's house."

Nicole protested. "It's so beautifully proportioned that it isn't a bit cramped. The rooms are all of a decent size, and what can you possibly want more than a room to feed in, a room to talk and read and sew in, a room to sleep in?" She turned to her mother again. "You can't imagine, Mother, what a homelike little house it is. It must always have been lived in by people with nice thoughts—decent people. . . . The cook showed us over, the sort of cook that is born, not made—you couldn't imagine her anything else, with a round rosy face and a large expanse of white apron. Thirty years she had served old Mrs. Swinton in the Harbour House. *Of course* I told her she must remain with us. Babs thought I was mad, before we had time to ask for references or anything, but her face was her reference. Mrs. Agnes Martin. That is your new cook, Mums." She turned to Mrs. Douglas. "To find a house and a cook both in one day! That was pretty clever, don't you think, in these degenerate days?"

"I should like to know more about both before I congratulate you," her friend said cautiously, as she rose to go. "I ordered the car at 10.30 and it must be long past that. Well—I'm glad you seem satisfied."

"Satisfied," said Barbara, with a groan, while Lady Jane sighed.

Mrs. Douglas turned to get her cloak.

"And what," she asked, "is to happen to all the furniture you can't get into this new house?"

"Oh," said Nicole, with an air of great carelessness, "didn't you know that the Jacksons are taking over the rooms as they stand?"

"What?" She stood staring at Nicole, who held her cloak. "Those heavenly old things! But not the portraits surely? Not your Lovely Lady?" She looked from one to the other of the three women, but no one spoke. "Give me my cloak, Nicole," and as the girl wrapped her in it she said, with tears standing in her angry blue eyes,

"It was bad enough to think of you being away, but I never dreamt of you being separated from your treasures. Nobody knows what Rutherfurd has been to me . . . not only because I loved every one of you, but because that room was to me a sort of shrine. You know," she turned to Nicole, "how the summer sun about six o'clock strikes through the west window and falls on the picture? I used to plan to be there to see it. . . . And now that fat woman tricked out in silly finery will sit there by the fire, and the shrine is desecrated, things that were lovely all made common and unclean. . . . Find my handkerchief, can't you, Nikky? It's in my bag. . . . What a fool I am. . . ."

She threw her arms round Lady Jane.

"I'm a Job's comforter, aren't I? Bildad the Shuhite should be my name! . . . But I promise you Mrs. Jackson won't enjoy her ill-gotten gains. She will sit in lonely splendour, I'll see to that."

"No, no," Lady Jane protested. "Indeed, Jean, I want you to be kind to her as only you know how to be kind. You are far the human-est person in these parts. Make things easy for her."

"Not I. Things have been made far too easy for her as it is."

"But, my dear," Nicole cried, "if it hadn't been the Jacksons it would have been some one else—probably very objectionable, pretentious people. In a way the Jacksons are benefactors. They have saved those things for Rutherfurd when they might have had to be all scattered abroad. . . . *Everything in its proper place*, Mistress Jean. You remember your Hans Andersen? Out we go, swept by the great broom of Fate. Exit the Rutherfurds. Enter the Jacksons."

Jean Douglas put both hands over her ears.

"Don't say it, I hate their very name. And how I shall hate them when I see them in the flesh!"

"No," said Nicole, "I defy you to hate Mrs. Jackson."

Late that night, when every one was in bed and the house very still, a light figure slipped downstairs into the dark drawing-room.

Quietly she pulled back the curtains and undid the shutters. Outside a full moon was shedding its ghostly light. How strange and dreamlike it looked, so distinct and yet so unreal—the wild thorns with their bare branches, the glimmer of the burn, the lawns like tapestry. Somewhere up on the Lammerlaw a wild bird cried strangely. Near the house an owl hooted. Nicole drank in the beauty thirstily. It was as if she were fixing it on her mind against a time when she would no longer behold it.

Presently she turned and went over to the fire-place.

In the moonlight the picture gleamed palely. The "Queen of Hearts" looked down on the girl kneeling on the fender-stool. It was nothing to her that the upturned face was very pale, and wet with tears.

CHAPTER VI

"Of many good I think him best."

Two Gentlemen of Verona.

Mr. Jackson bought Rutherfurd practically as it stood. He grumbled loudly at the sum it cost him, but in his heart he was as well pleased as the buyer in Proverbs: *"It is naught, it is naught," saith the buyer, but when he goeth away he boasteth.*

The house was what he had always vaguely dreamed of, always desired to attain to, for he had a real love and appreciation of beautiful things. He did not try to deceive himself about his own or his wife's fitness for their position; he knew they might be rather absurd in their new setting; his hopes were built on his son. Andrew, he determined, would play the part of the young laird and play it well. There was no need for him to trouble the Glasgow office much; he must shoot, and fish, and take to all country sports. His father had a picture of him in his mind's eye, going about in knickerbockers, with dogs, a member of the County Council, on friendly terms with the neighbouring landowners. And of course he would marry, some nice girl of good family, and carry on the name of Jackson. There was nothing to be ashamed of in the name; it stood for straightness and integrity. Jackson of Rutherfurd—it sounded well, he thought.

Mrs. Jackson, though very much excited at the thought of the change, was beset with fears. She called on all her friends and broke to them with a sort of fearful joy the news that the Jacksons were about to become "county." They were all very nice and sympathetic, except Mrs. McArthur, who was frankly pessimistic and inclined to be rude.

Mrs. Jackson would not have cared so much had it been one of her more recent friends who had taken up this attitude, but she had known Mrs. McArthur all her life and had always admired and respected her greatly.

"You're leaving Glasgow, I hear," she said coldly, the first time Mrs. Jackson went to see her after the great step had been taken.

"Have you heard?" that lady asked blankly. "I came to-day to tell you."

"Bad news travels fast," said Mrs. McArthur, sitting solidly in a high chair and surveying her friend as if she were seeing her in an entirely new light.

Mrs. McArthur was a powerful-looking woman with a large, white, wrinkled face. She belonged to an old Glasgow family and loved her city with something like passion. Holding fast to the past, she had an immense contempt for modern ways and all innovations.

"Ucha," Mrs. Jackson began nervously. "Mr. Jackson's bought a place and we're leaving Glasgow for good. It's a wrench to leave a town where you were born and brought up and married and lived near sixty years in—— And I'm fond of

36

Glasgow. It's a fine hearty place, and I'd like to know where you'd find a prettier, greener suburb than Pollokshields."

Her hostess said nothing, so she went on talking rapidly. "And the shops and all, and concerts and theatres; we'll miss a lot, but still—— Rutherfurd's a fine place and not that awful far away. I really don't know how I'll get on at all, entertaining and all that, and a butler, and taking my place as a county lady, but I'll just have to do my best. If only I'd had a daughter! What a help she'd be now. But it's no good blaming Providence, and Andy's a good boy to me."

She smoothed down her lap and sighed, while Mrs. McArthur gave a sniff and said:

"Well, I think you're making a mistake. Some people are fitted for a country life and some aren't. I'd hate it myself. We go to Millport every summer for July and August, and the coast's bright compared to the country, steamers and what not, but two months is more than enough for me. Indeed, I wouldn't go away at all, if it weren't that I value town all the more when I get back." She watched a maid put a large plump tea-pot on the tray before her and covered it with a tea-cosy embroidered with wild roses, and then continued: "A coast house is bad enough, but how anybody can buy 'a place' as they call it, a house away at the end of an avenue, removed from all mankind, dreary beyond words. . . ." She lifted her eyes to the ceiling in mute wonder, while Mrs. Jackson cleared her throat uncomfortably.

"Well, but, Mrs. McArthur," she began, "some people *like* the country, you know, and——"

"Some people have queer tastes, Mrs. Jackson. Look at the people that are always going away about the North Pole!"

Mrs. Jackson failed to see the connection, but she murmured, "That's so," in a depressed tone; then, more brightly, added: "You couldn't call Rutherfurd cold. Rather sheltered it is, with flowers blooming away like anything still, and we're putting in central heating—— Can you believe it, they had done all these years without it? Luckily, there's electric light."

"There is? Well, I prefer gas myself." Mrs. McArthur looked complacently round at her incandescent mantles in pink globes, then began to pour out the tea. . . . "Will the house need much?"

Her guest, glad of this slight show of interest, responded volubly.

"All the bedrooms need new paper and paint. The Rutherfurds were never very well-off for their position, and money's been getting scarcer with them every year. The hall and the public rooms will be left with all the furniture, just as they are; they're panelled, you know. . . ." She leant forward impressively. "Mrs. McArthur, would you believe it, there's no carpet on the stairs."

"Fancy! As poor as all that, are they? It's a good thing you've got a handsome one to lay down. It's just about two years since you got it. . . ."

Mrs. Jackson nodded. "Two years past in September. It *is* rich, isn't it? I'm awful fond of crimson, and it's a really good carpet, made for us. But——" she hesitated and glanced deprecatingly at her friend, "all the same, I don't think we'll put it down at Rutherfurd. It's not the thing if you've got a fine old staircase—

antique, you know—to cover it."

Mrs. McArthur laid down her tea-cup, and after a moment's pause addressed her old friend, gazing at her the while as if she had suddenly observed in her some new and most unpleasing trait.

"I must say I'm surprised at you, Bella Jackson, giving in to that sort of thing. At your time of life! It's all very well for artists, it's part of their trade to be daft-like, but I never thought to see you with a stair like a perpetual spring-cleaning."

"Oh, not as bad as that. You don't miss a carpet, somehow the bare steps are all of a piece with the rest of the house. You must come and see for yourself."

"I'll not do that," Mrs. McArthur said with great decision.

"Oh, mebbe you will. . . . The house is empty now. Lady Jane Rutherfurd and her daughter and niece have taken a small house in Fife. I'm sorry for them, I am indeed. It's not very easy to rise in the world, but it must be worse to come down. I'm going to ask the daughter to visit me. She's an awful nice girl with no airs at all. I think Andy'll like her, and she'll be a great help to me, for goodness knows what I'll do when all the people come to call!"

She sighed as she rose to go, and Mrs. McArthur, remaining seated, said: "Well, I'm glad I'm not in your place. You'll only regret once leaving Pollokshields and that'll be all the time. But *wha will to Cupar maun to Cupar.* I always knew your husband was a climber. Many a time I've said to myself: 'Look at that wee Jackson worming himself in here and there, doing public work for his own ends, thinking he'll get a knighthood out of it. . . .' But you were always an honest soul, Bella, and to hear you talking about 'the county' and 'Lady Jane' and not putting on a stair-carpet makes me fair sick. You can tell your husband from me that a queer sight he'll be as a laird."

She laughed unpleasantly, and rose to her feet, while Mrs. Jackson, flushed and distressed, meekly held out her hand.

"Well, good-bye. You'll be far too grand to remember me when you're the lady of Rutherfurd. I'll miss you, and I'll miss Andy. What does he say about all this?"

But Mrs. Jackson murmured something and fled from the place where so often she had found rest and refreshment, feeling that she had, in very truth, been wounded in the house of her friend.

What Andrew Jackson thought of the change no one ever heard. That young man was not given to confiding his feelings to the world at large. He was respectful to his parents—oddly so in this disrespectful age—and if he sometimes did permit himself to smile at them both, no one knew.

He was an ordinary-looking young man, neither tall nor short, with frank eyes, and a pleasant smile. His mother thought him wonderfully handsome. In the War he had won a well-deserved Military Cross, and since coming home to his father's business much of his spare time had been spent helping with various schemes for the boys and young men of his own city.

Sitting with his mother in her very own parlour one evening before they left Deneholm for good, he looked round the room, which with all its ugliness had an air of homely comfort about it, and said, "You've been happy here, Mother?"

Mrs. Jackson, who was tidying out a large work-basket, looked up at the question.

Andrew was lying back in one of the shabby red velvet chairs smoking a pipe, and watching his mother. She loved to sit so with her son. Her husband was always busy, out at a meeting or a public dinner, or looking over papers in his own room, but Andrew spent many evenings in "the parlour."

"Happy, Andy? Yes, of course I've been happy."

She spoke in an abstracted way, her attention obviously still on the work-basket. Presently she held out a photograph, saying: "It's queer to come across something you haven't seen for years. It's a school group. . . . That's me, that fat one in the front with the curls! Eh, my my, I couldn't sleep wondering what I'd be like, and I got such a disappointment. . . ."

Her son studied the faded picture gravely.

"Where was this taken, Mother?" he asked.

"At the first school I was ever at, a private school in Myrtle Park. My home was in Crosshill, of course. We sat on benches in an upper room and learned out of wee paper books. There were pictures to help us on, and I remember getting a rap over the fingers for spelling t u b—bucket. . . . I wore a white pinafore. Children never wear pinafores now. I daresay they're neater, but I don't know—there was something awful fresh about a clean pinny."

She was disentangling some silks and rolling them neatly on cards as she talked.

"The master was a queer man. I forget how it came up in the class one day, but he was talking about servants of God, and he said to me, 'Bella, have you ever seen a servant of God?' I said I had not, and he told me to come out into the middle of the floor, and he solemnly shook hands with me and said, 'Now you can say you've shaken hands with a servant of God.' . . . But, of course, I was thinking of prophets with long white beards. Jeremiah, you know. . . ."

"Of course," said Andrew.

"It was a queer Glasgow in those days. Crosshill was like a village, and there was a long stretch of vacant ground from it to Eglinton Toll. You'll hardly mind of it like that? And at the foot of Myrtle Park there were big pools or bogs or something that we could skate on in winter. And there were only horse-cars going in and out to town, and they didn't go further than the Park Gate. . . . I stayed at the Myrtle Park school till I was ten and then I went to another private school in Kelvinside till I was seventeen, but I don't think I ever learned much. . . . I got engaged to your father when I was twenty. He was a deacon in the church we went to, and read papers at the Literary Society. . . . He took to walking home with me from meetings and dropping in to supper, but it was long before I could believe he meant anything, for, you see, I wasn't clever, and he was a promising young man. We weren't married for some years because, of course, we had to save, but I was awful happy making my things, and going out with your father to concerts and socials."

She stopped to deal patiently with a very tangled skein, and her son asked where their first house had been.

"D'you not remember it, Andy? Uch, you must. We left it when you were six. It was called Abbotsford, a house in Maxwell Road, a semi-detached villa, just the six rooms and kitchen. We had been married five years when you came, so I can tell you we were glad to see you. And your father was getting on well, and in time he bought Deneholm. It seemed an awful lift in the world to me! We had just the one girl at Abbotsford, and we started here with three experienced women. My! I was miserable with them for a while: I always thought they were laughing to each other when I went into the kitchen, and so they were, mebbe, but I got used to it; and you've to live a long time after you're laughed at! The Rutherfurds' butler's staying on with us, that's a comfort, for he'll keep the other servants in order. He wanted to go with Lady Jane—quite the old family servant in a book—but they said they couldn't do with him in a small house. Miss Nicole said to me that it would never do for them to have a butler in Kirkmeikle, it would be 'trailing clouds of glory,' though what she meant by that I don't know. It's a hymn, isn't it? That's the worst of people like the Rutherfurds, you don't know half they mean; they so seldom talk sense. I can discuss a subject quite well if people'll stick to it, but when they suddenly fly off and quote things. . . . I want to ask you, Andy, d'you think I'll ever be able to take my place at Rutherfurd?" She did not wait for an answer, but went on:

"I was seeing Mrs. McArthur the other day and she fairly depressed me. I've known her so long and she's been such a good friend, and now she seems to have turned against me. I could see she thought I'd be a figure of fun at Rutherfurd, and she was quite bitter about your father, said he was a climber. . . . I think myself men are quicker at picking up things than women. I'm sure when your father married me he didn't know anything about pictures, and old furniture, and the things he cares so much about now. He was quite pleased with our little house, and worked in the garden on Saturday afternoons. I sometimes wish that we'd never got on in the world and that we still lived at Abbotsford."

Andrew knocked his pipe against the fender and put it on the edge of the mantelpiece.

"I wouldn't worry, Mother," he said, in his quiet voice. "You never pretend to be anything you're not, so you'll get on splendidly. Nobody's going to laugh in an unkindly way at you so long as you're sincere. And it doesn't matter greatly if we do amuse our neighbours. What would *Punch* do without jokes about the New Rich? It's better to amuse people than bore them, any day. You laugh too, Mother—then the laughter won't hurt you."

"I see what you mean, Andy. . . . But surely nobody would ever think of laughing at your father?"

"I suppose not. But the best-liked people are those that you can laugh at in a kindly way. And no one has more friends than you, my dear."

"In Glasgow—but I doubt there'll be none of my kind near Rutherfurd. Mrs. McArthur says . . ."

"Never mind Mrs. McArthur. She's a thrawn old body sometimes."

She still looked at her son with troubled eyes.

"And you're a beautiful speaker, Andy, from being at an English school, though I whiles wonder how you've kept it, for my Glasgow accent would corrupt a nation. I doubt Mrs. McArthur's right—but, anyway, I'll always have you. You've been my great comfort all your life."

"That's nonsense," said Andrew, beginning to smash up the fire.

His mother took the poker from him, for it vexed her economical soul to see a good fire spoiled.

"No, it's the truth. . . . Well, well, everything has an end. Somehow, I never thought we'd leave Deneholm. I wonder who'll buy it, and sit in this room? Mebbe children'll play here." She looked wistfully at her son. "I wish you'd marry, Andy. Mind, you're getting on. Thirty-two—and I never saw you so much as look at a girl."

CHAPTER VII

"Tush man—mortal men, mortal men."

Henry IV.

Kirkmeikle was a very little town, merely a few uneven rows of cottages, occupied chiefly by fishermen, and the workers in a small rope-factory, known locally as "the Roperee," half-a-dozen shops, and a few houses of larger size built a century ago. But, on the top of the green brae, crowning it hideously, stood three staring new villas.

The large square one, Ravenscraig, was inhabited by Miss Janet Symington.

It had many large windows hung with stiff lace curtains and blinds of mathematical neatness. Inside there was a bleak linoleum-covered hall containing a light oak hat-and-umbrella stand, a table with a card tray, and two chairs, a barometer hung on the wall above the table. To the right of the front door was the drawing-room, a large, light, ugly room; to the left was the dining-room, another very light room, with two bow windows, a Turkey carpet, and crimson leather furniture. A black marble clock stood on the black marble mantelpiece, and on the walls hung large seascapes framed heavily in gilt.

The late Mr. Symington had been a wealthy manufacturer, and profoundly pious. He was a keen business man, but outside his business his interest centred in religious work. He gave liberally to every good cause, he was not only a just but a generous master, and the worst that could be said of him was that he was a dull man. That he most emphatically was—quiet, dour, decent, dull. He never opened a book unless it was the life of a missionary or a philanthropist; he could not read fiction because it was not true, therefore a waste of time. He had thought highly of his minister, Mr. Lambert, until, one day, he found that honest man reading Shakespeare's Sonnets; after that he regarded him with suspicion. To Mr. Symington life was real, life was earnest, and not to be frittered away in reading Shakespeare.

His wife had been a delicate, peevish woman, who seldom went out, but who enjoyed amassing quantities of wearing apparel, more especially expensive shoes and gloves, which she never wore. She was proud of the fact that all her life she had never needed to soil her hands with house-work, and liked to hold them out to visitors saying, "Such *useless* hands!" and receive compliments on their shape and whiteness. She never read anything but the newspapers, and was not greatly interested even in her children. She died a few months before her husband, not much lamented and but little missed.

Janet was like her father. She had the same rather square figure and large head, the same steady brown eyes and obstinate chin. Mr. Symington had always looked like a lay preacher in his black coat and square felt hat, and his daughter dressed so severely as to suggest a uniform, in a navy blue coat and skirt, a plain hat of the sailor brand, and a dark silk blouse made high at the neck.

There had been a brother younger than Janet, but he had never been anything but a worry and disappointment. Even as a child David had resented the many rules that compassed the Symington household, while Janet had been the reproving elder sister, pursing her lips primly, promising that she would "tell," and that David would "catch it." At school his reports were never satisfactory, at college he idled, and when he entered his father's business he did his work listlessly and without interest. When war broke out he seemed to wake to life, and went "most jocund, apt, and willingly." That hurt his father more than anything. That war should be possible at this time of day nearly broke his heart, and to see David keen and enthusiastic, light-hearted and merry as he had never been at home, to hear him say that these were the happiest years of his life, simply appalled him. When it was all over David came home with a D.S.O. and the *Croix de guerre*, and a young girl with bobbed flaxen hair, neat legs, and an impudent smile, whom he had met in France and married in London when they were both on leave.

For one hectic month all abode together in Ravenscraig, a month of strained conversation, of long silences, of bitter boredom on the part of the young couple, and patient endurance on the part of the elder Symingtons. Then David announced that he could not stand life in the old country, and meant to try to make a living in Canada. His father, deeply disappointed but also secretly relieved, gave him a sum of money, and the couple set off light-heartedly to make their fortune. . . .

Three years later John Symington died, leaving to his daughter complete control of all he possessed, but this last act of his father's did not worry David, for before Janet's letter reached the ranch, David also was dead, killed by a fall from his horse. His widow, liking the life, decided to stay in Canada, and six months later married one of David's friends and sent David's son home to Kirkmeikle to his Aunt Janet.

The next villa, Knebworth, was a different type of architecture. It was of rough-cast and black timber, with many small odd-shaped windows, picturesque grates with imitation Dutch tiles, and antique door-handles.

Mrs. Heggie lived here comfortably, and, on the whole, amicably with her daughter Joan. Mrs. Heggie was more than "given to hospitality," she simply revelled in feeding all her friends and acquaintances. It seemed impossible for her to meet people without straightway asking them to a meal. It was probably this passionate hospitality that had soured her daughter and made that young woman's manner, in contrast, short and abrupt.

The third villa, Lucknow, was occupied by a retired Anglo-Indian and his wife, Mr. and Mrs. Buckler. They had two children to educate and had come to Kirkmeikle because it was quiet and cheap. Mrs. Buckler wrestled with servants, while the husband played golf and walked about with dogs.

There was a fourth house on the brae, much smaller than the others, more a cottage than a villa, which belonged to a Miss Jamieson, a genteel lady, so poorly provided with this world's goods that she was obliged to take a lodger.

She had been fortunate, she would have told you, to secure at the end of the summer season a single gentleman, quiet in his habits and most considerate. He had come to Kirkmeikle because he wanted quiet to write a book—something about exploring, Miss Jamieson thought. He had been with her for three weeks and expected to remain till early spring. His name was Simon Beckett. No one, so far, had made the acquaintance of Miss Jamieson's lodger except Miss Symington's six-year-old nephew, Alastair.

That young person had a way of escaping from his nurse and pushing his small form through a gap in the hedge that divided Miss Jamieson's drying-green from the road, and, on reaching the window of Mr. Beckett's room, flattening his nose against the glass to see if that gentleman was at work at his desk. If he were, Alastair at once joined him, and, with no shadow of doubt as to his welcome, related to him all the events that made up his day, finishing up with an invitation to join Annie and himself in Ravenscraig at nursery tea.

One afternoon in October, a day of high wind, and white-capped waves and scudding clouds, Alastair was returning with Annie from the shore where he had been playing among the boats. He was toiling up the hill, shuffling his feet among the rustling brown leaves and talking to himself under his breath, when Annie called to him to wait a minute, and forthwith dived into the baker's shop. It was a chance not to be missed. Off ran Alastair straight to Miss Jamieson's, walked boldly in at the front door and found his friend at his desk.

"Hello!" said Mr. Beckett, "it's you."

"Yes," Alastair said, panting slightly from his run. "Annie's in the baker's. I've run away."

"Shouldn't do that, you know."

"Why not?" said Alastair. "I wanted to see you. She'll be here in a minute." He looked out of the window and saw Annie already on his track. She was standing at the gate trying to see into the room.

Simon Beckett looked up from his writing and saw her.

"You'd better go, old man."

"I'd rather stay with you. Miss Jamieson's making pancakes for your tea. We only have bread and butter and digestive biscuits."

"I'm too busy for tea to-day. Come to-morrow at four o'clock."

He began again to write, and Alastair saw that there was no real hope of tea, and a story or a game. Still he lingered, and presently asked, "Do you mind coming out and telling Annie you've invited me to tea to-morrow?"

The face that he turned up to his friend was the funniest little wedge of a face, with a wide mouth and a pointed chin and pale blue eyes, the whole topped by a thatch of thick sandy hair; a Puck-like countenance.

Simon Beckett smiled as he looked at it. "Come on, then," he said, getting up and propelling Alastair before him, "we'll make it all right with Annie."

That damsel was not difficult to propitiate. When Alastair had tea in "the room," she had tea in the kitchen, and Miss Jamieson was known for her comfortable ways and her good cooking, so she blushed and said she would ask Miss Symington, and thanked Mr. Beckett in the name of her charge, calling him "Sir" quite naturally, a thing she had never thought to do, for she belonged to the Labour Party and believed in equality. As they were parting, all three on excellent terms, at the gate, Mrs. Heggie and her daughter passed. Joan would have walked on, but her mother stopped.

"Well, Alastair," she said, in the loud bantering tone which she kept for children, "what mischief have you been up to to-day, I wonder!"

Alastair regarded her in hostile silence, while Annie poked him in the back to make some response.

Mrs. Heggie turned to Miss Jamieson's lodger.

"You're Mr. Beckett, I think? How d'you do? Strange that we should have never met, but you're a great student I hear. It must take a lot of hard thinking to write a book. I often say that to Joan—my daughter, Mr. Beckett—for she's inclined to be literary too. . . . We would be so glad to see you any time. Could you lunch with us to-morrow?"

Joan trod heavily on the foot nearest her, and her mother winced but went recklessly on. "No? Then Thursday; Thursday would suit us just as well. 1.30. Then that's settled."

"Thank you," said Simon Beckett, in chastened tones. "It's tremendously kind of you. Yes, Thursday. Good-bye."

"I wonder," said Miss Joan Heggie, coldly, as they walked on, "what possible pleasure it gives you, Mother, to try to cultivate people who quite obviously don't want to be cultivated. You absolutely forced that poor man to come to lunch."

"Oh, I don't know," said Mrs. Heggie. "I think he's only shy."

"Not he, he's unwilling, and I don't blame him. Kirkmeikle society is far from enlivening. Oh, here comes Miss Symington. Don't stop, Mother, for goodness' sake."

But Mrs. Heggie was physically incapable of passing a friend or neighbour without a few words; besides she was wearing her new winter things, and was going to take tea with the doctor's sister, and altogether felt pleased and happy. She shook hands with Miss Symington, hoped she saw her well, and told her where she was going to tea. She rather hoped in return to receive a compliment about her new hat and coat, but none seemed forthcoming, so she said, "Well, good-bye just now, and do come and see us when you have time. . . . Could you lunch with us on Thursday? *Do.* 1.30." (Joan gazed despairingly at the sky.) "That'll be nice. Mr. Beckett is coming. Good-bye. . . . Oh, by the way, did you hear a rumour that the Harbour House is let? Our cook heard it from the postman. Let's hope it's a nice family who'll be a help in the place. Well, good-bye just now. . . ."

"Mother, what do you mean by it?" Joan asked as they walked away.

"I don't know," said Mrs. Heggie, "it just came out."

But there was no real repentance in her tone.

CHAPTER VIII

"Lady Alice, Lady Louise,
  Between the wash of the tumbling seas."

William Morris.

Jean Douglas insisted on taking Lady Jane to Kingshouse out of the way of the removal, and Nicole and Barbara, accompanied by two maids from Rutherfurd, an under housemaid, and a girl who had been "learning the table," set out for Kirkmeikle to make the Harbour House habitable.

It proved a comparatively easy task. Mrs. Agnes Martin had managed to chase out the painters in good time, and had every cupboard and floor scrubbed white when they arrived; the furniture fitted in as if made for the rooms, and very soon the house took on a look of comfort.

Now, after a week, Nicole, all impatience, was planning for her mother's coming.

"You'll go to Edinburgh and meet her, won't you, Babs? and I'll be standing on the door-step to welcome you both. Let's stage-manage it properly, for there's a tremendous lot in one's first impression of a new place. You'd better lunch in Edinburgh and come by the afternoon train—that's much the nicest time to arrive, about four-thirty or five o'clock." Nicole moved restlessly about the room—they were sitting in the drawing-room—altering things here and there, while Barbara sewed placidly.

"We'd better arrange for a car to be waiting at Thornton, don't you think? The first look of Kirkmeikle from the station is frankly ugly, and to jolt down here in a mouldy cab would be very depressing. If you motor you will come through clean harvest-fields, and beside green links, with glimpses of the sea, and then there would be the Harbour, and the open door, and inside familiar things everywhere for her eyes to rest on. . . . If *only* it would be the sort of day I want—a touch of frost and the sky sunset-red, the stars beginning to appear, and . . ."

"Don't expect it," said Barbara. "Rain and an easterly *haar* smothering everything—that's what's most likely to happen."

Nicole laughed. "In that case the house will look all the brighter . . . I'm pleased with it, aren't you? Everything has worked out so amazingly well. Mrs. Martin, for instance. I admit I was rash, but you must own that she looks like being a woman in a thousand, and is certainly a cook in five thousand."

Barbara shook her head. "You do exaggerate so wildly. But I must say she's a good cook, and in these days a cook that will do without a kitchen-maid is something to be thankful for. And I think she'll be good with the other servants; she seems to take an interest in them and tries to make things easy for them."

"I know. She said to me, 'Christina's a rale thorough worker, and Beenie too: they're baith wise lasses.' It's funny, isn't it, that sharp upward tilt in the Fife tongue after the slow soft Border? We'll get used to it in time, as well as to other things. The thing that matters is that Mother should feel herself at home."

Three days later, when the hired car drew up at the door, the scene was almost exactly as Nicole had pictured it. The tide was out, and beyond the low wall a stretch of firm, ribbed sand lay white in the half light; a very new moon hung bashfully in a clear sky; the masts of a sailing-boat stood up black beyond the Harbour; somewhere near a boy was whistling a blythe air. The open door showed a hall glowing with welcome. On a Jacobean chest stood a great bowl of brown chrysanthemums and red berries; sporting prints that had been in the gun-room at Rutherfurd hung on the walls; the clock, the chairs, the half-circular table, the rugs on the floor were all old friends.

When Lady Jane entered the drawing-room she cried out with pleasure.

The curtains had not been drawn, for Nicole liked the contrast between the chill world of sea and gathering dark outside and the comfort within, and from the four long windows in a row could be seen the tide crawling up the sand under the baby moon. Inside a fire of coal and logs blazed, and amber-shaded lights fell on the old comfortable chairs, the cabinet of china, the row of pictured children's faces over the mantelshelf. The tea-table stood before the sofa, with the familiar green dragon china on the Queen Anne tray; Lady Jane's own writing-table was placed where the light from the window fell on it, with all her own special treasures—the big leather blotter with her initials in silver which had been the combined gift of her children the last birthday they had all been together, the double frames with Ronnie and Archie, a miniature of Nicole as a fat child of three.

Barbara put an arm round her aunt and led her to her own chair.

"Well now, dear, we've got our journeying over in the mean time, and here is Christina with the tea and we want it badly after our exiguous lunch. The Club was so crowded, Nik, and the food so bad: everything finished except stewed steak with macaroni, and tapioca pudding to follow."

Nicole had been standing by one of the windows watching her mother's face. Now she came forward to the fire.

"You must have been very late, you foolish creatures. Pour out the tea, Babs, and I'll hand round the hot scones. See, Mummy, everything baked by Mrs. Martin! Yes, even that frightfully smart-looking iced cake. She's a treasure, I assure you, procured by me single-handed, because Babs was sceptical and cautious."

Lady Jane smiled at her daughter and took a bit of scone.

"Darlings," she said, "what a pretty room! I think our things look nicer than they ever did before. . . . These four windows with the seats looking to the sea—I almost seem to have seen the room before, I feel so at home in it."

"Then," said her daughter, "we shan't need to butter your paws. Isn't that what you do to make a cat feel at home?"

"Meaning me a cat! Trust Nicole to think of some absurd thing. No, there's no need for such extreme measures. I am more than happy to have my own dear things about me in this funny little sea-looking house, and my two girls to talk to. . . . I've all sorts of messages from every one. Jean's kindness was endless . . ."

"Tell us," said Barbara.

After dinner in the eighteenth century dining-room with its striped silk curtains drawn—an excellent dinner, for Mrs. Martin was anxiously determined to justify the faith Nicole had placed in her—they sat round the drawing-room fire. Lady Jane got out a strip of lace that she was making, Barbara knitted a child's jacket: Nicole sat in a low chair with a book in her lap, a large book with dull brown covers.

Her mother looked curiously at it. "What have you got there, child? It looks ponderous."

Nicole held it up for her mother's inspection.

"I found it among Father's books and it's going to be a perfect god-send to me. I hear the sound of Tweed while I read. . . . It's Sir Walter Scott's *Journal*. Every night I shall read a bit, it ought to last me quite a while for there are two stout volumes, and afterwards I'm going to read Lockhart's *Life*. I've got that too, in the closest print I ever saw, one fat calf-bound volume presented to Father as a prize in 1888—nearly forty years ago."

"But, Nicole," Barbara began, "you never could read Scott's novels. I remember Uncle Walter offering you a prize if you'd read through *The Antiquary*, and you stuck."

"I did. To my shame be it said. But that was only a tale, and this is true. I shall read bits out to you. It's the sort of book that simply asks to be read aloud."

Barbara passed her cousin a skein of wool. "Hold that for me, will you, while I wind? . . . Most of our time I suppose will be spent in this way, working a little, reading a little, talking, writing letters . . ."

"Yes," said Nicole, "I hope so. I do love a routine, doing the same thing at the same time every day. We shan't ever have to go out in the evenings now, so we'll have ample time to read and meditate. . . . I mean to read all Trollope. I've never had time before to settle to him. . . . Isn't it odd to sit here in this little house—we three— and not know anything whatever about the people who live round us. We who have always known every one for miles round!"

"Dear," said her mother, "Aunt Constance wants to know if you would like her to write to friends of hers—Erskine, I think is the name—who live not very far from Kirkmeikle."

Nicole bounded in her seat at the suggestion.

"Oh, Mother, beg her not to. Think what a disaster! Those Erskines would feel they had to come motoring over and invite us, and we would meet their friends, and before we knew where we were we would be in a vortex and all our beautiful peace smashed."

"Nonsense," Barbara said, impatiently tweaking the wool. "Do hold it straight, or how can I wind? Of course we want to know the Erskines. It will make all the difference."

"It's so like Aunt Constance to have friends in every out-of-the-way nook and cranny!" Nicole grumbled. "I thought we'd be safe here."

Barbara finished winding her ball, and said severely:

"You know quite well that there is no one here we could possibly be friends with."

"Isn't there, haughty aristocrat? Well, I can't keep myself to myself. I want to know everybody there is to know, butcher and baker and candlestick-maker. Yes, even the people who live in the smart villas. The Erskines would be exactly like all the people we have always known. Now that we are different I want to know different sort of people."

"How are we different?" Barbara asked sharply.

"We've come down in the world," her cousin told her solemnly.

"Ridiculous! Aunt Jane, isn't she horrid? Surely you don't want me to make friends with all and sundry?"

Lady Jane laughed. "I certainly think with you that we should get to know the Erskines, but it's pleasant to live on good terms with all our neighbours."

"Of course it is," Barbara agreed, "if we stop there, but Nicole never knows where to draw the line. She gets so disgustingly familiar with every one—I sometimes think she's a born Radical."

"What a thing to say about the Vice-President of the Tweeddale Conservative Association! Well, you make friends with these Erskines, Bab, and I'll confine my attentions to Kirkmeikle. I know I was born expansive. I can't help it, and really it makes life much better fun. And, Mums, you will sit here and watch the game, and entertain first Bab's friends then mine. It will be as entertaining as a circus."

"I wonder," said Lady Jane. "I wonder!"

CHAPTER IX

"Young fresh folkes, he and she."

Chaucer.

Barbara had once said of Nicole, and said it rather bitterly, that she might start on a journey to London, alone in a first-class carriage, but before her destination was reached she would have made the acquaintance of half the people in the train. An exaggerated statement, but with a grain of truth in it. There was something about Nicole that made people offer her their confidence. Perhaps they saw sympathy and understanding in her eyes, perhaps they recognised in her what Mr. Chesterton calls "that thirst for things as humble, as human, as laughable, as that daily bread for which we cry to God."

Certainly she found entertainment in whatever she heard or saw, and never came in, even from a walk on the moors round Rutherfurd, without something to relate. An excellent mimic, she made people live when she repeated their sayings, and "Nikky's turns," had been very popular with her father and brothers. Nowadays her recitals were not quite so gay: her mother and Barbara laughed, to be sure, but there was something wanting. However, as Nicole often told herself, the world was still not without its merits.

It was not likely that in such a small community as Kirkmeikle the Rutherfurds would be neglected, and, indeed, every one had called at once: the minister and his wife, Mr. and Mrs. Lambert; the doctor and his sister—Kilgour was their name; Mrs. Heggie dragging her unwilling daughter; Mr. and Mrs. Buckler, and Miss Symington. But they all called very correctly between three and four, and found no one in, for the new inmates of the Harbour House took long walks every afternoon to explore the neighbourhood.

Barbara took up the cards that were lying one day and read aloud the names:
"Mrs. Heggie, Knebworth.
"Miss Symington, Ravenscraig.
"Mr. and Mrs. Buckler, Lucknow."

Then, flicking the cards aside, she said: "How ghastly they sound! we'd better not return the calls for ages; we don't want to land ourselves in a morass of invitations."

"A morass of invitations," Nicole repeated. " 'Morass' is good. Each step taken, that is, each invitation accepted, leading you on until you get stuck deeper and deeper in the society of Kirkmeikle. . . . But what makes you think they would want to entertain us so extensively? It would only be tea—and that's soon over."

"Luncheon," said Barbara gloomily; "perhaps dinner."

"Well, even if they did! There are so few of them, we'd soon get through with it."

"Yes, but we'd have to ask them back."

"Why not?" Nicole asked. "Mrs. Martin would give them a very good dinner, and Mother would entertain them with her justly famous charm of manner; and you and I are not without a certain pleasing . . . I can't think what word I want."

Barbara shrugged her shoulders. "Personally, I have no desire to impress the natives. The names of their houses are enough for me. . . . Aunt Jane, have you fixed on the pattern of chintz you want? I'd better write before the post goes."

The next day came a breath of winter. The quiet dry weather that had prevailed for some time vanished, hail spattered like shot against the long windows, a wild wind tore down the narrow street and whistled in the chimneys, while white horses raced up the beach and threw spray high over the wall.

After luncheon Nicole came into the drawing-room with a waterproof hat pulled well down over her face, and a burberry buttoned up round her throat, and announced that she was going out.

"My dear, on such a day!" her mother expostulated.

"I'm 'dressed for drowning,' " Nicole assured her. "I only want to clamber about a bit and watch the waves. They'll be gorgeous along at the Red Rocks. . . . Won't you come, Babs?"

But Barbara, looking at the tumult of water through the streaming panes, shook her head. "It's a day for the fireside, and some quite good books have come from the *Times*, and I've work to finish—Do you mind?"

"Not a bit. I rather like to walk by my wild lone. . . . No, Mums, I will not take Harris, she's particularly busy to-day tidying clothes. No, nor Christina, nor Beenie—not even Mrs. Martin. They would tell us with truth that they had been engaged as domestic servants, not as props in a storm. I assure you I'll come to no harm. Don't worry. I'll be home for tea."

In spite of her daughter's reassuring words Lady Jane spent most of the afternoon looking out of the window, nor was Barbara at all comfortable with her new novel and her work, and when the early darkness began to fall and her aunt asked if she thought anything could have happened to Nicole, she became distinctly cross and said that it was extremely selfish of people to make other people uneasy with their whims and fancies. "So like Nicole," she added, "to want to go out and watch waves. I'm sure we can see more than we want of them from these windows. I don't know why we ever came to live by the sea. . . . But I suppose I'd better go and look for her—restless creature that she is!"

But even as she got up to go, the door opened and the wanderer appeared, her wet hair whipped against her face, her eyes bright with battling against the wind.

"Nicole," cried Barbara, relief in her voice, "you look like the east wind incarnate! The very sight of you makes me feel cold and blown about."

"Such fun!" Nicole gasped. "Yes, rather wet, Mums, and more than a little battered. Give me ten minutes to change. Here's Christina with the tea——"

They demanded to know, when she came down dry and tidy, where she had spent two and a half hours on such a day.

"We got so anxious about you that Babs was just starting to look for you when you came in," her mother told her. "And we had no idea where you had gone."

Nicole patted her mother's hand and Barbara's knee to show her penitence, and took a bite of buttered toast.

"It was wretched of me to worry you, but, you see, I've been making the acquaintance of some of our neighbours."

"On such a day!" cried Lady Jane.

Nicole laughed aloud. "You may say it, Mums, on such a day! . . . Give me my tea over here, will you, Babs? Having sat myself down by this gorgeous fire I must stay hugging it. Thanks! Now this is cosy, and I'll tell you all about it. . . . First, you must know, I went to the Harbour, which was quite deserted except for a boy lounging against the wall as if it were a summer day. A wave came over the top and nearly washed me into the water. I had to hold on to a chain."

"Then," cried her mother, "you must have been drenched from the very beginning. Oh, my dear, that was reckless of you."

"No, no. Salt water never gave any one cold. I gasped and spluttered for a bit to the evident amusement of the boy and said, 'Oh! *what* a storm!' He grinned again, and spat into the water. 'Storrum?' he said. 'It's no a' storrum, it's juist a wee jobble.' Wasn't he a horrid fellow? . . . I left the Harbour then, and walked along the shore to the Red Rocks. It took me about half an hour, for the wind seemed to clutch at me and pull me back; indeed when I reached the rocks I got down on my hands and knees and crawled; I thought it would be rather silly to risk breaking a leg. . . . The waves were fine. To watch them rush in and hurl themselves against the rocks so exhilarated me that I found myself shouting and encouraging them—— It's a good thing you weren't there, Babs, you would have been ashamed. I was just thinking of coming home when I suddenly heard, quite near me, a scream which almost immediately turned into a laugh, and turning round I found a small boy clutching his hair while his hat soared sea-wards."

"A small boy alone on the rocks?" Lady Jane asked.

"Not alone, Mums. There was a young man with him."

"A young man!" said Barbara.

Nicole's eyes danced. "An extraordinarily good-looking young man with a delightful voice, and, as far as I could judge among jagged rocks and gathering darkness and a wind blowing at a thousand miles an hour, some charm of manner. Aha!"

Barbara made a sceptical sound, and asked what such a being was doing in Kirkmeikle.

"Ah, that I can't tell you," Nicole confessed; "he didn't confide in me. The small boy is called Alastair Symington and lives with his aunt at Ravenscraig. When we call on that lady we may hear more."

"It's a matter of no interest to me," Barbara declared.

"I threw out feelers," continued Nicole, "to find out what he was doing here. I told him what *we* were doing here, but he offered no confidences in return. I think he must be in rooms near Ravenscraig, for the small boy kept hinting that he would

52

like to go to tea with him. . . . You'd like him, Mums, the small Alastair, I mean. He told me a long tale about the minister, Mr. Lambert, finding a gold comb on the sands, which he took home with him, and that night as he sat in his study somebody tapped at his window, and it was a mermaid to ask for her comb! According to Alastair the minister went with her to the Red Rocks and had dinner with her—cod-liver oil soup, which, it seems, is excellent, and a great delicacy—and she asked him what she could do to show her gratitude. There had been a great storm a little while before that, and many boats had gone down, and women had lost their bread-winners, and the mermaid gave the minister gold and jewels from the bottom of the sea to sell for the poor people."

Barbara looked indignant. "What a very odd sort of minister to tell a child such ridiculous tales."

Nicole helped herself to strawberry jam, and laughed as she said: "A very *nice* sort of minister, I think. Alastair was stumbling along in the storm looking for another comb. He said he thought it was the sort of day a comb would be likely to get lost, and he's very anxious to see a mermaid in a cave. Mums, we must call at once on Miss Symington, if only to get better acquainted with this Alastair child. How old? About six, I think. A queer little fellow and most pathetically devoted to this tall young man. To a boy brought up by women a man is a wonderful delight. The two escorted me to the door. I asked them in to tea, and Alastair was obviously more than willing, but the man said they were too wet, as indeed they were."

"Did you discover the man's name?"

"I did, from Alastair. He is called Simon Beckett."

Lady Jane wrinkled her brows. "Isn't there something familiar about that name—— Simon Beckett?"

"Aren't you thinking of Thomas à Becket?" Nicole suggested.

"No, no. I am sure I read somewhere lately of a Simon Beckett having done something."

"Crime?" said Nicole. "He didn't look like a criminal exactly. Isn't there a Beckett who boxes?"

"I know," cried Barbara. "I know where you saw the name, Aunt Jane. It was in the account of the last attempt made on Everest, more than a year ago. You remember? Two men almost reached the top and one died. Simon Beckett was the one that came back. You remember we read about the lecture to the Geographical? Uncle Walter was tremendously interested."

"Why, of course. . . . But this can't be the same man, Nicole?"

"Of course not," Barbara broke in. "What would *that* Simon Beckett be doing in Kirkmeikle?"

"*This* Simon Beckett certainly didn't mention Everest to me," Nicole said, as she began on a slice of plum-cake.

CHAPTER X

"O brave new-world
That has such people in't."

The Tempest.

A few days later Nicole and her mother—Barbara had pleaded excessive boredom at the prospect and had been let off—set out to return their neighbours' calls.

Nicole carried a card-case which she had unearthed from somewhere, and was very particular about what her mother should wear.

"The new long coat with the grey fur, Mums; it has such a nice slimifying effect—not that you need it. What a blessing that we are sylphs, you and I. Wouldn't you hate to feel thick, and to know that you had a bulge at the back of your neck? . . . You really are ridiculously young, Mums. You could wear your hair shingled, for the back of your neck is the nicest thing I ever saw, almost like a child's; and your little firm face is so fresh—only the eyes shadowed a little. And not one grey hair! How have the gods thus guarded your first bloom, as the poet puts it?"

Lady Jane, standing before the looking-glass pulling a small hat over her wavy hair, laughed at her daughter.

"All this flattery because I've consented to go with you and call! Or is there something more you want?"

Nicole stood beside her mother looking at the reflection in the mirror.

"We might easily be taken for sisters, Mums. In fact, I might be mistaken for the mother, for there is something stern in my visage that ages me. . . . How nice it is that now mothers and daughters can dress alike—the same little hats, long coats, and unimportant dresses. At one stage of the world's history you would have worn a bonnet and a dolman, Madam, and I should have had a sailor-hat tilted up behind (see old *Punches*) and a bustle. What we have been spared!"

"Come along, then, and get our visits over. I'm ready."

As they mounted the long street that led from the shore to the villas on the top of the brae, Lady Jane remarked, "I should think every one will be out this fine day."

Nicole pinched her mother's arm. "Don't say it so hopefully; you're as bad as Barbara. I want them all to be in. . . . Do let's speak to this woman; she's a friend of mine, a Mrs. Brodie."

They were passing a little house, the doorway a few steps under the level of the street, with two little windows each curtained with a starched stiff petticoat of muslin, and further darkened by four geraniums in pots. A large, cheerful-looking woman was standing at the door, holding a baby, while two slightly older children

54

played at her feet. She greeted Nicole with a broad smile, and when she said, "Mrs. Brodie, this is my mother," she gave an odd little backward jerk of the head by way of a bow. They admired the baby, and Lady Jane asked how many other children she had.

"Just the nine, no mony if ye say it quick eneuch," and Mrs. Brodie laughed loudly at her own joke. "Ma auldest's a laddie; he's leevin' the schule gin the simmer holidays. Then comes three lasses and the twins, an' thae three." She looked at the two playing gravely at her feet with a broken melodeon, then she chirruped to the baby, who leapt and plunged in her arms like a hooked trout.

"Ay," said his mother encouragingly, "I ken ye'rs a wee horse. I ken fine ye're a wee horse. By! ye're an awfu' ane."

Lady Jane's eyes met those of Mrs. Brodie over the head of "the wee horse," and she said, "You're a happy woman, Mrs. Brodie, with your children all about you."

"Ay, I mind ma mither aye said a wumman's happiest time was when her bairns were roond her knees, an' she gethered them under wan roof when nicht fell. I'm thrang eneuch, guid kens, but it's hertsome wark."

She nodded to the mother and daughter as they left her, remarking that they were getting a fine day for their walk.

Miss Symington was in, they were told, when they had rung the bell at Ravenscraig, at which intelligence Nicole cast an exultant glance at her mother.

There was no one in the drawing-room, and the housemaid lit the gas-fire and left them. The room had an unused feeling; no books lay about; in one of the big bow windows there stood on the floor an aspidistra in a yellow pot.

"It looks lonely," Nicole said, eyeing it.

Miss Symington came in, apologising for having kept them. She was dressed to go out, and looked oddly bulky in her coat and skirt and round felt hat beside the mother and daughter in their slim long coats and close-fitting hats.

It was obvious at once that if there was to be any conversation it would have to be made by the visitors.

Nicole, poising her card-case between the tips of her fingers, smiled gaily into the somewhat unresponsive face of Miss Symington and began to talk. She and her mother tossed the ball of conversation deftly to each other, appealing often for confirmation to the shadowy third, putting remarks into her mouth until that lady began to feel that she shone in company.

As they were leaving, "You have a nephew," Nicole said.

"Alastair," said Miss Symington.

"Yes, Alastair. He and I made friends on the rocks the other day. Is he in? I expect he'll be out this fine day?"

"He goes out every afternoon from two to four."

"Perhaps some day you would let him come to tea with us? My mother likes boys—don't you, Mums?—and Alastair is such a lamb. He must be a great delight to you."

Alastair's aunt seemed surprised at this assertion.

"I do my best for him," she said, "but I'm afraid I don't understand boys. I would never think of asking a boy to come to see me for pleasure."

Lady Jane leant forward, smiling. "Do bring Alastair to tea with us, Miss Symington, and we'll all try to amuse each other. Which day? Wednesday?"

"I've a Mothers' Meeting that afternoon."

"Thursday, then?"

"Yes, thank you. We shall be very pleased, though I don't see why you should be bothered having us. What hour?"

"Oh," said Nicole, "shall we say four sharp, then we'll have time to play after tea. That's fine."

As they walked down the gravel-path Nicole said, "I'm so glad I brought the indoor fire-works left from our last children's party. I nearly gave them away, not thinking that Kirkmeikle might produce a small boy. . . . Miss Symington's a nice woman, Mums, you think? Very, very well-meaning and decent."

Lady Jane looked back at the house as they went out of the garden gate into the road.

"It is odd that a woman can live in a house like that and make no effort to make it habitable. I wonder if it has ever occurred to her how ugly everything is. I didn't see one single beautiful thing. . . . She has nice eyes, Miss Symington, like clear pools, and I think she is utterly sincere."

Her daughter nodded. "I know, but she is inarticulate, isn't she? I felt ashamed of talking so much, but what could I do? . . . This is Knebworth. Here lives one Mrs. Heggie, with at least one daughter and, I daresay, others that we know not of. Quite a different type, to judge from the house. . . . Isn't this fun? Let's greet the unknown with a cheer. An electric bell this time, and, I expect, a much smarter parlour-maid. . . I thought so."

She followed her mother and the short skirts and high heels of the maid through an ornate little hall, complete with a fireplace and ingle-neuk and red tiles, into the drawing-room. It was a room of many corners and odd-shaped windows, comfortably furnished, the walls hung with reproductions of famous pictures. Tall vases filled with honesty and cape-gooseberries stood about, and a good fire burned on the red brick hearth. A small book-case fitted into a niche held a selection of the works of the most modern writers, while on a table lay some magazines.

Mrs. Heggie was seated on a low chair beside the fire, with a writing-pad on her knee, and a bottle of ink perched precariously on the rim of the fender. As she rose to greet her visitors paper and envelopes and loose letters fell from her like leaves in an autumn gale. She was a tall, stout woman with a round face and an all-enveloping manner.

"Well now," she said, as she held out one hand to Lady Jane and the other to Nicole, "isn't this nice? and to think I nearly went out this afternoon! If it hadn't been for some letters that I knew simply must go to-day nothing would have kept me in."

"But," said Lady Jane, "I'm afraid we are interrupting you—your letters ____"

"Letters," Mrs. Heggie said airily, thrusting her visitors into two arm-chairs, "they can wait: it's hours till post-time, any way." She subsided into her own low chair and asked in tones of deep interest, "And how d'you think you're going to like Kirkmeikle?"

"Very much indeed," Lady Jane replied. "We were lucky to get such a nice house. You know it, of course—the Harbour House?"

"I don't. The Harbour House is a sealed book to me, and I've always had the greatest desire to see inside it. There is something about it—the crow-step gables and long, narrow windows facing the sea—that fascinates me. I've often tried to see in when I passed! Mrs. Swinton was a queer woman. She never visited the other people in Kirkmeikle. I suppose she had her own friends and kept to them, and of course she was quite right, if that was the way she was made. People are so different. Now, I'm miserable if I don't know everybody. I don't think I'm a busy-body, but I do take the greatest interest in my neighbours and their concerns, and if I can do anything to oblige them I'm just delighted. Rich or poor, I like people and want to be friends with them."

"Hurrah!" said Nicole. "I feel like that too. Life is much too short to be exclusive in. One misses so much."

Mrs. Heggie beamed at the girl. "That's what I always say. You'll find Kirkmeikle very friendly—what there's of it. I suppose everybody has called?"

"Let me see," Nicole said gravely: "Miss Symington, Mr. and Mrs. Lambert, Dr. Kilgour and Miss Kilgour, Mr. and Mrs. Buckler—you and your daughter."

Mrs. Heggie nodded her head at each name. "That's all," she said. "Are you returning all the calls to-day?"

"We hope to," said Lady Jane, the corners of her mouth turning up. "We have just seen Miss Symington and are going on to the Bucklers."

Mrs. Heggie sat forward. "You've seen Miss Symington? She's very nice, quiet and solid, but very nice. Does a lot of good with her money. She's very rich, you know, though you wouldn't think so to look at her. She's like her father: all he cared for was missionaries and evangelistic meetings. D'you know, every week-end Miss Symington has a minister of sorts staying with her! She keeps up the Mission-hall her father started in Langtoun for his workers, and the preacher stays with her. Of course she isn't quite young; she must be forty-five anyway, and she's so discreet that it's quite all right, but I always expect to hear that one of them is going to hang up his hat—as the saying is."

The visitors were silent, not quite knowing what comment to make, and Mrs. Heggie continued:

"You'll like the Bucklers. Somebody told me that Mr. Buckler had quite a distinguished career in India, and I must say they are most obliging neighbours. I'm sorry for poor Mrs. Buckler with her servants. Now, you'll stay and have tea; I'll ring for it at once so as not to hinder you. It's early, I know, but you may not be offered it at the Bucklers, for they have a housemaid who objects to giving tea to visitors unless they come at tea-time. No? Oh, don't rise. You're not going already? Joan may be in any minute. She's all I have now. My husband died three years ago, and two boys in the Argentine. Joan is inclined to be literary—— Well, if you must go. . . .

57

When will you come for a meal? Let me see, this is Monday—Would lunch on Wednesday suit you? Friday, then? we *must* fix a day."

"If you don't mind," Lady Jane said in her gentle way, "we won't fix anything just now. We are still rather busy settling down and would rather have no engagements yet awhile. Might we, perhaps, propose ourselves for tea one day? That will be delightful, and you must come and see us in our funny little house when you can spare time."

"I'll do that," Mrs. Heggie promised heartily, "and you come here whenever you like. Just run in, you know. I'm always sitting here—except when I'm out somewhere. And when you feel like accepting invitations you'll come here first, won't you? I'll give a dinner for you. . . ."

Half an hour later when Joan came in and asked casually if there had been any visitors, her mother replied with studied carelessness, "Only Lady Jane Rutherfurd and her daughter. They were here quite twenty minutes—the *civilest* people I ever met. And I didn't ask one single question, though I'm just dying to know what brought them to Kirkmeikle. They're charming, perfectly charming."

Joan sat down heavily in a chair. "For any favour, mother," she said, "give that worn-out adjective a rest. Whenever you ask what sort of person some one is you're told—'Charming,' and when you meet her she's nothing of the kind. Charm is not the common thing people make it out to be."

"Oh well, Joan, I'm not going to quarrel with you about adjectives. You know far more about them than I do, but when you meet the Rutherfurds you'll be charmed with them, I know that. . . . The daughter looked at your books—what a nice friend she'll be for you. . . ."

Mr. and Mrs. Buckler received their callers with less excitement than Mrs. Heggie.

Nicole smiled up at Mr. Buckler as he put her into a carved chair with a brilliant embroidered cushion for a seat, saying: "The East in Kirkmeikle! I smelt it as soon as I came into the hall."

"You recognise it? You know India?"

"Only as a Paget M.P.—I was out for a cold weather when I first grew up, just after the War. I went out to an uncle and aunt who happened to be there. . . . Have you been home long?"

Mr. Buckler, a thin man with tired eyes in a sun-dried face, drew up a chair beside Nicole.

"I retired about five years ago," he said; "glad enough at the time to get away, but looking back at the life now, it seems the best on earth. Distance lending enchantment! I dare say if I went back I would be disillusioned. It's not the India I went out to as a boy, and loved. Things, they tell me, are altering daily for the worse —still it's India. . . ."

While Nicole and her companion recalled people and places Lady Jane listened while Mrs. Buckler told her of the trials of a retired Mem-sahib. She was a pretty, faded woman, with a vivacious manner.

"When I think of my jewel of a *Khansamah* who made everything go like

58

clockwork and produced anything you wanted at a moment's notice like a *djinn* in a fairy tale, I almost weep. Of course, we're as poor as rats now and we can't afford really good servants, and I know I ought to be thankful that at least we have honest women in the house, but, oh, Lady Jane, their manners! They never think of saying 'Mum' to me, and very seldom 'Sir' to Ernest. They seem to think it demeans them, whereas, as I tell them, all servants in good houses say it as a matter of course. They merely prove their own inferiority by not saying it. But how can one teach manners to women who don't know what manners mean? It was quite funny the other day, though vexing. A friend of ours had motored a long way to see us, and found no one in. Mrs. Heggie—our neighbour next door—came up to the door at the same time and heard the conversation. Our friend has a very forthcoming, sympathetic manner, and she said to Janet, the housemaid, who had opened the door: 'Now, tell me, how *is* Mrs. Buckler? Has she quite got over that nasty turn of influenza? Is she out and about again?' Janet stood quite stolid (so Mrs. Heggie said), then drawled in a bored voice, 'Och, she's quite cheery'!"

Lady Jane laughed. "It was rather funny, wasn't it? and most reassuring, and after all manners aren't everything: I wouldn't worry about them if I were you."

"We tried," Mrs. Buckler went on, "to be exceedingly polite to each other, Ernest and I, to see if that might have a good effect, but it hadn't. They merely seemed to think we were feeble-minded. . . . But as you say, we might have worse trials—and Janet isn't as bad as she was. The last time we had some people to dinner Janet's way of offering the vegetables was to murmur 'Whit aboot sprouts?' . . . But I really don't mind anything if Ernest and the children are happy."

"You have children?"

"Two—a boy at Oxford and a girl in Switzerland. That's why we live here. It is cheap and we can pinch in comfort—a contradiction in terms! . . . Must you go?"

Mr. Buckler walked down to the gate with the visitors, and as they stood talking a tall young man came towards them.

"Ah, Beckett, the very man I wanted to see! I heard this morning from the India Office. . . . By the way, have you met? . . . May I introduce Mr. Beckett? Lady Jane Rutherfurd, Miss Rutherfurd."

"Mr. Beckett and I have met already," Nicole said. "I told you, Mother— Alastair's friend. . . ."

As they walked away Lady Jane asked if they had done enough for one day. "It must be nearly tea-time," she said.

"Well," said Nicole, "we haven't time to attempt the Kilgours, but we pass the Lamberts' house, it's just here, this green gate in the wall—we needn't stay more than a few minutes. Come on, Mums."

The green door opened into a good-sized garden surrounded by a high brick wall on which fruit trees were trained. There was a lawn, wide borders which still held bravely blooming Michaelmas daisies and chrysanthemums, and plots of rose-trees—evidently a place on which was bestowed both labour and love.

" 'A garden enclosed,' " said Nicole, as they went up the path to the front door. "And what a pleasant-looking house!"

The manse was a rather long, low house built of grey stone. The front door stood open and children's voices could be heard. When Nicole rang the bell a very young servant answered it. She was not more than fifteen, but her hair was put tidily up, and she wore a very white cap and apron: her face shone with soap and rubbing.

"No, Mem," she said shyly. "Mistress Lambert's oot, but she'll be in to the tea aboot half five, and it's that noo. Would ye . . . come in?"

Nicole picked out a card while Lady Jane said:

"No, thank you—we shall hope to see Mrs. Lambert another time. . . . Who is this young person?"

A small fat child had trotted out, and now held the apron of the maid before her as a protection, while she peered at the visitor.

"That's Bessie. She's three," the rosy little maid said proudly, smiling down at her charge.

"I can skip, but Aillie can't," the baby informed them, and received the rebuke, "Dinna boast—Aillie canna walk, let alane skip."

The mother and daughter smiled to each other as they let themselves out of the little green gate in the wall.

"Doesn't she remind you, Mums, of the heroine of Jane Findlater's story? She's 'terrible bauld and firm.' *And* so trim and clean. A most decorous maid for a manse—— Oh, my dear, would you mind? Just one more place. There's an old woman here—Mrs. Martin told me about her—who comes from Langhope and wants terribly to see you."

"Yes, but need we go to-day?"

"Well, I'm just afraid she may be looking for us. Besides, it's so near—the Watery Wynd, the place is called. The first turning. This must be the place. There is the outside stair that I was told to look for. ' "On, on," cried the Duchess.' Take care, these steps are uneven. . . .'"

The short November day was nearly done, and Betsy Curle's kitchen was dark but for the firelight. She peered through the shadows at her visitors—"An' whae may ye be?" she asked.

Lady Jane went forward. "I hope you don't mind us coming," she said. "Mrs. Martin, our cook at the Harbour House, told us you came from our own part of the world and we wondered if we might come and shake hands with you. We're still feeling far from home."

Betsy rose to her feet painfully and tried to drag two chairs to the fire for her visitors.

"Let me," Nicole said. "You sit down in your own chair and tell us how you have strayed so far from the Borders."

"Ye may say it! Sit whaur I can see ye. I mind yer faither, an' yer grandfaither, an' yer great-grand-faither!"

"Oh!" Nicole leaned forward, her eyes alight with interest. "My great-grandfather! Tell me about him."

"He was handsome, like a' the Rutherfurds, and mad! as mad as a yett in a high wind." She turned to Lady Jane. "I mind fine o' yer leddy-ship comin' to

60

Rutherfurd—the bonfires and the flags. That was fower and thirty years syne come Martimas. Ye were but a young lass in a white goon and a hat wi' feathers, an' they ga'ed ye a bunch o' red roses."

Lady Jane nodded. "I remember both the hat and the roses. . . . Where was your home?"

"D'ye mind the white-washed hoose at the edge o' the pine wood afore ye come to Langhope? Ay, the keeper's cottage. I bade there; ma faither was heid keeper at Langlands."

"And what brought you to Fife?"

"Ye may ask! I mairrit a jiner. If I hed ta'en ma mither's advice—'Betsy, lass,' said she, 'there's little sap amang the shavin's.' . . . His folk cam' frae Fife, an' efter we'd been mairrit a wheen years, he got the offer o' a job here. I niver likit it—nesty saut cauld hole! No' like oor ain couthy country-side. I canna thole the sicht o' the sea, sae jumblin' an' weet. What wud I no' gie for a sicht o' the Tweed an' the Lammerlaw! But I'll never get hame noo, an' I canna see hoo I can lie quait in that cauld kirkyaird. Of course ma man's there, but it's an exposed place."

"Have you no children?" Lady Jane asked.

"Juist ae son leevin'—an' he's mairrit."

"Oh—but he's good to you, I hope."

"As guid as his wife'll let him be. O, ma guid-dochter's a grand gear-gatherer. She was a Speedie, and they're a' hard. She's big an' heavy-fitted like her faither. Handsome some folk ca' her! Handsome, says I, haud yer tongue! But I'm no' sayin' nae ill o' her, ye ken. She's welcome to a' she can get. I never grudged naebody naething their guid wasna' ma ill."

"Well," Lady Jane rose to go, "I hope you'll let us come again. I want to talk to you about home. . . . Don't get up. I'm afraid you've bad rheumatism?"

"Ay, it cam' on me aboot five years syne. I was as soople as an eel till then. . . . Hoo's Agnes Martin pleasin' ye?"

"Oh, she's a treasure. And I hope she's happy with us."

"Happy eneuch, I daursay. She's the sense to bow to the bush that gie's her bield," and Betsy lowered herself slowly into her chair, while her visitors went down the stairs feeling rather snubbed.

CHAPTER XI

"This for remembrance."

Hamlet.

Though Barbara had professed herself unable to endure the boredom of calling on her new neighbours, she greeted her aunt and cousin with interest on their return.

"Well," she said, as she roused the fire to a blaze, and lit the wick under the lamp for the teapot, "how have you fared, intrepid spirits?"

Lady Jane had left her coat in the hall and stood, looking absurdly girlish in her straight black dress, her bright hair escaping from under the close-fitting hat, warming her hands at the fire.

"We've done a good afternoon's work," she said, smiling at Barbara, "and enjoyed it."

"You haven't had tea, I hope? for Mrs. Martin has baked a very special cake —a reward for well-doing, I suppose."

"I'm glad to hear it," said Nicole; "I'm hungry. Mrs. Heggie wanted to give us tea, but Mrs. Buckler didn't offer because of a disobliging maid. Wasn't it luck we got three out of the four at home?"

"You call it luck?" Barbara said.

"And," continued Nicole, "we've put our first foot in the morass of invitations you dreaded so. Miss Symington brings her nephew to tea on Wednesday."

Barbara groaned. "I knew it! The thin end of the wedge. . . . What are they like, Aunt Jane? I want your unbiassed opinion and not a rose-tinted appreciation from Nikky."

Lady Jane sipped her tea contemplatively for a minute, then said:

"Nice people, I think. We called first at the three large villas. Miss Symington's is most depressingly bleak and ugly, but Miss Symington herself seems a quiet inoffensive woman. Almost entirely silent, though. Nicole and I had to talk all the time to avoid embarrassing pauses. Some people seem to feel no responsibility about keeping up a conversation. I wonder if it is shyness——"

"Sheer laziness," said Nicole. "I'm sure I'd much rather be silent; it would be easier than keeping up a bright vivacious flow of talk."

Her mother laughed sceptically and went on. "Then we went to Knebworth, a type of modern villa that is all right in London suburbs but should never be seen in Scotland. The bleak Ravenscraig goes better with the East wind and the sea birds and the high sharp voices of the people—— But it was comfortable and, in a way, pretty, with its absurd ingleneuks and latticed windows, and Mrs. Heggie herself is a character. She is one of the people who help to make the world go round. She lifts, and doesn't merely lean. You couldn't please her better than by using her. But she's lost in a place like this, her energies need freer scope."

Nicole nodded. "Not only a good sort, but an amusing good sort. She reminded me a little of Mrs. Jackson. . . . To-day I felt she was constrained, and we were strangers, but I should like to be there when she really lets herself go. . . . I wonder what the daughter is like. I expect the books were hers. Evidently a modern young woman, an admirer of the latest lights. I don't think, somehow, I'll ask her to come and read Scott's *Journal* with me."

"The third house," said Lady Jane, "is called Lucknow, and appropriately enough shelters an Anglo-Indian family. . . ."

"Ah, but, Mother," Nicole broke in, "don't lay that to their charge. It was christened before they took it—Mr. Buckler told me."

"What are the Anglo-Indians like?" Barbara asked.

"Well, there's always something rather pathetic about retired Anglo-Indians. I know it's great impertinence to find people pathetic who in no way desire sympathy, but it must be such a change to come back from an important position with 'a' thing braw aboot ye,' to live an unoccupied life in an ugly little villa, among people who take no interest in the thirty years you have given to the Empire, and don't want to hear anything about the things that have been more than life to you. Mrs. Buckler is a nice woman and not nearly so discontented as she might be. She takes her servant troubles humorously, and she's proud of her children."

"Why, Mums, have they children? They struck me as being distinctly childless. I'm glad they have. . . . I liked Mr. Buckler so much. And, Babs, we met the young man I told you of the other day, and—wasn't it silly?—I clean forgot to ask any one if he really is the Everest man."

"But," said Barbara, "you haven't called on the whole population of Kirkmeikle? There are others, surely."

"We called at the Manse but Mrs. Lambert wasn't at home, but we didn't reach the Kilgours."

"I must say they sound a dull lot," Barbara said as she poured out tea.

"They're not exciting, perhaps," Nicole confessed. "But, Babs, I want you to come and see an old woman—Betsy something, who comes from Langhope. To hear her speak was like a drink of water in a thirsty land. . . ."

Nicole took a bun and her cup of tea and went and curled herself into one of the window-seats. She liked peering out at the Harbour in the dusk, watching the lights along the shore come out one by one.

"I wonder," she said in a little, "how the Jacksons are getting on. Jean Douglas has never said she has called."

"Too busy, I expect. By the way, Christmas isn't very far away. What are we going to do about it this year?"

Nicole smiled lazily at her cousin. "Need we do anything about it? Are 'the last sad squires' expected to keep Christmas? We've shed all our responsibilities, haven't we? I expect Mrs. Jackson will do great things at Rutherfurd. Do you

63

remember . . ." She stopped realising that to recall other and happier days was not wise.

"I must see in time about boxes for my old people," Lady Jane said. "I wouldn't like them to feel forgotten. The next time you go to Edinburgh, Babs, you'll see about it, won't you?"

"Yes, Babs, you're our shopper-in-chief. Please get me a selection of useful articles also. . . . I believe, Mums, that this wise virgin has already heaps of presents, all made by herself, stored neatly away. . . . Oh, letters!"

Barbara took them from Christina. "Three for you, Aunt Jane, two for me, the rest for Nikky."

Nicole looked with distaste at her lot. "Bills, I think. I don't believe I'll open them."

"Isn't that one from Jean Douglas?" Barbara said, and Nicole pounced on it with the cry, "Now we shall have some news."

A few minutes later Lady Jane looked up from her letters and said, "Well, Nikky, what does Jean say?"

Nicole handed over the sheets to her mother who began at once to read, while Barbara, perched on the arm of the chair, looked over her shoulder.

"I wish, dear Nikky," so the letter ran, "that I could go with this letter across the Forth Bridge, and slip into the Harbour House about five o'clock in the afternoon, and find you three sitting in the room with the four long windows. I expect I would be able to greet everything in the room as an old friend! I would take my own chair and draw it up to the fire, and with my feet on the fender, listen to all you have to tell me.

"Tom has been laid up with lumbago which has kept me pretty much at home, but on Thursday last I fulfilled my promise and went to call at Rutherfurd. I simply hated going. Every inch of the road brought back some memory, and to go through the gateway and wave as usual to the curtseying Lizbeth, and to know that I would find no Rutherfurds at Rutherfurd, made me both fierce and tearful, so that I was in no mood to be pleased with the new owners.

"The place is very well kept, leaves most carefully swept up, and gravel raked, not a twig out of place, and oh, my dear, how beautiful it is! It came back to me with a sort of surprise the exquisiteness of the lawns running up to the mouth of the glen, the burn with its turf bridge, the bracken-covered hill-sides, and the long grey front of the house. No wonder the Jacksons coveted it!

"It was a comfort to have Johnson open the door. His manner was perfect—I always admired the artistry of Johnson—chastened with regret that times had changed yet subtly exuding loyalty to his new employers.

"The hall, as of course you know, is the same, except that Mrs. Jackson has introduced a few little conceits of her own, a bronze boy now supports a lamp, another figure holds a tray for cards. There are also masses of hot-house flowers, an opulent innovation which I resented, and I missed—but what is the good of tearing your heart with what I missed, you who will miss it 'until the day ye dee.'

"I was shown into the drawing-room. Nothing could spoil that gracious room, and Mrs. Jackson, to do her justice, hasn't tried. I told you I would hate her, but when she rose to greet me in a smart velvet gown complete with a hat covered with Paradise-plumes, and an ermine stole, I thought she was about the most pathetic thing I had ever seen. She gave me a very warm welcome, and as I sat beside her on the sofa she confided in me that, except for the minister and his wife, I was her first caller.

" 'I wish they'd come,' she said wistfully, 'for the cook bakes special things for tea every afternoon, and I dress myself, and when nobody comes I hardly know where to look. I'm a wee bit afraid of Johnson anyway—— D'you mind telling me, are there many people round about to call?'

"I told her truthfully the names of every one from the Duke downwards. She sighed. I fear she finds life rather a burden.

"The son came in while we were at tea. 'Andy,' his mother called him. I like 'Andy.' His manner to his mother was perfect, he had an amused, protecting smile on his face as he watched her sitting there in her Paradise-plumes and her ermine. He told me with the greatest frankness that he knew practically nothing about country life, and felt very much in a mist, so I asked him to come to Kingshouse and let Tom put him wise about a lot of things. Mrs. Jackson and I had a very interesting talk, mostly about you people. She wanted to know everything I could tell her about you all, and she is pathetically eager to model herself on your dear mother. It is funny, but I know you won't laugh. I confess that you were right, there is something about Mrs. Jackson that melts one's heart. I range myself by her side, and I'm going straight away to hustle people up to call. I simply can't bear to think of the poor dear dressing up for people who don't come, and feeling shamed in the eyes of her servants. . . . Nikky, I can't tell you how I miss you all, how every one misses you. Tilly Kilpatrick even, and Alison Lockhart twisted that wicked amusing mouth of hers at me the other day, and said: 'I'm a worse woman because Jane Rutherfurd has left the district.' Tell your mother that though it sounds obscure I feel sure it is a compliment. Write to me very soon, and promise that you will come for Christmas. It's going to be quite gay, two hunt balls, and several private dances, not to speak of theatricals at Langlands. Won't you be tempted? A fortnight? Or even one week? Please think about it, and tell my dear Lady Jane I ask as a great favour that she should add her persuasions to mine. She would have Barbara with her and she is a host in herself.—All love from Mistress Jean——."

"Will you go, dear?" Lady Jane asked, as she handed back the letter.

"Is it likely? Leave you and Babs our first Christmas in a strange place. Why, Mums, there aren't so many of us now that one can go without being missed. Besides, I'd hate it above everything."

"I thought you were so fond of the Douglases?" Barbara said, as she got out her work.

"So I am, but—oh, don't let's talk about it. I should feel like a ghost going back to dance among ghosts. Some day I've promised to go to Mrs. Jackson, but that's different. Then I wouldn't be going for my own pleasure. . . ." She looked into the fire with unseeing eyes for a minute, then jumped up. "Now I'm going to have my hour with Scott's *Journal*: that takes me back in the spirit to my own country, I don't want to go back in the flesh."

"Poor Mrs. Jackson," said Lady Jane. "I'm glad Jean likes her. She will absolutely bully the Jacksons into popularity. Can't you see her?"

"What surprises me," Nicole said, "is that she seems to like the son so much. Somehow I had the impression that 'Andy'—I like the soft drawl his mother gives his name—was a sort of suburban *knut*, but he can't be."

"It's comparatively easy," Barbara put in drily, "to like a young man with prospects. Indeed, you will find that the Jacksons, vulgar as they are, will go down very well. People will smile and tell stories about them to each other, but their cheques for all the numberless causes will be very acceptable. And, remember, there are a lot of girls in the district and no superfluity of unmarried men."

Nicole laughed. "That's quite true, Babs. Mums, had you realised what benefactors we are?"

CHAPTER XII

"It is a gallant child, one that makes old hearts fresh."
The Winter's Tale.

On the morning of the Thursday that he had been invited to tea with the Rutherfurds, Alastair and his friend and attendant, Annie, disported themselves among the boats at the Harbour. It was not usual for them to be down on the shore in the morning. Generally, Annie "did" the nursery, and Alastair played in the garden, and then they went for a walk; but to-day Miss Symington had gone after breakfast to Langtoun, the sun was shining, and Alastair had begged so hard for the Harbour that Annie had skirmished rapidly through her work, cast care to the winds, and raced with him down the brae.

It was exceedingly fortunate, Alastair felt, that his aunt had gone away that day, for his friend Mr. Beckett had given him a repeater pistol complete with ammunition (caps), and, also, there was a Norwegian boat in the Harbour manned by strange-speaking but wonderfully friendly sailors. He and Annie had been invited on board and had sat in a fascinating cabin and drunk strong black tea out of gaily-painted bowls. It was a good thing Miss Symington had been spared the sight, but it had all been so novel and exciting that neither had ever thought for a moment they were doing wrong.

Now they were pirates. Alastair was a quaint figure in an overcoat made for his growth, inclined to be humpy at the back, and a dark grey felt hat; but if his appearance suggested a lay preacher rather than a law breaker, his spirit left nothing to be desired. As he stamped about shouting hoarsely what he fondly believed to be curses, Annie said he made her blood run cold. That damsel's idea of the behaviour of a pirate was an odd one. She leant languidly over the side of the boat and sang a song which she was much addicted to, beginning, "When the spring-time comes, gentle Annie."

Alastair was firing his new pistol so recklessly after what he called a "retreating craft," that he did not notice Nicole Rutherfurd until she leant over and shouted to him:

"I know who you are. You're Paul Jones. He was a tremendous pirate and he came from these parts."

"Oh?" said Alastair politely. "Would you care to see my pistol? It goes on firing as long as there are any caps."

"And then what happens?"

"It stops. I'm coming to your house this afternoon."

"You are," said Nicole.

"Yes. I was going to ask you, only Annie wouldn't let me ring your bell, would you mind if Mr. Beckett came with me rather than Aunt Janet?"

"But—does Mr. Beckett want to come?"

"No," said Alastair truthfully, looking very straight into Nicole's eyes, "he hates tea-parties, but he might come if he was asked. He says you can't very well not accept, when ladies ask you. That's why he went to Mrs. Heggie's."

"I see. And what about your Aunt Janet? Would she rather stay at home too?"

"She'd stay at home if you asked her to," Alastair said, and received a prod in the back from Annie, who was struggling with suppressed giggles. "Give over this meenit," she whispered hoarsely, "or I'll tell yer aunt." Then, to Nicole, "Please be so good as not to heed him, Miss"; and again to her charge, "Come awa' hame, ye ill laddie."

But Alastair heeded her not, for, walking along the shore, he spied his friend Mr. Beckett and flew to him like an arrow from a bow.

Nicole and Annie followed, the latter apologising incoherently as they went.

"Naebody pits the things he says into his heid: he juist oots wi' them afore ye ken whaur ye are. He's daft aboot Maister Beckett—— Ye see, he's fair seeck o' weemen, for he sees nothing else. He didna mean to be impident to you, for he's an awfu' polite laddie. I dinna ken whaur he gets his manners, they're no' Kirkmeikle anes onyway."

Nicole shook hands with Simon Beckett, and remarked on the freshness of the morning.

"Yes, too good to work in. The mornings have been so good lately and the afternoons so bad, that I'm trying the plan of walking in the morning and writing the rest of the day."

"Oh, you write?" said Nicole with lively interest.

"Not to say write. . . . I'm doing a job—trying to write an account . . . an unholy mess I'm making of it." He looked so embarrassed and ashamed of himself that Nicole changed the subject by asking him if he would give them the pleasure of his company at tea that afternoon.

The tall young man looked suspiciously at Alastair, while Alastair looked out to sea, and Nicole said, "I know it's too bad to ask you, for like all men I expect you loathe tea-parties, but if you would come and support Alastair in a household of women you would be doing a kindness. . . . Then we may expect you? Why, Alastair, we'll have quite a party, shan't we? You and your aunt and Mr. Beckett and three of ourselves—enough to play musical chairs!"

Before four o'clock another man had been added to the party.

Lady Jane, who had taken a liking for Mrs. Brodie, the woman with the nine children, had gone along with something for the baby and had found the household in trouble. The eldest boy had been brought in with a bad cut on his forehead and a broken arm. The doctor was with him, a clean-shaven elderly man with a weather-beaten face.

Mrs. Brodie was standing near, holding her youngest, the "wee horse," under one arm. "Eh my!" she said, wiping her face with her apron, "folk gets awfu' frichts in this warld. Ye're niver lang wi'oot something—a family's a sair trauchle. I was juist thinkin' we were a' quat o' the measles an' here we are again!"

"Wull I dee? Wull I dee?" wailed the patient, a freckled fair boy of fourteen.

"Not you," said the doctor, "but you deserve to, hanging on carts as I've seen you do fifty times. If you had dropped off before a motor instead of a gig where would you have been, I'd like to know? . . . Now, then, Mrs. Brodie, he'll do all right if you keep him quiet. Don't let him sit up on any account. I'll look in again before bedtime. Be thankful he's got off so easy." He pinched the cheek of the baby. "That's a fine child. He's the best you've got, and they're not a bad-looking lot taking them as a whole. Good day to you."

Lady Jane and the doctor went out into the street together. "Which is your way?" he asked.

"Down here—to the Harbour House."

"Ho! so you are one of the new-comers? My sister called on you—Kilgour's the name—but she found you out. I think you must be Lady Jane Rutherfurd?"

"I am, and I'm hoping to meet your sister soon——— What a nice place Kirkmeikle is!"

"I'm glad you like it. I've lived here all my life and I think there's no place to compare with it. Are you interested in old things? No one is about here; like the ancient Athenians they follow after new things, and they don't know their own old town. I haven't much time, being an Insurance slave, but there's a spare hour or two nearly every night when I can shut myself into my den. My sister has an ill will at my craze: she says I waste both coal and light, but bless me! a man can't live by bread alone and it's an innocent pastime delving in the past."

"And are you going to give to the world the result of your delving?"

Dr. Kilgour laughed. "Ah, that's another matter. I doubt if any publisher living would take the risk of bringing out a book that would only interest a few. . . . But we'll see. I go off here."

He stopped and held out his hand.

"But we are almost at the Harbour House," Lady Jane said, "Won't you come in and have some tea before you go on with your rounds? I'm sure you need it."

Dr. Kilgour hesitated. "I'm afraid my sister would say I wasn't dressed for company. I've on a terrible old coat, but the thought of tea is tempting. And I'm very fond of your old house. I knew it well in Mrs. Swinton's time, for I was her doctor for nearly thirty years."

"Oh, so you knew Mrs. Swinton? She seems to have been something of a veiled prophet in Kirkmeikle. No one seems actually to have known her."

"Ah well, you see, she didn't visit in Kirkmeikle—she wasn't a woman who made friends—and she always drove to Aberlour to the Episcopal Church there. A fine woman in her way, but the most reactionary old Tory I ever met. She would have turned an ordinary moderate man into a howling red Bolshevist in ten minutes. And yet you couldn't help admiring her somehow——— Many a time she ordered me out of the house and got Barr from Aberlour or Dawson from Langtoun, but she always came back to me again. And never was a bit abashed to send for me either, that was the funny thing. Like an old woman here, Betsy Curle, who says: 'I've tried Barr, an' I've tried Dawson, but I've juist had to fa' back on Kilgour!' There's a great deal in being used to a doctor; it's natural to like a change, but when people are really ill they want back their old one."

Lady Jane laughed as she ran up the steps and opened the door.

"There's more in it than that," she said. . . . "I think we'll find the girls in the drawing-room, and tea will be ready shortly. We're having it early to-day, for Miss Symington is bringing her nephew to see us."

"A party!" said Dr. Kilgour. "I'm being punished for coming out so shabby. But I might wash my hands at least. . . . Yes, I know the cloak-room, thank you."

Tea had to be in the dining-room that afternoon, and the striped curtains were drawn at the windows, and candles in red shades gave a festive look to the table. There were crackers too, red crackers, for this was Alastair's party, and a great iced cake, stuffed not only with raisins and peel, but with threepenny bits and rings and thimbles.

Alastair had never seen such a table in his life and looked at it with grave concerned eyes, saying nothing.

"It's either a belated Hallowe'en party or a premature Christmas party," Nicole explained, as they took their places. "Hallowe'en we'd better call it, for we're going to 'dook' for apples. Alastair, are you good at 'dooking'?"

The child swallowed a bit of bread and butter and said, "I don't know. I've never tried."

"Alastair has hardly ever been to a party," his aunt explained. "There are so few children of his age within reach that he rarely has any one to play with."

But Alastair, not liking to be pitied, broke in:

"I've got Annie: she plays, and Mr. Beckett knows heaps of games."

"I don't believe, however," Nicole said, "that Mr. Beckett has ever 'dooked' for apples."

"I haven't," that gentleman confessed. "What exactly is the rite?"

Nicole nodded at him. "Wait and see," she advised.

Dr. Kilgour had already drunk two large cups of tea, and was enormously enjoying the hot scones and the feather-light "dropped" scones.

"Curious eerie time, Hallowe'en," he remarked; "cold winds, cabbage runts, red apples, and looking-glasses! You know the superstition that if a girl looks into the glass at midnight on Hallowe'en, she'll see the man she's to wed? A farmer's wife near here, I've been told, advised the pretty kitchen-maid to go and look. The girl came back—'Sic blethers,' she said, 'I only saw the maister an' his black dowg.' 'Be kind to ma bairns,' said her mistress, and before Hallowe'en came round again she was dead, and the kitchen-lass reigned in her stead. . . . What d'you think of that, Miss Symington?"

"It's not very likely to be true," Miss Symington said prosaically.

Lady Jane laughed. "It's a good tale, anyway," she said. "Pass Alastair the chocolate biscuits, Nikky. Babs dear, will you cut the cake. . . ."

Immediately after tea a small wooden tub half full of water was set on a

70

bath-mat by the careful Christina in the middle of the drawing-room floor, the apples were poured in, and Barbara stirred them about with a porridge stick, while Nicole knelt on the seat of a chair, with a fork in her hand.

She was as serious and absorbed as a child as she hung over the back of the chair waiting an opportunity to drop the fork among the rosy bobbing apples. She chose her time badly and the fork slid harmless to the bottom of the tub.

"No good! Now, Alastair, you see how it should be done—or, rather, how it shouldn't be done." She knelt beside him on the chair, one arm round him. "Now— very careful. Wait until they slow down a bit and drop the fork into the thick of them. . . . Oh, well done, you *almost* got one there: the fork knocked off a bit of skin."

Immensely encouraged, Alastair descended to the floor, and asked whose turn it was next. "Mr. Beckett's, perhaps?" he suggested.

"Miss Symington first, I think," Nicole told him, "and then comes my mother and Barbara."

Miss Symington found herself meekly accepting the fork and mounting the chair. It was a thing she had never expected to do again in this life, but she dropped it with precision, and it was fished out sticking in a large apple.

Barbara wiped the apple and presented it to the victor.

"We'll put Mr. Beckett next," Lady Jane said, and Alastair nearly tumbled into the tub in his anxiety that his friend should succeed: but he failed.

"It was too difficult," Alastair said loyally, "they were going round so fast."

"If Barbara wouldn't stir so lustily," Lady Jane complained. "Let them settle. Now, you see, I've got one."

Alastair secured half-a-dozen apples before he could bear to see the tub removed, and endeavoured to stow them all about his person for future consumption.

"Fireworks now," Nicole told him.

"I must go," said Dr. Kilgour. "I've stayed far too long already, but it's been fun. Thank you for my good tea, Lady Jane. . . . I'll send you that book, Beckett, I think it'll interest you."

The fireworks were produced and set off, to the almost solemn joy of Alastair. Everything was warranted harmless, but the place stank of brimstone, and when Miss Symington saw confetti bombs explode, and sparklets shed flying sparks of light in all directions, and fire balloons ascend to the ceiling, she felt that this was no amusement for the drawing-room.

She stared in sheer amazement at the almost girlish abandon of Lady Jane, who was the most reckless conductor of fireworks. "Apply a light," she said, without troubling to read the directions, and immediately applied a light to anything she saw which had an end sticking out. And these girls, too! working so hard to make a child happy, throwing themselves heart and soul into his entertainment, not playing down to him but playing with him, and obviously enjoying it. All this trouble about a little boy! Miss Symington could not understand it. She had been brought up to believe that children should be seen, not heard. Alastair would be past bearing if he were made to feel so important. Mr. Beckett spoiled him, too; Annie said he played with

71

him for hours, just like Lady Jane and these girls. They were all quite different from the people she was accustomed to meet—much simpler and at the same time very puzzling, full of fervour about things of no moment, and quite off-hand and careless about really serious matters. Very good to look at, she admitted, glancing across the room to where Nicole sat cooling herself in one of the windows. She wore a straight tight black satin dress, with a soft white pleated ruffle starting from the shoulder and continued all down one side. The wicked extravagance of a white ruffle! Why, it wouldn't go on more than once or twice. . . . And to sit there with the window open and the night air blowing in on her bare neck!

Simon Beckett crossed the room and stood by Nicole, who smiled up at him, inviting him to admire the outlook.

"I sit here always after tea," she told him, "and look out at the sea and the lights. . . . We do enjoy these quiet evenings. Mother plays Patience or writes letters, Barbara sews, and I watch the lights when I'm not reading." She twisted the blind-cord and asked, "D'you write in the evenings?"

Simon nodded. "At least I try to, but I get so stuffy and restless that I'm generally glad about nine o'clock to dash out for an hour and tramp about."

"Is it a novel you're writing?"

"Oh, Lord, no." He looked aghast at the idea. "I'm only putting into as decent English as I know how, the record of our expedition in the Himalayas."

"Yes," Nicole said, "I thought you must be that Simon Beckett."

"You see," Simon said apologetically, "there's no one else to do it, or you may be sure I wouldn't have attempted it."

"It must be fine, though, to have a job like that to do; something you've *got* to begin every morning, something that no one else could do. I envy you."

"Oh, I don't know. I don't suppose it matters much to any one, but I'd feel a slacker if I didn't do it. . . . But the worst of it is I'm no manner of use at writing, I sit for hours over one sentence. I never had much of a head . . ."

He stopped and pulled at his tie, then said bashfully:

"I wonder—would it be an awful bore to you—if any time I'm in a worse hole than usual I came and asked your advice? I'd be awfully obliged if you'd sometimes give me a hand."

"I'm afraid," said Nicole, with unusual diffidence, "that I don't know much about style."

Simon laughed aloud. "Style! If I can make it sense I shan't worry about style."

"In that case we shall feel honoured—I speak for mother, Babs, and myself —if you will come down some night and dine and talk over any difficulty. Mother can spell really wonderfully, and Babs is clever. . . . To write a book must be far worse than attempting a high peak."

Simon Beckett groaned. "The next time I go out I'll settle there. Nothing again will ever induce me to attempt to lecture or write on the subject."

"Oh, you lecture too?"

"I have lectured twice. But never again. It was an awful exhibition . . ."

He turned to Alastair who had come up to him, saying:

"What is it, Bat?"

"Aunt Janet says I've got to go home?"

Simon looked at his watch. "By Jove, it's going on for seven o'clock. Past your bedtime, old man."

"Why d'you call him 'Bat'?" Nicole asked.

"Because," Alastair explained, "my name's too long and he thinks I'm like a bat. He calls Annie 'Gentle Annie.' "

"Your aunt's waiting for you," Simon interrupted. "Yes, I'm coming too."

Alastair departed reluctantly, comforted, however, by the fact that his pockets were full of nuts and apples; and Nicole had put into his hands a box of chocolates and an electric-torch as parting gifts. "So that you may light them home," she told him, as he trotted away his hand in Simon's.

He chattered all the way home to his friend, but Miss Symington walked deep in thought. When she opened her own front door and went into the hall she stared round her as if she were seeing it for the first time. After the Harbour House how bare it looked, how bleak. The unshaded incandescent gas made an ugly light. Before her she saw the hall she had just left, the soft-shaded lamps, the coloured prints on the walls, the polished table reflecting the big bowl of bright berries, the chests with their brass trays and candlesticks and snuffers, the blue and yellow of the old Chinese rugs, the warm pleasant smell of good fires and good cooking and well-kept furniture. She sniffed. Her own house did not smell so pleasantly. There was a mixed odour of hot iron and something burning in the kitchen range, for the cook had an economical but unpleasing habit of putting potato-peelings and such things in the fire.

Miss Symington went into the dining-room. The fire was low, and one gas burned dully. A green chenille cloth covered the table, and there was an arm-chair on either side of the fire, and eight smaller chairs were ranged along the wall under the oil-paintings. Presently a tea-cloth would be laid corner-wise on the green cloth and her supper set. How dull it all seemed! She was not a woman who greatly cared for comfort and good food and pretty things about her, but to-night she felt that something was lacking.

"You'd better go to bed, Alastair," she said. "Annie will be waiting for you. D'you like Lady Jane and the two young ladies?"

"Yes, they're kind and pretty and they smell nice!"

Miss Symington was rather scandalised—fancy a child noticing that! but she merely said:

"Run away to bed."

"Yes." He was collecting all his treasure to show Annie. "Good night, Aunt Janet."

But Miss Symington did not reply. She was looking at herself in the mirror above the mantelpiece.

CHAPTER XIII

"This is the flower that smiles on every one."
Love's Labour Lost.

A few days later when Nicole was coming home from a tramp over the golf-course, she met Janet Symington at her own gate. They talked for a few minutes, then Janet on a sudden impulse asked Nicole to go in, and she went. Janet took her guest into the dining-room, remarking that she generally sat there.

The daily papers lay on a small table by the fire, along with a Bible and a pile of hymn-books and a work-basket. Janet motioned Nicole to the arm-chair at one side of the fireplace and seated herself in the other. She had wanted to see this girl again, but now that she had got her seated at her own fireside she found nothing to say.

"I suppose," she began awkwardly, "things will seem strange to you. I mean to say Kirkmeikle. . . ."

"Strange? Well, I've never lived in a little town before, and it's all very new and interesting. We enjoy it—mother, Babs, and I. Perhaps I enjoy it most, for I believe with Mr. Pope that the proper study of mankind is man! Mother and Babs are more—well, withdrawn. I mean to say they would be content to sit up in a tower, hardly troubling to look out of the window, whereas I would want to be down jigging with the crowd in the market-place."

"Oh!" said Janet. Then, after a pause, "I suppose you will always have lived a very gay life?"

"Oh dear, no! far from it. You see, when I grew up the War was just finishing, and my two brothers had been killed, and my father was beginning to be ill, and there wasn't much thought of gaiety in any of our heads. Of course, I have had some very good times; my aunts have me in London for months at a time, and I had a cold weather in India; but I've lived a great deal quietly at home in the country. . . . When my father died we found we couldn't keep up our house—Rutherfurd; and we were very lucky to get the place sold almost at once; we heard of the Harbour House, liked it, took it, and here we are! Mine is a very simple life-story so far, I must really get it coloured up a bit. It's ridiculous to be twenty-four and to have done so little."

Miss Symington clasped her hands in her lap. "I'm forty-seven," she said, "and I'm beginning to think I've done nothing at all."

"Oh, but you," cried Nicole, with her usual swift desire to make people pleased with themselves, "you are an important person, directing a household of your own, and with a nephew to bring up—that in itself is a big job. And you do a lot of good works, I hear."

"I expect you're an Episcopalian, Miss Rutherfurd?"

Nicole, rather surprised, said, "No. The Rutherfurds have always been Presbyterian, except perhaps before the Reformation, when I was an Irish rat, which I can scarcely remember."

Miss Symington held on to the first part of the sentence, which had been sense, and replied to it. "I'm glad of that, for I always feel that a difference in the form of worship makes a barrier."

"I never thought about it," Nicole said truthfully. "Mother was brought up in the Church of England. Have you lived alone long?"

"Since my father died four years ago. My mother died two years earlier, and my only brother died in Canada about the same time as my father."

"Oh." Nicole clasped her hands. "I know what it means . . . but I always had my mother. Anyway, you have Alastair. I do envy you him. What we would give to have a little boy in the house! . . . And you're rich, aren't you? That must be rather jolly."

Miss Symington shook her head. "My money has never given me any pleasure, and I've never found that people have liked me any the better because of it. Of course, I give systematically to deserving charities."

Nicole stared at Janet, sitting holding the *Scotsman* between her face and a by no means too hot fire.

"But how dull!" she said. "I wouldn't give systematically to anything—not though the Charity Organisation Society clapped me in jail for not doing it! All the fun of giving is giving where and when you like, and I don't believe it does the harm they say, anyway." Nicole lay back in her arm-chair and glowered defiantly.

"Money is a great responsibility," Miss Symington said primly.

"So it is, but if I were you I wouldn't let it weigh on me. Give half a crown to the next tramp—or five shillings if you want to make a 'gesture' as the papers say —and see if you don't enjoy the look on his face."

"Oh, I never give to beggars."

Nicole made a face. "I give to every single one," she said, and laughed. "You see what a thoroughly unsatisfactory person I am—selfish and sentimental and wayward, everything you're not."

"You're willing to let me have all the virtues but you keep the graces." Miss Symington smiled and flushed as she spoke, astonished at her own repartee, then went on, "I quite agree you have everything I haven't—youth and . . . I suppose you would call it charm."

Nicole flung out her hands. "Not that, not charm; don't accuse me of that— I'm so sick of it. 'Charrum—a kind of a bloom on a woman,' doesn't Barrie call it?"

"Does he? That will be in a play. I never go to the theatre."

Nicole was aghast. "But—oh, but what you are missing!"

"I daresay, but I couldn't sit comfortably in a play-house. I'd be like the two old ladies in Edinburgh who were persuaded to go, and were hardly seated when a cry got up of 'Fire', and the one turned to the other and said, 'And we'll go straight to the Pit because we're on the Devil's territory—and to think, too, that it's Prayer-Meeting night!' "

Janet's eyes had a slight twinkle as she told the story, and Nicole cried, "The lambs! But you don't really believe that, do you? That it's wrong to go to a play?"

"It would be wrong for me. . . . But to go back to charm. D'you know what Alastair said of you and your mother and cousin when he got back from the Harbour House? 'They're pretty and kind and they smell nice.' . . . I was brought up to think it wrong to spend much time or money on my appearance. My mother had a passion for fine underwear and silk stockings, and we thought it just part of her illness. My father despised all that sort of nonsense. He gave his time to higher things, and I've tried to follow out his wishes—about the Mission Hall he started in Langtoun, and all his other schemes."

"I know you do a tremendous lot," Nicole assured her; "and don't you have a parson of sorts staying with you every Sunday?"

"Yes. I arrange for a speaker every week for the Hall, and of course I give hospitality. It's nothing,—only supper on Saturday night, and there's a fire in the library and they sit there; then Sabbath's a busy day with services and classes, and they go off on Monday morning. We often have very good speakers. If you would care to come some Sabbath? . . ."

"Yes, thank you, I would. . . . D'you never go away, Miss Symington? never take a holiday?"

"Oh yes. I go for a month to Crieff Hydro, every summer. A lot of ministers go, and it's very nice."

"I see." Hearing steps on the gravel Nicole turned her head. "You're going to have visitors, I'd better go."

"No, please. It's only Mr. and Mrs. Lambert. I go to their church. Do stay and see them."

Mr. Lambert was a man of about five-and-thirty, small and thin, with a whimsical, puckered face. He was afflicted with a slight stammer and had a funny way when he came to a difficult word of helping it out by giving little slaps to his trouser-leg. His wife was a slim, dark girl, with a gentle manner and a frank smile. They both shook hands cordially with Nicole, and regretted that they had been out when she called with her mother.

"But I saw your small daughter—and I know something of you, Mr. Lambert, from Alastair. He told me the story you told him about the mermaid's comb and the cod-liver-oil soup."

Mr. Lambert looked shy, and stammered when he spoke.

"I sometimes t-t-ell him stories when I meet him on his walks. . . . I hope you like Kirkmeikle, Miss Rutherfurd?"

"I do. It's a likeable little town."

"And the inhabitants?"

Nicole appealed to Mrs. Lambert. "What am I to say? Criticism is never welcome."

"We don't mind it in Kirkmeikle," the minister told her. "We're used to it. Fife folk are hard critics, so say away?"

Nicole shook her head. "But I've nothing to say. I haven't seen anybody more than once, and that once they were very pleasant. It's very difficult, don't you think, to find horrid people except in books? The worst you can say of most people is that they are dull, and I expect that is a wise arrangement, for dull people are much easier to live with than scintillatingly brilliant people."

"Talking of books," said Mr. Lambert, "unless you're a great reader you'll find it very dull here in the winter. We've a small book-club among ourselves that's a great help. But you may belong to a library?"

"We get our books from *The Times*. Whenever you want a new book, let me know and I can order it for you."

"That would be kind," the minister's wife said eagerly, "for sometimes we wait months before we get a book we're keen about. Indeed, we've only now got *Page's Letters*—but they were worth waiting for."

"Really, Mrs. Lambert," Janet said, as she knelt down to pick up a coal that had fallen on the hearth, "I don't know how you find time to read, with two infants and so much housework."

"Ah, but there's always time to read, odd half-hours, and even ten minutes aren't to be despised that give you a refreshing page or two to go on with."

"In that case," said Nicole, "you must only read the best. It would be too bad to waste those precious snatched minutes on rubbish. . . . If I come across anything specially good, may I bring it to you? Just now old books suit my mood best, and I'm utterly behind with new books."

"Oh, do you read according to your mood?"

Nicole had risen to go, but at Mrs. Lambert's question she sat down on the arm of her chair and said:

"Yes; don't you? I like contrasts. If I'm having a tremendously gay time in London I read dull memoirs to recall to myself my latter end! In India I used to like to sit at the end of the long Indian day and listen to the monkey-people, and watch the kites swoop down, and hear the conches from the temple, and read Barrie—all about Jess and Leeby and the intimate details of the Thrums kitchen. It was like seeing a minutely painted Dutch interior against the background of the Matterhorn!"

"And tell me," said Mrs. Lambert, "what d'you read when life is terribly ordinary, and everything seems to smell of boiled cabbage?"

Miss Symington looked in a surprised way at her minister's wife, but Nicole laughed and said, "I know—'when nothing is left remarkable.' Why then, I read of glowing places like the Taj Mahal, and of people like Shah Jehan. Shah Jehan with his elephants and his peacocks, his queens and his palaces . . ."

She stopped. The minister's wife was enthralled, but Miss Symington wore a doubtful expression as if she feared that this young woman was not going to prove a very uplifting influence in Kirkmeikle.

"I must go," said Nicole, "for I'm talking far too much. Good-bye, Miss Symington." She smiled at the Lamberts. "I shan't forget the books," she promised, and was gone.

Mrs. Lambert gave a sigh as the door shut behind her, and said. "I never met any one like her. Her voice . . . and her eyes. She's like warmth and light. I seem to feel chilly now she's gone."

Her husband shook his head at her. "You're a born worshipper, Jeanie. I suppose now you'll go home and dote on this Miss Rutherfurd. And she hasn't wanted for worship, that young woman."

Nicole went home so silent and thoughtful that her mother, in some alarm, asked her if she felt quite well.

"Oh yes, thanks. . . . I've been to see Miss Symington."

"What," cried Barbara, "again? You seem to have a morbid desire for that woman's society."

"No. I met her at her own gate and she asked me to come in, and she's one of those sincere people who would never think of asking you unless they really wanted you. We talked—— Do you know"—very solemnly—"I don't believe any man has ever said anything more intimate to Miss Symington than, 'A bright day, but rather chilly.' "

"And do you propose to introduce passion into her life?" Barbara asked drily.

Nicole laughed. "You do make me sound a fool, Babs. You're the best bubble-pricker that I know—— But don't you think it is very sad for Miss Symington to have all that money—didn't Mrs. Heggie say she was very rich?—and get no good out of it?"

"But she does good with it," Lady Jane reminded her.

"Oh, but in such a dull way, just giving large impersonal sums. She doesn't know how to give, and she doesn't know how to live, and she doesn't know how to love—— Rather neat that, what? No, but really, I can't bear to see waste. I looked at that woman to-day and I just longed to spend some money on her. The house is *awful* —I shouldn't think there is one single beautiful thing in it. She sits in the dining-room, Mums, with a green plush cloth on the table and an aspidistra in a pot—and if there is a soul-destroying thing on earth it's an aspidistra! She entertains preachers for the week-ends. I can see her sitting talking so painstakingly to them, telling them what she has read in the *Scotsman.* . . . D'you know, she doesn't even realise what a treasure she has got in Alastair: he's just another thing for her to be conscientious about. I tell you she doesn't know *how* to enjoy."

Barbara yawned. "Oh, do let's talk about something else. I'm frankly bored with the whole population of Kirkmeikle. . . . I'm tired of solid worth. Is there anything really wicked in the house that I could read?"

Her aunt laughed. "Poor Babs! But you've found a way of escape to-day." She turned to Nicole. "Aunt Constance's friends the Erskines called to-day when you were out. Very friendly people they seem. We are all invited to Queensbarns next Wednesday."

"Oh, are we?" said Nicole.

CHAPTER XIV

"It is a rule with me, that a person who can write a long letter with ease cannot write ill."

Jane Austen.

A week or two later Nicole wrote to her friend Jean Douglas at Kingshouse:

You blame me for not writing, and ask what I can possibly have to do except write, but you'd be surprised how full the days are and how quickly they pass. Anyway, for me. Barbara still kicks against the pricks. Mother smiles her absent smile and accepts things as they are, but I think perhaps she hasn't been quite so "absent" lately—you know what I mean, present in the body but her thoughts not of this world. She is sometimes quite like her old self when she is talking to Alastair. I told you—did I?—about him. He is a small boy, the nephew of Miss Symington who lives in the biggest of the red villas, six years of age, plain of face, superficially quite unattractive. You know how my heart always did melt to small boys, and there is something about Alastair that appeals to me mightily. He reminds me in the strangest way of Ronnie and Archie, and I think Mums must feel the same, for I've seldom seen her so absorbed in any one as she is in this child. He is old enough to begin lessons, but there is nobody available in this place to teach him, and his aunt doesn't want a resident governess, and—actually—mother offered to give him lessons for two hours every morning! So punctually at ten o'clock he arrives with his nurse—a large Fife girl, quite young and full of common-sense—we call her Gentle Annie, because of her liking for a song of that name—whom he admires exceedingly. (When we read to him about a beautiful princess, he asks, "*As* beautiful as Annie?").

Alastair sits at a table with an exercise book and a pencil and learns to recognise and make letters and read little words. So far his progress is not striking. I heard Mums going over with him a n, an, with great patience, then she said: "Now, Alastair, tell me what is that word?" and Alastair with the most charmingly helpful air said, "I'd tell you in a minute if I knew."

You say you want to know all about the people here. Barbara says they are the dullest crowd she ever struck, and indeed they are utterly ordinary—what are we ourselves?—and very far from exciting, but I like them.

Mrs. Heggie, who can't see any one without offering hospitality, came to tea with her daughter the other day. The daughter was calm and collected and condescended to us a good deal, but her mother was absolutely simmering with excitement. It seems she has always had an intense desire to be inside the Harbour House, and she was like a child at her first pantomime. I escorted her through every nook and cranny of it—we even visited the coal-cellar—and she gasped out admiration at everything she beheld. She was so interested in the few photographs she saw in the bedrooms, that we raked out boxes of them, and I believe she would have sat entranced till bedtime listening to the life-histories of people she had never known existed. The daughter, Joan by name, dragged her away in the end, evidently ashamed of her exuberance. She writes, this girl, but I can't quite gather what. She is rather plain, with a long nose and chin, and an ugly laugh.

Miss Symington, Alastair's aunt, is a woman of about forty-seven, quite good-looking if she knew how to make the best of herself; rich, free to do what she likes; and here she stays all the year round in a hideous house, eating badly cooked food, wearing ugly clothes, seeing nothing beautiful, hearing nothing beautiful, hardly, I think, aware that there is such a thing as beauty. What could one do to wake her up?

Her minister and his wife are so different. The Lamberts live in a plain little grey stone house in the middle of a walled garden; you enter by a green door in the wall. They have £300 a year to live on, and it shows how little money really matters, for they are absolutely happy. They have everything that any reasonable being could desire, a house where love is, good health, good books and a good fire. Also, by a merciful dispensation of Providence, they have a small servant called Betha, a wise and virtuous child, and she and Mrs. Lambert between them cook, clean and look after the two children. Always by one o'clock Betha has got on her black dress, ready to carry in the early dinner, and when she has washed the dinner dishes out she goes to give the two little girls their daily walk. Mrs. Lambert makes all the clothes for her babies, besides visiting the congregation, presiding at meetings, and reading every book she can lay her hands on. Mr. Lambert is rather a pet. He has a most engaging stammer and helps out the words by giving himself little slaps; but he also has what his wife calls "a dry manner," and isn't sufficiently affable to his congregation. Small and thin, with a sort of twisted smile, he is like a benevolent gnome; but his sermons are excellent, and he is a man of wide reading.

Then there is Dr. Kilgour and his sister. He delves in the past and writes of what he finds without hope of it ever seeing the light of publication; and his sister collects pretty well everything—old glass, china, furniture, brass. Her house is like a very nice museum; everywhere you turn there is something worth looking at, not the least being Miss Kilgour herself. Quite old—seventy, I believe—round and comfortable, with such white hair and blue eyes, she is full of funny old rhymes and stories of the people who once lived in Kirkmeikle, and the rise of the new people in Langtoun. There is a bite in her talk which is refreshing; it is so tiresome when everybody says nothing but good of everybody else!

As to men, I've already mentioned Mr. Lambert and Dr. Kilgour. Then there is Mr. Buckler, the retired Indian judge, and—Mr. Simon Beckett. I've kept him to the last like the bit of icing on a cake, for he is no less a person than the Simon Beckett who almost succeeded in climbing Everest. You remember Beckett and Cullis were together, well on their way to the top, when Cullis was killed and his companion had to return?

We couldn't believe that it was the same Beckett, it seemed so utterly unlikely that he should be here; but it appears that when he was a small boy he and his brothers came here for sea-bathing, and the little quiet town remained in his memory, and he thought of it when he wanted a place in which to write in peace. For, you must know, he is writing an account of what happened on that expedition, thus late in the day because he was for long ill and broken.

I like him for his kindness to the small Alastair, who follows him with dog-like devotion.

Poor old Babs sniffs at the whole of Kirkmeikle, but—thanks to Aunt Constance whose acquaintance list I am convinced ranges from Kew to Kotmandu—we have got to know one family with whom she can feel at home, people called Erskine, who have a place about ten miles from this, Queensbarns. They are very pleasant people and are full of schemes for amusing us. "What d'you *do* here?" one of the girls asked me, and for the life of me I couldn't tell her. I could only assure her that I didn't play bridge, and that stunned her into silence. Babs and I went over and played badminton the other day at Queensbarns: it was very nice, but oh! how glad I was to creep back to our own funny little house.

Could you help liking a town that contained a place called *The Watery Wynd?* and another of the name of *The Puddock Raw*?

I like Kirkmeikle, but I ache all the time for my own countryside. D'you remember what the old woman said to Dorothy Wordsworth when she told her she lived in a pretty place? "Ay, the water of Tweed is a bonny water" . . . Isn't there a text about "Weep not for him who is dead but weep sore for him who goeth away. . . ."

All the same, I'm happy.—Your loving

Nicole.

CHAPTER XV

". . . as to not meeting with many people in this neighbourhood . . . I know we dine with four-and-twenty families."

Jane Austen.

Mrs. Jackson was going to her first dinner-party from Rutherfurd. It had lain like a weight on her since ever she had got the invitation. She had gone to bed every night dreading it, and wakened in the morning weighed down by the thought of it. She was almost thankful that the day had come—to-morrow would be free from the oppression.

She had kept her fears to herself until, at tea-time on the fatal day her son had said carelessly, "By the way, aren't we going out to dinner to-night?" when she could contain herself no longer.

"Oh, Andy," she wailed, "you can say it like that as if it was nothing, something that had just come into your head, when the thought of it has been like a nether mill-stone round my neck for a week."

Andrew was helping himself to jam, and he paused with the spoon in his hand and looked at his mother.

"Nonsense, Mother," he said, "a dinner-party's nothing to you. You didn't mind them in Glasgow, you enjoyed them."

"Ah, but this is a very different thing. The Glasgow ones were all more or less official, I knew what I was there for, and all that was wanted of me, but this ——" Mrs. Jackson threw out a despairing hand,—"I suppose this'll be to meet our county neighbours, and I'm *terrified*. I know how frozen these kind of people can be, and the way they look at you."

Andrew laughed. "A few perfectly harmless people hoping for a decent dinner and not too boring company. . . . You know you liked the people who called. Mrs. Douglas——"

"Oh, if it had been Mrs. Douglas's dinner I'd have gone like a bird, but I've never set eyes on these Langlands. I was in Glasgow the day Lady Langlands called and she was away when I returned it."

"Well, it's very civil of them to ask us; it's just a pity Father had to be in London. Don't, for goodness sake, worry about it, you silly wee body, nobody's worth worrying about. What good cakes these are."

"Yes, oh yes. Mrs. Asprey's a good baker. . . . Andy, what'll I put on to-night? I've three dresses laid out."

Andrew considered for a moment. "Well, if you really want my opinion I like the black velvet one with the funny train best."

Mrs. Jackson's face fell. "I was afraid you'd say black," she said resignedly. "And I've got a new one I'd like fine to wear, a sort of tomato-red, a lovely shade and awfully fashionable this winter."

Andrew had a vision of his stout mother swathed in tomato-red, the cynosure of all eyes in Lady Langlands' drawing-room, and he said gently, "You must keep that one to cheer us up at home, but you know I never think you look so well in anything as in black—and black velvet gives your pearls a chance."

"Well, that's true, but all the same I would have liked to show these people that I've some smart clothes. I don't know whether they're dressers in this part of the world or not. . . . Of course, Mrs. Douglas is awfully smart. Her clothes are London, I could see that, but to my mind Glasgow's every bit as good. . . . Black, you think, and my pearls?—I believe I'll go and lie down for an hour before I need begin to dress, and then I'll mebbe not get so flustered and excited. Whatever will I talk about? Is there anything much in the papers, Andy, except murders and politics? Oh, if only it was eleven o'clock to-night what a happy woman I'd be!"

"Not you, you'll be quite sorry the party is over. When you hate the thought of a thing beforehand you always enjoy it when it comes, and anything short of the tortures of the Inquisition will seem pleasant to you to-night!"

She picked up her work-bag and a book she had been reading and prepared to go upstairs, when a thought struck her.

"But I've never even seen Lady Langlands. Mercy, Andy, how'll I know which is the hostess?"

"I suppose she'll hold out her hand, won't she, O Manufacturer of Mountains out of Molehills?"

Mrs. Jackson sighed. "Oh, I daresay . . . I just hope I'll be given grace to hold my tongue to-night. I always mean to be perfectly calm and dignified, and before I know what I'm doing I'm just yattering away. Uch, Andy, you needn't laugh. . . ."

Exactly at a quarter to eight Mrs. Jackson and her son were being admitted into the hall of Langlands. Mrs. Jackson's heart, she would have told you, was in her mouth, but she got a crumb of comfort as soon as the door opened and it was this— the Langlands' butler could not compare either in looks or deportment with Johnson. She felt oddly uplifted by the fact, and was able to leave her cloak, and follow the butler with something like equanimity, though for days the thought of the moment when she would be ushered into a gathering of strangers had almost made her swoon.

There were only about half-a-dozen people in the room when her name was announced, and she stotted forward on her high heels towards the out-stretched hand of a tall lady in a soft grey gown who was hastening to greet her.

"Mrs. Jackson. I'm so glad to meet you at last. I've been so unfortunate missing you twice. . . . My husband——"

The next thing Mrs. Jackson knew was that she was sitting on a comfortable high chair talking to her host, at least, Lord Langlands was talking and she was making little gasps of assent. She looked round her. Lady Langlands was talking to Andy, very thin she was, not young, but striking looking, with a small head like a deer.

"Mrs. Jackson, I don't think you know Mrs. Kilpatrick." Her host was speaking, and she found herself shaking hands with a young woman with a bright colour and a fashionable head. Her dress was cut very low and finished prematurely, revealing a pair of stalwart legs and somewhat unfortunate ankles, her lips were painted an unconvincing carmine, her voice was shrill and she spoke with an affected lisp, but she was very pleasant, and assured Mrs. Jackson that she would have been to call on her long ago, but her infants had chicken-pox.

"A troublesome thing," said Mrs. Jackson in her comfortable voice that made one think of warm nurseries and soft little garments and violet powder. "It's such a long infection. Three weeks, isn't it? I mind Andy—my son, you know—had been playing with a wee boy who took it, and we kept him in quarantine, as they call it, for a whole three weeks, and the day he should have gone back to school there were the spots!—real provoking. But it's an easy trouble once you get it. I hope your children are better?"

"Oh, thanks, I think so. Nurse says they're perfectly all right. I haven't seen them myself for about a week. Tim and I have been away and only got back to-night."

"Is that the way of it?" said Mrs. Jackson, and with that dinner was announced.

"We're a man short," Lady Langlands said, "but it doesn't matter, for we'll walk in just anyhow. Jean, lead the way. . . ."

It was a round table, and Mrs. Jackson found herself between her host and a small horsey-looking man who, she saw by the name-card, was Major Kilpatrick, the husband of her vivacious young friend. Having cast one glance at him she decided that she could do nothing for him in the way of conversation, so she turned her attention to her host. Her first remark was somewhat unfortunate. Looking round the room she said, "My! this is a fine house for a big family."

"Yes," Lord Langlands said, without enthusiasm. The nurseries at Langlands were empty. . . . "How do you like Rutherfurd?"

Mrs. Jackson looked him full in the face, gave one of her beaming smiles, and said, "We like it *fine*. At first, you know, I wasn't sure about living in the country, always being used with the town, and not caring much for country sports or gardening or visiting cottages, but we've settled down wonderfully. Andy, my son over there, has taken to it like anything and tramps about in knickerbockers quite the country gentleman. Mr. Jackson, of course, has to be a great deal in Glasgow—he's in London to-night, that's why he's not here—but he's quite pleased with Rutherfurd too. Of course, you know the place?"

Lord Langlands laid down his soup spoon. "Walter Rutherfurd was my greatest friend. We were at school together, and Oxford together, and his boy Archie was my namesake."

"Is that so? You'll miss them. Ucha! I'm awfully sorry for poor Lady Jane losing her boys and her husband like that. Indeed, I don't know how she goes on at all, and yet she's wonderfully bright, too."

Lord Langlands murmured something, and his companion continued.

"Have you heard how they're liking Fife? Fancy having to go to a house in a street—I understand it's not even a good villa in a garden—after Rutherfurd! Mind you, some people are tried in this world."

At that moment Lord Langlands' attention was claimed, and Mrs. Jackson turning her head met the glance of Major Kilpatrick and had, perforce, to make some remark.

She smiled shyly and said, "Isn't it wonderful weather for the time of year?"

"Oh, not bad, not bad. . . . D'you hunt, Mrs.—eh—Jackson?"

"Me?" Mrs. Jackson began to laugh. Was this jerky little man trying to be funny? "I never was on a horse in my life. You see, I've always lived in Glasgow, in Pollokshields. D'you know Pollokshields? It's an awfully nice suburb."

"Oh, I've been to Glasgow," said Major Kilpatrick. "At the Motor Show, you know, and catching trains and that sort of thing. Bit grimy, isn't it? What!"

Mrs. Jackson at once rose in arms. "Not a bit grimier than any other big town. Bless me, its smokiness is just a sign of its prosperity." She gave a sigh. "It's a fine place, Glasgow. I'm proud, I can tell you, to belong to it."

"Quite right. By Jove, yes. Stick up for the place you belong to, that's what I always say. But this part of the world's not bad either, you know, and Rutherfurd's far the nicest place round about. What times I used to have there with Ronnie and Archie. It was dashed hard luck that they had to sell it." Major Kilpatrick ate a few mouthfuls rapidly, and continued: "Not that it's not jolly nice having you there, you know, Mrs. Jackson, but the Rutherfurds—well, the Rutherfurds, we all know them, don't you see?"

"That's what I said myself," his companion assured him. "The first time I went to look at the place they were so kind and pleasant to me, and I just said, 'What a down-come from Lady Jane Rutherfurd to Mrs. Jackson.' "

Major Kilpatrick laughed uncomfortably. "I wouldn't say that. Oh, by Jove, no, I wouldn't say that. . . . By the way, does your son hunt?"

"He never has, but he's going to learn. You see, since ever he came home from the War he's been pretty close kept at it, learning the business, but now that we've bought a place, Mr. Jackson wants Andy to be more or less a country gentleman, if you know what I mean? Father's not what you'd call an old man— sixty-four; that's nothing, when you see pictures of people quite spry at a hundred— and he's quite able to look after the business himself—in fact, he prefers it. He has a wonderful business head, Father has, as sharp as a needle. I think, mebbe, Andy's more like me, inclined to be dreamy-like. And he likes the country; he's as fond of that old house as if his ancestors had lived in it for hundreds of years."

"Is he though? By Jove."

"Yes. I sometimes think it would comfort Lady Jane to know that the one who'll come after us likes the place so well."

Major Kilpatrick agreed, and in the pause that followed addressed a remark to the lady on his other side.

Mrs. Jackson sat crumbling her toast and watching her fellow-guests. Andy was talking to Mrs. Douglas and laughing at something she had said. His mother decided that he was much the best looking man at the table. Lord Langlands had a big nose, and stooped, and was rather like some great bird; Major Kilpatrick was an ugly little man with a comical face; Colonel Douglas was red-faced and bald; but Andy looked really well in his white tie and waistcoat, not handsome exactly, but solid and kind and dependable. He glanced her way and she nodded and smiled to show that all was well with her. . . . She liked Lady Langlands, she decided; she had a grave, almost a sad face, and a gentle manner. Mrs. Douglas seemed quite an old friend and Mrs. Jackson felt a proprietary pride in her very smart appearance—how well she put on her clothes. Mrs. Kilpatrick of the carmine lips she mentally shook her head over, and thought what a silly couple she and her husband were. The only other woman present she did not think she liked the look of—Miss Lockhart, she thought her name was. She nibbled a salted almond and considered her. She was well dressed and had beautiful pearls, but Mrs. Jackson did not care for the arrogant look in her face. This lady, she thought, was probably given to keeping people in their places.

"I was saying, Mrs. Jackson"—her host was addressing her—"that there is a great deal to be said for seeing the winter through in Scotland. Only we who have endured hardships can properly appreciate the first snowdrop, and those who have flown to Egypt or the Riviera haven't the same right to watch the daffodils. Don't you agree?"

"Oh yes. Yes, indeed," she said, rather confusedly, turning from watching Miss Lockhart's attractive though rather wicked mouth as she talked to Colonel Douglas, to the solemn countenance of her host. "I love the spring days after the dark and cold, and the sight of the crocuses always reminds me that the spring-cleaning's coming on. I wonder if you've noticed an advertisement—it's awful clever—a picture of a great bunch of delphiniums and a bottle of furniture polish? It fair makes you smell a newly-cleaned room."

Lord Langlands looked slightly surprised. "Eh—quite so," he said. "Are you going south after Christmas?"

"Oh, mercy, no. We're just newly settled into Rutherfurd. Such a flitting as we had! I'm sure we'll not want to stir a foot from home for ages. I'm not fond of continental travel myself. The language, you know, and the queer food. I'm terrified they give me snails. . . ."

When Mrs. Jackson returned to the drawing-room with the other ladies she glanced surreptitiously round for a clock. Dinner had lasted so long, surely it must be after nine, and the car was ordered for ten o'clock. Only another hour to get through!

"Is that chair comfortable? Do let me give you another cushion," and Lady Langlands tucked in a cushion behind Mrs. Jackson, while Jean Douglas seated herself in a low chair beside her and began to talk.

"I want to tell you how nice you look. There is nothing so becoming as black velvet and pearls. . . . And how's Rutherfurd? I had a letter from Nicole the other day; she always asks about you."

"Yon's a nice girl," Mrs. Jackson said earnestly. "I wonder—d'you think it would be all right for me to ask her to visit us some time? I wouldn't dare ask the cousin, but Miss Nicole was so kind and helpful, she made me realise what it must be like to have a daughter. I'd love to have her if she'd come."

"Then I'd ask her if I were you." Jean laughed a little. "As you say, Miss Burt is a different matter—though, remember, there's a lot of good in Barbara, but she lacks something that Nicole has, that touch that makes the whole world kin. We all liked her, but no one exactly loved her, whereas Nicole has had all her life a surfeit of love—if such a thing is possible. It made it hard for poor Babs."

"Ucha. Well, I thought we might be giving a dance later, and Miss Nicole said she'd help me any time I needed her. But, of course, it might be trying for her coming back, too."

"Oh, if she refused you would understand why, but—— What did you say, Tilly? No, this isn't my month to visit the Nursing Home."

The talk drifted away from Mrs. Jackson into a maze of Christian names, and events of which she knew nothing. They knew each other so well all these people! She felt a little lonely sitting there, wearing a fixed smile, and listening to Tilly Kilpatrick lisping out gossip about meets and dances, and the whereabouts of this one and that, and her thoughts wandered, and presently she nodded. Lady Langlands' voice saying her name made her sit very straight, and look incredibly wide awake.

"We are hoping, Mrs. Jackson, that you will take Lady Jane's place in our Nursing Association. Perhaps you will go with me one day and see over our little hospital? It is part of our War Memorial, and we're very proud of it."

Mrs. Jackson nodded amiably. "I'm sure I'll be very glad. I'll do anything but speak in public—that I *can't* do, but I'll sit on Committees, and subscribe money and all that sort of thing. . . ."

"That's the kind of member we want," said Jean Douglas, while Mrs. Kilpatrick said, "Oh, Jean!" and giggled.

Driving home with her son Mrs. Jackson was a happy woman. The ordeal was over, and a wonderful plan was in her head. Nicole would come to Rutherfurd, Andy would love her at sight. Already she heard the sound of wedding bells. To have a daughter to entertain for her . . . to hear Nicole's laughter in the house—— A rosy and golden haze seemed the future as she peered into it.

CHAPTER XVI

"Be this, good friends, our carol still—
  'Be peace on earth, be peace on earth
  To men of gentle will.' "

W. M. Thackeray.

The Rutherfurds had settled down in the Harbour House in a way that surprised themselves. It seemed almost unbelievable that a bare three months ago they had known nothing of Kirkmeikle and its inhabitants and were now absorbed in the little town.

Nicole's desire to know only Kirkmeikle, and Barbara's determination to know as little of the town and as much as possible of the county, had resulted in a compromise. People from a distance were welcomed and their visits returned, and Barbara suffered Nicole's Kirkmeikle friends, if not gladly, at least with civility. The Bucklers she liked, and the Lamberts and Kilgours, but Mrs. Heggie and Miss Symington she could not abide, and marvelled at her cousin's tolerance for those two ladies.

"The appalling dullness of them, their utterly common outlook on life, their ugly voices and vacant faces, how you can be bothered with them, Nikky, passes me."

"But it's the way you look at them," Nicole protested. "You expect to find commonness, so of course you do. I find nothing but niceness in Mrs. Heggie. Just think what fun she is to feed. I met her the day after we had had her to luncheon and she went over the whole *menu* with reminiscent smacks. 'The grape fruit! delicious: and that new way of doing eggs . . . and such tender beef I never tasted . . . and the puddings were a dream. I simply couldn't resist trying both, though I know it was rather a liberty the first time I had lunched with you, and the whole thing so *recherché*!' Isn't it worth while to have some one like that to a meal? I think it is. As for Joan Heggie, she is rather ugly and awkward, but she can write poetry. . . . Miss Symington interests me."

"You like them," said Barbara, "because they make a little worshipping court for you; you shine against their dullness."

But Nicole only laughed, and called heaven to witness that she had a very rude cousin.

As for Lady Jane she was gently civil to every one who came, but preferred Mrs. Brodie and her noisy brood, and old Betsy with her talk of Tweedside, to any of them.

December is a month that, for most people, "gallops withal," and it seemed to be Christmas before any one was prepared for it at the Harbour House.

It was the morning of Christmas Eve, and the drawing-room did not present its usual orderly appearance. White paper, gay ribbons, boxes of sweets and candied fruits, and crackers for the out-going parcels lay about on the big sofa, while the long table at the far end of the room was piled with parcels which had arrived by post. Nicole gazed round her ruefully, remarking that everything must be packed before luncheon, whereupon Barbara came briskly to the rescue.

"Say what's to go into each parcel," she said, "and I'll tie them up. These are the local ones, I suppose?"

"Thank goodness, yes. All the others were packed days ago. I wish I hadn't gone to Edinburgh yesterday and I wouldn't be in such a state of chaos to-day! Are you sure you can spare the time? . . . Well, first a parcel for Mrs. Brodie from mother; just oddments to make a brightness for the children. Is there a box to put them in? These gaudy crackers, sweets, dates, shortbread, and sugar biscuits: a tin of tea for Mrs. Brodie, and those toys for their stockings. Will they all go in? Good. That's the only really bulky parcel. You do tie up so neatly, Babs. Providence obviously intended you for a grocer."

"What about this?" Barbara asked, holding up a large flat box.

"That only wants a ribbon round it and a bit of holly stuck in. It's for old Betsy; shortbread. I had it made with '*Frae Tweedside*' done in pink sugar—a small attention which I hope she'll appreciate. Mother is sending her tea, and other things. The framed print is for the Bucklers, they haven't many household gods; the Bond Street chocolates are for Mrs. Heggie, she has such a sweet tooth; the book of Scots ballads for Dr. Kilgour."

"I can't see that Mrs. Heggie needs anything," Barbara said, as she wrapped each thing in white paper and tied it with a red ribbon. "It will only make her insist on us all going to dinner at her house." . . . She looked round at the articles remaining and asked, taking up a Venetian glass bowl with a lid, "Who is this pretty thing for?"

"It is pretty, isn't it? I'm going to fill it with my own special geranium bath-salts, put it in a white box, tie it with a length of carnation ribbon and present it to Miss Janet Symington." As she spoke Nicole looked impishly at her cousin, who said, "Ridiculous! What will she do with such a present?"

"Nothing, probably, but I'm determined she will have at least one pretty thing in her possession. Pack it, Babs dear, very gently, with cotton wool and lots of soft paper. . . . These are all the things for Alastair's stocking. He's coming here after breakfast to-morrow to get the big toy Mums has for him. The Lamberts are having him for early dinner and tea, so he'll have quite a cheerful day."

"You spoil every one," said Barbara.

"I like spoiling people, but I quite see I'm a horrible trial to you. You would have liked this house to keep up its reputation for exclusiveness, wouldn't you, poor pet? . . . But we're not really over-run by my new friends. They never come unless they're asked, and we have quiet jolly times, old Babs, you and Mother and I. I sometimes think it is almost unbelievable that we can be so happy after— everything."

Barbara touched her cousin's hand. "I know—— I didn't approve much of coming here, as you know, but I'm bound to say I think Aunt Jane has been the better of it. She takes more interest in people and things than she did. I was really afraid for her before we left Rutherfurd, but now she is less of a gentle spirit and more of a living, breathing mortal. It pleases her to have Alastair so much with her, and she likes Mr. Beckett. D'you notice how she looks at them sometimes—the little boy and the grown man? I think it hurts her to see them, and yet the pleasure exceeds the pain. When Alastair plays round preoccupied and busy, talking to himself, she sees again Ronnie and Archie, for all little boys are very much alike: and in Mr. Beckett she sees them as they would have been now."

Nicole nodded. "I'm rather dreading to-morrow for her. One can go on from day to day, but these special times are difficult. . . . What do outsiders matter after all, Babs? It's we three against the world—though you and I do bark at each other *whiles*!"

After luncheon and a belated post had been discussed, Lady Jane and her niece settled down to cope with the last of the preparations, while Nicole set out to deliver parcels.

It was about three o'clock before she started. The frost of the morning had increased in intensity, so that walking was difficult on the cobbled stones, and Betsy's outside stair, which had been recklessly washed, was now coated with ice.

Betsy herself was sitting wrapped in a shawl by the fire. "Come in," she cried, "I kent yer step. Bring forrit a chair and get a warm. It's surely terrible cauld?"

"It's a perfect Christmas Eve," Nicole told her, walking over to look out of the little window. "I can see the moon already, though the sun's only going down now, and the red tiles have got snow on them, just a sprinkle. I do like your view of chimney-pots and roofs. It makes me think of storks, and Northern Lights, and Christmas trees in every window."

This harmless remark seemed to provoke the old woman. "Gentry," she said peevishly, "are aye crackin' aboot *views*. I never felt the need o' a view if I had a guid fire. An' I dinna haud wi' Christmas. It's juist Papacy. It fair scunners me to hear the wives aboot the doors a' crackin' aboot Christmas here an' Christmas there. Ye canna blame the bairns for bein' taen up wi' Sandy Claws an' hingin' up their stockins, but it's no' for grown folk. . . . Whae tell't ye that Christ was born on the 25th o' December? It's no' in the Bible that I've ever seen. Juist will-worship, that's what ma auld minister ca'ed it, an' he kent. The verra word's Popish—Christ-Mass."

Nicole left the window and sat down by Betsy.

"Does it matter about all that?" she asked. "Isn't it a good thing that we should keep one day for kind thoughts and goodwill to all men, because long ago in Bethlehem a baby was born?"

Betsy sniffed. "Ay, but I dinna haud wi't. It was aye the New Year we keepit at Langhope. Thae were the days!"

"Did you have presents?"

"Na, we hed nae money for presents, but the bairns dressed up and went frae hoose to hoose playin' at 'Galatians' and singin'

'Get up, auld wife, an' shake yer feathers,

90

Dinna think that we are beggars:
We are but children come to play—
Get up and gie's oor Hogmanay.'

An' we got oatcakes and cheese, and a lump o' currant-loaf, and shortbreed, and we carried it a' hame in oor pinnys."

Nicole was sorting out parcels from her big bag.

"I don't suppose," she said, "that this shortbread will taste anything like as good, but it says on it '*Frae Tweedside.*'"

"So it does." Betsy gazed admiringly at the sugar inscription. "It's faur ower bonny to eat, I'll juist pit it in a drawer." Nicole exclaimed at the idea, and produced tea, and a warm woolly coat.

"These are from my mother with her best wishes. She hopes to come to see you very soon."

Betsy sat with her hands on her gifts. "I dinna ken what to say. I'm no' üsed bein' noticed. Naebody ever brocht me things afore, no' as muckle as a mask o' tea. Lady Jane's kindness is fair nonsense, but ye'll tell her I'm muckle obleeged."

"Mrs. Martin told me to tell you that she'll be along this evening with some 'kail.'"

"Ay, weel, it's no' a'body's kail I'd sup. God gies the guid food, but the deil sends the cook. . . . But Agnes Martin's a rale guid haund at kail."

"Well, good-bye, Betsy, and—a Merry Christmas."

"Na, I'm for nane o' yer Christmases. I'll gie you a wish for Ne'er day, for fear I dinna see ye—'The awfullest luck ever ye kent and *a man afore the year's oot.*'"

Nicole left her chuckling, and took her perilous way down the slippery stair to the home of Mrs. Brodie.

Mrs. Brodie was busy cleaning for the New Year and, like Betsy, seemed to take little stock in Christmas.

"Ay," she said, leaning on her besom as Nicole produced her box, "the morn's Christmas, but it maks nae odds here. It's juist wark, wark, the same. The bairns get an orange an' a screw o' sweeties in their stockins, but that's a' the length we gang. It's rale guid o' yer mither to send thae things—Jimmie, I'll warm yer lugs if ye dinna let that alane!—Is she gaun tae gie me a look in wan o' thae days? I like fine to hae a crack wi' her. Weel, guid day to ye, an' thanks."

Nicole left her parcels at Lucknow and at Knebworth, and then turned into the gate of Ravenscraig.

Miss Symington was, as usual, sitting in the dining-room, making up the accounts of one of the many societies she was interested in. There was no sign of festivity anywhere, not so much as a sprig of holly. To-night Alastair would hang up his stocking and she would go in on her way to bed and put some things in, she had these lying ready—a shilling and some walnuts in the toe, a pair of warm gloves, an orange, and a small packet of chocolates. *Chatterbox* would be laid on the breakfast-table, also a game sent by Mrs. Heggie, and a box of Meccano from the Bucklers. It was too much for one child, she thought, and she meant to tell him how many children had nothing but a crust of bread.

She added up columns rapidly as she sat, putting very neat figures into a pass-book. Then she put the books away and fetched some brown paper and string from a table in the corner. Nicole came springing in on her like a gay schoolgirl.

"Am I disturbing you? No, please go on packing. I've been at it for the last week, and to-day I'd never have got through if Barbara hadn't given me a hand. She takes time by the fetlock, as my brother Ronnie used to say, and is always well beforehand."

"These are just a few things that Annie will take out this evening," Miss Symington said, cutting the end of a string carefully.

Nicole, watching her, said, "You don't keep Christmas much in Kirkmeikle, do you? My efforts to be seasonable have been rather snubbed this afternoon; but Alastair keeps it, I'm sure. Will you put these things into his stocking, please? They are only little things, but they may amuse him. And this is for you. You won't open it till to-morrow morning—promise? Now, I'm not going to stay a moment longer. A very Happy Christmas to you. No, don't come to the door. . . ."

She heaved a sigh of relief as she left the dreary villa, and stood on the brae-face looking over the tumbled roofs to the sea, and saw the lights along the coast begin to twinkle greeting to the stars in the frosty sky.

"Quite like a Christmas number, isn't it?" a voice said behind her, and she turned quickly to find Simon Beckett.

"Where are you wandering to, sir? I've been playing 'Sandy Claws,' as old Betsy puts it. . . . I thought you would have gone away to spend the festive season—falsely so called."

Simon turned and walked by her side. "Watch how you go: it's pretty slippery. . . . No, I'm not going away. I've only cousins to go to, anyway, and they don't particularly want me. Besides, it hardly seemed worth while to go so far just now. I'm keen on getting my job done, and . . ."

"How are you getting on? You haven't asked for any advice yet?"

"No—you see I've only now got the rough draft done: I've taken an age to it. It's when I re-write and polish that I'll be most grateful for help—only, I hardly like to bother you."

"We'll be enormously flattered and not in the least bothered. You know that. . . . I've been at Ravenscraig with some things for Alastair's stocking. It was all so hopelessly uncheery for the poor lamb. When I think of our childhood—the fuss that was made, the thrill of the preparations, the mystery. It does make a difference having a mother, an aunt given to good works isn't the same at all."

Simon agreed. "I've got a train for him," he said, "with rails. It only came this morning and I was in a perfect funk that it wasn't going to turn up in time. He's been fearfully keen to possess one. I hope it'll come up to his expectations."

"Sure to, trains never fail one—— What are you doing to-morrow?"

"Nothing special. I thought I'd treat myself to a really long walk."

"We're quite alone," Nicole told him. "After your walk it would be a kind act if you'd eat your Christmas dinner with us—7.30—and afterwards we'll sit round the fire and talk. . . . Isn't it jolly to-night? The moon and the snowy roofs and the lights in the frosty air. And look at that little steamer, plugging along! Where are you going to, you funny little boat? Don't you know what night this is?"

CHAPTER XVII

"Go humbly; humble are the skies,
  And low and large and fierce the Star;
  So very near the manger lies
  That we may travel far."

G. K. Chesterton.

When Alastair had almost finished dressing on Christmas morning, Gentle Annie suddenly dumped a parcel on the dressing-table, announcing, "That's ma present."

Alastair looked shyly at it, making no effort to discover its contents.

"Open't. Here! See!" Annie quickly whipped off the paper and disclosed, on a stand, a round glass globe containing a miniature cottage, which, when shaken, became surrounded with whirling snow-flakes.

"It's a snow-storm," she declared triumphantly. "It cost one shilling and sixpence."

"Oh, Annie, how could you afford it?" Alastair asked anxiously.

"Aw, weel, I wanted a strong ane this time. The last I got was a shilling, an' I brocht it back from Langtoun in aside ma new hat, for I thocht that would be a safe place, but when I won hame I fand it had broken, and a' the water and white stuff—I think it's juist bakin' soda—was ower ma hat."

Alastair shook the globe and produced a most realistic snow-scene.

"Is the snow really only baking soda?" he asked rather sadly.

"Ay, but it does fine. We'll pit it on the mantelpiece for an ornamint, an' juist shake it whiles, an' then it'll no get broken in a hurry. . . . By! but ye're weel off gettin' a' thae things in yer stockin'. . . . Dinna brush yer hair till yer jersey's on. D'ye no see ye pit it a' wrang again?—Noo, rin awa' doon to yer breakfast, like a guid laddie, and be sure and say 'a Merry Christmas' to yer auntie."

But Alastair, very pink in the face, was thrusting something into Annie's hand.

"It's my present, a purse. I bought it at Jimmie Nisbet's when I was out with Mr. Beckett. D-d'you like it?"

"By! it's a braw ane," said Annie. She saw that it was really a tobacco pouch, but Alastair had bought it for a purse and she wouldn't enlighten him. "I'll keep ma chance-money in't, and aye carry it when I'm dressed."

Alastair, blushing with pleasure to hear that his present was valued, and carrying the contents of his stocking, ran downstairs. He was well content with the beginning of his day, and ready to enjoy anything that might turn up.

"Good morning, Aunt Janet," he said; "a Merry Christmas," his eyes all the time fixed on his place at the breakfast-table. *There were parcels there!*

"Good morning, Alastair. A Happy Christmas. I hope you're a grateful boy to-day. Just think of all the poor children who will get no presents. . . . No, sup your porridge, and eat your bread and butter before you touch a parcel."

Miss Symington had never much to say to her nephew except in the way of reproof, and breakfast was eaten more or less in silence. When they had finished the bell was rung for prayers, and the servants came in and sat on chairs near the door, while their mistress read a chapter and a prayer, and Alastair said the text which Annie had to teach him every morning. At first she had opened the Bible and chosen a verse at random, and Alastair had come down and repeated, "*All the Levites in the Holy City were two hundred, fourscore and four,*" or something equally relevant, until Miss Symington gave her a text-book which she was working steadily through.

"Your text, Alastair," his aunt said on this Christmas morning, and Alastair's flute-like voice repeated gravely, "*Remember now thy Creator in the days of thy youth, while the evil days come not, nor the years draw nigh, when ye shall say, I have no pleasure in them.*"

To Alastair there was no sense in the words, but he liked the sound of them, the rhythm . . . *Remember now thy Creator.* . . . "May I open my parcels *now?*"

Miss Symington had not much to open. The postman would bring her some cards and booklets, doubtless. Mrs. Lambert had sent her a tray cloth, her own work, and Mrs. Heggie—with a thought, perhaps, of Alastair—a box of candied fruit. And there was Miss Rutherfurd's box. It stood on the sideboard, a seductive-looking parcel wrapped in white paper and tied with carnation silk ribbon. What could it be! Surely not chocolates. . . . Slowly she untied the ribbon, undid the paper, took off the lid of the box and lifted out the fragile gilt bowl. She sniffed. Bath salts—geranium. That was the scent Miss Rutherfurd always used. Well, really! Miss Symington sat back in her chair and looked at the frivolous, pretty thing. No one had ever thought of giving her such a present before. A thought came vaguely to her that the gift was like the giver, the glow of it, the brightness, the fragrance.

While Alastair played, absorbed, she gathered up the box with the bowl, and the ribbon, and carried them up to her room.

The window was wide open to the frosty air, the bed stripped, and airing. She looked round for a place to put her present. The dressing-table was covered with the silver brushes and mirror her parents had given her on her twenty-first birthday. There was a large pin-cushion too, and two silver-topped bottles that would not unscrew. It looked crowded, and she remembered Nicole's dressing-table when she had once been taken into her room to see something, a table, old and beautiful in itself, covered with plate-glass, with nothing on it but a standing mirror and a bowl of flowers. Everything else, Nicole had explained, lived in the drawers of the table: it was tidier so, she thought.

Janet then tried the bowl on the mantelpiece, but decided at once that it couldn't stand there. It was an ugly painted wood mantelpiece, with a china ornament at each end and a photograph of the Scott Monument in the middle, and the Venetian bowl looked forlornly out of its element, as a nymph might have looked at an

Educational Board meeting.

There was a fine old walnut chest of drawers opposite the window. It had a yellowish embroidered cover on it which Janet whisked off, leaving it bare. That was better. The wood was beautiful, and the bowl stood proudly regarding its own reflection in the polished depths.

Janet was surprised at her own feeling of pleasure and satisfaction in her new possession. After all, there was, she thought, something rather nice about having pretty things about one. But, the worst of it was that one pretty thing was apt to make everything else look uglier. That wall-paper! It had been chosen for its lasting qualities, but she acknowledged to herself that it was far from beautiful. Suppose the walls were made cream? It would make a difference . . . Perhaps when spring-cleaning time came round she might have it done, though it did seem ridiculous to fuss about one's own room. A guest-room was a different matter. . . . She lifted the lid of the bowl and the light sweet scent stole out. What had Alastair said, "Soft and warm and nice-smelling." She supposed many people considered it worth while to do everything in their power to make themselves and their surroundings attractive, but in this fleeting world was it not a waste of time? So soon we would all be done with it. *A few more years shall roll. . . .* She wondered if Nicole and her mother, among their pretty things, ever thought of another world, and of the importance of working while it was day. The shadow of the night that was coming had always lain dark across Janet's day of life.

The sound of voices disturbed her train of thought. Looking out of the window she saw her neighbour, Mr. Beckett, standing on the gravel holding a large box, while his dog, James, leapt on him, and Alastair ran about giving excited yelps. Janet felt almost ashamed of herself for noticing how good the young man was to look at standing there in his light tweed jacket and knickerbockers. He was bare-headed, and the winter sun turned his fair hair to gold.

"Ask your aunt if you may come in with me next door. My room's the best place to fix it up in," she heard him say, and went quickly downstairs to the front door.

"It's a train," Alastair shouted, roused completely out of his habitual gravity, "a train for me! May I go with Mr. Beckett and see how it works?"

Janet met the eyes of the tall young man, who smiled boyishly as if he were as keen on the game as his small companion, and she found herself telling him, with quite a warm inflection in her usually so colourless voice, how good he was to trouble about her nephew, and she hoped Alastair was as grateful as he ought to be.

Alastair, in no mood to study inflections in his aunt's voice, tugged at his friend's arm, saying, "Come on, then, oh, *do* come on," but Simon felt compelled to suggest that perhaps Miss Symington would accompany them to see the train work.

Alastair's face was anxious until he heard his aunt decline, graciously, the invitation. She added that Annie would call for him at eleven o'clock to take him to the Harbour House, and, about twelve, he was going to the Lambert's.

"My word, Bat, you're having a day," Simon told him.

"I'm afraid he will be spoiled among so many kind people," Janet said

96

primly.

"Come on, oh, *do* come on," Alastair insisted, jigging up and down impatiently, feeling that all this talk was quite beside the mark; so Simon, with a smile to Miss Symington, allowed himself to be led away.

Evening had fallen on another Christmas Day. Everywhere tired children were being put to bed, some cross, some dissatisfied, all, more or less, suffering from over-eating. It is doubtful whether the long-looked-for day ever does come up to expectations, but no matter how disillusioned they go to bed, in the morning they are already beginning again to look forward to that bright day which lies at the end of the long year ahead.

The Rutherfurds, having long since put away childish things and having no expectations of extra happiness but rather the reverse, had been surprised to find themselves thoroughly enjoying their first Christmas in Kirkmeikle. Alastair and the postman had taken up the morning, after luncheon they had, all three, walked round the links, and finished up at the Lambert's garden-enclosed house, which was full of all happy cheerful things, toys and children's voices, music and firelight. Mr. Lambert had told a wonderful story of pirates in Kirkmeikle, with Alastair as hero, and they had played games and sung carols.

Now dinner was over, and they were sitting round the fire in the long drawing-room, drinking their coffee, Lady Jane in her own low chair, Nicole beside her on a wooden stool with a red damask cushion, Barbara on the sofa, and Simon Beckett comfortable in a capacious arm-chair.

Barbara wore a dress the colour of Parma violets, Nicole was in white, with a spray of scarlet berries tucked into the white fur which trimmed it.

They had been talking animatedly, but now a silence had fallen. So quiet was the room that outside the tide could be heard rippling over the sand. A boy passed whistling some popular song, a gay tune with an undertone of sadness.

After a minute, "Well," said Lady Jane, "what are we going to do to amuse our guest?"

"Let's play at something," Nicole suggested.

"But what?" asked Barbara.

"Oh, anything," Nicole said lazily. "Just let's make up a game! Suppose we each tell what strikes us as the funniest thing we know."

"The best joke, do you mean?" Simon asked.

"The best joke, or story, or episode in a play, or something that happened to yourself. The thing that has remained in your memory as being really funny."

"Far too difficult," Barbara declared. "I laugh and forget."

"And I," said her aunt, "have such a primitive sense of humour that it's the most obvious joke that makes me laugh: to see somebody fall over a pail of water convulses me. But I never can remember good stories, can you, Mr. Beckett?"

"I seldom remember them at the right moment," Simon confessed.

"I'm glad of that," Barbara said, getting out her work. "I do think those people are a bore who are constantly saying, 'That reminds me of a story. . . .' "

"I think you're all very stupid," Nicole said.

"But I do remember one thing, Miss Nicole," Simon said, "one of A. A. M.'s *Punch* articles on how to dispose of safety-razor blades. The man had been in the habit of dropping worn-out blades on the floor, and his wife protested that the housemaid cut her fingers and dropped blood on the blue carpet. 'Then,' said the husband, 'we'll either have to get a red carpet or a blue-blooded housemaid. . . .' I always think of that when it comes to discarding a razor-blade, and laugh! What is your funniest thing?"

"I was trying to think," Nicole said, hugging her knees, "but everything has gone out of my mind. There's one story that always cheers me about Braxfield, the hanging judge; I think it was Braxfield, but it doesn't matter anyway. He was crossing a burn in spate, and by some mischance his wig fell off. His servant fished it out and handed it to him, but the judge refused it, petulantly remarking that it wasn't his. 'A weel,' said his servant, '*there's nae wale o' wigs in this burn.*' Don't you think that's a good story?"

"Very," said Simon, collecting the coffee cups and putting them on a table. "What does 'wale' mean?"

Nicole dropped her head in her hands. "To think that I've been trying to tell a Scot's story to a Sassenach! 'Wale' means choice. It's the cold sense of the answer that makes the story seem so good to me. I thought you looked a little blank. Like the Englishmen dining at some inn and waited on by a new recruit of a waiter. They were waiting for the sweets, when he rushed in and said: '*The pudden's scail't. It was curds, and it played jap ower the dish and syne skited doon the stairs.*' The poor dears realised that they were to get no pudding, but they never fathomed why."

"I don't suppose," Lady Jane said to her guest, "that you understood a word of that? I know it was Greek to me when I came first to Scotland. . . . I wish you'd tell me about your writing. How, exactly, do you proceed?"

"Oh, well," Simon said, lighting a cigarette, "my job would be the merest child's play to some people. I haven't to invent anything, only to put down facts. . . . I thought it would be the easiest thing to write a simple account, but I'm beginning to think that simplicity is the most difficult thing you can try for. You'd laugh at the struggle I have sometimes!"

"But," said Nicole, "it must be great fun when things do go right. Don't tell me you haven't successful moments when you say to yourself, 'Well, that's jolly good, anyway.' "

Simon shook his head. "Those moments hardly ever occur. Now and again when I get past a nasty snag I seize my hat, and walk five miles over the head of it! No wonder my work doesn't make rapid progress."

"How long does it take to write a book?" Barbara asked. "I mean, of course, an ordinary-sized book, not a Decline and Fall."

Simon laughed. "I daresay an expert could do it in a few weeks, but it's taken me months to write the first rough draft—doing nothing else either, except golf a bit and motor a bit, and walk a good deal. But what I'm thankful for every day of my life is that my lecturing is over. However I stood up and jabbered to all those people I don't know."

"It is dreadful," said Lady Jane. "Mine have only been small things like opening bazaars and flowershows, but I made myself quite ill dreading the day. But when once I was on my feet and realised that my audience was not made up of ravening wolves waiting to devour me, but of friendly people who wished me well, then I was quite all right."

"Women are less self-conscious than men," Simon said. "I felt such a fool!"

"I wish I'd been there to see you," Nicole told him unfeelingly. "But, you know, one should always make a point of doing things one simply hates doing, it's such a lovely feeling afterwards. Besides, it's nice to look back on heart-diseasy moments; long uneventful days are jolly at the time, but it's the heart-diseasy moments that really count, as you know, much better than I do. What a nice old age you'll have!"

"I like that from you, Nikky," her cousin said. "What kind of old age you'll have I don't know, for at present you live like an old lady, visiting in the day, and in the evening reading dull books by the fire. . . . Well, aren't we going to do anything?"

"Won't you sing, please?" Simon suggested.

"Oh, do, Babs. Sing what you sang this afternoon—'*On Christmas night when it was cold.*' D'you know it, Mr. Beckett? Such an old carol."

Barbara went to the piano and struck a few chords softly. Lady Jane, as if drawn by the music, moved close to her.

> "For his love that bought us all dear,
>   Listen lordings, that be here
>   And I will tell you in fere
>   Whereof came the flower delice . . .
> On Christmas night, when it was cold,
> Our Lady lay among beasts bold. . . ."

Barbara sang the words as if she loved them.

Nicole, in her white frock and her scarlet berries, sat looking into the fire; her lips were parted and her eyes bright as if she were seeing pictures in the flames, lovely pictures.

Simon sat forward with his hands clasped between his knees watching Nicole's face as she dreamed——

"Whereof came the flower delice . . ." sang Barbara.

CHAPTER XVIII

"Two lads that thought there was no more behind
  But such a day to-morrow as to-day,
  And to be boy eternal."

The Winter's Tale.

Two days after Christmas, breakfast at the Harbour House was a somewhat prolonged meal, for the post, arriving in the middle, brought a letter which needed immediate discussion.

"Mums," said Nicole, "here's a letter from Bice saying that Jane and Barnabas have taken scarlet fever. Happily, Arthur has been in the country with Aunt Constance, so he isn't in quarantine, and he can't go home, of course, so this is an S.O.S. from Bice asking if she may send him here for the rest of his holidays. She is very worried, poor dear. See what she says."

"What a sad thing to happen in the holidays," Lady Jane lamented, taking the letter, while Barbara, coming back from the sideboard with her tea-cup, stood staring gloomily out of the window. Nicole, who was watching her cousin's face, said:

"Quite so, Babs. We're for it, I fear. We'll have to take the child for at least a fortnight, and cart him back to school at the end of it. . . . Personally, I don't mind; boys are always a delight to me, only I don't quite see what the poor little chap will do in Kirkmeikle."

"How old is he?" Barbara asked moodily. "Twelve, isn't he? If we had been at Rutherfurd it wouldn't have mattered. He'd have gone out with the keeper, and there would always have been something to amuse him, but a boy cooped up here. . . ."

"At an age, too, when women are a bore and a nuisance."

"And," said Barbara, "we haven't seen him for ages. He's probably one of those frightfully superior schoolboys who despise more or less everything. I met one at Langlands once and I never felt so shy in my life. I hardly dared address him, and he only just condescended to answer me. . . ."

"Ah! not Bice's boy—he wouldn't be like that. Bice herself is such a simple creature. . . . Well, Mums, what do you think?"

Lady Jane laid down the letter and began to butter a bit of toast. "Of course he must come here, poor boy, but I am so sorry for Bice missing his holidays. When I last heard from her she was planning all sorts of treats for Arthur's Christmas holidays, and Barnabas, who adores his big brother, was going back with him to school. Now, I suppose, he will be weeks late, and spoil his first term . . . we must wire at once. If they put him in charge of the guard of the night train we can meet him in Edinburgh to-morrow morning. Which of you will go?"

"I'd better," Nicole said, as her cousin remained silent. Barbara might greet him as Miss Murdstone greeted David Copperfield: "Generally speaking, I don't like boys: How do you do, boy?" "What shall we do with him, I wonder?"

"Arthur will be quite happy," Lady Jane said serenely.

"Doubtless, but how do you propose to entertain him?"

"Why, he'll amuse himself, Nikky. The harbour, and the rocks, and golf . . ."

"Well—I hope so, Mums, but I foresee a strenuous time for us all. You see, he's pretty old—twelve; almost ready for Eton, and he may have large ideas. Besides, remember he's coming here, you say, disappointed of all manner of treats in the way of plays and pantomimes and parties. However——"

The next night Arthur Dennis was settled in the Harbour House, and as much at home as if he had been born and bred there. Nicole and he had arrived with the four-thirty train, having spent most of the day at the Castle and the Zoo, and after tea Arthur sat answering gravely all the questions put to him, but otherwise contributing nothing to the conversation, and when Lady Jane suggested that he might like to unpack he rose with alacrity and went out, leaving the door open.

"Well?" said Nicole, looking from her mother to her cousin.

"A dear boy," said Lady Jane.

"He has Bice's beautiful eyes," Barbara said, "and what lashes to waste on a boy!"

Nicole poked the fire. "I like his grave way of speaking," she said, "and that sweet infrequent smile. He nearly went out of the carriage window trying to find out how the Forth Bridge is made. I've promised to take him to see it close at hand. He isn't superior, Babs, and he tells me he's 'frightfully bucked' to be here. Coming up alone in a sleeper had been a great thrill. I think you were right, Mums; he'll be quite happy. Though speechless at present, he talked a lot on the way. He tells me his chief horror is what he calls 'civilisation,' meaning, I find, char-a-bancs that popularise remote places. He says, personally, he can't get far enough away from people and shops. His idea of bliss is Loch Bervie—forty miles of rough road between you and a railway station. They spent the summer there last year, you remember? and he got a taste for solitude—— Dear me, to judge from the noise our whole staff is helping him to unpack."

The next morning Nicole set out with the guest to climb among the rocks and watch the sea-birds, for Arthur, it turned out, was deeply interested in birds.

On their way home they met Simon Beckett striding along as if celebrating some victory over words. They stopped to talk and Arthur was introduced—"Arthur Dennis. Driven from home in the holidays by scarlet fever."

"Rough luck!" said Simon. "What school are you at? No? That's my old prep. Is Snooks still there? By Jove . . ."

Nicole stood watching the two eager speakers, well pleased to be forgotten, realising that here was a solution of the entertainment problem. If only Mr. Beckett in his spare time would take some notice of Arthur, what a help it would be!

They strolled home together and Simon was easily persuaded to join them at luncheon. Nicole managed to whisper to Arthur that this was the Everest Beckett, and his eyes were large in adoration. Later, when Simon invited him to go to the golf course with him and have tea at his rooms, he went, almost dazed with happiness.

"And, Arthur," Nicole said to him, as Simon Beckett was taking leave of her mother, "if there's another boy to tea, Alastair Symington, be kind to him, won't you? I know how good you are to Barnabas, and this poor little chap has no father or mother. Of course, he's much too young for you, only about six, but Mr. Beckett makes quite a companion of him."

There followed for Arthur a fortnight of complete bliss. There are worse fates than to be an only boy in a household of women, each of them at his beck and call. Mrs. Martin cooked only what she knew he liked, and Christina cared not how muddy his boots were, or how many snowy towels he wiped half-washed hands on. Beenie tidied up after him without a word: a smile of approval from the young sultan was all they asked. Nicole was his very good friend, ready always for fun; Barbara patiently stitched sails for the boats he made; "Cousin Jane" was the one he liked best to sit with him after he was in bed and tell him stories of Rutherfurd, and Ronnie and Archie.

Almost at once Arthur developed a strong affection for young Alastair, "The Sprat" he called him, and was never so happy as when he had him trotting at his heels. At the same time he was a frank and fearless commentator, and did not hide his disapproval of certain traits in the Sprat's character.

One day Simon Beckett suggested that he would take the two boys to St. Andrews, show them the places of interest, and give them luncheon at an hotel, and asked Barbara and Nicole to be of the party. Barbara happened to be engaged, but Nicole was delighted to accept the invitation.

Simon had meant to go by car, but the boys were both keen on a train journey, so they set off, crowding into a carriage that already contained an elderly stout man and his equally stout wife. Nicole and Simon sat facing each other in the middle and the boys were given the corner seats.

As there were strangers present Arthur never uttered a word, but looked out at the dreary winter fields with an impassive face. Alastair, alas! seemed unaware of how the best people behave when travelling. First he removed his hat, then he drew from his pocket a mouth-organ and, sitting hunched up in his seat, began to play on it earnestly.

Arthur stood it for a minute or two, then he leant forward and said, "Stop that, can't you!" But Alastair, like the deaf adder, stopped his ears instead and went on playing, his usually pale face quite pink with exertion, his hair standing up in what Gentle Annie called "a cow's lick."

"Pan in an overcoat!" whispered Nicole to Simon. "Did you ever see such a freakish little face?"

Again Arthur leant forward and admonished his friend:

"*Don't behave like a beastly tripper.*"

Alastair stopped playing, but still holding the mouth-organ to his mouth with both hands, said simply, "I am a tripper," and started again. With a snort of wrath Arthur turned away and devoted his whole attention to the landscape.

Later, at luncheon in the large and splendid hotel, he resumed the subject. "Sprat, why d'you like playing a mouth-organ when you're among people you don't know?" he asked when they were both attacking plates of roast-beef, Alastair very carefully, for he had only lately been promoted from a fork and spoon to a knife and fork. "Why *do* you?"

Alastair held his knife and fork upright, which he had been told not to do, as he considered the question.

"Because it makes me happy," he said at last.

"But—don't you *mind* people seeing you play the fool?"

Alastair shook his head:

"Then," said Arthur, "I believe you're Labour."

"Yes," said Alastair.

"What is Labour, Sprat?" Nicole asked him.

"It's what Annie is. There was an Election in Kirkmeikle once, and I wore a red ribbon to show I was Labour."

"And I suppose," Arthur said bitterly, "that you like char-a-bancs full of trippers throwing empty ginger-beer bottles about?"

Alastair lifted his head, his eyes the eyes of one beholding a vision.

"How lovely!" he said.

Nicole and Simon laughed, and Nicole said: "Never mind, Sprat, I like char-a-bancs and trippers and ginger-beer bottles too!"

"I bet Mr. Beckett doesn't," Arthur declared.

Alastair looked wistfully at his friend, who said, "Have some ginger-beer now, both of you," and the boys were nothing loath.

"Now we must explore," Nicole said, when the excellent meal was over.

"Shall we buy a guide-book?" Simon asked. "Or how shall we manage?"

"Just let's wander down South Street. I was here once as a child and I remember we went along South Street to the Tower and the dungeons."

"I want to see the dungeons," said Arthur, "don't you, Sprat?"

"Yes," Alastair said firmly. Then—"What are they?"

"Queen Mary's house is somewhere here," Nicole said, as they walked along the old street. "I've forgotten my history-books but I remember *The Queen's Quair*. It says that in St. Andrews the Queen lodged in a plain house where simplicity was the rule, and that the ladies wore short kirtles, and gossiped with fish-wives on the shore, rode out with hawks over the dunes, and walked the sands of the bay when the tide was down. And Darnley came here, that 'long lad.' St. Andrews will always in a way belong to Queen Mary. I wonder if the story will ever lose its magic?"

"Never," said Simon, "so long as there are men and women to listen."

Alastair was holding Simon's hand. "Tell me the story," he begged.

Simon looked down at the small face. "I'm afraid, my Bat, it wouldn't interest you. Mary was Queen of Scotland, but she had been brought up in France and had learned to love sunshine, and gaiety, and courtly manners—everything we haven't much of. Then she came to Scotland and found grey skies, and thought the people rough and unmannerly. And all round her were enemies, and though she had

103

some loyal friends they couldn't keep her from making nets for her own feet, and the enemies put her in prison and in the end they killed her."

"What a rotten shame!" said Arthur.

"But why did they kill the Queen if she was good?" Alastair asked. "She was good, wasn't she?"

"Perhaps not always," Nicole said, "but she never had a chance." She turned to Simon. "I'm always being rebuked for my tiresome habit of quoting things so now I hardly dare to, but do you know the lines Marion Angus wrote?" and she repeated
—

> "Consider the way she had to go,
> Think of the hungry snare!
> The nets she herself had woven,
> Aware or unaware,
> Of the dancing feet grown still,
> The blinded eyes—
> Queens should be cold and wise,
> And she loved little things,
> Parrots
> And red-legged partridges
> And the golden fishes of the Duc de Guise
> And the pigeon with the blue ruff
> She had from Monsieur d'Elbœuf."

"Poor little soul," said Simon. "Queens should be cold and wise. Imagine her here in this grey place, surrounded by men who wished her ill, she who loved little things!"

When they reached the ruins of the cathedral, "Who knocked it down?" Alastair asked.

"Perhaps Arthur can tell us," Nicole suggested, but that worthy shook his head. "Don't know," he said, "but anyway it wasn't me," a reply which struck Alastair as the height of wit.

"Now, listen," Nicole said. "John Knox had it destroyed. '*Pull down the nests,*' he said, '*and the rooks will fly away.*'"

"The old blighter," said Arthur. "What about the poor rooks? They'd have to build other nests."

"By rooks he meant priests," Nicole explained, "or anyway, papists. Oh, he was a root-and-branch man this same John Knox. Old Betsy says, 'Mary was a besom, but auld John Knox was a guid man, and he made a graund job o' oor Reformation.'"

"John Knox is a friend of Aunt Janet's," Alastair announced. "We've a picture of him in a long white beard. . . . Are these all tombstones, like we have in Kirkmeikle?"

"Yes," said Nicole, reading one here and there. "I've all my countrymen's passion for a graveyard. I can wander contentedly for hours and read epitaphs. Just look at this one." She spelt out the name, and made out that the man who lay here had once occupied the Chair of Logic in St. Andrews University. . . . "And his family extends to both sides of the stone. I make fifteen: how many do you make? Ensigns and cornets—most of them seem to have gone to India. Well, I do call that a good day's work—three wives, fifteen children, and a long useful life teaching logic. . . . And now it's going to rain so we'd better see the dungeons at once."

After the dungeons had been gloated over, the rain drove them into a cinema for an hour before tea. It was the first time Alastair had ever been in one, and Arthur instructed him. "They're not real people, you know, they're only pictures."

But even in the cinema Arthur was tried by his friend's too spontaneous behaviour, for not only did he laugh long and loud at the funny parts, but he insisted on addressing the actors who were "featured" on the screen. "I don't like the look of you," he told the villain. Against the driver who did not stop the train as quickly as seemed necessary when the hero and his horse lay helpless on the line his rage knew no bounds. Standing on his feet, with his hands clenched, he muttered against him. Towards the heroine he felt nothing but disgust. When in the "close-up" she was shown with large tears in her eyes, he could hardly bear it, and when the hero clasped her in a close and prolonged embrace, he nudged Arthur crossly to know what they were doing. "Kissing," hissed Arthur shamefacedly, adding, "The silly asses!"

One wonders what Miss Symington thought of her nephew's adventures when he related them on his return—a medley of mouth-organs, beer in hotels, bottle-dungeons and John Knox, Queen Mary being killed by wicked people, ladies kissing men, and trains that wouldn't stop though a poor horse was going to be run over.

Alastair had yet another new experience during these Christmas holidays.

"Nikky," Arthur said to his cousin one night, "the Sprat's fearfully keen to go to something called a 'Swaree.' He says you get a 'poke' and 'a service of fruit,' and he wants me to go with him."

Nicole laughed. "But, Arthur, have you any idea what a church *soirée* is like? True you get tea and a poke, but after that there are speeches and all sorts of dull things. I know what has fired the Sprat's imagination—the service of fruit, but I'm afraid he'd find it very disappointing."

"I don't think so. Anyway, it'd be fine to come home late. The Sprat's never been out at night."

"When is it? To-morrow? Well, I'll see what Miss Symington says."

The next morning Nicole went to the Manse to ask for particulars, and found Mrs. Lambert in the study with clean towels over her arm. "I've got stuck here," she explained, "when I should be getting the spare room ready for Mr. Bain of Kirkleven; he's coming for the Sunday School Social to-night. You see, John has to take the chair, and I'm trying to give him some useful hints."

"I wish you'd let it alone just now," said Mr. Lambert. "Dear me, girl, can't you see I'm busy?"

"Yes, but this is your job just as much as the other—— *Please* don't go, Miss Rutherfurd. Take that chair by the fire and help me to convince my husband that a chairman must be both bright and tactful."

"T-terrible!" said Mr. Lambert.

"Terrible indeed," agreed Nicole, "but necessary. I've taken the chair myself sometimes, and I know how one has to smile and smile and be an idiot——"

"And whatever you do, John," his wife continued, "be sure and praise Mr. Lawson, or we won't see the right side of his face for weeks." She turned to Nicole and explained: "Mr. Lawson is the superintendent of the Sunday School, a decent man, but dreadfully easily slighted. And talk about the teachers, John, and say something encouraging about their work. And when some one is singing, don't just say coldly, 'Miss So-and-so will sing,' as if she had forced her way in; say something about how fortunate we are to have Miss So-and-so with us to-night—you know the sort of thing."

"Yes, yes, girl, I'll remember about Lawson and the teachers, only do stop now. . . . Miss Rutherfurd, I wonder who invented Social Meetings; he did an ill turn to ministers."

"Not to all ministers," his wife reminded him. "Mr. Bain simply lives for them. He's the best *soirée* speaker in these parts, Miss Rutherfurd, and we're very lucky to get him to-night."

"Please tell me," said Nicole, "may any one go to-night?"

"Adults ninepence," Mr. Lambert responded gloomily.

"Oh! Does that cover a poke and a service of fruit? Because both Alastair and Arthur are keen to taste of those delights, and I'm going now to beg Miss Symington to let Alastair go with us."

"Do come. It would be so cheering to see you there," Mrs. Lambert said, but her husband only smiled sardonically.

Miss Symington gave the desired permission. Alastair might go with Arthur and Nicole, and Annie, who would also be at the Social, would take him home. The show began at seven o'clock, so Lady Jane said instead of dinner there would be supper at nine o'clock. Nicole tried to persuade Barbara to join the party but she refused; Simon Beckett, however, accepted an invitation given by Arthur, and the four started in great spirits.

The *soirée* was held in the church, which seemed odd to Simon's English eyes, but Nicole told him that in her opinion it could not hurt even a sacred building to see a lot of happy children have tea, even though they did explode their "pokes," when empty, with a loud bang.

The "poke" in question consisted of a cookie, a scone, a perkin, and an iced cake from which the icing had peeled and distributed itself over the other contents.

In the choir-seat a table was spread with a white cloth covered with more choice viands than were provided for the multitude, and at it sat Mr. Lambert, the superintendent of the Sunday School, and Mr. Bain who had come to speak. Mr. Lambert wore a strained expression.

When Nicole volunteered to help with the tea, Mrs. Lambert, very busy with tea-kettles, pointed her to the choir-seat which was doing duty as a platform. "If you'd take them that tea-pot. There's cream and sugar on the table; they don't get

106

ordinary ready-mixed *soirée* tea."

Nicole nodded. "I see—'How beautiful they are, the lordly ones!' "

She mounted the platform and was introduced to the two men she did not know, and gave them tea, and received in turn many fair speeches from the jokesome Mr. Bain. Simon, meanwhile, helped Mrs. Lambert with the heavy kettles.

"Boys all right?" Nicole asked as she passed him.

"They seem so, and the way the Bat's wolfing the contents of that bag is a poor compliment to the tea Miss Jamieson gave him a short time ago."

"Ah, but think how good, how *different* things taste when eaten out of a poke, in a hot steamy atmosphere, along with fifty other children. ... I think everybody's about finished eating now. I wonder what happens next?"

A hymn was given out, an old-fashioned hymn, which the children knew and sang with gusto, "*When Mothers of Salem*," then Mr. Lambert rose to his feet. He smiled nervously and said he was glad to see such a good turn-out of children, and also of parents. Then followed a few sentences in which Nicole recognised an attempt to follow his wife's advice to try to be bright. It was galvanised mirth and she was thankful when he ceased the effort, and gave a very short, very sincere address to the children. He finished and sat down, and his eyes wandered to where his wife sat. She was obviously dissatisfied. What message was she trying to send him? Ah! the superintendent—the teachers: he got to his feet again: the situation was saved.

A stalwart young woman sang "*The Holy City*," then came the feature of the evening. Mr. Bain, advancing to the front of the choir-seat, and rubbing his hands as if in anticipation of his own treat, began. It was *soirée*-speaking in its finest flower. Everything in heaven and earth seemed to remind the speaker of a funny story and his audience rocked with laughter.

"Look," whispered Nicole to Simon, "do just look at Arthur and the Bat."

Arthur was sitting looking absolutely blank, evidently thoroughly bored with Mr. Bain's efforts. Alastair, on the other hand, seemed to sympathise with the theory that "every chap likes a hand," for he was applauding vociferously, his face radiant.

"Arthur," said Simon, "evidently believes with Dr. Johnson that the merriment of parsons is mighty offensive."

The meeting was over before nine o'clock, so they carried Alastair and Gentle Annie back to the Harbour House for a drink of lemonade, a beveridge which Alastair's soul loved.

Arthur, who was in great spirits about staying up late and having supper with Simon Beckett, nudged Alastair and asked, "Did you like it, Bat-Sprat? Was it fine?"

And Alastair lifted his face from the lemonade glass and said: "*Fine*. ... This lemonade's so nice and prickly."

"You get treats here, Arthur," Barbara said. "A 'swaree' is far before a pantomime."

"Rather like a pantomime, Cousin Barbara. The chap who kept on being funny wouldn't have made a bad clown. Silly kind of clergyman, though."

"But tell me," said Lady Jane, "what *is* a service of fruit? I've been so anxious to know."

"It was an orange," Alastair said gravely, producing from his pocket a somewhat shrivelled specimen of that fruit.

"Have mine, Sprat," said Arthur; "mine's a goodlier one."

"*An orange!*" said Lady Jane. "And I expected at the very least bells and pomegranates!"

CHAPTER XIX

"What's to come is still unsure."
Twelfth Night.

Barbara took Arthur back to school, as she professed herself unable to live any longer without a breath of London air and the sight of her friends.

It was quiet and strange to Nicole and her mother without the boy. In the short time he had lived with them he had made a place for himself, and every way they turned there was a gap.

"Barbara was wise," Nicole said. "It's the people who stay at home who do the worst of the missing."

She and her mother were sitting in the dusk doing nothing.

Arthur would never have allowed them such a time of idleness. He had always clamoured for light, in order to go on with whatever particular bit of business he was engaged on at the moment, which might be anything from an attempt to make a wireless set to the laborious penning of a blotted epistle (he was no scholar) to his fever-stricken brother and sister.

"Yes," Lady Jane agreed, "it was wonderfully nice having a boy in the house —the sound of his heavy boots on the stairs, the way he had of knocking up against things, the way he whistled and sang refreshed one, somehow. There is something stagnant about the air of a house that contains only women."

Nicole laughed. "My dear, you make the most remarkable statements in that gentle voice of yours. How angry some women would be to hear you! I know what you mean, and in a way I agree. No matter how well women get on together, how much at one they are, there's a lack of vibration, so to speak. We are too neat, too tidy, too regular in our ways. A man is like a strong wind blowing through the house; his boots are muddy, and he smells of fresh air, and pipes, and peat-smoked tweeds. And his views on life are different, and his voice—— One gets tired of women's voices, they're so peepy."

Just then, Christina's voice in the dusk announced, "Mr. Beckett."

"How odd," said Nicole, as the visitor found his way cautiously to the fireside.

"What is?"

"That you should come in at this moment . . . We were talking, Mums and I, about men, and agreeing that life is a little stagnant without them—almost too peaceful. We're missing Arthur, you see—— We'll not have the lights yet, Christina."

"I'm missing Arthur too," Simon confessed, as he settled himself into a chair. "He's a fine little chap. He ought to do well at Eton—he has such a tremendous respect for tradition."

109

"He has indeed," Nicole laughed. "Can you imagine two boys more utterly different than Arthur and Alastair? Arthur rather arrogant and intolerant, as self-conscious as he can be, and with it all a very decent chap, and Alastair, the friendliest little mortal on earth, not caring what any one thinks but quite set on his own odd opinions! And they were such good friends. Arthur adored the Sprat. I don't wonder. There is something about that fantastic little face and the too-large overcoat that makes my heart turn to water in the most ridiculous way. . . . By the way, we didn't ask have you had tea?"

"Yes, thanks. I'm just back from a long tramp."

Nicole laid cigarettes and matches on the table beside him, while her mother said:

"Nikky, you've always been a slave to little boys. Providence must have intended you to be matron in a preparatory school. You would so utterly have enjoyed comforting them when they arrived homesick, and giving them a good time when they had measles and mumps."

"Yes, I only wish I had been Alastair's aunt instead of Miss Symington. Not that she isn't good to him, and she's certainly a far better instructor for youth than I am, but—a child cannot live by bread alone."

Simon reached for an ash-tray. "The great lack about Miss Symington," he said, "is that she can put no glamour into things. Life to her is just so many days to be devoted to work, meals, and—in strict moderation—play. Everything is what it seems, and she is merely grieved when the Bat tries to liven up things by telling her he has found an elephant's nest in the garden. Whereas, some people can make even a dull job like supping rice-pudding into a thing of delight to a child. . . . I remember my mother used to make a quarry in the middle and fill it up with milk, and tell us a story about it, until it all went down. I can't imagine Miss Symington telling a story, I can't imagine her 'making believe.' I daresay all that sort of thing can be carried too far, but when it's never there at all the child misses a lot."

Lady Jane took up her embroidery frame. "I shouldn't think," she said, as she chose her various silks, "that your childhood was wanting in glamour."

Simon turned to her with a smile.

"No," he said. ". . . There were three boys of us with no sister, but my mother was so young and jolly we never missed one. She loved to bird-nest with us, and didn't mind a bit lying for hours in swampy places, and she rode with us, and played cricket and tennis. . . . My mother used to say that she had to be extra kind to me because I was the middle one. Ralph was important being the eldest, and Harry, as the youngest, had been petted, but I had to fight for my own hand. The three of us were pretty near an age, and tremendous friends. . . . I can remember getting home for holidays in winter, when mother made toffee and roasted chestnuts in the school-room, and we tried who could tell the weirdest ghost story; and spring mornings when we got up at six and went away through the meadows; and long summer nights in the Highlands where my father rented a stretch of river. . . . My mother died in 1916, when we were all away from her. Ralph was with his ship, I was in the trenches—Harry had been shot down while flying. She worked too hard and got

110

pneumonia, but it was really Harry's going, and the anxiety about Ralph and me that killed her. Father said so."

There was silence for a minute, then Simon said:

"Ralph died at Zeebrugge. . . . My father was a good deal older than my mother and after she went he seemed suddenly to become an old man—not keen and interested any more—just as if he had come to an end of hope. When the news came that Ralph had gone he just seemed to give it up, and only lived a month after him—so I'm alone you see, and . . ."

His voice trailed into silence.

Nicole knelt down to stir the fire. In a little, "We must have light," she said. "Can you find the switch, Mr. Beckett? . . . Dear me, how we blink! Like owls in the sunlight. . . ."

She got up to pull the curtains, standing for a few minutes to look out. When she went back to the fireside her mother and Simon were deep in talk. Simon was speaking:

"I was always very keen on climbing and had done a good deal, and it was a tremendous chance to be allowed to join the Everest Expedition. And then, you see, I had nobody to be anxious about me. I suppose I was lucky not having to feel selfish about leaving people—but that cuts both ways, for I admit it was pretty beastly to come home and have no one to tell. . . ."

"And the book?" said Lady Jane. "I'm afraid you must have got very little done lately, you gave so much of your time to Arthur."

"Oh, you'd wonder! I've begun to rewrite and polish. At present there's hardly a decently put sentence in it, so I've my work cut out for me."

"Don't they say, 'hard writing makes easy reading?' Probably what you write will be much pleasanter to read than the outpourings of a facile pen. I should think that must be the undoing of many writers—the knack of writing blithely on and on?"

"Perhaps," Simon said; "anyway, it's beyond me. I sit in awe of the people who can write page after page about nothing. Bare facts baldly narrated—that's my style!"

He laughed and took a cigarette.

"And when you finish it," said Lady Jane, "will you leave Kirkmeikle? For in that case . . ."

"Finished or not, I must leave in March. The preparations for the next Expedition are being made, and I'm going out before the others. There's a tremendous lot to do—you'd wonder—both here and out there."

Lady Jane was threading her needle with a strand of bright silk. She stuck it into the embroidery and leant forward to the young man.

"But—you don't mean that *you* are going to make another attempt? that you are going back? Oh, surely not!"

Going back! Simon! Nicole sat very still and said not a word.

Simon looked at Lady Jane gratefully. "It's jolly nice of you to care . . . your kindness to me has been wonderful.—Of course I'm going back. I was desperately afraid I wouldn't be fit enough, but the doctors say now I'm all right, and Kirkmeikle

111

air has completely set me up. . . . Odd how reluctant I am to leave the little town ____"

The door opened. "Mr. Lambert," said Christina, and the little clergyman ambled in, a book under either arm.

"I'm not going to stay," he murmured. "Good evening, good evening. I only came with these books in case you wanted to return them." He looked at the books as if loth to part from them, and laid them on the edge of a table, from which they quickly descended to the ground accompanied by a glass of flowers. "D-dear me! what a mess. Flower vases are awkward things."

"So they are," said Nicole, springing to the rescue. "The books are hardly touched; we'll rub them up and they won't be a bit the worse. Once I put marmalade on *Marius the Epicurean* and it improved him vastly, gave him a lovely polish."

"I d-daresay," Mr. Lambert began, "that if Pater . . ." then he stopped, for Simon was on his feet saying good-bye. "Wait a moment, Beckett, and I'll go with you. There's something I want to talk to you about. . . ."

But Simon hurriedly apologised and left.

CHAPTER XX

"From you have I been absent in the Spring."

Sonnets by William Shakespeare.

The days passed, short, stormy, January days melting into February with its hint of spring.

One mild day when the blackbirds were trying their notes, Nicole wrote to her friend Jean Douglas.

... This is the sort of day that makes me simply long for Rutherfurd. The snowdrops will be in drifts by the burn-side now. How often I've stood under a steel-grey sky, with a north wind blowing, and looked at the brave little advance armies of spring poking their heads through the beech-leaves of a dead October. To-day I'm positively hungry for Rutherfurd. How gladly would I turn the Jacksons out neck and crop, if only I had the fairy whistle! *Everything in its proper place* I would pipe, and positively laugh to see them scuttle. ... After that outburst I shall write, I hope, in a better spirit. You see, I can only say it to you. I daren't breathe a word of discontent here in case of rousing sleeping fires of desire in Mother and Barbara. Poor Babs does miss the old life so badly. Mother never says she misses anything, and is always cheerful and willing to be amused, only—laughter can be sadder than tears sometimes. She still, at times, has an air of sitting so loosely to the things of earth that Babs and I want to clutch at her skirts to keep her with us at all.

Things amble along as usual. I said this morning, "I *do* wish Mistress Jean would pay us a visit." The others echoed the wish, only Babs was sceptical about our power to entertain you. But, I think you would be quite well amused.

What fun it would be to get the best guest-room ready for you: to find flowers for it—flowers are a great difficulty here, as the nearest florist is in Langtoun and he sells mostly vegetables!—and to choose books for your bed-table that you would like. And you would lie in bed in the morning and listen to voices underneath your windows, fisher laddies talking their Fife lilt, foreign sailor-men, fish-wives crying "Hawdies, fresh hawdies," and smell through the lavender of the bed-linen the salt, tarry smell of the harbour.

And what else can I offer you? We would explore the East Neuk, you and I, and I wonder if you know St. Andrews? If not, there are fascinating things to see there. And, of course, you would meet all our new friends—I shouldn't wonder if Mrs. Heggie made a dinner party for you, and you would enjoy the comedy of that good lady and Barbara. Barbara is always putting Mrs. Heggie in her place, but her efforts are quite lost on the dear soul, for she has no notion what the place is or that she has ever strayed from it. She admires Barbara immensely—licks the hand that beats her, so to speak. She tells me Mother is her idea of a *grande dame*, but she doesn't quite understand where I get my democratic ways. *Alas, poor Yorick!*

Miss Symington you would have to go and see, though, probably, you'd find her supremely uninteresting, with her ugly clothes, and her bleak house, and her still ways. But I think you'd like Dr. Kilgour and his nice funny sister, and it would be most disappointing if you didn't appreciate my friends the Lamberts. It does make me feel ashamed of myself when I go to the Manse of a morning to take the babies out to find Mrs. Lambert conning over her address for the Mothers' Meeting while she stirs a milk pudding for the early dinner! Her great cross is having to speak in public, and open meetings with prayer, but she does it, the valiant little person, she does it. I now and again go with her to the Mothers' Meeting, to help with the singing and play Sankey's hymns on the harmonium, and to hear her read the Bible is an inspiration. It is no dusty far-away history when she reads it. She is so interested in it herself that she makes it sound like Dumas, and the women sit back with a sigh when she finishes.

She has a small transparent face like a wood-anemone, and I'm always afraid she wears herself out of existence, but you mustn't think Mr. Lambert is idle. He helps her in a hundred ways, writes his sermons with a baby rolling on the floor at his feet—and very good sermons they are. He keeps the garden, and goes messages and does all the odd carpentering jobs about the house. The only thing his wife cannot get him to do is gush. To her most frantic appeals to be "frank" to some person he can only manage a cold hand-shake and a bald sentence. I've seen her turn on him a face half vexed, half amused as she said: "Oh, John, you're *a dry character!*"

Odd, isn't it, that there are one or two words that have a different meaning in Scots? English people mean by "frank" honest and open; here "frank" means free: a "frank" manner is a forthcoming, gushing manner. "Canny" is another word. It really means cunning, but in Scotland it means gentle—"Canny wee thing."

Well! is that all I've got to offer you? Not quite. Barbara will want you to know her friends, the Erskines. They are a great support to her, and she goes over a good deal to their place and meets people she likes, and they come here. Mother and I like them very much, but it's difficult taking an interest in new people, I find. Babs retorts that I manage to be interested in the Kirkmeikle people, but they are different, more human, somehow, and pitiful. The Erskines are so sure of themselves, prosperous, invulnerable.

And you might possibly be invited to lunch with Mr. and Mrs. Buckler. Their lives have been full of colour and interest—thirty years in India—but they haven't brought much of either away with them. They are oddly interested in things like disrespectful parlour-maids . . . so after all what does it profit a man to see the world?

I wonder if you stayed a week with us consorting daily with Kirkmeikle people, would you say, like Babs, that you were sick of honest worth? She says she is driven to Mr. Michael Arlen in sheer self-defence. To forget Mrs. Heggie and Miss Janet Symington she reads of ladies reclining in slenderness on divans, playing with rosaries of black pearls and eating scented macaroons out of bowls of white jade!

This is a long letter all about nothing. Your last letter was a joy. Cannes must have been lovely. How could you tear yourselves away?—but of course I know that

Colonel Douglas is never really happy anywhere except at Kingshouse. You will be home now, lucky people. Write when you have time and tell me all about everybody.

Your loving

Nikky.

Nicole, having finished her letter, sat on at the writing-table, looking before her. A letter all about nothing indeed! But, somehow, there was nothing of interest anywhere these days; life was flat and stale, and Simon Beckett was going away.

Well: Nicole gave herself a mental shake as she put her letter into an envelope, and straightened the writing things on the table. It must be the hint of spring in the air that was making her feel foolish and sentimental; besides it was Saturday afternoon, always a depressing time somehow, and her mother and Barbara had motored off to have tea at a distance, and Alastair had gone with Simon, in the latter's car, to Langtoun, to see a football match. She had preferred to stay at home, thinking it would be pleasant to have a long afternoon for letter-writing, but she found she wasn't liking it at all. She would go out, she decided, and talk to old Betsy for a little, and then walk very fast round the links and try to walk off this curious depression which had suddenly enveloped her.

She found Betsy in a distinctly bad humour. Saturday afternoon seemed to have cast a blight on her spirits also. She had paid somebody twopence to sand her stair, and was not pleased with the way it had been done.

"And it's juist like everything else," she grumbled. "The folk nowadays winna work. They dinna ken what work means: them and their eight hours day! Labourites they ca' theirsels. What they're lookin' for is a country whaur folk wad be hangit for workin'. . . . An' the Government's tae support a'body! Ye'd think to hear them that the Government could pick up siller in gowpins . . . Ay, thae folk next door ca' theirsels Labour, but efter the way the wumman washed ma stair, I'll naither dab nor peck wi' them!"

"But," said Nicole, "the stair looked to me very clean. I just thought as I came up how fresh everything was, all ready for the Sabbath day. . . . And it's February, Betsy, and almost spring. The last time I was here it was Christmas."

"Weel, better something lang than naething sune, but I was wonderin' what hed come ower ye. But her leddyship's awfu' attentive. I div like tae see her, an' we've sic graund cracks aboot oor ain place. An' she reads to me whiles, for ma sicht's no' what it was. Sic a bonnie speaker she is! There's a lot o' folk awfu' queer pronouncers o' words, ye wud suppose they were readin' the buik upside doon. The man next door came in and read me oot o' a paper, but losh! I was nane the wiser when he feenished. . . ."

"You've lots of visitors, Betsy, haven't you? And you take such an interest in everything that goes on."

"Oh, I dae that, an' though I canna steer ower the door verra little passes me. There's aye somebody to gie me a cry in an' tell me what's gaun on. Ye see, I'm aye here, an' folk like a listener. . . . Did ye hear that ma son's been lyin'? Ay, it sterted wi' influenzy and syne it was pewmony. Ma gude-dochter cam' to see me the nicht afore last. She's that ill at Dr. Kilgour, the dowgs wadna lick his bluid efter the names she ca'ed him."

"Why?" asked Nicole, startled. "What has Dr. Kilgour done?"

"Oh, when he cam' an' fand Tam sae faur through he gaed her a ragin' an' said he shuld hae been there lang syne. An' he sterted an' pu'ed down the winday—she keeps the windays shut for fear o' dust comin' in—an' he was that gurrl aboot it that he broke a cheeny ornament."

"But your son's getting better?"

"Oh, ay, he is that. Dr. Kilgour's a skilly doctor, but he's offended ma gude-dochter." Betsy smiled grimly. "An' he tell't some o' the wives aboot here that they hed nae richt to hev bairns at a', they didna ken hoo tae handle them. That's true eneuch. I've aften said ye wad suppose it was broken bottles they hed in their airms."

Nicole laughed as she rose to go. "Dr. Kilgour's not afraid to speak his mind." She looked out of the little window. "See the sun on the water, Betsy! You'll admit Kirkmeikle is a nice little town?"

But Betsy shook her head. "I see naething in't. I never cared for a toon. I aye likit the hill-sides and the sheep. Eh, wasna it bonnie tae see the foals rinnin' after their mithers, an' the mears stannin' still to let them sook?"

"Very bonnie. And now I'm going to put your tea ready for you. Mrs. Martin sent a ginger-bread, and I know you like a bit of country butter and some cream at a time. These are fresh eggs. . . ." Nicole was unpacking the basket as she spoke.

"Weel," said Betsy, watching her, "what's guid to gie shouldna be ill tae tak'. It's sic a thocht to move an' I'm that blind, that whiles I juist dinna bather aboot ony tea, but a cup'll be gratefu' the noo. Thank ye kindly, Miss. . . . Na, na, I manage fine. Agnes Martin comes in every nicht when she gets the dinner cooked, an' sees me tae ma bed, an' pits a'thing richt for the mornin'. Ay, I'm weel aff wi' her. . . ."

When Nicole was going up the brae towards the links she met Janet Symington walking with a man. She immediately found herself wondering who he could be, and smiled to think she was becoming as inquisitive as Betsy herself. Then she remembered that it was Saturday. Of course this was one of the preachers.

He was a tall man with a large soft face, and, evidently, quite a flow of conversation, for Miss Symington was walking with her head bent listening attentively. Looking up she saw Nicole and half stopped. Nicole also hesitated, and presently found herself being introduced to Mr. Samuel Innes. He held out a large soft hand ("He shakes hands as if he had a poached egg in his palm," thought Nicole), and uttered a few remarks about the weather in the softest voice she had ever heard in a man.

"Mr. Innes is going to speak at the Hall to-morrow night," Miss Symington said. "It's always a great treat to have him."

"Not at all," said Mr. Innes, while Nicole faltered, "That is very nice. I hope it'll be a good day."

"There's always a good turn-out when it is Mr. Innes," said Miss Symington, looking up at her companion with what in any one else would have been called a smirk.

Mr. Innes repeated "Not at all," and Nicole, making hasty adieux, fled.

"Now I wonder," she said to herself, as she stood a minute looking out to sea, "I wonder if that gentleman means to hang up his hat, to use Mrs. Heggie's descriptive phrase. . . . Mr. Samuel Innes. What a perfect Samuel he makes——"

CHAPTER XXI

"The only difference between the sentimentalist and the realist is that the sentimentalist's reality is warm and beautiful, while the realist's is glacial and hideous, and they are neither of them real realities either. . . ."
Reginald Farrer.

They were apt to linger over breakfast at the Harbour House. It was a pleasant time of day in the dining-room with its striped silk curtains and Hepplewhite chairs, more especially when the tide was high and the water lapped against the low wall, but always pleasant with the feeling of morning activity all round, voices from the harbour, children shouting as they went to school, wives having a gossip before they began their daily round.

The postman came, as a rule, when they were at the marmalade stage, and they read bits out of letters to each other. It had been so, too, at Rutherfurd. Something this morning took Barbara's mind back to the old times when they had all been together in the sunny morning-room that opened on to the lawns and the brawling burn. Nicole had been a schoolgirl, swallowing her breakfast and rushing out with her brothers to get every minute out of the day, while she, in the restraint of new grown-upness, had sat with her elders sipping her second cup of tea and listening to Sir Walter reading out bits of news from the *Scotsman*.

There never had been, Barbara thought, a more truly good man than her uncle, so gentle and magnanimous, so full of humour, such a sportsman. Often, laughing, they had told him that he was in danger of the Woe promised to those of whom all men speak well. He was always asked to take the chair at political meetings that promised to be rowdy, because he was so courteous, so full of sweet reasonableness that the rudest were disarmed. She remembered how all his life his first thought had been his country. In his youth he had been in the Army, and when his father died he settled down at Rutherfurd, making the ideal landlord. When war broke out he had at once offered for service, and worked patiently through the four years at a dull but necessary job at the War Office, stinting himself of all but the barest necessities when food became scarce.

He was cheerful till Ronnie and Archie died. After that his laugh was seldom heard, though he went about among his friends and neighbours with his old kindly smile, always willing to listen, always ready to help. At home they had seen the change in him. The big man seemed to have shrunk, his clothes hung loose on him. He wandered much alone, and the men about the place shook their heads and told each other, "He's sair failed, the maister; he's gettin' awfu' wee buik. . . ."

Barbara came back to the present with Christina bringing in the letters. There were a few for Barbara and Nicole, but most of the budget went to Lady Jane.

"Why, Mother," Nicole said, "I never saw any one get so many letters. You might almost be a Cinema Star."

"It comes," said her mother, busily opening envelopes, "of being one of a large and united family. This is from Constance."

Nicole took up her own letters, looked through them and laid them down again to go and strew the usual meal on the window-sill for the birds. She sat half outside the window for a few minutes breathing in the fresh salt air.

Lady Jane looked up from her letters. "Anything interesting, Nikky?"

"Nothing much. There's one from Mrs. Jackson asking me to Rutherfurd in the beginning of March. If I can come she means to send out invitations for a dinner on the 10th, and a dance on the 11th. Heard you ever the like?"

"It is very kind of Mrs. Jackson," Lady Jane said.

"It is—very. She gives me no information about how things are going with her, but in a postscript remarks, 'We are liking our new home quite well.' I must say I call that rather cheek! Liking it quite well indeed! I feel inclined to say to her what Thomas Carlyle said to the lady who told him she accepted life. 'My God, Madam, *you had better.*'"

Lady Jane laughed. "I had forgotten that," she said; but Barbara glowered and asked, "Will you go? Could you bear to go?"

Nicole looked at her cousin thoughtfully. "It won't be easy. In fact . . . but, you see, I'm afraid I did promise that I would go and help her if she wanted me. It's so fatally easy to say something kind when you are saying good-bye to people you don't expect to come much into contact with; Mrs. Jackson seems to be depending on me. I know, Babs, you think I would consult my own dignity if I refused. What do you say, Mums? Ought I to accept or not?"

Lady Jane gathered up her correspondence. "My dear, you know best yourself. Mrs. Jackson is a nice woman and she was very considerate to us. It won't be easy, but it might be kind. You'd be a great help to her, and you needn't stay more than a few days."

"I might have to stay a week."

"I daresay you would survive it."

"And," said Barbara, "I defy Nicole not to get a great deal of amusement out of the most unpleasant duty. It's your lucky nature. I don't think I could go, but I'm not likely to be asked. Naturally they want the more romantic figure, the dispossessed heiress, golden hair and all!"

"What nonsense, Babs!"

"Great nonsense, my dear, but true . . . By the way, I've a note here from Marjory Erskine. She wants us to go over this afternoon. Some people have arrived unexpectedly whom they'd like us to meet."

"But I can't, Babs, I'm so sorry. I've promised to go to tea with Miss Symington—a special invitation in writing. I haven't seen her for weeks. They've had the painters in, and Alastair has said several times that his aunt was from home. It is unfortunate. I'd have loved a run with you this fresh good day. . . . Here comes Alastair with his shining morning face and his bag on his back, the complete scholar! Well, old man, is bat still t a b this morning? . . ."

That afternoon, having half an hour to spare before going to Ravenscraig, Nicole looked in at Knebworth, and found the Heggies, mother and daughter, at home.

"This is nice," said Mrs. Heggie, rising large and fresh and rosy, in her black dress and white frillings, to greet her visitor. "We do see you seldom! Surely you'll stay to tea?"

"I'd like to," Nicole assured her, "but I'm engaged to drink a dish of tea with Miss Symington. Invited by letter. I thought it must be a party, but it can't be if you're not going."

"Oh, it may be, it may be, but we're not invited. In fact, I haven't been asked inside the door of Ravenscraig since well before Christmas."

"Oh well," Nicole said soothingly, "Miss Symington may perhaps want to talk to me about something. I expect I'm the party! It's much better fun when there are several."

"Yes. She hasn't much conversation and it's difficult getting into a good comfortable talk with her. You've just to ask her how the Girls' Guild's getting on, and the Mothers' Meetings, and talk about the price of food and how cooks waste. She's not interested in anything you've been reading, and she'll not gossip. I must say I like a more varied 'crack'!" Mrs. Heggie laughed. . . . "And how's Lady Jane?"

"Very well. She's so busy writing letters this afternoon that she wouldn't stir out to take the air. You see, she has five sisters and three brothers and numerous nieces and cousins, and they all love her dearly and write constantly."

"Wonderful!" ejaculated Mrs. Heggie. "It's so unlike all I've ever heard of the aristocracy! . . . Joan's glaring at me, but I'm not saying anything wrong, am I?"

Nicole smiled at Joan, and reassured Mrs. Heggie.

"Of course not. You mean that from novels and the daily papers you would think the 'aristocracy' were thoroughly debased, engaged all the time in being divorced, and spending hectic days and nights gambling, drugging, swindling and dancing at night clubs—all that sort of thing! And, I suppose, it's true in a way of a certain section, a small but very vocal section. But you would be amused if you met the members of my mother's family and their friends. Some, I admit, are not bright and shining lights, but the majority are quite hopelessly respectable, and full of 'high ideels,' working away obscurely and conscientiously to leave the world a little better than they found it: husbands and wives quite loving and loyal; children brought up to respect the eternal decencies; master and servants liking and respecting each other! Even the people labelled 'smart' in the picture papers, whose names you see reading from left to right, are often quite dull-ly respectable. I'm afraid it's disappointing!"

Mrs. Heggie nodded. "But far better," she said. "Of course I knew Lady Jane was good, you can read it in her face, but I thought mebbe she was an exception, for, I'm sure the stories you hear. . . . And what is Miss Burt doing to-day?"

"Oh, Babs is off in her little car—I tell her she's like a child with a new toy —to spend the afternoon at Queensbarns."

"I suppose the Erskines are a very smart sort of people?"

"They certainly dress well," Nicole said.

"I mean that they keep up a lot of style—a butler and all that, and go to London for the season. They're not what you'd call provincial."

"Perhaps not. . . . Anyway, they're very kind."

"Oh," said Mrs. Heggie, "they're kind to *you*, naturally. But I'm told they're a bit stand-offish. Mrs. Thomson—you know, Joan?—they simply ignored her."

"I don't wonder," said Joan.

"Oh!" her mother protested. "She's quite a nice woman and awfully willing to be hospitable."

"A pusher and a climber," said Joan.

"Oh well," said Mrs. Heggie, with her usual large charity, "it's only natural that she should want to better herself, as the servants say!"

"Miss Joan," said Nicole, "do tell me, where do you do your writing? In some eyrie?"

Mrs. Heggie replied for her daughter. "Upstairs. Joan, take Miss Rutherfurd up to see."

Joan looked uncertainly at Nicole, who said eagerly, "Won't you? I'd love to see your workroom."

The two girls went upstairs together, and Joan opened a door, remarking, "It's not as tidy as it might be. I like to keep it myself."

It was a small room looking to the sea, with the floor stained black and covered with one or two bright-coloured rugs. The cream walls were hung with a medley of prints and photographs. A small figure of the Venus of Milo stood on the mantelshelf. A book-case entirely filled one wall.

Nicole went to it and began conning over the books.

"You've got Raleigh's *Shakespeare*—one of my first favourites. I think I can almost say it by heart. And what a line of poets—Walter de la Mare, A. E. Housman. . . . Do you sit at this table and write solemnly?"

"No. I generally crouch before the fire with a writing-pad on my knee. But I never write anything worth while, so what's the good of it?"

"Well, I don't pretend to be much of a judge, but your mother let me see some verses which seemed to me to have a touch of real magic."

"Oh yes, I've got a certain facility in the writing of verses—but that's not what I want to do. I want to write a book about life, a strong book, going down to the depths and rising to the heights, a book that talks frankly—not the pretty-pretty sentimental stuff that my mother and so many women love to read. I've heard them in book-shops at Christmas time: 'I want a book, a *pleasant* book. . . . Are you sure this is pleasant all through?'"

Joan sat gloomily in a wicker chair filled with brilliant orange cushions. Her skin looked dingier than ever against the cushions and the many-coloured Fair Isle jumper that she wore, and Nicole wondered why such a wholesome-looking mother should have such an unwashed-looking daughter.

"If you want to write a book like that, why don't you?" she asked.

"Because I can't," said Joan bitterly. "I don't know whether it's my upbringing or my subconscious self or what, but no matter how untrammelled my thoughts may be, when I put pen to paper I become so moral as to be absolutely maudlin."

She hunched up her shoulders and sat forward, staring hopelessly into the fire.

"What a book I might write about Janet Symington, for instance, about all the thwarted forces of her nature going into good works, what a study I could make of her! But I can't put down what I want to say, my pen seems to boggle at it."

Nicole giggled, then abjectly apologised. "I'm so terribly sorry, but it is rather funny, you know. . . . And I can't help being rather glad that you don't feel equal to writing such a book, it would be neither elevating nor entertaining. The sort of books you talk about don't shock me at all, I enjoy the cleverness with which they're written, but I finish them with relief and push them away. Isn't it better to try to write a book that people will go back to again and again? . . ." She looked at her wrist-watch. "Good gracious! is that the time? . . . Good-bye. Thank you for letting me see your den. Won't you come and see us soon? Mother would love to talk to you about poetry. . . ."

It had always been dusk when Nicole had gone to tea at Ravenscraig, but now the days were drawing out and the thin bright light of early spring lay over everything as she stopped to look at the clumps of snowdrops in the border, and the grey-green shoots of daffodils, and the first bold yellow crocus.

But what had happened besides the spring? Surely there was a difference! The stiffly starched lace curtains had gone from the windows, gone also the brown Venetian blinds, and in their place were hangings of fine net. The large sheet of stained glass in the inner door had been replaced by small leaded panes, and when the door opened she found that the hall had been changed out of recognition. Instead of the imitation marble there was a soft grey paper; the wood was painted black, and soft powder-blue carpets covered the stairs and lay on the tiled hall. An old oak chest bearing two heavy Chinese lamps had taken the place of the hat-and-umbrella stand.

Nicole glanced round distractedly, feeling as if she had fallen out of a dream, inclined to clutch the solid arm of the servant to prove to herself that she was really awake, but the drawing-room door was being opened, and she stumbled through to greater surprises.

Was this the bleak room with its gaunt bow-window, its dingy walls hung with pale water-colours and enlarged photographs, its carpet a riot of chrysanthemums on a brown ground, its unwelcoming gas fire?

Nicole forgot her manners in her astonishment. She left her hostess standing with outstretched hand, while she stared, and stared again, gasping at last, "But it isn't the same room; it can't be."

To begin with, it seemed twice the size. The walls were a warm apricot, the floor was polished, and bare, except for a fine Persian carpet in the middle, and a much smaller one at the fire-place, round which were grouped some capacious armchairs. The window was hung with curtains of blue and green and gold, beautiful glittering stuff that made one think of peacocks strutting in the sunshine. In the middle of the window was a small divan heaped with cushions covered with rich stuffs.

A grand piano stood in one corner, and the wall opposite the fire held a long low table with bowls of spring bulbs, above which hung the only picture the room contained, a glowing Eastern scene of hot sunlight and dark shadows. There was a long, slim gilt mirror over the mantelshelf, on which stood four old crystal candlesticks. In place of the gas fire with its baleful gleam, a fire of coal and logs sent flickering lights over tiles that gleamed like mother-o'-pearl.

Nicole shook hands with the owner of this room and sustained another shock, for Miss Symington was exactly the same. That she, too, should have suffered a change into something rich and rare was, perhaps, too much to expect, but it was, nevertheless, rather disconcerting to find her still in a blue serge skirt and a silk blouse and with an unfashionable head.

She looked rather bashfully at her guest as she said, glancing around the room, "We've been having some alterations made here, you will notice."

Nicole sank into one of the arm-chairs and found it supremely comfortable. "Alterations!" she said. "I should think you have; but, tell me, was it your own idea, this room?"

"No," said Miss Symington, looking rather affronted. "Could you imagine me thinking of anything like this? . . . I don't know how it was, your house looked so different, but I had no idea how to set about improving mine, so I went to the best furnishing shop I knew, and they sent a man to see the house and advise me. He was quite young—he looked like an artist—and he told me this was his profession, advising people how to make their houses pretty. Isn't that a queer profession for a young man?"

"Rather a jolly one, I think. So he thought out this scheme?"

"Yes. He said in this sort of villa there wasn't much to work on, but he managed to change things a good deal."

Nicole still gazed round the room. "Your young man seems to me a magician. You like it, don't you? And is all the house changed?"

"I think I like it," Janet said, rather doubtfully, "at least, I think the rooms that aren't changed look odd. The dining-room is just as it was. You see, there are the preachers over the week-ends, and they might not feel at home in this sort of thing!" She waved a hand towards the new splendour of colour. "Only this room, and the lobbies and stairs, and my own room and the best spare-room are changed. You must come up and see them after you've had your tea."

"But—d'you mind me asking?—what made you decide all of a sudden that the house wasn't just as you liked it?"

Tea had been brought in and Janet was pouring it out in her deliberate way. She passed Nicole a cup, and in her slightly complaining voice said, "It was your crystal bowl that started it all."

Nicole poured some milk into her tea and waited for enlightenment.

"On Christmas morning," Janet went on, "I took it up to my room, and it was so useless and so pretty that my room didn't seem the place for it at all. It made everything else look dull and ugly. I thought it was the wall-paper, and I got that changed; then the chintzes looked dingy and the carpet, and the bed, somehow, was wrong, and the light wood furniture—then I called in an expert."

She stirred her tea in the genteel way that always amused Nicole, and sat very straight on the edge of a great comfortable chair. All round her was beauty and colour, but she was provokingly drab.

Nicole leaned forward. "There's one thing still left to do," she said coaxingly. "You've made your house beautiful, now give yourself a chance. Blue serge is very nice, but it's not the most becoming wear for you. I want to see you in something softer—let me take the place of the furnishing young man and adorn you!"

Janet Symington flushed, pressing her lips firmly together, and Nicole cried, "I know what you're thinking, but that seems to me such a mistake. Would God have troubled to make this world so beautiful if He had wanted us to go about all sad-hued and dreary? You simply don't know how much harm is done by good women not knowing how to dress. I remember as a child, when I helped my mother to entertain Mothers' Unions and Girls' Friendlies and things like that, wondering why the best people—meaning the most serious, good people—nearly always had badly hung skirts! And to-day, when clothes are so easy and so suitable and so varied, it's conservatism run mad not to wear what other people are wearing. You would never wear a blouse and skirt again if you knew the comfort of a little frock. You always look nice and tidy, but I could make you look so attractive. . . . Let's go to Edinburgh and have a buy! It would be such fun. . . ."

About an hour later Nicole burst into the drawing-room at the Harbour House to find her mother listening to Barbara, who had just come in full of her afternoon at the Erskines'.

"I was to tell you, Nik, that they were very sorry you couldn't come; but they quite understood that Kirkmeikle had great attractions."

"I should think so indeed!" Nicole said, squatting down on a stool at her mother's feet. "Kirkmeikle's the most exciting place I ever struck. What do you think? When I went into Ravenscraig to-day I found the whole place changed as if a magician had waved a wand. Mums, you know what it looked like the first day we went to call? Lace curtains, sprawling flowery carpet, gas fire! Pouf! Gone. Now, lovely exotic colours, space—comfort. Some furnishing firm sent a man to advise, and this is the result. It's all as modern as can be, of course, you know the sort of villa he had to cope with, but quite beautiful. The staircases are grey and powder-blue, with black-framed etchings on the walls: the best bedroom is striped grey and white with pale-yellow silk curtains: Miss Symington's own room is prettiest of all. *And* the dining-room is the same old room—red leather chairs, green table-cover, aspidistra in a pot—because the preachers mightn't feel at home if it were changed. Isn't that delicious? Now, Babs," to that young woman, who was standing with her coat over her arm ready to go upstairs, "tell me if your Erskines ever do delightful exciting things like that? *Never!!*"

CHAPTER XXII

"Why should calamity be full of words?"
King Richard III.

In the first week of March Nicole went out one day with Alastair looking for star-fish at low tide, slipped, and fell into a deep pool. Often she had done it before and had never been a penny the worse, and this time she laughed and made her wet shoes "chork" to amuse Alastair, and continued the search. But a wind came out of the east, a nipping and an eager air—and Nicole shivered and went home. The next morning she woke with a sore throat and a cough and a temperature, and it was evident that Rutherfurd would not see her that week. She admitted it herself, sitting up in bed, flushed with fever and distress at her own stupidity.

"Who would have supposed that I would take cold?" she croaked, "a thing I almost never do. And no one would want me for a visitor, coughing and sneezing and infecting everybody! I must give up the thought of Rutherfurd, and I hate to fail Mrs. Jackson when all her arrangements are made. . . . Babs, won't you go in my place? You would be twice as useful anyway."

"My dear, I couldn't possibly offer myself."

"No, but send a wire now, and if she writes suggesting you . . ."

"We'll see," said Barbara.

Mrs. Jackson's letter when it came was a wail of despair. How was she to cope with her festivities with no one to stand by her to counsel and direct? What did Nicole suggest? Would Miss Burt think of coming? And Barbara, after much persuasion, consented to go.

"I'll be a sort of death's head at the feast," she predicted. "You know I never can be gay to order as Nikky can. And I'll hate the Jacksons when I see them really installed in our house. I feel already like Banquo's ghost, or something like that."

"You're not ethereal enough for that," Nicole reminded her, laughing. "I don't see you flitting spectral fashion. . . . Oh, don't make me laugh, for then I cough. You look so nice, my dear. Assure Mrs. Jackson that you aren't bringing her influenza, that this is only a common chill got through wet feet in an east wind, and I'm really better already. . . . Be sure and tell me what you think of 'Andy.' "

Barbara departed in the morning, and after luncheon Nicole announced that she couldn't stay in bed one moment longer.

"Do let me get up and sit by the drawing-room fire," she begged her mother. "Bed does me such a lot of harm. It has the same effect on me that having his hair cut had on Samson. And it's so boring in bed; if I were up I could find a thousand things to do. And you needn't tell Dr. Kilgour."

"But you look so comfortable lying there with your pile of books and these lovely roses—Mr. Beckett must have sent to Edinburgh for them. . . . Have you read all the last batch of books that came from the *Times*?"

"Never looked at them," Nicole said cheerfully. "You don't want to read new books in bed, they're too wearing. These are all 'tried favourites,' as we say of puddings."

Lady Jane bent over to read the titles. "*Starvecrow Farm*, surely that's an old book?"

"Don't you remember it, Mother? The runaway bride and the splendid old hostess of the inn. I know no book that gives you a more wonderful feeling of atmosphere. You absolutely live in that comfortable inn among the mountains, through these November days, and suffer with the girl and her lover. . . . And *The Good Comrade*. Why, Mums, you surely haven't forgotten 'Johnnie' and the stove called 'Bouquet,' and the Dutch bulb-growers? . . . Apart from the great books, what a lot of jolly good books there are in the world!"

"Yes," said her mother, "but to go back to the subject of staying in bed, I'm afraid you'll feel very wretched up."

"Not in the least. I've no temperature, and I'm not such an unsightly creature now that the cold has left my head and settled comfortably on my chest."

Lady Jane ceased to argue, and Nicole rose and dressed herself, adding as an invalid touch a rose-red satin dressing-gown with slippers to match, and assisted by Harris carrying things, took her way to the drawing-room. It was only five days since she had been in it, but she looked round appreciatively as if she had come back from a long journey, and settled down in one of the large arm-chairs by the fire with a sigh of satisfaction. After bed, she thought, what a joy to sit in a chair. A table drawn up by her side held a flask of eau-de-Cologne, a large bottle of smelling-salts, a tin of home-made toffee, and Simon Beckett's roses, as well as her letter-case, in case she should think of working off some letters.

"Now, Mother, you sit opposite with your work. It is so jolly to have you there and not feel that I should be begging you to go downstairs and not bother to sit with me. I do hate being unselfish!"

Lady Jane picked up her work and smiled at her daughter.

"It did seem a most unnatural thing to have you in bed. I hardly ever remember you being ill. Barbara was inclined to take bronchitis as a child, but you and the boys were like Shetland ponies. Even when you had measles and other childish ailments you were hardly ill."

"No. Measles was a very happy time. I remember hot lemonade as one of the chief joys, and *The Just So Stories* heard for the first time. I can feel the thrill of 'the most wise Baviaan,' and the tone of your voice as you read the delicious snatches of verse:

. . . comes Taffy dancing through the fern,
To lead the Surrey spring again. . . .

How long ago it seems!"

Nicole turned to tidy a pile of books on a stool, and presently said, "It does seem queer without Barbara. I always miss her so when she goes. Three o'clock.

She'll just be starting from Edinburgh. They're to meet her at Galashiels. . . . D'you know, Mums, I believe Babs will be glad to be back at Rutherfurd even as things are. She pines for it: it meant such a lot to her. She felt secure there, impregnable. She will never be really happy in Kirkmeikle."

Lady Jane put down her work.

"No," she said. . . . "I can't help worrying sometimes about Barbara. You are different. You have the gift of taking things as they come, and finding happiness in little things. I shouldn't be unhappy about you though you missed what most women crave for most, but Barbara can't make her own happiness, so to speak, it has to be made for her. It was always so as a child. . . . As you say, she misses Rutherfurd—it gave her a setting."

Nicole clasped her hands round her knees. "What a pity there isn't a male Erskine needing a wife, or would châtelaine be a more imposing word? That would be a setting. . . . I suppose people are like jewels, dull and lustreless when badly set, glowing and sparkling in their proper environment—— Why, the sun has come out, Mums. You must go out and enjoy it. You've been terribly stuck in the house these last few days. Walk along to the Red Rocks or look in and see Mrs. Brodie. Have you been to see Betsy lately? She greatly relishes your visits."

Lady Jane looked out at the bright afternoon, then uncertainly at her daughter. "But are you sure you'll be all right? Have you something to read?"

"Indeed I have. By the way, have you finished Mr. Beckett's manuscript?"

"Yes, I have."

"Well?" said Nicole.

"Well—— It is good, I think, well told and clear, and written with more sense of style than, somehow, I had expected. But it's so devoid of feeling as to be almost wooden. He could have made so much of the final scene, and he makes nothing. . . . Of course, there it is.—This is the man who was there, who did the thing, and he can't talk. Whether would you have the story from him, or from the professional writer who was not there, but who can write beautifully about what he has heard, who can touch the heart and the imagination, thrill you, make the story live? Remember, I don't say that Mr. Beckett couldn't, if he liked, but he won't. I may be entirely wrong, but reading, I had the feeling that he was giving us the bald narrative in case we weren't worthy of anything else. This was his friend. He won't cheapen his memory by making appeals to the emotions.—It's the silent Englishman carried to excess."

Nicole nodded. "I see what you mean, and I agree. But I liked it—the reticence in the telling. I'm so tired of writers that fling themselves about, emptying themselves of all they ever thought or felt, or being whimsical and elfin, that a plain, straightforward narrative delights me."

"It's very refreshing," her mother said, as she put a log on the fire. "Now don't move out of the room. Shall I tell Christina to keep out callers?"

"Oh, dear, no. A caller would be rather a treat! And I don't want dry toast for tea, I want it buttered."

"You're no use as an invalid," Lady Jane told her as she went out.

Just before tea Simon Beckett was shown in. He had been tramping over the links and brought a breath of the sea and the east wind into the quiet room. He stood at the door, hesitating—"Christina said you would see me, but I'm afraid I may give you more cold coming straight in out of the air."

"Oh, do come in. Of course shake hands. It freshens me to see you. My head's still fuzzy with quinine, and I seem to smell nothing but beef-tea made the old-fashioned way, and eucalyptus, but I'm really quite all right again, and properly ashamed of myself. . . . What a humiliating thing a cold is! If people can like you through a cold they'll like you through anything. I wonder if Cleopatra ever snuffled!"

Simon sat down in the arm-chair on the other side of the fire-place, and said, laughing, "You're not much accustomed to being ill, are you?"

"I don't think I've ever had a temperature before, and I hardly know what it is to have a headache. Rude health is what I enjoy, and you're not much of an invalid yourself," and she laughed, as if the sight of the robust young man opposite amused and pleased her. They talked together, and Nicole was conscious of the feeling that she always had in Simon's company, a feeling of comfort and content, of being able to dabble in the shallows of talk, knowing they would both be equally at home in the depths.

Presently she lifted the pile of manuscript that lay beside her on the table.

"Let's speak about this," she said.

Her companion at once became acutely miserable.

"Oh, I say, don't," he moaned. "You don't know how horrible it is to have to talk about one's own writing. I tell you what, write me a note about it: I'd like that."

"But why should I, when there's lots of things in it I want to discuss with you here and now? You don't know how interesting it is for some one who can't write to talk to a person who can. I've read so many books I ought to be a judge, but I don't suppose that follows." She patted the neatly typed sheets on her lap. "You are no tripe-merchant, my friend."

Simon asked what exactly she meant by that.

"It's a phrase of my brother Archie's. When he thought an author spread himself too much, and blundered into pits of bad taste and made one hot with shame, he said, 'Tripe-merchant.' You are almost, if I may say it, too little of a tripe-merchant."

Simon rumpled his hair miserably. "Say anything you like," he said, "only get it over quickly."

"Well, my crab about your book is that you make it all sound too easy. The first part is excellent, couldn't be better. The description of the going, and the places you passed through, and the people you met, is delightful. You've got humour, and the human touch. But the actual climbing, the last arduous bit, the disaster, the coming back, you seem to me to shirk. You say, for instance, 'We went from camp 5 to camp 6.' Just like that! A ten minutes' stroll on a pleasant path! The carrying of a parcel from Tottenham Court Road to Euston Station! a trifle! Remember, we're not at all an imaginative people, we need to be told things, to be made to see them, if we

128

are to realise. . . . And the disaster—well, reticence there, one can well understand. Still—he was your friend. Couldn't you have said a little more—or couldn't you bear to?"

Simon sat forward in his chair, his hands clasped between his knees. There was a boyish, perplexed look on his face that made Nicole think of the Bat.

"You see—I had to think of Cullis. He hated advertising. I never met such a chap for avoiding notice. I didn't want to write the beastly book at all, but they said I must for I was there, but I'd hate Cullis to feel that I'd given him away. He was my best friend."

Nicole said nothing, and in a minute Simon went on:

"If only he'd succeeded! Then I shouldn't have minded. But to die like that when it seemed as if we were going to manage it—— Still, it was a great end. I like to think of him there among the heights—it was what he always wanted. And he died satisfied, I think, for he knew we wouldn't leave it at that. He knew we'd come back. . . . Lots of people think that Cullis threw away his life—funny, isn't it?"

"It seems like madness to many," Nicole said.

"But you don't think it madness?"

"No, but I see the tremendous pity of it. . . . In a war you must fight, but here you take your life and . . . Don't you *care* whether you come back or not?"

"I?" . . . Simon cleared his throat. "When I came home ill and broken-up, all I asked for was to go back and lay my bones beside Cullis."

The door opened and Christina appeared with the first preparation for tea, while just behind her came Lady Jane, saying:

"So you *have* a caller! How d'you do, Mr. Beckett? It was kind to come and cheer the invalid."

CHAPTER XXIII

"How blessed are we that are not simple men."

The Winter's Tale.

To say that Mrs. Jackson was disappointed on hearing that Nicole Rutherfurd was unable to fulfil her promise to help with the festivities is a poor, bald way of describing the utter despair that filled that poor lady. As people in moments of peril are said to see all their past life before them, Mrs. Jackson, still clutching the telegram, saw herself alone, unaided, exposed to the full battery of the county. It had been bad enough the thought of it all, the big dinner and the dance, even with Nicole beside her to bear the brunt, to receive, so to speak, the first shock of the encounter. On her would have depended the success or failure of the undertaking. But now—it was more than she could face by herself, and desperately she got on to her feet and went to look for her son.

She found him in the library, smoking a pipe, deep in a book, and, bustling towards him as fast as her high heels would permit, she wailed:

"Andy, *she's not coming!*"

Andrew laid down his book, and getting up with his pipe in his hand, said, "Who?"

"Miss Rutherfurd, of course. She's in bed with a chill and there's no chance of her being able to travel, and all these people coming—— Andy, I'm nearly demented."

"It's a pity, but surely we can manage ourselves."

"We can *not* manage ourselves"; and in her despair poor Mrs. Jackson nearly burst into tears. "A bonnie-like mess of things I'd make with no one beside me to tell me what to do! You know quite well that if I can put my foot in it I do it, and I can't talk. And, oh! the dance! the orchestra and the purveyors. . . . Oh dear, dear, what made me think of trying to entertain? It was you, Andy, that said we should give a dinner to pay back, but the dance was a bit of show-off on my part."

"Wouldn't Mrs. Douglas help us?"

Mrs. Jackson dismissed the suggestion with an impatient shake of her head.

"It wouldn't be the same. With Nicole Rutherfurd beside me playing the daughter of the house I could have faced anything. Andy, could we not send wires to every one that we've got something? Influenza or a nervous breakdown. . . . I'm sure I've got that right enough."

Andy thought for a minute. "Isn't there another Miss Rutherfurd, a cousin? Wouldn't she come?"

"She's called Miss Burt, and she's a stand-offish thing; not a bit like my girl. Besides, she wouldn't come."

"You could ask her."

As a drowning man clutches at a straw, so Mrs. Jackson clutched at this possibility. "You send a wire then, Andy, an urgent wire so that they'll see things are desperate.—Or mebbe I'd better write. . . . She'd be a lot better than nobody."

It was now the 9th of March, and Miss Barbara Burt might arrive any minute. Andrew had gone to meet her in the car, much against his own inclination, but spurred thereto by his mother's eagerness.

"It would never do to let her arrive and find no one but a chauffeur. Besides, you know Father'll not let Renwick leave the car for a minute, so it would be very awkward. I'd go myself, but I dread the thought of having to talk to her all the way back. It's nothing to you to talk. I've often watched you chattering away like anything."

Andrew looked slightly dashed at this description of his conversational powers, but he only said, "Well, I don't expect to 'chatter' much to Miss Burt. When does the train come in? All right. I'll be there."

When Barbara got out of the train and stood looking about her for a porter to take her luggage to the car which she had been told would be waiting, a voice said, "Pardon me, but are you Miss Burt?" and she saw before her a young man in a light tweed suit, with pleasant grey eyes, and a smile that revealed very white, even teeth. She smiled and nodded. "And you are——?"

"I'm Andrew Jackson. We're most awfully grateful to you for coming. How is your cousin?"

"Better, thanks, though not fit to travel. She is greatly disappointed, for she had been looking forward to this visit. . . . The cane trunk and the hat-box, and the case. Yes. That's all."

Andrew turned to the porter. "Bring 'em along, will you? The car's outside. I'll take the dressing-bag."

They went out of the station, Andrew explaining that his father did not like the chauffeur to leave the car, in case the little wanton boys that abound round a station did it an injury.

"It seems a pity to worry," said Andrew, "but there it is."

"What about the luggage? Doesn't Mr. Jackson object to that?"

"He does, if there's a lot," Andrew confessed, "but yours is modest. . . . Is that all right, Renwick? Now, we're off."

Barbara had looked forward with much distaste to this enforced visit to her old home, but she had made up her mind that, so far as in her lay, she would do her best to make it a success. She would try never to think about herself and her own feelings, but to enter into the feelings of others. She set Nicole before her as an example, for nobody knew better than Barbara herself that she was not always a social success.

Now, carried swiftly along the well-remembered road, she told herself that things had begun well. She liked this young man with his kind simple manner and his honest eyes, and she felt flattered that he wasted no time on the preliminaries of friendship, but plunged at once into what interested him.

131

Some remark was made about the countryside, and Andrew said, "I wish you'd tell me something about your uncle and cousins. . . ."

Barbara turned to him with a very charming smile.

She said, "You've chosen *the* subject I like best."

"Everywhere I go," Andrew went on, "I hear about them, and every one I meet has some story to tell me about them. It is rather remarkable, you know, the affection they seem to have inspired. Sir Walter Rutherfurd is still a name to conjure with in these parts, and I would very much like to know wherein lay the secret of his influence. You see, it's frightfully interesting to me, who, in a way, must follow him. I hope you don't think this is cheek, but I'm very keen to carry on the tradition. I'm not saying it'll be easy, for we've everything against us—we're strangers, city folk. . . ."

"The Rutherfurds were deep-rooted in the soil," Barbara said, leaning forward to see some familiar landmark.

Andrew nodded. "That's it. . . . They grew up with all the people round, their fathers had been friends, their grandfathers, away back . . ."

"Uncle Walter was the best of all the Rutherfurds," Barbara said. "The others, my grandfather, my great-grandfather, and further back were all fine men, but some of them were eccentric and queer; but he was the sanest, most reliable of men. There was something about him so big and kind and simple. He was austere too, in a way, and absolutely unshakable about what he thought was right and wrong. And Ronnie and Archie promised to be very much the same."

"They died young?"

"Twenty and twenty-two. Do you wonder their parents' hearts were broken? I sometimes think the War killed more fathers than mothers. Perhaps women's hearts are made to stand more, or perhaps it's because it is easier for them to speak out what they feel, but I've known several cases where the mother was able to go on, but the father, saying very little, just slipped out of life. Uncle Walter did that. It was as if something had broken that we couldn't mend. We tried to hold him back, but something far stronger drew him away. . . . Oh, it hasn't been easy these last years."

"And giving up Rutherfurd must have been very bad," Andrew said gently.

Barbara had a sudden and almost overpowering inclination to burst there and then into a flood of tears. She turned and stared unseeingly out of the window . . . and they had reached the gates of Rutherfurd before she felt sure of keeping her voice steady.

When the car drew up at the door Mrs. Jackson stood waiting to receive them. She wore a smart gown, a hat with ospreys, and an ermine stole, determined to do full honour to her guest. Enormous fires blazed everywhere, and hot-house flowers scented the air. "Not a word till you've had tea," was her greeting, "you must need it badly after such a long journey. Come right into the drawing-room. There now, sit there. Is that cushion quite comfortable? Would you like a footstool?"

Barbara, feeling like seventy and decrepit at that, refused a footstool, but gladly accepted tea, while her hostess poured into her ears details about the arrangements. . . .

"The dinner I could cope with—we've given dinners before—but it's the dance. They keep telling me that the men'll do everything, prepare the floor and put everything right, but I don't know. The question is can you trust them? Wouldn't it be awful if there wasn't enough to eat, or if something went wrong with the orchestra? That orchestra! It fair weighs on my mind. I never had anything to do with them except just listening, of course, but I've often heard how difficult choirs are to manage, and I doubt orchestras will be worse. . . . It's a big undertaking, look at it any way you like."

Barbara soothed her, and assured her everything would be all right. "When you go to a good firm they've a reputation to keep up, they won't fail you. . . . It ought to be a charming dance. I don't know if there has ever been a dance at Rutherfurd before. There was to have been one when I came out, but the War stopped it. Tell me, how have you arranged about the dancing . . . ?"

Later Mrs. Jackson, having with great wealth of detail described all arrangements, at last conducted Barbara to her room, and flung open the door impressively. Barbara almost recoiled.

The room was heated by radiators, but a large fire had been ordered as well. The walls glowed rosily, the carpet also was pink, and very thick. A crystal bowl of pink geraniums and maiden-hair fern stood on the dressing-table.

Mrs. Jackson clasped her hands before her and beamed.

"It doesn't need the fire for heat, but I thought it would be a nice welcome. I always think a fire's just a friend." She looked round complacently. "The room's changed a wee bit. I hope you like it. Can you mind what it was like before?"

Could she "mind"? This had been Lady Jane's own room and Barbara remembered every detail of it. The wall-paper had been white with a tiny sprig, and on it had hung water-colour drawings of her aunt's old home, rather vague and amateurish, but treasured by their owner. There had been a fine four-poster bed with chintz valance round the top. In this room Nicole and Ronnie and Archie had been born.

Barbara was grateful that Nicole had been unable to come. Aloud she said, "There is a most wonderful difference. How did you manage to keep it all pink and get everything to tone so beautifully?"

"I like pink," said Mrs. Jackson, "it's such a cheery colour; and I wanted a complete change, for it was awful washed-out looking before."

"Nothing had been done for a long time."

"Oh, of course, we quite understood that. Besides, it's far more satisfactory, I think, to do up a house to suit your own taste, and if it's been fairly recently done it seems extravagant. I wouldn't dare to meddle with the reception-rooms, for I'm not sure of myself, if you know what I mean, but in the matter of bedrooms I could let myself go. Our own room is yellow. Ucha! Carpet and all. They wanted me to have pale lemon walls and a grey carpet, and mebbe it would have been more artistic, but I like something strong. It's not to call orange exactly, but it's tending that way. I'll let you see it. It's lovely. Then we've a pale blue room, and two other pink rooms, and two pure white, suites and all—— But there, you'll see them all to-morrow. Here am

I keeping you standing all this time. Would you like to rest till dinner-time? Your luggage is all in the dressing-room so as not to litter your room. Esther'll be unpacking it now. Isn't that a queer name for a housemaid—Esther? I always think of the King, you know, and the poor girl going in to beg for her people, and Haman being hung and all that. Aren't there some queer stories in the Bible? Well—I'll leave you to yourself for a bit. . . . I'll mebbe take a rest myself, for what with all the things I've got to think of, and you coming, I'm real worn out." She still lingered, then, "Well, ta-ta," she said, with a wave of her hand, and left her guest feeling both dazed and exhausted.

At dinner Barbara met for the first time the new owner of Rutherfurd. It was surprising to see such a rich man so thin, and he had an oddly detached air as if he had no connection with his surroundings. She found him fairly easy to talk to, but then, as she reflected, a man is always interesting when he talks his own shop.

After dinner Mr. Jackson went off at once to his own den, and Barbara talked by the drawing-room fire with her hostess and Andrew. Very soon Mrs. Jackson's head began to nod, and her son rose and put a cushion more comfortably behind her head.

"Oh, thank you, Andy." She roused herself to say apologetically to Barbara, "Was I nodding? Sleep comes on me like an armed man. I must ask you to excuse me. . . ."

The young people continued to talk for a little, then Andrew asked if Barbara played the piano.

"I do, but——" She looked towards her sleeping hostess.

"It's all right," he assured her, "it won't disturb my mother. Will you play for me?"

They went together to the piano, and Andrew produced a pile of music.

"I play these with one finger. They're mostly Gilbert and Sullivan. But play anything you like. I'm tremendously keen on music. . . ." So Barbara played what she could remember, and Andrew listened. Presently she broke into the music of *Patience* and they sang together "*A magnet hung in a hardware shop*" and "*Prithee, pretty maiden.*"

Mrs. Jackson woke up at intervals and pretended to beat time, only to doze off again.

When Johnson brought in the tray at ten o'clock he coughed discreetly to waken his mistress, and she promptly sat up, put on her slippers, which she was apt to kick off as the evening advanced, and, looking very alert and wakeful, said in a loud Englishy voice, "What a treat to have a little music. Andy, you're in luck to-night."

Barbara left the piano and came over to the fire.

"We've had quite a concert, haven't we?" she said, holding her hands to the blaze. "Your son has a delightful voice; you should make him take lessons."

"D'you hear that, Andy? It's what I always say, Miss Burt. He had always a nice voice. I mind when he wasn't more than three, he would sit beside me and sing, "*Lord, a little band and lowly*" and "*Bonnie Charlie's noo awa*'," as sweet as sweet.

134

He had golden curls, Miss Burt, though you wouldn't think it to look at him now, and he wore a wee blue velveteen suit, sort of made like a sailor but trimmed with lace —— He was an awful nice wee boy!"

Andrew looked at his mother with a quizzical expression as she retailed these confidences to their guest, but only said:

"Here's your hot water, Mother—Miss Burt?"

"May I have some hot water?"

"That's right," said Mrs. Jackson, "there's nothing like it, I think, a glass of hot water every night gives you a wash inside. As my mother used to say, 'The stomach's an ill dish to clean'—I'm sure I hope we'll all get a good sleep to-night and be well for to-morrow."

CHAPTER XXIV

"Withal it is a kindly face and belongs to one who is without pretensions."
Glasgow in 1901.

When Barbara went down to breakfast the next morning at nine o'clock she found her hostess alone in the morning-room.

"Come away. Did you sleep well? That's right. Mr. Jackson's away to Edinburgh to some sort of meeting, and Andy's taken him to Galashiels, so we'll have breakfast cosily together. . . . I've the hot rolls and scones and toast down by the fire to keep hot, and I've just this moment made the tea. Or would you prefer coffee? They're both here, so say the word."—She patted Barbara into a chair and hovered round her. "Now will you begin with fish? No? Well then, kidney and bacon." She peeped into another hot dish: "And here's poached eggs."

"But"—Barbara got up and joined her hostess at the sideboard—"I'm not going to let you wait on me like this. I expect you were up seeing Mr. Jackson away and you must want your breakfast. Please sit down and let me look after you. Everything looks most tempting; what will you have?"

"No," said Mrs. Jackson firmly. "I never take anything but a cup of tea and a bit of dry toast. I'm no great breakfast hand. Indeed, for all so stout's I am, I don't make much of any meal. But you're a young thing. Sit down, and don't mind me waiting on you. I like it. Indeed, I don't get half enough of it for Father gets kind of irritated if I fuss him, and Andy waits on me—— I hope you don't mind getting your breakfast in here. I thought it would be as well to leave the dining-room free all day. Indeed, I think I provoked Johnson suggesting it should get a sort of thorough clean-out. But it's always been my way if people are coming to give the dining-room a good do-out. When I had only the one girl I did it, and at Deneholm if there was a party on I would say to the housemaid, 'Give the room an extra good do-out, so that there'll be some pleasure in making it all nice with flowers and that.' "

"A very good plan," Barbara agreed.

"Of course I could do that in a house like Deneholm, but here it's different. Can you tell me if the rooms were turned out regularly in your time? for I can't get any satisfaction about it. . . . I said to the head housemaid that I'd always been used to having the rooms turned out on regular days, and she said, 'Yes, madam,' but for the life of me I can't tell you whether she meant to do it or not, and you can't always be asking at superior servants."

"No," said Barbara, "but after all they are your rooms——"

"The bedrooms are done all right: it's the hall and all the reception rooms. Unless they're done before breakfast they're never done. So I said very mildly to Johnson that I thought the dining-room and drawing-room would be the better of a special clean, and I don't think he liked it."

"But you don't mind Johnson, surely? He's as gentle as a lamb though he looks like an archbishop. My cousins once locked him into his own pantry!"

"Fancy that!" Mrs. Jackson looked awed. "How did they dare? . . . I wish you'd advise me what to do about the ladies to-night, I mean about taking off their wraps. Any time we've dined out round here I just left my cloak in the hall, and never a glass to look into. I don't like that sort of comfortless way of doing, and yet it's a day's journey to take them to a bedroom—— Though, of course, it would show them more of the house."

"Why not put a table into that funny little room that opens into the library, with a mirror and brushes, and a maid to help?" Barbara suggested.

Mrs. Jackson looked thoughtful and said, "The very thing! I wonder I never thought of it, and it's so convenient to the front door. Well—if we just had the dinner well over we could give our whole minds to the dance. . . . There's one thing, I can trust Mrs. Asprey. I needn't give a thought to how things'll come up, and I'm sure it's a mercy, for goodness knows I'll have enough to do trying to make conversation with Lord Langlands. I'll have to go in with him, though he fairly paralyses any little mind I've got. You know the slow way he speaks, and the sort of intent way he stares at you while he's speaking? I simply can't meet that gaze of his, my head jerks in spite of me, and I try crumbling toast and doing things with my hands or I don't know what I might be driven to do—scream, mebbe."

Barbara laughed. "I know. It's his solemn way: he's entirely without humour."

Mrs. Jackson sighed. "I've only really enjoyed myself once out, and that was at Kingshouse. Mrs. Douglas has a real knack as a hostess. She never lets any one feel out of it and she makes everything go. . . . Have another kidney, my dear. No? A wee touchy cold ham? Well—some marmalade?"

"Thanks. . . . But you are beginning to feel at home, aren't you?"

Mrs. Jackson was sitting with her elbows on the table and her cup held in both hands. "Yes," she said. "Uch, yes. Of course I see fine how the people about here regret the Rutherfurds and just receive us on sufferance, so to speak. They're civil, of course, and they make the best of us, but I see myself what a change it is. Here was Lady Jane that they all adored, and Miss Nicole, and you, and the house so pleasant and all their interests in common, and now they come stiffly to call, and we speak about the weather and the Nursing Association. . . ."

"Oh, tell me, how is that doing?" Barbara cried.

"Oh, fine. . . . If you've finished, I'll let you see the house. But I'd better see first about the ladies leaving their wraps."

So Barbara followed her hostess and heard her giving the order.

"In here," she directed Johnson. "A table, you said, Miss Burt? Would any sort of table do? We could hardly bring down a dressing-table."

"Oh no. Any table—a writing-table: and have you a standing mirror?"

"There's one with two side wings that used to be in my room, but I put it away because it always gave me a shock to see my profile. It stands."

"The very thing. And hair-pins, and powder, and that sort of thing."

"I'll let you see the glass, it's in the pale-blue room," and Mrs. Jackson began to pad hastily across the hall to the stairs, followed by Barbara.

Once upstairs they inspected every room with some thoroughness, Mrs. Jackson talking busily all the time. It was long since she had had such a happy, well-occupied morning, and she was agreeably surprised to find her guest so easy to get on with, so appreciative a listener and so helpful with sympathy and suggestion.

"This is the pale-blue room. A little cold, perhaps, at this time of year, but pleasant in summer. I'm very fond of pale blue myself. I always wanted to have a wee girl to dress in white muslin with a blue sash. . . . That's the glass."

"The very thing," Barbara declared. "You can see your head all round, and that's such a comfort in these days of tidy heads when every hair must be in place."

"Uch, yes, but I never heed. Yours is very neat. . . . You were asking about the Nursing Association."

"Yes. My aunt took a tremendous interest in it, and we had a Sale here every year."

Mrs. Jackson sat down heavily on a chair, and held up her hands playfully.

"You don't need to tell me that, my dear. The times I've heard it! The Committee meetings are a treat. Lady Langlands sits at the head of the table with the matron beside her and all the members sitting round, and my! I would just like some of my Glasgow friends to see the way they're dressed. A Viscountess and all, and you wouldn't give tuppence for all she's on. A wisp of a scarf round her neck, and the plainest of coats and skirts, and a bashed sort of hat, and big thick shoes. I wonder her maid can bear to let her out. . . . Some of the ladies are real smart, but all to the plain side—just tweeds and that. But I never heed. I go in my sables, with all my rings and so on; not being a Viscountess I can't afford to be shabby."

Mrs. Jackson stopped to chuckle at her own wit, and Barbara said brightly:

"I know these Committee meetings. Do they bore you badly?"

"Not me! I'm amused. . . . It came up the other day about the Sale Lady Jane always had, and what a help it was to the funds, and what could take its place, and so on. And Lady Langlands looked kind of helpless and said, 'Couldn't we have an entertainment of some kind? *Tableaux vivants*, perhaps?' and nobody said yes or no, but they looked at each other, and I looked out of the window. Goodness knows, I wouldn't mind writing them a cheque for the amount of the Sale, but I won't be hinted at. They should ask me straight out to have the Sale, don't you think so?"

"Well"—Barbara smiled—"it isn't easy to ask, is it? I quite know what you feel, but it would be noble of you to offer. . . . Is Miss Cumming still matron? She was such a nice woman."

"Didn't you know? She's married. Ucha! Married to a widower with five children but quite well off, and we gave her two silver entrée dishes, small but solid, for a present. . . . I never speak a word at these meetings for I never can think of anything intelligent to say.—But I'm keeping you here all morning, and you'll have letters to write, no doubt. Lunch is at one fifteen. . . ."

Andrew was in to luncheon, and afterwards he and Barbara went for a walk up the glen to the farthest shepherd's cottage. It was a fresh March day and they

138

found it pleasant to stride over the springy turf and leap the hill burns swollen with February rain.

For most of the way they walked in companionable silence. At the top of the glen, while they stood looking at the rounded hills crowding round them, Andrew said, "I think you like walking in silence; I do myself."

"Yes," Barbara agreed. "Walkers should talk only when the spirit moves them; to try to make conversation among the hills would be ridiculous. How I love the heather burning! I think of Rutherfurd oftenest in early spring weather: steely blue skies and burns running full with rain, and grey smoke hanging on the hillsides."

Andrew leant behind a dyke lighting his pipe.

After a minute, he said, "It must have been a hard job for you to give up Rutherfurd, I've only lately realised how hard. Your cousin—did she feel it very badly?"

"Nicole!" Barbara gave a little laugh. "It's so hard to say what Nicole feels. She doesn't talk much about her own feelings, she's so interested in other people's. . . . You say you love Rutherfurd after a few months; what do you suppose it means to the people who . . . oh, don't let's talk about it. . . ."

When they got back they had a merry tea at the end of the long refectory table in the hall, and then went in to see the dinner-table.

"This is charming," Barbara said. "I do like glass so much better than silver."

"Awfully fragile, though," Mrs. Jackson reminded her. "We got these lace mats in Italy."

The long table was bare but for the lace mats. Down the centre were placed three wide glass bowls filled with pink tulips, and six tall glass candlesticks with pink shades.

"What are you wearing to-night, may I ask? Black and white? I just hoped it might be pink to go with the decorations. I'm awfully fond of having everything in keeping, but with my figure I can't wear pink. Not but what quite elderly women wear it now, and look well, but they always tell me that black's best for me. I'm brightened up to-night, though, with silver embroidery all down the front—beautiful. To-morrow, for the dance, I'm wearing gold tissue. As I said to Andy there, it would depress the whole company to see the hostess in black, and besides I think gold tissue'll look awfully well against all that black oak, eh? Did I tell you there are three young men coming to stay, friends of Andy's? I think we'll have more men than girls, and that's a good fault at a dance. Every house in the district nearly is bringing a party, but I'm not going to think of it for I get so nervous."

Barbara laid her hand on Mrs. Jackson's arm and said, "You'll be thoroughly tired before eight o'clock for you've been seeing after things all day. Come up to your room and let me tuck you up on the sofa with a book, and you'll be asleep before you know."

"Well—I believe I will. Andy, see that Father doesn't go to the study when he comes in; send him straight up."

At a quarter to eight they all waited in the drawing-room. The door opened. . . . Mrs. Jackson moistened her lips and took a step forward, while her husband retreated to the fire-place.

After that, Mrs. Jackson was only confusedly conscious of shaking hands and trying to say things, of watching Barbara being greeted by every one and going happily from one to another, of realising between the measured remarks of Lord Langlands that it was an excellent dinner, and that surely things were going well. . . .

About eleven o'clock they all stood round the fire again, in the reaction that follows a strain, Mr. Jackson inclined to be mildly facetious, and his wife happily loosed from bonds.

"Well, that's over," said Andy.

"And well over," said his mother. "I declare I'm quite looking forward to to-morrow now."

"It only needs a beginning," said Mr. Jackson, beginning to wind his watch. . . . "I'm going away to my bed."

"So am I," said his wife, "though I'm too excited to sleep." She trotted up to Barbara. "Good-night, my dear. You were both an ornament and a great help. If you don't mind I'd like to kiss you."

CHAPTER XXV

"I should like balls infinitely better if they were carried on in a different manner. It would surely be much more rational if conversation instead of dancing made the order of the day."

"Much more rational I daresay, but it would not be near so like a ball."

Jane Austen.

Fortune continued to smile on Mrs. Jackson, and her dance passed off without a hitch.

The dreaded orchestra arrived, did their work, and departed with approbation. Everybody seemed happy, the dancers, the bridge players, and those who looked on. The supper was something to dream of, the decorations charming and not overdone, and above all there was that air of jollity without which no party can be called a success.

Barbara thought this was largely due to the hostess herself. She was so obviously eager that every one should have a good time, so beamingly happy to see her guests enjoy themselves, so all-pervadingly kind and cheerful.

Mr. Jackson, on the contrary, added nothing to the gaiety of the evening. He stood about looking rather dazed, the festive look of the flower in his buttonhole belied by his face. Melancholy seemed to have claimed him for her own. He had nothing to say to any one; sometimes he played a tune on his teeth with the nail of his forefinger (a trick he had when bored), and every now and then he yawned widely, with no attempt at concealment.

Barbara owned to herself that never had she enjoyed a dance so much. She had been made to feel important. Old friends had crowded round her. She had been conscious of looking her best, of being gay and pleasing, desired as a partner, a real asset to her hostess.

She and Andrew had not danced much together, but when they passed each other they had exchanged understanding smiles which seemed to establish an intimacy that no amount of talking could have done.

Lying in bed the morning after the dance, Barbara thought things over. She had only been a few days at Rutherfurd, but already Kirkmeikle seemed far away and unimportant. She stretched herself in her most comfortable bed, appreciating the fineness of the linen and the lace that trimmed it, and looked around her. She did so like the space, and the feeling of the big quiet house worked so smoothly by efficient servants. She liked to think of the lawns, the gardens, the moorland that lay all round. It gave her a feeling of being apart, not merely one of the multitude, which was pleasant.

She had thought she would hate being in a Rutherfurd that belonged to strangers, that all virtue would have gone out of the place for her, but to her surprise she found that it was not so. Why it was she could not tell, but it actually seemed to belong to her now in a way that it had never done before. The present owners seemed not to matter, to be merely accidental, and as for their son—he mattered certainly; he seemed to belong too, to belong to her.

Barbara looked the matter straight in the face. She did not disguise from herself that her intention was to marry Andrew Jackson. He could give her what she wanted. All her life Rutherfurd had come first with her. As a child she had been aware of her own passion, and had sometimes almost hated her cousins for their light acceptance of such an inheritance. They had not seemed to care, but she had always cared. . . . If she married Andrew it would be hers. The loathed Burt part of her would pass away and be forgotten. People would say—"Mrs. Jackson of Rutherfurd —you know, of course, that she was one of the old Rutherfurds? Yes, so suitable."

And surely it had been meant. Surely it was Fate that had sent her here. She remembered with complacence that the visit had been none of her arranging, she had not plotted or planned. She had come to oblige her cousin, to perform an unpleasant duty, but as soon as she had met Andrew at the station she had known that her task would be a light one. And on his side there seemed to be the same attraction. He had walked with her, and talked and laughed with her, had sought her out, had seemed pleased at her success with his mother.

But if Nicole had been able to come herself?

Barbara sat back against the pillows and folded her arms.

"What he likes about me," she told herself, "are the Nicole bits."

She had been aware that she was quoting her cousins sometimes when she talked with Andrew, and it was then that he had looked at her with bright interested eyes.

"He cares for things in the way she cares for them. In a way I'm winning him on false pretences, but I don't care. It isn't as if I were hurting Nicole or defrauding her of anything. She doesn't want him; her whole thoughts are for Simon Beckett. I believe she'd help me if she knew I cared so much."

Barbara shook back her hair impatiently. She could rest in bed no longer. She must get up and be active and not think.

Bathed and dressed, she studied herself in the mirror. She was very good-looking, with regular features, and clear eyes that looked out from under straight brows. A handsome, wholesome woman endowed with no disturbing charm, but eminently fitted to be a good wife and mother, a competent, dignified mistress of a house. But Barbara sighed as she turned to go downstairs.

Mrs. Jackson she found in the morning-room reading the *Glasgow Herald*.

"Here you are, as fresh as a daisy," was her greeting. "And everything tidied up as if there hadn't been a soul here. Entertaining's easy after all, and very repaying. I'm sure it was a pretty sight, and you looked a treat, my dear. You were as smart as could be but not overdone, if you know what I mean. Father was a little upset at the sights some of them had made of themselves. Hardly clothed, you might say. I'm sure I was sorry for the gentlemen who had to dance with them. Say what you like, so much bare skin's not pretty to see. Disgusting, I call it."

142

Barbara laughed and agreed, and Mrs. Jackson went on happily:

"Did you get your breakfast comfortably? The papers have just come. Here's the *Herald*. Perhaps you prefer the *Scotsman*? We take both, of course, but it's the *Herald* I'm used to: I've read it all my days and I can't find my way about the *Scotsman*; besides, you miss a lot of deaths. It's queer, you'd think people would put their deaths into both papers, but they don't. I suppose for the East the West hardly exist, and the other way round. Births too, of course, but deaths are more important, for people are wonderfully touchy about you not writing.... Well, well. The gentlemen have gone out. Andy's taken his friends a motor run to see the country. They were sorry you weren't down in time, but you were quite right to take a long lie.... Mrs. Douglas made me promise to take you there to lunch to-morrow, and Lady Langlands wants us on Saturday, and——"

"Oh, but—I'm afraid I ought to go home to-morrow."

Mrs. Jackson raised both hands in protest.

"Never! Never in the world! You came here to do us a kindness, and what I'd have done without you I don't know. And now you are here you must stay for a bit and see all your friends that are so keen to see you. And Andy has lots of places he wants to take you.... I've just been thinking it would be awfully nice if your cousin, Miss Nicole, could join you here. The change would do her a lot of good after the nasty turn she's had, and you'd be so happy together among your old friends. D'you think your aunt would spare her just for a few days? I'll write this very minute, and you might write too and urge her, say what an awful pleasure it would be for us all. Don't you think it's a lovely plan?"

"A very lovely plan," said Barbara, and if her tone carried no conviction Mrs. Jackson noticed nothing as, well pleased with herself, she went off to write to Nicole, leaving Barbara to toy with the *Herald*.

Andrew and his friends were back in time for luncheon, which was a somewhat trying meal, for Mrs. Jackson's idea of entertaining young men was to subject them to a constant stream of light banter, which so exhausted them that they retired to the smoking-room and there slept peacefully till tea-time.

Barbara went upstairs to put on her outdoor things. She was standing in the hall idly looking at a magazine that she had taken from the neatly arranged selection on a table, when Andrew appeared.

"Oh, you're going out?" he said. "Anywhere particular?"

Barbara laid down her magazine. "No. I just felt I wanted a walk on the hills. Will you lend me a stick? I didn't bring one."

"Come and choose. May I come with you or would you rather go alone? Tell the truth, please."

Barbara laughed. "Oh, I'm a horribly truthful person always, I shall speak 'sad brow and true maid.' If your friends don't need you—how polite we are—I shall be very glad of your company. To tell you the truth, I'm terrified of tramps. That's why I asked for a stick, though it'll only be a moral support: I'm quite sure I could never hit even the most belligerent beggar."

As they went out Mrs. Jackson came bustling in from a visit she had been paying to the chauffeur's wife.

"Going for a walk? That's right. It's a cold wind but fine and bright. I've been to see Mrs. Renwick's baby, and—what d'you think, Andy?—it's to be called after you."

Andrew looked rather abashed, but his mother was radiant.

"I think it's awful nice. We've never had anyone called after us before. We must see about a present, something really handsome but useful too.—Well, see and have a nice walk. T'Ta."

That night as the owners of Rutherfurd were going to bed in their yellow room, Mrs. Jackson, who had been thoughtfully putting her hair into curl-pins, said:

"Father, d'you think Andy likes Miss Burt?"

"How should I know?" said her husband, much embarrassed.

"Well, *I* think he does, and it's not what I intended. Since that first day that I came to look at Rutherfurd I've had one wish, and that was that Andy would marry Nicole. That's why I was so anxious to give the dance—you thought I was daft, I know—it was an excuse to bring her here and get them acquainted. I was quite sure that Andy, whenever he saw her, would take a fancy to her like I did. And here——" Mrs. Jackson threw out her hands.

"Would Miss Burt take Andy?" Mr. Jackson asked.

His wife gave a short laugh. "There's not much fear of that."

"Well, she's quite a nice girl." Mr. Jackson crawled into bed.

"If you've never seen the other one," said Mrs. Jackson, who sat looking into the fire. "Miss Burt's been all that is kind and helpful, and it little becomes me to say anything against her, but there's all the difference in the world between her and her cousin. Miss Burt helps you because she's there to do it, and it's her duty: Nicole does it as if she loved it. . . . Miss Burt thinks in her heart that we—you and me, Father, not Andy—are the lower orders, but with Nicole there's neither Jew nor Gentile, as the saying is. It was Nicole I wanted to live here with Andy. . . . But mebbe it's not too late yet. . . . I've written and begged her to come, and I'm hoping that when Andy sees her. . . ."

Mr. Jackson tapped his teeth with his forefinger in a perplexed way.

"It's hard on Miss Burt," he said.

His wife took off a very ornate dressing-gown and hung it on the back of a chair.

"So it is," she said, "but somebody's always got to be hurt in this world."

Mr. Jackson was not satisfied.

"I never thought you were so hard-hearted, Mamma," he remarked.

"I've got Andy to think of," said his wife.

CHAPTER XXVI

"Oh, stay at home, my lad, and plough
   The land and not the sea.

Oh, stay with company and mirth
   And daylight and the air;
Too full already is the grave
Of fellows that were good and brave
   And died because they were."

A. E. Housman.

Meantime, at Kirkmeikle, Nicole absorbed in her own affairs had little thought to spare for the doings of her cousin at Rutherfurd.

On the day of the dance the sun shone brightly in the early afternoon, and Nicole looking wistfully from the window said she thought she would go out.

"Only to air myself, Mums. Only where the sun is bright on the sands road. Oh, *surely!*"

"It's a pity to be rash," her mother cautioned.

"So it is, and selfish in the extreme. If I got pneumonia it would be a horrid bother for every one. But, still—I feel quite all right. Isn't it funny how you go about miserably shaky and breakable, and quite suddenly—you can almost name the hour —you begin to feel yourself again?—And nobody was ever the worse of fresh air and sunshine."

"I don't know," Lady Jane said placidly, "wasn't it too fresh an air that gave you the chill? But if you wrap up warmly I expect you'll be all right. Keep a scarf over your mouth."

But when Nicole shut the front door behind her she had no air of a muffled invalid. She wore a new spring coat with a bunch of violets pinned in front, and a becoming little black hat with a white mount pulled down over her bright hair.

Out on the sheltered sands road it was delicious. She lifted her face to the mild heat of the March sun, she breathed in the salt air and was glad. Having walked to the far end of the road she was tempted to go farther. It was absurd to go back and sit in the house on such a living day. A little bit along were the Red Rocks and a favourite seat of hers, a sort of throne hewn out by the waves, which the Bat thought must be used by the mermaids when they came up to comb their long hair with combs made of ivory and pearls; she would go there.

How good it was to be out again, to be free of the feverish choked feeling that a bad cold brings, to feel the sea-wind in one's face, to watch the gulls sweep over the water, and to know that spring was on its way, that the winter was over and gone.

Not that it had been a bad winter. She remembered pleasantly the walks and the games, the merry tea-parties in the Harbour House, the long evenings when they had read and worked and talked in the room with the four long windows; the short winter days with frosty sunsets, the red roofs of the little town, the moon making a silver highway on the sea. And the people—old Betsy with her passion for the Borders and her contempt for every other place; Janet Symington, narrow and dull, yet surprisingly human; kind Mrs. Heggie; harassed, happy Mrs. Lambert. . . . How good it had all been! And even as she confessed it she felt a twinge—ought she to have been so happy? Did it not show a certain lightness, a lack of feeling? Barbara had not been happy, she had made that fairly obvious. And her mother? Well, with her mother it was different; in a way, for her, life seemed finished.

How strange, Nicole thought, to be done with life, not to waken in the morning wondering what new and glorious thing might be going to happen, not to expect to meet round every corner Romance. How dull, oh! how dull, to wash and dress knowing that the day would only hold meals, and letters with dull domestic news, and conversations about trifles; to look forward to day after day filled with comfortable commonplaces, a level plain, with no heights of rapture, no depths of despair.

But then, she reflected, her mother had known it all, the expectations, the uncertainties, the raptures, the despair. She had had more, perhaps, of loving and living than most people, more of suffering too, and now she was serene, as the seas are calm when the storm is over.

Nicole walked slowly with her eyes on the sea, and did not notice Simon Beckett until suddenly he stood before her.

She looked up into his face and saw there what she had been seeking unconsciously always.

Neither spoke.

Then Simon took her, as Torquil took his Neuha, by the hand, and they crossed the rocks to the mermaid's throne. Nicole seated herself and Simon knelt at her feet.

They whispered each other's names as if they had made a great discovery.

"Simon."

"Nicole."

Then Simon blurted out: "I'm going away. I've just heard; I've got to leave on Saturday morning."

"And this is Wednesday!" said Nicole.

"And this is Wednesday," Simon agreed.

Nicole sat very still. . . . "Two whole days together," she said at last. "Well, that's not so bad. We mightn't have had any. You might have gone without knowing."

"I've always known."

"Then why in the world didn't you speak? I'm afraid you're a bit of an idiot, Simon dear."

"Well, but—why didn't you let me see?"

146

"Ah! it wasn't my place." Nicole dimpled at him as if it were a new game. "But it's sad to have lost so much time in this little flash of a life. Was it the day we met here in the storm, when the Bat fell into the pool, and we could hardly see each other for spray or hear each other for crashing waves, that very first time that ever we met, that you . . . ?"

"That very first day," said Simon solemnly.

"Then we didn't really waste any time, did we? Kiss me, Simon."

They sat there oblivious of everything, trying to crush into an hour all they had to tell each other, in case these flying minutes were all they were to have together.

And yet it was not much that they said after all. Little more than "*I love you!*" and again, "*I love you!*"

At last prudence woke in Nicole and they turned to go home.

"Nobody must know," Nicole decreed.

"Not your mother?" Simon was surprised.

"It's because of Mother that it must be a secret. Simon, she's had so much. I can't have her burdened with this anxiety. . . . Besides, it's partly selfishness on my part, it will be easier for me to bear it alone. I hate pity. I hate to be fussed over. If nobody knows, I can keep cheerful and talk rubbish all the time, but if people are watching me——"

Her voice broke and she turned away her head.

Simon looked at her miserably.

"But you see, don't you, that I have to go?"

Nicole turned, her eyes shining with unshed tears, and said gently:

"My dear, I wouldn't say one word to keep you. Of course you must go. I'd be a poor creature if the first thing I wanted to do to my love was to clip his wings. I wouldn't love you half as much if you were content to stay. I'm glad and proud to see you go, only—come back to me, my love, come back to me. If you don't, well, some of me I suppose would go on living, but most of me would die."

"Oh, I'll come back all right. I'll be so deucedly careful this time. No risks for me, only what's got to be done. . . . The nuisance is, you won't hear from me much once we've started, but there'll always be the cables in the papers."

"Oh yes," said Nicole, "there will always be the papers."

When they reached the Harbour House Nicole said, "You'll come in?" but Simon shook his head, looking at his wrist-watch.

"It's the Bat. I asked him to tea and said we'd play at trains afterwards. I couldn't disappoint him?"

"No," said Nicole, "you couldn't do that."

"May I come in after dinner? And what shall we do to-morrow and Friday?"

Nicole thought, leaning against the doorway.

"To-morrow I think we should give the Bat a treat. You've no idea how the child will miss you.—He has never forgotten that day at St. Andrews. Let's take him somewhere to lunch and give him a good time. He yearns to see another cinema. . . . And Friday must be our own day. Let's go away together somewhere in the car, it

147

doesn't much matter where, so that we have every minute of the day together. And you'll come to dinner with Mother and me and we'll talk and laugh, and read bits to each, and not think of anything. And next morning you'll be gone. . . ."

Nicole went in and had tea with her mother, and Lady Jane said, "You look much the better for your walk. I was afraid you were staying too long. Where did you go?"

"Oh, just round the Red Rocks. . . . I met Mr. Beckett and he told me he had got his marching orders. He goes to London on Saturday morning. Won't it be perfectly ghastly without him? The Bat will be inconsolable, and, Mums, I'm afraid you will miss him badly. We were planning to take the Bat somewhere to-morrow for a treat; won't you come too? . . . And I asked him to dinner on Friday night. That's all right, is it? . . ."

Later, about six o'clock, when Nicole was sitting alone by the fire thinking, Miss Symington was announced.

Nicole sprang up to welcome her, for Janet was shy and needed a good deal of encouragement.

"This is nice.—Come over to the fire and settle into this really comfortable chair. Why didn't you come to tea? Mother's just gone to her room to rest before dinner; she will be so sorry to miss you."

Janet was looking extremely handsome in some of the clothes that Nicole had persuaded her into buying; in fact, it was difficult to recognise the Miss Symington of the sailor-hat and the pulled-back hair, in this comely woman in soft browns and fawns, her hair softening her face under a most becoming hat, but her manner was as stiff as ever, and she said:

"It wasn't convenient for me to come to tea.—Are you better?"

"Quite better, thanks, but I daresay I still look a wreck. It's refreshing to see any one look as well as you do. I *do* like your new hat!"

Janet gave it a little tug. "I feel queer in it, but I'm told it's the fashion."

Nicole assured her that it was, and conversation languished. Subject after subject Nicole tried, only to find it dropped by Janet, who seemed oddly ill at ease.

At last, Nicole said rather desperately, "Well, and how is life with you?"

To her surprise her companion blushed and, fixing her eyes on the carpet, said, "I had a proposal yesterday—my first."

Nicole blushed also, in sympathy, and murmured incoherently, "But—how very nice! And how good of you to tell me. . . . Did you accept?"

Janet fumbled with her gloves. "It was a letter, and of course that gives you more time to think. It's Mr. Innes. I think you've met him."

Nicole remembered the rather unctuous gentleman with the soft voice that she had met walking with Miss Symington.

"Oh yes," she said. "He came to preach, didn't he?"

"Yes. He has been a number of times, but I never thought . . . that he thought of me like that. But I did notice when he was here a fortnight ago that he looked at me a lot more than he ever did before—I was wearing one of my new dresses, and you had taught me how to do my hair differently, and I thought mebbe he found me unfamiliar, for I felt very queer myself. And he did say several times in a surprised sort of way that I was looking very well. I've known him for several years and we get on very well together. We never run out of conversation as I do with the other preachers. But—I don't know. . . . He's a widower with two girls away at school, and lives in Morningside. He's got a confectionery business, but all his spare time is taken up with Christian work. He's a really good man, and earnest, but I don't know. . . . The children are a difficulty, of course. . . ."

"But," said Nicole, "does anything really matter except whether you care for him or not?"

Miss Symington stared. "You've got to look at it all round," she said. "You see, it means giving up a lot. My house is a real pleasure to me now, and I don't know if I'd like Edinburgh. And, remember, I'm nearly forty-seven, and at that age you don't make changes lightly. The question is, is it worth while? It's difficult knowing. . . ."

CHAPTER XXVII

"... now I find thy saw of might,
'Who ever loved that loved not at first sight?' "

As You Like It.

Somewhat to her mother's surprise, Nicole had at once said she would go when Mrs. Jackson's invitation had come, followed by Barbara's less impassioned appeal.

"I could go on Monday for a few days, and bring Barbara home with me," she said. "Mums, does it strike you that Babs isn't terribly keen on me going to Rutherfurd?"

"Why shouldn't she be?"

"No reason ... Are you sure you would be all right alone for a few days? I somehow feel I would like to get away just now. ..."

"The change will do you good," Lady Jane said, "and don't give a thought to me. I'll be perfectly all right."

Mrs. Jackson was in a state of simmering excitement over Nicole's coming, though what she expected to happen it would be difficult to say. To Barbara she was almost overpoweringly kind, guiltily feeling that she was deliberately doing her an injury.

As for Nicole, her mind was so full of other matters that this coming back to Rutherfurd—at any other time a most poignant experience—hardly moved her at all. Sitting in the train, watching the familiar landmarks come one by one into view, she did not feel herself to be alone. Simon was with her. To him she turned when again there swam into her ken her beloved Border hills, his hand she grasped when the links of Tweed among their green pastures greeted her eyes.

Mrs. Jackson met her, explaining that Barbara had gone with Andrew and some friends to a Point-to-Point meeting. "And I daresay," she said as she tucked the rug round her guest in the car, "you'll be glad enough of a little peace and a rest in your own room before you see any one. I know what it's like to be recovering from a chill, your legs feel like brown paper."

Nicole, thinking how Simon would have enjoyed Mrs. Jackson, looked into the kind, concerned face turned to her and said:

"As a matter of fact, my legs feel more like growing trees than brown paper. I'm really quite all right.—I was so sorry about failing you, but I'm sure Barbara was of much more use than I would have been. She's so splendidly practical."

"She's all that, and a great help she was. Indeed I couldn't have got on without her at all. Andy laughs and says I always need somebody to stand beside me and give me moral courage, but I do like somebody who knows how things should be done and could check me if I was going to make some big mistake. Johnson is all very well, but you can't just *lean* on a butler.—You see, I feel so unsure of myself among all these people."

"You needn't," Nicole assured her. "They all like you so much. I hear from Jean Douglas and others what a kind, hospitable place Rutherfurd continues to be."

"Ah, Mrs. Douglas! if they were all like her! She's such a grand laugher."

"Isn't she? And don't you like her white hair, and her eyes so blue in her nice open-air face? . . . And I hear the dance was an immense success. Everything so well done, and the food divine! You're nothing short of a public benefactor, and how the girls must have blessed you at this dull time of year!"

Mrs. Jackson purred like a stroked cat. "Oh, well, I don't know, but they all seemed glad enough to come.—And how's Lady Jane?"

"Well, thank you. I believe that Kirkmeikle is really rather a good place for her. She is away from the people who would constantly remind her of what she has lost, and she takes quite an interest in some of our new friends. You know, we live right in the town, on the sea-front, among a huddle of houses occupied by fisher-folk and others, most delightful, I think, and Mother can go in and out among them. They love her.—No, that is, perhaps, rather an exaggerated way to put it, for Fife people are not expansive. Let's say they don't mind her, they welcome her and tell her all their troubles. And Mother doesn't seem to mind that there is almost nothing to do in Kirkmeikle. She is the least restless of women."

"I think she's a noble character," said Mrs. Jackson.

Nicole laughed. "She'd be very much amused to hear it. The thing about Mother is that she never thinks of herself at all.—Ah, here's Rutherfurd."

"Yes, yes," said Mrs. Jackson nervously. "You'll try not to mind. I know it's hard to come back like this, but here's Johnson. . . . I'm sure you're glad to see Miss Nicole back, Johnson?"

Nicole was out of the car in a moment, shaking hands with Johnson, and asking for his wife and his son in London. "But I'll be in to see you and hear about everything," she told him.

"Very good, Miss, thank you. Her ladyship is well, I hope?"

"Quite well, thank you. . . . I'll leave my coat. . . ."

"Tea's in the drawing-room," said Mrs. Jackson. "Unless you'd rather go straight up to your room and have it there? No. Well, go right in, I needn't show *you* the road."

After tea she insisted on taking Nicole to her room, and when there remained to talk and tell her favourite some of her troubles in the new life.

"But you're beginning to feel at home, aren't you?" said Nicole.

"No," said Mrs. Jackson, "that's what I never will be. You see, I can never be natural: I've to watch myself all the time, for the things I say, just ordinary things, seem to surprise the people here. And my voice sounds so queer. They say their words so clear cut, and I say mine so slushy, somehow. But uch! What does it matter! Andy gets on fine with them, and that's the great thing. They make a great fuss about him, and he's asked out a lot, and away to stay and all. But I'll tell you one thing I've told nobody. When Andy takes a wife, Father and I'll be very glad to creep back to Pollokshields. Father has no use for the country—it was just a notion he took to have a place. If Andy's here that'll please him, and he'll work away quite contented in his office. People'll laugh at us, I know that. Mrs. McArthur'll say to me, 'What did I tell you?' but I don't care. I've had about enough of being 'county,' and I must say I'd like to spend my last years comfortably, not always straining after appearing what I'm not. I'd like a nice new villa, not too far out for concerts and things, with a bit of a garden and every modern convenience, so that it could be worked by two servants. I plan it to myself every night in my bed—but I mustn't stay here chattering, you'll be fair wearied."

Andrew Jackson and Barbara got back only in time to dress for dinner. They had had a very good day and came home much pleased with each other. As Andrew dressed his thoughts were full of Barbara. She seemed to like being with him as much as he liked being with her. He admired her warmly, and was contentedly aware of the direction in which he was drifting.

It was time he married: this was an eminently suitable arrangement, and he felt perfectly content at the thought of a future spent with Barbara. If she saw things in the same light, so much the better, but there was no hurry: things were very pleasant as they were.

Always a punctual person, Andrew found himself downstairs, as he thought, before any one else. He was just about to turn on the lights in the drawing-room when he heard a sound. Looking round the heavy screen that sheltered the fireside from draughts, he saw, kneeling on the fender-stool, a girl. At first he thought he was dreaming, for the slim white figure bathed in the rosy light of the fire seemed more a thing of fire and dew than an ordinary mortal. He leant forward. She was speaking, addressing the picture, as a lover addresses his mistress. And what a voice! by Jove, what a voice!—deep, soft, caressing. . . . What was she saying?—

"You meaner beauties of the night,
   That poorly satisfy our eyes . . .
   You common people of the skies,—
   What are you when the moon shall rise?"

Then Andrew realised that this was the expected guest. This was the girl his mother had so often talked to him about. This was Nicole.

He slipped out of the room and turned over papers in the hall till the others came down.

Nicole jumped up from her kneeling position and went to turn on the lights. She had dressed early and been ready for Barbara when she ran in to greet her on her way to dress, and had come downstairs anxious to have a short time alone in the room she so loved. The sight of the picture had made her forget everything. . . . What a blessing no one had come in and found her kneeling there talking to a picture! She turned, as her host and hostess came in:

"Down first!" said Mrs. Jackson. "This is Father," taking her husband by the sleeve and leading him forward like a reluctant schoolboy.

152

"Pleased to meet you," he murmured. "Did you come from Fife to-day?"

Nicole said she had, and that it had been a pleasant journey.

"Left your mother well?"

"Thank you, quite well."

"That's right," said Mr. Jackson, and retired from the conversational arena.

Barbara came in, followed by Andrew.

"Oh, Andy," said his mother, "you haven't met Miss Rutherfurd."

"No," said Andrew, and shook hands gravely.

Dinner was a lively meal, the hostess being in uncommonly good spirits. "What! no champagne," she cried, when Nicole refused wine. "Uch—you should try a wee drop. No? Well, champagne's my temptation, and," as Johnson approached, "I'm going to succumb."

It sounded worse than it was, for she only "succumbed" to the extent of one glass, but it seemed to inspire her, for she kept the conversation almost entirely in her own hands, chiefly recalling episodes of her life in Glasgow: "D'you mind, Andy? ... Father, what was yon man's name that was always making jokes?" ... Later on, as they sat round the fire in the drawing-room, Barbara demurely stitching, the others idle, Mrs. Jackson looked at the picture above the fire-place and said:

"Who is it again? You remember you told me once, Miss Nicole, but I always forget."

"Elizabeth of Bohemia."

"Uch, yes, and who was she exactly? I get mixed with these foreign princesses."

Nicole turned to the son of the house. "Have you got 'Q's' *Studies in Literature*? You have?—then you must remember what he says about my Lovely Lady?"

"Only vaguely, I'm afraid," said Andrew. "I tell you what, I'll get the book and you'll read it to us."

"That'll be nice," Mrs. Jackson said comfortably. "I like fine being read to, but I nearly always fall asleep."

"No, no," Nicole cried, putting out a hand to stop Andrew. "It would be too wooden to read you solemnly a long extract. 'Q' talks, don't you remember, about the certain few women in history who in life fascinated the souls out of men, and still fascinate the imagination of mankind. Helen of Troy was one, of course, and Cleopatra another ..." She was sitting curled up in her favourite position on the fender-stool looking up at the picture, and she now turned smiling to her hostess, and said with a little confidential air, "What men call enchantresses, but what you and I would call *besoms*!" Then she continued: "But Joan of Arc was a third, a saint above saints, and Catherine of Siena—another saint; and a fifth was Mary Queen of Scots, who was what you will—except a saint; and that brings him to Mary's grand-daughter, Elizabeth of Bohemia, and there 'Q' rains out a perfect flood of adjectives, 'wayward, lovely, extravagant, unfortunate, adorable, peerless'—I forget them all. Then he breaks into Wotton's lines:

"You meaner beauties of the night,

That poorly satisfy our eyes
More by your number than your light;
   You common people of the skies,—
   What are you when the moon shall rise?

"Oh," she threw out her arms, "how I adore people who can be really enthusiastic!"

It was Andrew she addressed, Andrew who was sitting spellbound watching her, but it was Barbara who replied, looking coolly up from her work at the rose-flushed face and shining, eager eyes of her cousin.

"For my part," she said, "I see nothing fine, but merely silly, in going into raptures over a woman who has been dust for centuries," and dropped her head again over her work.

Nicole laughed and made a rueful face to the picture. "Yes, it's you she is talking about. . . . Never mind, Queen of Hearts, you had your day, for no man came into your range but knelt your sworn knight.—You rode conquering all hearts, and lifting all hearts to ride with you—to ride with you 'over the last lost edge of the world.' "

She almost whispered the last words, and clasped her hands tight. It was not the pictured lady she was thinking of now, it was Simon, her Simon, who had gone into danger without her. How blessed were they who rode *together* over the last lost edge. . . .

She shivered, but in a moment recovered herself, and smiled at Mr. Jackson, who was looking slightly affronted. He was not accustomed to the society of young women who sat in unconventional attitudes and apostrophised pictures.

"Well, I'm sure," said Mrs. Jackson. After a minute she added, "I knew a girl once—I was at school with her—and she had such a way with men. A little quiet thing to look at she was, I never knew how she did it, but men fairly flocked round her." She pulled a cushion into a more comfortable position for her back and continued meditatively: "And she made a poor marriage after all, a large bakery business, but not very steady, so it just lets you see . . ."

Presently Mr. Jackson slipped away to his own room, Mrs. Jackson fell asleep, and Nicole and Andrew sat on a sofa and talked, while Barbara stitched and stitched.

When Johnson brought the tray in, Mrs. Jackson, waking from uneasy slumber, said, "No music to-night? I've quite missed it.—We've been having great concerts these last few nights. . . . Your cousin sings awfully well, Miss Nicole, and Andy has a nice voice too."

"Oh, why did nobody suggest music to-night?" Nicole cried. "What I've missed!"

"Oh, we were much better employed to-night," Barbara said coolly.

Nicole looked from one to the other. So this was what had been happening! She had greatly enjoyed the talk with Andrew—they had only discussed books and reminded each other of this and that character and incident—but she had not understood that she was more or less of an intruder and had probably spoiled the evening for both Barbara and Andrew.

She felt very contrite as she followed Barbara into her room for a good-night talk. But Barbara was rather aloof, though asking questions about her aunt and the household at Kirkmeikle and politely interested in everything her cousin told her. And when questioned in turn her replies were cool and crisp. Yes, she had a very good time at Rutherfurd; the dance had been delightful: the Jacksons everything that was kind and considerate. No, she did not mean to go home yet. At the end of the week she was going on to Langlands for a short visit, and then to the Kilpatricks.

And Nicole presently slipped away to bed rather forlornly, wondering why she had left the Harbour House and her ever-understanding mother.

Next morning when they were idling over the newspapers Mrs. Jackson demanded to know what the plans were for the day.

"Would you not like a nice round in the car, Miss Nicole?" she asked. "You haven't seen this countryside for a while."

"What I'd *like* to do," said Nicole, "is to go for a really long walk. Up the Farawa, and down into Langhope Glen and home by the Moor Road.—If we might have a sandwich with us? We'd be home in time for tea. Who will come?"

Andrew, throwing down the *Glasgow Herald*, sprang up, and Nicole could have slapped him for the eager light that was in his eyes. She knew that though Barbara appeared immersed in the *Scotsman* she saw it too.

She turned to her cousin. "Barbara, you'll come."

"I'm afraid I can't. I'm going with Mrs. Jackson to make a lot of calls this afternoon," and Barbara turned to her hostess for confirmation.

"So we are," said that lady in a delighted voice. "So, Andy, you'd better go with Miss Nicole, she might easily meet a tramp. I'll see about sandwiches." She bustled out of the room.

Nicole looked thoughtfully at her cousin, whose head was again bent over the newspaper, and then turned to Andrew:

"Will you come, Mr. Jackson? . . . I'll go and get ready, for it's a fairly long walk."

Mrs. Jackson not only saw that they were well supplied with sandwiches, but begged them to have some sustenance before they started. She had an idea that if people were more than an hour or two away from the offer of food they must collapse.

It was a steel-grey day with a high wind rustling the dry heather and the bent grass, and sweeping the clouds across the sky. Nicole and Andrew walked together in almost complete silence. Nicole was realising that Barbara had reason to feel coldly towards her. She had arrived at exactly the wrong moment, and Andrew, by some evil mischance—she could not feel herself to blame in the matter—seemed inclined to turn aside from the path he was on and take an interest in her unlucky self.

Well, she had to put it right somehow, even if it meant a sacrifice. . . . No one knew of her love for Simon Beckett, she held her happy secret warm in her heart, it was like a lamp that lit her days, but to speak of it seemed like sacrilege. She had not meant to tell a soul till Simon came back, but now she turned to her companion.

"It's lovely, lovely." She swept her arm around.

"Yes," said Andrew, "but I feel an intruder here. The place is yours, will always be yours; the fact that we have bought it makes no difference. We go out and in, but the spirit of the place is yours."

"No. No. I'm *glad* you're here. I don't know of any one I'd prefer to be here. —I'm afraid that sounds rather cheek, for what business is it of mine after all? I believe, really, that it's a good thing we had to go to make room for you."

Andrew shook his head. "I can't bear to think that we turned you out. I never realised what we'd done until I went into the drawing-room last night and saw you kneeling in the fire-light before the picture——"

"What? Did you come in? What a posing idiot you must have thought me! The fact is—I used to do that as a child. My father taught me Wotton's poem, and I used to kneel on the fender-stool and say it to the picture. My Lovely Lady, I called her."

Andrew went on—"I've always been a very prosaic person, but last night when I heard your voice . . ."

Nicole broke in—"Did you by any chance feel that we were meant to be friends? Because I did, whenever I saw you. Your mother had talked of you so much I seemed to know you quite well. And because I believe we're meant to be good friends I can't bear you to have that foolish idea of being a usurper. . . . I'm going to tell you something that nobody knows, not my mother, not Barbara. I'm not to be pitied. If we hadn't left Rutherfurd and gone to our funny little salt-sea house in Fife I'd have missed the most wonderful thing that ever happened or ever could happen to me." She stopped and looked away for a minute, then turning again to Andrew, said: "There I met a man—Simon Beckett. At first he seemed to me only an ordinary quiet, rather dull Englishman.—No, that's not true. I tried to tell myself that, for I was ashamed of my own feelings, but from the first moment I saw him I knew, quite without doubt, that he was the one man in the world for me, and most wonderful of all he saw in me the one woman. . . . He's an explorer, a mountaineer.—And now he's gone, Andy, he's gone! He sails for India this week to make another attempt on Everest."

Andrew cleared his throat. Presently he said, "So he is that Beckett. I heard him lecture once at the Geographical."

Nicole had flushed into one of her moments of sudden loveliness.—"*You saw him?*" she said, and poor Andrew felt that he had taken on an entirely new interest in her eyes. "Tell me, was he very bad?"

"Oh—it wasn't much of a lecture, he never let himself go, but I wouldn't have missed it for anything. Why, just to see him was enough! This was the man who had been *liaison* officer between the gods and mortals . . . And what a good-looking chap he is!"

"Isn't he?" Nicole laughed softly. "He always said he was such a rotten lecturer, but you see he was there—I like that idea of yours about the *liaison* officer —it was he who left his friend dead and struggled back alone, so how could you

156

expect him to be eloquent? He could only harden his poor voice and repeat it like a school lesson."

Andrew nodded, and they walked on, Andrew slightly in front.

Presently he turned and said, "It was most awfully good of you to tell me this. Thank you. I've always taken a tremendous interest in men who did that sort of thing—I mean to say, attempted what seemed impossible heights, went to look behind the ranges. I'd never do it myself, I was born cautious, but I like to think that there are such men—it seems, somehow, to make life more spacious. . . . I wonder if you noticed in the papers not very long ago the death of a man—an ordinary business man—who had been on a climbing expedition with some friends in the West Highlands, and lost his life in an attempt to get a golden eagle's nest? Wasn't that rather fine?"

"Yes," said Nicole, "it gives one a thrill to think of it. The commonplace regular life, going backwards and forwards to an office, and then the wild romantic end. I'm glad you don't condemn it. So many people can't for the life of them see anything but idiocy in it, a wilful throwing away of life. Anyway, there it is. . . ."

"Yes," said Andrew, "there it is"; and he sighed.

CHAPTER XXVIII

Viola. Ay, but I know——
Duke. What dost thou know?
Viola. Too well what love women to men may owe.
Twelfth Night.

Barbara was far from happy. She had, to her own rather horrified disgust, dreaded the coming of Nicole, and what she had foreseen had almost at once come to pass. Andrew had obviously eyes only for her cousin, and Barbara did not blame him, she had never suffered from too good a conceit of herself, and she did not underrate Nicole's charm. Andrew, she realised, though prosaic enough to look at and talk to, had hidden depths of romance and poetry, and to these depths Nicole, that "fairy's child," appealed. And there was no use in blaming Nicole. She had not willingly enchanted him, she did not want his worship. When Andrew found that out, Barbara wondered, would he come back to her? She was very humble now, this Barbara, for the truth had come to her that it was not Rutherfurd that counted with her, it was Andrew alone.

While she sat in the car as they made their round of calls, and laughed and chatted to Mrs. Jackson, her thoughts were all the time with the two who were walking over the hills. . . . What were they talking about? Was Andrew going at every step farther from her?

They refused tea when calling, and got home about five o'clock.

"Now I wonder," said Mrs. Jackson, "would they go in somewhere and get their tea or come home? What d'you guess? Will they be home before us?"

"I guess," Barbara said, as she got out of the car, "I guess that they're ravenously devouring tea in the drawing-room at this moment."

"You're right, here they are!" Mrs. Jackson cried as she burst into the room. "Well, what kind of day have you had?"

"Fine," said Andrew, springing to his feet, "and we've eaten all the tea, so I hope you aren't hungry——" He rang the bell as he spoke.

"Poached eggs and plum-cake," said Nicole. "I feel like the greedy king in the fairy-tale. But it has been lovely. . . . Has calling given you an appetite? Barbara, how disgustingly nice you look." She put up both hands to her face. "What with the hill winds and the fire and my greed for tea my face is like a harvest moon! We were too hungry even to wash our hands or smooth our hair: we just rushed at the food with a cry. Now I'm gorged I must go and tidy. But tell me first whom have you called on?"

"Well, we were awfully fortunate about getting people out," said Mrs. Jackson, "so we got over quite a lot.—I'll not give you this tea, my dear, they'll be bringing fresh tea in a minute.—The only one we found at home was Mrs. Scott at the Manse, and she was as kind as could be, I must say that. She would have us to stay to tea, the maid was in with a table and a cloth over her arm before we had hardly sat down, but we said No, quite firmly. She's a good manager, yon woman; I knew it before the door opened. Such a clean mat and bright scraper, and inside everything as shining and neat as you like—tasteful too."

Nicole nodded. "Mrs. Scott's a noted manager, and cannot only get servants herself, but manages to find them for other people. . . . Wasn't she frightfully glad to see Barbara? We used to go to parties at the Manse when we were all children."

"She told me that," Mrs. Jackson said. "Oh, she made a great fuss of Miss Barbara, and they had so many things to talk about that I had plenty of time to sit and look at the room. It's awfully nice, I must say, to meet old friends: I quite envied them their talk!"

"I always liked Mrs. Scott," Barbara said, helping herself to bread and butter, "and I enjoyed our talk. I'm afraid, though, you must have been bored, Mrs. Jackson. We had so many things to recall. She was telling me, Nikky, that James is doing extraordinarily well in India."

"I can well believe it. D'you remember how he was always held up to Archie as a pattern? and poor Archie said bitterly, 'He's so beastly clever that he's abnormal!' Oh, James will get his 'K' in no time, and then won't his mother be proud!"

"The only thing," said Mrs. Jackson, "that I don't like about the Manse is having the churchyard so near. The funerals come past the front door!"

"Quiet neighbours, Mother," Andrew said.

"Uch, Andy, be quiet—I suppose you get used to it, but I must say I'd hate to sit there alone on winter nights, thinking of all the graves outside, and not very healthy either. . . ."

That evening Nicole went to her cousin's room and asked her what dress she meant to wear. Barbara looked at the bed to see what Esther had laid out, and Nicole protested, "Not that, I don't like you in that." She went to the wardrobe and began to pull things about. "This, I think," producing a white dress embroidered in black. "Now, let me do your hair. I haven't done it for ages and I do enjoy it."

"Why this sudden interest in my appearance?" Barbara asked, not quite sure whether to be pleased or provoked.

"Because, my dear, I didn't think you were looking your best last night. . . . I saw some one with her hair done like this and I thought at the time it would suit you. —Now, that's very nice. Tucking your hair in like that shows the shape of your head. Do you like it?"

Barbara considered herself in the looking-glass. The new style was a distinct success, and she said so.

Nicole looked over her cousin's shoulder and made a face at herself in the mirror. "What a horror I look! I must do something about it." She yawned. "I'm really very sleepy. It was a gorgeous walk to-day, Babs, I do wish you had come. . . . Andrew *is* a nice fellow. I knew he must be good and kind and dependable or his dear funny mother wouldn't have adored him so whole-heartedly, but I also thought he

159

would be very dull. He's anything but dull. No wonder everybody about here likes him."

"Yes," said Barbara, studying the back of her head in a hand-glass, "he makes a very interesting companion," and her tone was as light and placid as if Andrew was nothing to her but the merest acquaintance, but Nicole was not deceived.

That night Barbara did not feel out of it; rather, though how it was she did not quite know, she found herself the centre of things. It was easy for her to be amusing and amused; a becoming flush and a sparkle in her eyes transformed her. Barbara's looks depended greatly on the mood she was in. Bored, and feeling unsuccessful, she was a handsome but somewhat heavy-looking young woman; appreciation lit a lamp in her eyes and gave a witty edge to her tongue.

She sang, and Andrew hung over the piano. "Sing this, please," he begged . . . "you sang it the first night you came. . . . Don't you sing, Miss Nicole?"

Nicole sadly shook her head. "Alas, no. Barbara is the only talented member of our family. Sing '*Lady Keith's Lament*,' Babs, I love your voice in that; the deep notes make me feel as if I were on a swing!"

She was sitting beside her hostess, keeping her awake by telling her stories of Kirkmeikle. Mrs. Jackson was immensely interested in Mrs. Heggie and her daughter who wrote, and in Miss Symington and her house.

"Mrs. Heggie must be a fine hearty body," she said.

"Oh, she is," Nicole agreed. "She's the sort of woman that if you sat next her on a railway journey and told her your chimney at home smoked would never rest until she found a remedy for it. You must come and visit us some day, and then you'll meet every one."

"That would be fine. . . . I like your mother awful well. . . ."

Nicole left Rutherfurd to go home the day Barbara went to Langlands. Mrs. Jackson implored her to stay, but Nicole pleaded that her mother really needed her and that she had to go.

While Barbara was at Langlands Andrew rode over one morning and asked her to marry him.

They were standing together in the little winter garden opening from Lady Langlands' sitting-room, looking at a climbing rhododendron, and Barbara answered nothing for a minute, just went on looking thoughtfully at the white blooms. Then she turned to him and said, "Are you sure you want me?"

He flushed a little but met her eyes steadily.

"Quite sure." He took her hand. "I think I could make you happy, and I shall count myself a very lucky man if you will take me."

"Well . . ." Barbara let her hand lie in his, and gave a sigh which ended in a laugh. "You realise, don't you, that in me you would get a most ordinary unexciting wife, not too costly to wear everyday! . . ."

Andrew, as in duty bound, protested and added: "Where would you find a more ordinary workaday fellow than I am? Andrew Jackson, born and bred in Glasgow, in trade up to the neck, distinguished in no way at all! I wonder I have the impudence to ask you."

Barbara smiled and said, "Andy." It was enough. He was answered.

That night Andrew told his mother. They were alone, Mr. Jackson was in Glasgow, and Mrs. Jackson had been nodding over a magazine while her son pretended to read a book.

"Mother," he said suddenly; "I've got something to tell you. I'm going to marry Barbara Burt."

Mrs. Jackson stared at her son as if she had not understood him. "But—I thought, I thought . . . Oh, I did *hope* it would be the other one," and suddenly, she began to cry.

Andrew threw the cigarette he was smoking into the fire.

"Mother," he said, "it isn't like you to be cruel."

"Me cruel?" Mrs. Jackson sniffed convulsively.

"Cruel to Barbara. What would she feel if she heard you."

"Well, I can't help it. Everything's gone wrong. If only Nicole had come to the dance and you'd seen her first you'd never have looked at Miss Burt."

Involuntarily Andrew looked up at the picture.

You meaner beauties of the night . . .

What are you, when the moon doth rise?

He sat down by his mother and put his arms round her shoulders. "Mother," he said, "you're the best mother ever man had."

"Oh, Andy, I'm not. D'you think I don't see how I affront you at every turn ____"

"And for my sake I want you to be good to Barbara. . . . And, Mother, I want you to understand, once for all, that Nicole Rutherfurd would never have looked at me, so don't worry yourself about what might have been. And you like Barbara and get on well with her, you know you do."

Mrs. Jackson sighed. "She's all right, but she's a buttoned-up creature compared to my girl. . . . I don't know how it is but when I'm with Nicole I just feel as easy and comfortable as if I were sitting at the parlour fireside at Deneholm with a daughter of my own beside me. When I'm with Barbara and kick off my slippers and lose my handkerchief and specs, and do any of the daft-like things I'm always doing, she wears a sort of long-suffering expression, but Nicole's down on the floor picking up my things and laughing, and fitting my slippers back on my feet, saying, 'There, there,' so comforting like. . . . But Barbara's your choice so I'll say no more. It might have been worse. If it had been one of those half-naked girls that came to the dance . . ."

She sat up and dried her eyes and smiled at her son.

"Oh, Andy, I hope you'll be happy, my dear. And she's a very handsome girl to show to our friends. I suppose we'd better send it to the papers, that is after Father knows, and Lady Jane. . . . How would you put it '. . . to Barbara, daughter of the late Somebody Burt'? We'd better put 'and niece of the late Sir Walter Rutherfurd and of Lady Jane Rutherfurd, the Harbour House, Kirkmeikle.' That sounds quite tony . . . I wonder what Mrs. McArthur'll say when she reads it in the *Herald*?"

CHAPTER XXIX

"O, think'st thou we shall ever meet again?"
Romeo and Juliet.

Nicole had thought she wanted to get away from Kirkmeikle, but all the time at Rutherfurd she had pined to be back. She saw the place where she had known Simon through the haze of her dreams, it was beautified by her memories, she felt there must be a virtue in it that would help her to courage and patience.

But going back was not all she had pictured.

It was a day grey with east wind. Edinburgh was at its rawest and bleakest. The Gardens had a dejected look as if they had ceased to believe that it could ever be warm and sunny again, even the Castle seemed a mere dull hulk. At every street corner passers-by clung to the collars of their coats for the blast was biting.

Nicole had meant to do some shopping and get the afternoon train, but she felt so discouraged by the prevailing gloom that she was thankful to escape. She settled herself in the corner of an empty carriage, but discomfort dogged her steps, for there entered a bronchial lady in a sealskin coat who immediately demanded that the windows be closed, the result being a sort of cold frowst.

Nicole stared out of the window. The Firth was sullen and grey. One by one they passed, the dreary, dripping little stations, then Kirkcaldy with its tall factories and "queer-like smell," and, at last, Kirkmeikle. She sprang out and looked eagerly round. There was no one to meet her, of course; she was not expected till the next train, nevertheless she felt neglected. A young porter came along kicking at a stone, and whistling, and she pointed out her boxes and, asking him to see that they were sent down to the Harbour House, set off walking.

There is something about an east wind on a March day that seems to lay a weight on the spirits. As she walked down the familiar steep street Nicole felt supremely sorry for herself. Here she was, alone, Simon every minute going farther from her, her mother living with her memories, Barbara engrossed in Andrew Jackson.

As she passed Mrs. Brodie's little house with its steps leading down to the front door she looked eagerly, but the door was close shut; she was not even to be cheered by a sight of "the wee horse."

She stole into the Harbour House like a thief in the night, and went straight to the drawing-room. Here, anyhow, was comfort. The bleakness of the March day had no power to chill the gentle colours of the quiet room. Here was peace.

The fire was purring to itself as little flames licked the seasoned logs. Lady Jane sat at the bureau. She had been writing one of her long family letters, and had stopped to think for a little, head on hand. A small glass of deep blue grape hyacinths stood beside her on the bureau, the three miniatures that never left her were ranged there. On the wall above were other miniatures, older, much older, with the tremulous look that such meek little pictures of the past have: the modern ones looked almost blatant beside them. A small frame with a bit of embroidery in the making lay on the arm of a chair, the *Cornhill* open beside it.

Nicole, having opened the door without being heard, stood, holding her breath in the quiet. How contented the room looked, the very furniture seemed to like to be there! It was her mother that made it so, she thought. Some rooms are as restless as their owners, one could not imagine any one sitting down in them to read or think, or to be "lonely and happy and good." They seem only meant for sprawling about in with an illustrated paper, for smoking and drinking cocktails, for light talk and lighter laughter.

Lady Jane's rooms were sanctuaries, sweet with fresh flowers, gently gay with choice embroidery and rugs, wise with old books.

"Mother," Nicole said softly.

Lady Jane sprang up, her face suddenly warm with colour, her eyes bright and expectant. She saw her daughter: "My darling—you!" she cried, and put her hand to her eyes for a second. "I'm getting old, Nikky, and wandering. When you spoke just now I thought . . . your voices were all so much alike.—But where have you come from? I meant to be at the station to meet you at six o'clock."

"I know, I know. I ought to have sent a wire. It was such a terrible day in Edinburgh I had no heart to shop, so I rushed and caught the early train. And there was a woman in the carriage who loved a frowst, and it was so sad seeing no one at the station, and I'm dreadfully cold and it's a mischievous world. . . ."

Ten minutes later, sitting well "into the fire" with a cup of hot tea in her hand, Nicole gave a long sigh and said, "Mums, I don't believe there's an ill in the world that a good fire and a good tea can't do something to lighten. Even when your heart's nearly broken there's a slight consolation to be found in these two blessed things, and, when added to them, one has a mother like you, well—— I don't believe I'm going to take pneumonia after all. . . ."

"That's a good thing," said her mother. "Now, if you're sufficiently warmed and comforted, perhaps you'll tell me something about your visit. Your letters were wonderfully unilluminating."

"I know." Nicole looked at the fire. "You see it was rather difficult. . . ."

Lady Jane looked at her daughter's averted face, and said: "Barbara seems to have enjoyed her visit."

"Yes, oh yes—Mums, I rather expect we'll be hearing some news from Babs soon. She and Andrew Jackson have made great friends. I expect Babs will go back to Rutherfurd as mistress. Funny, isn't it?"

"Very. You liked the young man?"

"Oh, I did, enormously. He's quite one of the nicest people I've ever met. He's got something of his mother's simplicity, along with very good brains and excellent taste. He'll make a fine laird of Rutherfurd. Babs is in luck. And so is he. It'll make all the difference to Babs to have a house of her own and an assured position. . . . I've been thinking, Mums, it can't always have been easy for her living

164

with us. Of course she adores you quite as much as if you had been her own mother, and you've never made the slightest difference between us, but when I grew up I must have been a horrid snag, always in the way. I rather wonder she didn't hate me —a smaller-natured person would have, for I can see looking back how often I must have spoiled things for her, but I believe in spite of everything she is fond of me.— We'll miss her terribly, won't we, Mums? I do like tart people. Babs was like the cloves in an apple-tart, she gave things a flavour! . . ."

"But, Nikky, are you sure of this?"

Nicole nodded. "Quite sure. Barbara, as I told you, went off to-day to stay with the Langlands. I give Andy—I love the way his mother says it, 'A-andy'—just two days to miss her, to realise where he stands, and to go over to Langlands and propose. And Barbara, dear thing, knows where her happiness lies. That I am sure of too. If there was ever in her heart any feeling of superiority, of stepping down to accept, it is gone now," she laughed softly. "She looks at Andy as if he were a knight in armour instead of a little Glasgow merchant!"

Lady Jane stitched for a minute or two in silence, then she said, "As you say we'll miss Barbara very badly, but I confess, I'm glad to hear of this. I've often worried about her, and sometimes I've felt that I wasn't quite fair to you in my efforts not to make her feel out of it. . . . It was often hard for her, but I'm glad you never realised it till now or things would have been more difficult.—Then, will Barbara settle down at Rutherfurd with the parents?"

"I think not. I believe the elder Jacksons will go back to Glasgow. Mrs. Jackson will never be really happy at Rutherfurd. She's proud of it but feels herself entirely alien. She tells me her dream is to get a new villa in a Glasgow suburb, with two good servants and a little garden, and 'Father' less busy, and her old friends round her. She says she is tired of being 'county' and prefers to be suburban. Sensible woman, she knows what she wants. She really is a dear, Mother. I loved listening to her stories, and going round the place with her, and hearing her talk to all the cottage women, taking the deepest interest in all the details of their cooking and housework and management of their children. They must be fond of her, I'm sure. And all the people round like her so much."

"Does Barbara get on well with her?"

"Oh yes. Quite fairly well. I think she jars, you know. Babs is ultra-sensitive and Mrs. Jackson has a somewhat free way of expressing herself, but I expect it will be all right. They are united in one thing—love for Andy. . . . Mr. Jackson is rather like a rat, a nice rat of course, out of *The Wind in the Willows* perhaps, a little depressing to live with I should imagine. If he isn't at work in Glasgow, or buried in papers at Rutherfurd, he doesn't seem to know what to do with himself. He's a man 'perplexed wi' leisure.' He keeps tapping his top teeth with the nail of his forefinger, and answers invariably, 'Is that so?' Once he broke into an anecdote, but though I laughed immoderately I couldn't see the point: I doubt if there was one. . . . And now tell me your news. What have you done since I left?"

Lady Jane smiled as she pulled a thread through the linen she was working on.

"Missed you, Nikky dear, mostly. And I've read and walked and sewed, and written some of my endless letters, and the servants have been most attentive, almost embarrassingly so—set on, I suppose, by you. Christina kept making errands into the room every hour, watching me like a nurse with a mental patient! I was driven to go out more than I would otherwise have done, in consequence. And the Bat came every day for his lessons, and once he lunched with me. He's an extraordinarily idle little boy! If I don't watch him after I've given him a task, he simply folds his hands and sits: he has no real thirst for knowledge!"

"Has any boy?" Nicole said and laughed.

"And I visited Betsy," her mother went on. "She is at war with her daughter-in-law. There has been a new baby and Betsy hasn't been invited to inspect it, and her pride won't let her go unasked. She makes a virtue of remaining away, and says, 'It's a guid dowg that disna bark till it's askit,' and adds, 'She'll never hae to soop her floor efter me.' "

Nicole laughed. "Poor Betsy, she has a saying for every crisis in life. And 'the wee horse'? I brought him some *gundy*."

"Oh," said Lady Jane, "there has been a crisis in the Brodie household and Mrs. Brodie had no proverb ready! The poor 'wee horse' took suddenly ill on Wednesday. I heard about it and went in about three o'clock in the afternoon to see if I could do anything. I found Mrs. Brodie white-washing the kitchen ceiling, with all the younger children *including the invalid* stacked in the kitchen bed to keep them out of the dirt! When I expressed surprise that she should have chosen such a time for such an undertaking, she replied that Dr. Kilgour was bringing another doctor to consult, and she couldn't let a strange doctor see her with a black ceiling! There were no bad results, indeed the child had begun to improve when the two doctors arrived."

"Amazing!" said Nicole, "and what of our friends on the hill? Has Mrs. Heggie asked you to any meals?"

"None in particular. I met her one day and she asked me to 'any meal I cared to come to.' Mrs. Buckler's new housemaid goes in and out of the front door instead of the back, which is causing friction. Miss Symington I haven't seen. I think Mrs. Lambert must be spring-cleaning. As I passed the garden-gate yesterday, the little stalwart Betha was beating chairs furiously . . . you know, you've only been away for the inside of a week though it seems much longer. It's a week to-day since Mr. Beckett went away—I must say I've missed him a lot, I hadn't realised quite how much his visits meant, how much I looked forward to them. Things seem a little flat and stale, now that I know I won't hear Christina announce 'Mr. Beckett.' He once said he felt ashamed to hear himself announced so frequently and thought he ought to change his name to create a diversion! I think he liked coming."

"Well," said Nicole, in an even voice, "I knew I liked him coming. He was almost as much my friend as the Bat's. The poor Bat must be missing him terribly. I must take him out and devise some sport, but I'll be a wretched substitute for his beloved Simon. Heigh-ho! I wish nice people didn't always want to put the thick of the world between themselves and their friends and well-wishers! and the dull, tiresome ones remain, sticking closer than a brother."

CHAPTER XXX

"Consider Mr. Collins' respectability, and Charlotte's prudent, steady character. Remember that as to fortune it is a most eligible match; and be ready to believe . . . that she may feel something like regard and esteem for Mr. Collins."
Jane Austen.

Wondering much what was happening to Miss Symington, Nicole made an early opportunity to call at Ravenscraig.

The ten days which had elapsed since their last meeting had made a decided change on Janet. She carried herself with more importance, as if the coming dignity of matrimony was already casting its shadow. She spoke with more weight, was inclined to lay down the law, to treat Nicole rather patronisingly as a mere spinster.

Events had moved rapidly, and everything was arranged for an early marriage.

"Samuel says there's no sense in delay," she said with a little conscious laugh.

"No," said Nicole.

"And the housekeeper's leaving in May anyway. She isn't at all satisfactory, Samuel says, very lax about the amount eaten in the kitchen."

"Does that matter?" Nicole asked carelessly.

"Of course it matters. It's not right not to be careful, no matter what your means may be."

"I daresay not, but it seems a pity to make a fuss and have no end of unpleasantness. . . . I'd rather be cheated."

"I don't agree," Miss Symington said, pursing her mouth. "I couldn't be happy if I thought waste was going on. I've just parted with my cook—very inconveniently—simply for waste. The woman had no conscience about dripping."

"Hadn't she, poor soul? Well, well. And have you decided where the wedding is to be? In Mr. Lambert's church, I suppose?"

"No. We're going to have a very quiet wedding in the Caledonian Hotel in Edinburgh. Samuel doesn't care for church weddings, he doesn't like display, and there will only be the nearest relations present."

"Oh," Nicole said, looking dashed. "It won't seem much like a wedding, will it, in a hotel?"

"Oh, I don't know. A church wedding is such a parade, and with Samuel a widower and me far from young, it would be quite out of place.—I've been to see the house and the children."

"Oh, you have? I hope you liked what you saw of them."

"Quite. Quite. I'm not awfully fond of Morningside, and it's just a house in a terrace.—I'll miss the space we have here, and there's a basement flat which I don't like, but you can't have everything. I'm sorry now I was at all the expense of doing up this house. If only I had known what the future held for me—but Samuel never gave me an inkling of his intentions, and I never imagined such a thing possible, though I always admired him. . . . But Samuel has consented to sell his drawing-room furniture—it was furnished by his first wife on her marriage, quite handsomely but without much taste—and I'll put this furniture into it. . . . It'll require to be redecorated, of course, something the same as this I should think." She looked thoughtfully round the pretty room. "It's been practically unused since the first wife died, for, of course, there was no entertaining done. All the house is thoroughly well-furnished and stocked. I suppose I'll need to get rid of nearly all my things. There's no room for them."

"Why not let Ravenscraig furnished; or keep it as a summer house?"

Miss Symington looked thoughtful. "Well, that's an idea, and it would let me keep my things. I'll need to think it over and see what Samuel says. It's a different thing when you've got a man to consult." She sighed, not unhappily.

"And the daughters?" Nicole asked. "Are they agreeable creatures?"

"Ye—es. Agnes is just finishing school, she's seventeen. Her father's going to send her for a year to Paris, and then she'll be at home."

"Pretty?"

"Not very. She's a lank kind of girl with a long pale face and an Edinburgh accent; she seems inclined to lounge."

"Perhaps she has grown too fast, and her spine's weak," Nicole suggested cheerfully. "Paris ought to smarten her up a bit."

"They've been very carefully brought up," Janet went on, "never been taught dancing, or allowed to go to the theatre."

"Oh—well, I daresay it's possible to be quite happy without dancing or going to the play. They'll be allowed to play games, I suppose, and go to concerts?"

"Oh, I think so, and the circus. My father hated the theatre, but he said a circus was different—the horses, you know. . . . The younger girl, Jessie, struck me as being rather a monkey. She has a dimple, and a good deal of colour, and I distinctly saw her wink at Agnes behind her father's back! But she's only fifteen, so I shan't have much to do with her for a few years, except, of course, in the holidays. But when I saw those girls, Miss Rutherfurd, and the basement I couldn't help thinking I'd taken on a good deal."

"I think you have," Nicole told her frankly. "To run a house with a basement in an Edinburgh suburb, and make a man and two young girls and, incidentally, yourself happy!"

"Of course," said Miss Symington, "I'm giving up a lot, my own house, my freedom, and—and———" She looked round vaguely as if in search of something, and continued. "But there will be great compensations. I'll be Mrs. Innes. It's only now I realise how much I've always wanted to be a Mrs. . . . And Samuel's a highly respected man with a very good position. And we've exactly the same tastes; I *will* enjoy going with him to meetings, and I'll take a real pleasure in seeing that he's comfortable. I don't believe the housekeeper looked after his clothes as she should have done, and, of course, the girls were too young to care. And then I'll have a large circle of new acquaintances, and my life will be full. I've often felt Kirkmeikle very cramping; the people are so uninteresting. ...: I wonder you stand it, for you're young."

Nicole laughed. "But I don't find the people dull," she said.

Janet nodded her head sagely. "It's all very well for you, you've just alighted here like a bird and will be off again whenever the spirit moves you. That was what Mr. Lambert said about you when you came, and I thought it was so true. You look so interested in everything, and seem so keen, but your real life isn't here at all."

"The difficulty," said Nicole, "is to have a real life anywhere.—But what I want to know is, *have you got your clothes?* What will you wear in the Caledonian Hotel on your wedding day?"

Janet blushed becomingly. "Well, that's what I want to ask you. Samuel liked the last things you chose for me, indeed, I'll always treasure that brown dress with the orange, for I was wearing it when Samuel first saw he cared for me. . . . He went home, you know, and wrote.—I don't want to be a laughing stock. Talmage once said that nothing made him laugh so much as to see a middle-aged woman dressed like a girl, and I've never forgotten it."

"Who was Talmage?"

"He was a minister, American, I think, who wrote every week in a paper called the *Christian Herald.*"

"Well," said Nicole, "I don't think I care for Mr. Talmage's kind of humour. If a woman dresses becomingly no one will laugh at her. Of course, if a middle-aged woman shingles her hair and reddens her lips and wears skirts to her knees, they might laugh, but the decent ones would feel more inclined to cry. . . . What do you think you'd like to wear yourself?"

"Well," again Janet blushed, "Samuel likes brown in all shades."

"Oh, well that includes fawn and that's quite wedding-like. Why not have a very pale fawn with long tight sleeves and some embroidery—rather vivid—with a cloak of the same with a beaver collar for softness, and a hat repeating the colours in the embroidery, and shoes and stockings and gloves all in palest fawn."

Janet's eyes shone. "I'd like that. I couldn't think of a single thing except grey and pink, and grey is so cold, and doesn't suit me. . . . I'm afraid I'm being very troublesome, but will you come with me to Edinburgh and explain just exactly what you mean to the dressmaker? Middle-aged woman as I am she makes me feel like a school-girl and I just do whatever she suggests, but if you were there to support me ——"

"Of course I'll come. Weddings are so interesting, and I love having a finger in the pie."

She rose to go, and Miss Symington said, "Had you a good time when you were away? I've been talking away about my own affairs, and probably you have more exciting things happening to you which you never speak of."

"Epoch-making events!" laughed Nicole. "How is the B—— Alastair?"

"That's another complication," Miss Symington said, looking worried. "It seems a shame that Samuel should be saddled with the child, and yet he's rather young to be sent to school."

"He's not seven yet." •

"I know. It's very difficult knowing what to do. The house in Morningside isn't large, and we couldn't spare a room for a nursery, and yet a child coming to meals and always about is such a nuisance. And I don't want to take Annie, and yet who would take the child out and look after him? It would just come on me. Of course I'm fond of Alastair, but I never did understand him. Samuel's very good about it, and says 'Bring him along,' but I don't know. . However, it's no use worrying about it. . . . Good-bye, just now."

Nicole went home very thoughtful, and finding her mother alone at once began: "Mums, I'm worried about the Bat."

"Why, isn't he well?"

"Oh, quite, I think, but Miss Symington's marriage is going to change things for him!"

"I hope so, poor darling. He has a dreary life with her here."

"I'm afraid he has," Nicole agreed; "though she honestly tries to do her best for him. But, Samuel's house, it seems, isn't large enough to take in the Bat, and . . ."

"Samuel?" Lady Jane raised puzzled eyes.

"The man Miss Symington's going to marry—Samuel Innes. I told you about him. I've just come from Ravenscraig. Mother, she's so changed. She talks now, quite a lot, and actually simpers. Often middle-aged marriages are lovely things, intensely happy with a grateful happiness that is the very innocence of love; but somehow Samuel and his house in Morningside with a basement and pert school-girl daughters! Poor Janet Symington! And yet what right have I to call her poor? She is almost triumphant. She says her life will be so full, and she is looking forward to going to meetings with Samuel. Isn't life the most laughable, pathetic jumble? I wonder what Miss Symington's religion really amounts to! Does she want to do good because Christ died for her, and for His sake she must be loving and giving, or is it only an inherited fear of a jealous God Who will send her to Hell if she doesn't heap up, ant-like, little bundles of good deeds and works of mercy? I don't know. I don't know. But it's the Bat I care about. Wouldn't it be possible, Mother, if Miss Symington were willing, for us to take him? He could stay with us until he was old enough for school, that's all we need say at present, but gradually he would become our own. Boys mean so much to you and me. . . ."

There was a silence, then Nicole said:

"Wouldn't you like to have him for your own, Mother, the funny little Bat? To have a boy to look after again, to see about his clothes and his tuck-box, and welcome him back for the holidays? Miss Symington never really wanted him, I think she disliked his parents, and I can't bear to think of him an unwelcome presence in that Morningside house, with Samuel and the lank girl that lounges, and the pink girl that winks."

Half-laughing, half-crying, she laid her head on her mother's knee, and Lady Jane, stroking her hair, said:

170

"I think it would be an immense comfort to have the Bat—if it can be arranged. We've lots of room, and time, and everything. The first moment I saw the child I felt drawn to him, in fact, I can't explain to myself the curious sympathy there is between us. And he is so small and solitary in the world. When he gets on that too-large overcoat, and gravely salutes as he goes away with Gentle Annie, I yearn over him! And now that his friend is gone for the time being we've more responsibility . . . will you see Miss Symington, Nik, or shall I?"

"I think I'd better. I've promised to go with her to Edinburgh to choose clothes—isn't it good of her to want me to help? I'll have lots of opportunities. But I don't think she will make any serious objection. It's a way out of the difficulty for her, and for us—— Oh, Mother, won't it be lovely? Let's plan now about his room. . . ."

CHAPTER XXXI

"Oh isna she verra weel aff
To be woo't an' mairrit an' a'?"

Scots Song.

Events worked out even as Nicole had predicted. Barbara wrote to her aunt from Langlands saying that she had promised to marry Andrew Jackson. It was not an ecstatic letter, indeed there was a sort of gravity about it that made Lady Jane wonder, and hope that Barbara was not marrying for any but the one reason. She questioned Nicole. "She cares for him, you think?"

Nicole reassured her. "She certainly cares for him. Rutherfurd matters to her too, of course, but it comes a long way behind Andrew Jackson. Have no doubts, Mums. Happiness is rather startling, you know. She would be but little happy, if she could say how much. When is she coming home?"

Lady Jane returned to the letter. "Wednesday, she says. I'll write at once."

"So shall I, but I'll send a wire with our love first thing. Is there a form there? Christina will fly with it."

Barbara came back and was petted and made much of to her heart's content, and it was a changed Barbara, softened, warmed, willing even to see good in Kirkmeikle now that she was leaving it.

"Why, Babs," Nicole cried, "I believe you're quite interested in Miss Symington's approaching nuptials? You and she seemed to be having quite a heart-to-heart talk. Own she isn't so intolerable as you used to find her."

Barbara laughed rather shamefacedly. "I own I was a cantankerous creature, but it does make such a difference to know I'm only sojourning here, not tied, not caged. Now I can see all the good points both in the place and the people. I never would admit they had any, would I?"

Nicole agreed that it was easy to be a sojourner. "Then you haven't to be consistently pleasant, that's what gives people nervous breakdowns. But there's something else, Babs. Your whole outlook on life has changed. Happiness makes people wonderfully kind." And she lightly kissed the top of her cousin's head as she went out of the room.

It was arranged that the marriage would take place very quietly in the beginning of June in the Rutherfurd church, and afterwards at Kingshouse. Jean Douglas insisted that it should be so.

"After all," she wrote, "Fife is a *fremt* place, with which you have no links, whereas there isn't a soul in this countryside that won't be interested. You must all come to me for at least a week before. Thomas says that he can see that my fingers are itching to get started, and I must say I do like to manage things. Of course I know

172

you will want a quiet wedding, but you must have all your oldest friends. It's a most satisfactory marriage. Andrew Jackson is a thoroughly good sort, and Barbara will make the best of wives. I went to see Mrs. Jackson yesterday. She said she was very pleased—as well she might be! But I thought her rather quiet and dull. I daresay she feels giving up her only son. And she and her husband are going back to Glasgow, so she told me. Probably a wise step, but I can't help feeling sorry. I shall miss her. I've got a sincere liking for her, and I could listen for hours to her conversation. I shall miss her, too, at the Nursing Meetings. It always cheered me to meet her shrewd eyes and exchange a furtive smile; she and I shared many jokes. . . . By the way, I've just heard that the Bothwells are giving up their delicious little house: it would be so beautifully perfect for you and Nikky. Leave your old Harbour House and your sea-mews and come back to your own country-side. . . . But of this more anon——"

It was all arranged about the Bat. Miss Symington had protested, had taken council with Samuel, and finally accepted Lady Jane's offer. If she had qualms about it she salved her conscience with the assurance that she was really doing a good turn to poor Lady Jane. "And the keep of a child doesn't amount to much," she told herself, "and father left him enough to pay for his education, so he won't be much expense."

She told Alastair one morning at breakfast.

"You know, Alastair," she said, "that I'm going to be married to Mr. Innes and live in Edinburgh?"

"Yes," said Alastair, polite, but uninterested.

"And Lady Jane has kindly asked you to come and live with her."

Alastair's hand holding a bit of bread and butter was suspended in mid-air while he fixed his eyes on his aunt's face.

"To live? To take my pyjamas and my tooth-brush and sleep at the Harbour House, not come back here at all?"

"No, of course you won't come back here. This house will be shut up."

"And Annie?"

"Yes, Annie's to go with you, though you're far too big a boy to have a nurse —— Where are you going?"

Alastair was scrambling from his chair. "I'm going to tell Annie," he said.

"Nonsense, you haven't finished your breakfast. . . . Are you so glad to be going to the Harbour House that you can't wait?"

"Yes," said Alastair.

"Aren't you sorry to leave me and leave Ravenscraig?"

Alastair got rather pink and said "Yes" without much conviction.

"Run away then," said his aunt, and to herself she said rather bitterly: "Unfeeling, like his father before him."

Miss Symington had decided recklessly to defy superstition and be married in May. Samuel wished to attend the General Assembly of his church, so it was on the last day of the sitting of that august body that Janet stood up in the Caledonian Station Hotel to become Mrs. Innes.

It was an exciting time in Kirkmeikle with preparations for two weddings, and it is doubtful if Mrs. Heggie had ever been quite so happy. All barriers went down before her kindly interest, and she trotted—no, that is not the word to describe this large, hearty lady, rather she sailed, like some old-fashioned vessel with all sails set, between Ravenscraig and the Harbour House, inspecting each present as it arrived, gloating over the soft stuffs and fine lace of the two trousseaux.

Miss Symington's presents were rather scanty, for she had few friends and fewer relations, but Samuel and his connections had risen to the occasion, and Janet was more than satisfied. Her expression became positively smug, so much so that Mrs. Heggie, calling one evening at the Harbour House on the chance of seeing anything that was to be seen, said:

"I never in my life saw anybody so changed as Miss Symington."

"Changed?" Lady Jane lifted her eyebrows questioningly.

"In every way," said Mrs. Heggie. "A year ago you wouldn't have seen a duller or more dejected figure. I used often to say to Joan that she was a typical old maid. Always neat and tidy, you know, but just a person you looked at once and then looked away. And her conversation! It wasn't there! Fond as I am of tea-parties, I quite dreaded going to tea with her. I had to bear the whole brunt of the conversation. Not," Mrs. Heggie chuckled, "that that was any real effort to me, for I'm a great talker, but you can understand it wasn't very interesting. And her house was as depressing as herself. With all her money I don't think she ever had a luxury. Luxury! She was so busy looking for waste that she hardly gave the household proper food. Of course she did give away a lot to deserving charities, and worked away herself on all sorts of committees, and went to meetings, but, I may be wrong, it never seemed to me that she did it for the love of it. It was all duty with Miss Symington, and duty's a cold thing. I never heard of her being a comfort to any one in trouble, or doing an impulsively kind thing, and perhaps at heart she's still the same, but what a difference on the outside! You could have knocked me down with a feather the first time I went to call after I saw the workmen had left, and the curtains were up. Joan said the drawing-room reminded her of *Hassan*—that's a play, you know—and Miss Symington herself with her hair brought forward over her ears (I couldn't have believed she had such pretty, soft hair for she wore it scraped back, indeed she always reminded me of the man who shaved his beard, saying, 'A' face that wull be face!'), and a dress of soft brown with some colour about it to warm it! I tell you I almost forgot my manners and said, 'My dear, what have you done to yourself?'—It was like a transformation scene. I wonder what put it into her head. Joan says she must always have been in love with Mr. Innes and that this was a last effort to attract him—but I don't know. Joan writes, you see, and literary people have queer notions about things, besides, Miss Symington was too nice-minded to want to attract.— What do you think, Miss Rutherfurd?"

That young woman was sitting in one of the window-seats showing Mrs. Lambert a beautiful book which had just come for Barbara, between intervals of listening to Mrs. Heggie's conversation. Barbara, in another window-seat, was sewing a fine seam.

"Oh," said Nicole, "to my way of thinking there's nothing actively immoral

174

about trying to make oneself attractive, but you'd be safer to ask Mrs Lambert." She turned to her friend. "What do you think?"

Mrs. Lambert's face flushed as she said:

"I think it's only right for every woman, young or old, to look as attractive as possible, but, dear me! it's terribly difficult when you're busy all day and at night simply long to tumble into bed. For making yourself attractive takes time, hair brushing, and attending to your hands, and keeping your skin smooth. And in the morning one is so apt to twist up one's hair anyhow and run, when there's the breakfast waiting to be made, and the children to bath and dress, and the whole house depending on you to freshen it up for the day! But deliberately to make oneself attractive for an object doesn't seem to me quite nice, and I don't believe Miss Symington ever had such an idea. I think she was immensely surprised herself when Mr. Innes asked her to marry him."

"What kind of man is he?" Lady Jane asked.

"Quite a personable man to look at," Mrs. Heggie said, and Mrs. Lambert put in, "John says he's a good man."

"I'm glad to hear it," said Nicole, "for 'John' ought to know: he's a very good man himself. D'you know what I'm going to start in Kirkmeikle?—a society for speaking ill of our neighbours. It's perfectly ridiculous the way every one says only nice things about every one else, and *thinks* them, too—that's the worst of it. It's so *dull*."

Mrs. Heggie laughed appreciatively. "You'd like our old cook. She smooths her apron and begins. 'I suppose . . .' and tells you the most terrible tales of every one. And there's not a word of truth in them, that's the best of it."

"Or the worst of it!" said Nicole.

"Oh, I don't know," Mrs. Heggie said. "I don't like to have to think ill of anybody." Then in a stage whisper. . . . "Any more presents, Miss Burt?" and Barbara in her new kindness and patience smiled at her and offered to take her up to see what had come lately.

"Let's all go," said Nicole, and they all went.

A large unoccupied bedroom had been given over to Barbara for her dresses and presents, and very delightful it looked that evening to the visitors, with the spring sun pouring in through a west window on tables stacked with offerings.

Among many rare and lovely things there was the usual pile of silversmith's boxes containing tea-knives and spoons, toast-racks and sugar-sifters, ink-pots and paper-knives, mustard and pepper-pots complete with salt-cellars.

"What you're going to do with them all, Babs, I know not," Nicole said, "because it isn't as if you were starting a house. Rutherfurd's stocked with everything."

Barbara shook her head. "Most of them will remain in the silver chest, I'm afraid."

"It's extraordinary," said Lady Jane, "how one's mind goes when one starts out to buy a present. There are so many things to give, but everything at the moment is forgotten, and I can think of nothing but silver candlesticks or an inkstand—and I

175

hate both, and always use glass candlesticks and ink-pots. But you've been lucky, Barbara, getting so many really charming things. Show Mrs. Heggie the old Waterford glasses you got to-day, and the painted tray, and the lovely lace dinner-set, and the lacquer table."

Mrs. Heggie gloated over everything, patting the things for pure pleasure.

"I do like my Kirkmeikle presents," said Barbara. "I mean to use your tea-caddy every single day, Mrs. Lambert. See how beautifully it goes with this tray and the Worcester cups! And your present, Mrs. Heggie, just speaks of comfort."

"Like Mrs. Heggie herself," put in Nicole.

The present in question was an eider-down quilt, large, thick, lustrous.

"It's a homely sort of gift," Mrs. Heggie said, as she proudly eyed her offering displayed over the end of the bed, "but useful."

"*Very*," said Barbara. "This Chinese panel is from the Bucklers. Isn't it a nice splash of colour?"

"Everything's perfect," sighed Mrs. Heggie, "but are we not to have a chance of seeing Mr. Jackson himself?"

"Oh, I hope so," Lady Jane said, "but we've been meeting in Edinburgh as a half-way house. Andrew is very busy just now, as you may suppose. I met him for the first time last week and was delighted with my new nephew. . . . Shall we go downstairs now?"

It was a beautiful day, Janet's wedding-day, very clear and golden, and as Nicole walked towards the Caledonian Hotel from her Club where she had been lunching, she thought that never did Edinburgh look so well as on a bright May afternoon.

It was the last day of the Assemblies and Princes Street was full of black-coated figures hurrying to catch trains that would take them back to their different homes. Some were well dressed, with glossy silk hats, and walked importantly, looking as if they had flourishing congregations and were frequently mentioned in the *British Weekly* as outstanding preachers. Some looked rather shabby and careworn; these Nicole judged to be men who had a hard row to hoe, and she hoped they had warm, kind homes to go back to, and understanding wives to give them a welcome.

One man she noticed in particular, a thin little man with a travelling-bag in one hand, and several parcels in the other, parcels of which she thought she could guess the contents. The flat one was a book from Andrew Elliot's for the minister himself, the oblong parcel in white paper was Ferguson's Edinburgh rock for the children, and the thick package was cake from Mackie's, good rich cake that his careful wife would put away in a crock, and which would come out to grace several tea-parties. Nicole looked very kindly at the little hurrying figure, and amused herself picturing the reception he and his parcels would get when they arrived at home.

Nicole was invited alone to the wedding, indeed it was rather a concession that she was there at all, for only relatives were supposed to be present, but Janet had made a point of her being there.

"I'll feel safer," she said, "if I know you're there. It's not as if I know

176

Samuel's relations at all intimately, and I know they'll be there to criticise. When I come into the room I'll look at you, and if you give a nod, I'll know I'm looking all right."

Nicole was prepared to enjoy everything, and when she was taken to a large room half-full of people she looked about at once for some one she knew. She found they were all strangers to her except Mr. and Mrs. Lambert, who were at the other end of the room. With them was Alastair, resplendent in a new white man-of-war suit, but wearing a subdued expression.

No one seemed quite to know whether they ought to behave as if they were in a church or not, but the social atmosphere was so chilly that to warm it Nicole began at once to talk to the people on either side of her, though she had never seen them before, and they evinced no desire to become better acquainted with her.

Some one at the piano broke into a wedding-march, and the two ministers, with Samuel and his best man, moved into position, and Janet came in on the arm of her uncle, an aged and confirmed hypochondriac who lived in complete seclusion, but who had been forcibly resurrected for the occasion by his strong-minded niece.

The eyes of the bride sought her friend, and Nicole gave her a radiant nod, and indeed Janet had never looked so well in her life. Samuel, in a frock-coat, seemed to think so, for his smile was more unctuous than ever.

Mr. Lambert, looking acutely miserable, assisted by the bridegroom's minister, married them, and the short, unadorned service was soon over.

"It doesn't take long to do a great deed," a chinless young man remarked solemnly, and Nicole laughed suddenly.

Seeing that there was no chance of getting near the bride and bridegroom yet awhile, she made her way to where the Lamberts were sitting and soon had Alastair supremely happy drinking lemonade through a straw.

Mr. Lambert had gone to look for tea for his wife, and appeared with a cup which was mostly slopped into the saucer.

"John's no use at a wedding," Mrs. Lambert said sadly. "Just look how Mr. Robson is making everyone laugh!"

She cast a rebuking glance at her husband who said stiffly, "I see no p-point in being facetious at a wedding."

"Well, if you can't be facetious, be useful, and get Miss Rutherfurd some tea." But Nicole thought it wiser to make her own way to the buffet, and there she enjoyed an excellent meal.

She shook hands with the newly-wed couple and was introduced to the stepdaughters. They talked for a little, and she liked them, they were good laughers and quite unaffected, and she felt that unless Janet erred grossly the household at Morningside should go fairly smoothly.

The bride moved up to Nicole. "Well?" she said.

"Splendid. You look quite, quite charming, and everything has gone off so well. They have done things nicely, haven't they? Such good cakes and ices!"

Janet looked round complacently. "Quite. Quite. And it's such a blessing it's a good day. A nice-looking lot of people, don't you think? Practically all Samuel's relations."

"Yes, and I like your stepdaughters. Give them a good time, Miss—*Mrs.* Innes!"

Janet nodded. "I'll do my best for them, you may be sure. I'm going to change now. We're leaving about four—*motoring to Crieff,*" the last in a hoarse whisper.

When the bride and bridegroom departed amid a little genteel throwing of confetti and many good wishes, Nicole stood looking after the departing car. "I *hope* they'll be happy," she thought, "and anyway, they've done us a good turn." She held the hand of the Bat and smiled down at his small upturned face on which content lay like a sunbeam. He was going back that very night to the Harbour House. Gentle Annie was there already with all his belongings, and it seemed to the child that life was now going to be like a fairy-tale come true.

CHAPTER XXXII

"You to your land and love and great allies."
As You Like It.

The Harbour House was in a state of pleasant turmoil until the wedding was over.

To Alastair it seemed as if Paradise had opened its gates to him. There was no time to think of lessons, so he and Gentle Annie spent hectic days flying backwards and forwards to the Post Office with parcels and telegrams, and two days of pure bliss helping the man who came from Edinburgh to pack the precious things safely. Alastair was hopelessly at sea about the reason for the preparations, and when he heard Christina talk of "Miss Barbara's bridegroom" he said, "Oh, so she's going to marry Mr. Innes too?" the word "bridegroom" suggesting to him only the frock-coated Samuel.

"I daursay no," said Christina, tossing her head in an affronted way. "Miss Barbara's mairryin' a braw young man."

An anxious frown puckered Alastair's brow. "But, Christina," he said, "where'll we find him? Will he be walking about?"

Christina laughed. "Oh, she's fand him richt eneuch! . . . Eh, I'd like fine to gang to Rutherfurd to see the weddin'! . . . It's sic a bonnie wee kirk, an' a' green an' quait aboot it; an' the windays are clear, a' but the big yin at the end, an' ye can see the sheep feedin' on the knowes sae canny-like. I dinna like thae stained-gless windays!"

Alastair looked interested. "Church can't be so bad," he said, "when you can see out, not so like being in prison. . . . Tell me more about Rutherfurd."

"Och," said Christina, polishing a glass—they were together in the pantry —"I'm nae guid at describin' things. Ye'll see it for yersel', for I heard Miss Nicole sayin' that Mistress Douglas hed askit ye to Kingshouse. It's a braw bit, I can tell ye, ye've naething like it aboot here.—But it's a' different yonder. The roadsides are fu' o' flowers, buttercups, and ragged robbin, and crawfit, an' they smell sae bonnie. And on the hill-sides ye find wee yella pansies, an' thyme, an' heather bells, an' whiles"— she nodded her head at the Bat—"an' *whiles* ye git a deil's snuff-box."

"Ooh! What is it, Christina?"

"They're brown things juist like wee bags, an' when ye squeeze them stuff like snuff comes oot."

Alastair drew a long breath, and presently asked, "And is there a sea?"

"Na" Christina pursed up her lips and shook her head. "There's nae sea, but we can easy dae wantin't, we've sic fine burns gaun joukin' through the heather and loupin' ower linns. Whaur ma hame is there's a burn juist at the back door, an' a brig, a wee wudden brig wi' steps up an' doon, an' there's a muckle flat stane whaur ma mither kneels when she taks oot the pots an' pans to scour them in the pool. An' mony a time I've guddled under the stanes—ye ken ye lie doon on the bank an' pit baith yir haunds verra cautious roond a stane, an' whiles ye catch a troot."

"Yes. Arthur catches trouts with a fishing-rod: he told me. They're like poddlies, aren't they?"

"Poddlies! Na. They're a faur higher breed o' fish. They've brown backs, an' they're speckled wi' red and white, an' the big yins lie in the pools an' lauch at ye, but the wee yin's are easy catch't, bein' innocent."

Christina put the silver forks and spoons carefully into the baize-lined basket and Alastair sat watching her.

"Christina," he said, "why did you leave your home at Rutherfurd?"

"Deed ... I whiles speir that masel! But ma mither said, 'Gang wi' her leddyship, Christina,' an' then, ye see, I was betterin' masel. An' I like Kirkmeikle no' that bad, and her leddyship and Miss Nicole tell us a' the news they hear aboot hame, an' there's auld Betsy Curle aye gled to crack aboot it—but I wadna settle here. Na. Ma laud's at Rutherfurd. He's a mole-catcher."

Alastair gasped. The fascinating and unusual things they did in that wonderful place that was called Rutherfurd—guddling, and mole-catching, and looking for "deil's snuff-boxes"!

"Ay, an' when we've gethered eneuch we'll get mairrit—aboot the New Year I wad like it to be, I've aye a notion to be mairrit then—an' live in a wee hoose beside a burn. I ken the yin I want, an' it'll mebbe be empty when we're ready for't."

"And is there a flat stone for you to kneel and scrape your pots?"

Christina laughed. "Ye're a queer bairn. Ay, I'll see to that, for I maun keep a'thing terrible clean. I'll hae nae siller forks an' spunes an' tea-pots, but I'll scrub ma tables white, an' aye hae a tidy fireside an' a warm denner for ma man."

"It'll be lovely, Christina; and will Barbara do that when she's married?"

Christina laughed in rather a shocked way, and sketched for Alastair the sort of life "Miss Barbara" would lead, with motors and balls and troops of servants.

To Alastair it sounded deplorably dull.

"She wont have half such good fun as you'll have, Christina. But I don't suppose there are many mole-catchers to marry ... Could I be a bridegroom, Christina?"

"Oh ay, some day."

"Then I'll marry Annie."

"Ye'll change yer tüne or then, ma man!" Christina said, as she folded away the dusters. "Awa' noo an' find Annie, for I'm gaun to lay the lunch."

When everything was more or less packed and they were ready for the removal to Kingshouse for the wedding, Barbara went with Nicole after tea one evening to pay farewell calls.

"Isn't it odd," she said as they mounted the brae, "how quickly a place takes hold of one? Only eight months ago we had never heard of Kirkmeikle or any of its people, and now we're bound to them by ties of kindness and sympathy—they *have* been decent to me at this time."

"My dear," Nicole reminded her, "eight months ago we had hardly heard of the Jacksons, and now——"

It was odd to see Ravenscraig shut up, and Barbara expressed a hope that all went well with Mr. and Mrs. Innes at Crieff.

Nicole laughed. "I do hope so. I can't think why that sober and well-reasoned union should seem to me so farcical. I do wonder how that household will work!"

In the Knebworth drawing-room Mrs. Heggie archly asked Nicole when they were to have the pleasure of presenting her with a wedding present.

"Surely," she said, "you're not going to let Miss Symington beat you, as I tell Joan."

Joan sat with a disgusted face, in a window, looking down at the sun on the pansies that filled a plot just beneath her, and to change the subject, Nicole turned to her and said:

"I was just thinking as we passed Ravenscraig that you should write a story about Miss Symington's marriage, or rather about the household after the marriage; Samuel and his two daughters and the house in Morningside with a basement. Wouldn't it make an interesting study, Miss Heggie?"

"It ought," said Joan. "But why don't you try it yourself, Miss Rutherfurd? You must have gained such an insight into the lives of villa residents in the last few months that you should be quite competent to do it. . . . It would be rather interesting if we both did it, and I'm quite sure no one would recognise it as the same household. Yours would be such a sweet picture of family life, you would throw a glamour and a charm over these exceedingly ordinary people and transfigure even the basement. Mine would be a merciless study: I would enjoy doing it. I wouldn't leave a rag on Samuel, and I'd lay bare the barren recesses of Janet Symington's soul."

Mrs. Heggie clicked with her tongue in a shocked way and murmured—"Did you ever hear the like?" Nicole laughed aloud.

"I believe that's a very true picture of what my attempt would be. Somebody once told me that I was meant to be satirical but that I varnished all my statements over with so many coats of the milk of human kindness that they became without form and void! But I don't believe in your 'merciless study' either. You know and I know that Samuel is no villain, but a decent dull man, a little puffed up with conceit about his gifts as a speaker, but honestly striving to do some good. His wife is a good sincere limited woman——. Let live. What's the good of being clever and merciless? But I admit that may be sour grapes on my part, for I couldn't be either if I tried!"

"And this is really good-bye?" said Mrs. Heggie, who was much more anxious to discuss details of the wedding than to talk of cleverness. "When d'you go?"

"To-morrow!" said Barbara, "to-morrow as ever was. I can hardly believe that I'm really leaving Kirkmeikle for good and going back to my old home. It will be nice having the few quiet days at Kingshouse before the wedding, and it won't mean such a rush for my aunt; but it has been a business deciding what is to be sent to Kingshouse and what will go direct to Rutherfurd. I'm quite prepared to find we've confused everything and that my wedding gown and my cousin's dress will arrive here after we've left."

"Oh, I hope not. What's Miss Nicole to wear?"

"Blush pink, and a very pretty head-dress of pink rose-buds, and roses in her hand—I wanted her to look like a rose at my June wedding."

Mrs. Heggie nodded agreement. "And I'll mebbe see the dress later on . . . What about the cake?"

"The cake? Oh, it's going straight to Kingshouse. We're having an extra tier to please Andrew's mother. She wants all the people on the place to have a good slice, and she and Mr. Jackson are giving a supper and dance on the night of the wedding at Rutherfurd."

"Very nice. You're evidently fortunate in a mother-in-law, and I hear from Lady Jane that the parents are leaving the place to you young people at once. That's very wise, I think, and unselfish. What? Are you going already? It was good of you to spare the time—— Well, I can only wish you health and happiness. . . ."

There was something wistful in her face which made Nicole say, "I wish you had been coming to the wedding, Mrs. Heggie, but I'll tell you every single detail when I get back, and take snapshots for your special benefit of the happy pair."

As they made their way to Lucknow Nicole said:

"I rather think that Mrs. Heggie and her daughter are inclined to get on each other's nerves to-day. Poor Mrs. Heggie would so love to have a daughter who was going to be married, a nice, pretty, come-at-able daughter, who would sit beside her and make *crêpe-de-Chine* camisoles and talk about really interesting things like clothes and weddings and cooks, and instead, she has the plain-faced Joan who affects to despise men and shuts herself up in a room and writes. And Joan, I am sure, realises this, and feeling that she falls short, gets bitter, and talks nonsense about 'merciless studies.' She doesn't like me much ('I don't blame her,' as the Bat said when I told him that Mrs. Fred Erskine had three little boys and no little girls!), and suspects me of taking an interest in Kirkmeikle people in order that I may laugh at them, which doesn't worry me at all, it's too far from the truth. . . . Now for the Shield and Buckler!"

Having received the parting blessing of the Bucklers, the Kilgours, and the Lamberts, Barbara thankfully turned her steps homewards, but her cousin begged her to tarry for a minute at Betsy Curle's.

"Five minutes, Babs, not a moment more. And she's so old and frail and crippled, and it would be such a joy to her."

But Betsy betrayed no sign of considering the visit a joy.

Her little room, which seemed cosy enough on a dark winter day, was stuffy and dark to come into from the shining June day outside, and she herself sitting crippled and helpless by a handful of fire, wrapped in a grey woollen shawl, seemed to belong to a different sphere to the two happy-eyed girls in their light summer frocks.

"I've come to say good-bye, Betsy," Barbara said, bending to her. "You know that I'm going to be married and going back to Rutherfurd."

"... Gaun back to Rutherfurd! It's guid to be you. I'll never gang back to Rutherfurd——"

Nicole broke in. "Nothing but marrying and giving in marriage, Betsy. First Miss Symington, now my cousin."

"Ay, I doot there wadna be muckle competeetion for Miss Symington, rich as she is. Never mairry for money, ye'll borrow it cheaper—that's a true sayin'."

"Why, Betsy, I don't believe you ever saw Miss Symington."

"I've heard plenty aboot her onyway, clippit cratur! Nae servant wud bide wi' her she was sae suspicious, oh—ay——"

"Well now, I want you to say something very nice to Miss Burt."

Betsy fixed her dim eyes on Barbara. "I wish ye weel, Miss Burt, but I wish a Rutherfurd hed been gaun back to Rutherfurd——"

Nicole hastily broke in: "You can't possibly say anything against Kirkmeikle in this weather, Betsy... It isn't cold and it isn't dirty, and just look at the sea to-night!"

"I dinna want to look at it," Betsy said. "I tell ye I dinna like it. It wasna for naething the Book said that the wicked were like the sea."

"Like a *troubled* sea, Betsy; to-night it's like the sea of glass mingled with fire. . . . Oh, Babs, I do hope we get a day like this next Wednesday. Rutherfurd kirk is perfect when the sun comes through the end window! You know it well, Betsy?"

"Rutherfurd kirk," said Betsy to herself, then to Nicole, "But ye'll no mind what it was like afore they spiled it? Na, it was lang afore ye were born. I sat in a sate under the poopit, an' the precentor, auld Jimmie Hislop, aye haunded ma faither his snuff-box afore the sermon sterted. An' in thae days they took up the collection in boxes wi' lang handles, an' ae day Dr. Forman forgot an intimation aboot some collection, an' he got up efter to gie it oot. Adam Welsh, the beadle, was pokin' the box up the pews sae pushin' like, until the auld Doctor got fair provoked, and he cries, 'Stop, Adam, that's just what I'm talking about.' . . . Aye, they spiled the kirk when they took oot a' the auld straight-backed sates an' pit in new wide yins. Tam Moffat, the shepherd, awa' up Harehope Glen, he juist cam' the yince efter the alterations. 'I canna find ma sate,' he said; 'it was in that sheugh by the poopit an' it's gane,' an' oot he walkit."

The two girls laughed, and Barbara said:

"But, Betsy, Rutherfurd kirk is still bonnie. You'll wish me well when I stand there next Wednesday, won't you?"

Betsy looked at the bright face bent to hers, and smiled a little grudging smile. "Ay," she said, "I wull that, but ye're gettin' a lot o' this warld's guid, an' mind —a full cup's ill to cairry!"

The sun did shine through the end window in Rutherfurd kirk when Barbara stood up beside Andrew Jackson. It fell on the bride tall and straight and beautiful in her wedding gown, on Nicole's rose-crowned head as she stood with serious eyes, listening to Mr. Scott's precise voice as he talked of the duties of the married state, on Lady Jane dreaming of days that were gone, on the Bat enjoying the rapturous present.

Though Nicole looked so intent it is doubtful if she heard a word the minister said. She was imagining another wedding, a quiet ceremony in a bleak little church by the sea, with no guests to speak of, and no parade. John Lambert to marry her, a few friends round her who really cared, and were glad in her happiness—then to go away with Simon. She crushed the roses in her hands as she thought of it. Would it ever be?

It was the prettiest of weddings. Every one said so. A young and happy couple in a perfect garden, in June sunshine—it was roses, roses all the way.

And it was all so beautifully managed. When Jean Douglas entertained there was no crowding, no dull waiting, no luke-warm tea or tepid ices. There was an abundance of little tables placed in the shade, with steady chairs to sit on, the sandwiches were of every variety, and all appetising, the cakes fresh and crisp, the strawberries were abundant, the cream sweet, the sugar within every one's reach. And as always happened at Kingshouse, people found the people they most wanted to talk to miraculously beside them, so that there was that look of content on the faces of the guests that makes any gathering a success.

Mrs. Jackson was resplendent. Andrew had not had the heart to restrain his mother on this occasion, and for once she felt herself really smart. Her dress, which she would have told you was of 'champagne shade,' was most wonderfully embroidered. Over it she wore a coat also of 'champagne,' and a large hat covered with paradise plumes. Her shoes, which were of the same pale shade, were so tight that her feet seemed to bulge out of them; she carried a bouquet of orchids.

Mrs. Douglas and Nicole saw to it that every possible attention was paid to her. The Duke, who happened to be paying one of his infrequent visits to the neighbourhood, had ten minutes conversation with her on the lawn and Mrs. Jackson was happily aware that she was the cynosure of all eyes.

When the guests were beginning to depart, Nicole missed her friend, and after some searching found her in a corner of the deserted drawing-room. She had last seen her smiling bravely and waving her bouquet after the newly-married couple as they drove away, but now dejection was in every line of her and Nicole saw that large tears were rolling over the flushed face, tears that she was making no effort to deal with. And as Nicole looked, a deep depression that she had been grappling with all day rose up and conquered her so that she went up to the fat homely figure, so smart in 'champagne shade,' and, laying her head on the broad bosom, she too began to cry. Mrs. Jackson's arms went round her and she at once roused herself to try and comfort.

"There, there. Don't you cry, my dear. You're my girl, and always will be. . . . Never you mind. There's good fish in the sea. . . . You'll be the next bride, and my! you'll be the bonnie one!"

But Nicole shook her rose-crowned head, and said, "Who knows?"

Then they both sat up and mopped their faces, and laughed a little.

"I don't like weddings," said Mrs. Jackson, sniffing. "I sometimes think a funeral's cheerier, but what can you say? People will always marry. . . . And this is a sort of end of things to me, if you know what I mean. It's the end of Andy as my boy, the end of our life together. Father and I'll just be left like two paling stabs!"

"What nonsense!" Nicole said. "Andy will be more to you than ever, you'll see. Barbara would never want to take a man away from his mother. And you will pay them long visits and see that they do things as you would like them done. And they'll visit you in your new house. . . ."

"Well, we've got a nice house. Here, listen, will you come and stay with us some time? That would be something to look forward to."

"Indeed, I'd love to. And you'll give tea-parties for me, won't you? and show me all the sights? Oh, believe me, dear Mrs. Jackson, I know very well what you must be feeling just now, but you'll look back on this day as one of the happiest days of your life."

Mrs. Jackson straightened her hat, gave her face a rub with her handkerchief, and said, "Mebbe I will. I'm sure I hope so. Now, I must find Father and go away home."

"Come and say good-bye to Mother first. She will want to see you, I know"; and having deposited Mrs. Jackson beside Lady Jane, Nicole went to look for Mr. Jackson and found him wandering lonely as a cloud. She also collected Jean Douglas, so that when the couple drove away back to Rutherfurd they were tucked into their car by friendly hands and sent away a good deal comforted.

CHAPTER XXXIII

"Farewell:
  If we do meet again, why, we shall smile."

Julius Caesar.

Nicole sent her own account of the wedding to Simon:

I feel that I am scattering bread on the waters when I write these letters, and when I watch them slide down the brass maw of the post-office I wonder if it is possible that they will ever reach you. But, anyway I must go on, for writing to you is my one comfort.

We have just got home again, all the excitement of the wedding behind us. The nicest thing about the wedding-day to me was that that very morning I got a lovely thick letter from you, from Darjeeling. I should like to have done what all well-conducted young women in novels do, worn it next my heart. But I think that could only have been successfully done when people filled their clothes, or, to be exact, had clothes to fill! In the wisp of a dress I wore as bridesmaid—blush pink, Simon, with roses round my hair!—there was nothing to hold a letter in its place next my heart, it would simply have slipped through and got lost; but anyway, I thought of you all the time.

It really was a very pretty wedding. Barbara never in her life looked so well, and I was proud to stand behind her and contemplate the grace of her bearing. And Andrew Jackson looked so nice, and listened with such a serious good face to Mr. Scott's homily. I'm afraid I didn't listen much. I was thinking if it had been our wedding-day—Simon—Simon.

All our old friends were there, and Jean Douglas had spared no pains to have everything perfect. I was so thankful Providence seconded her efforts by sending a good day.

Mrs. Jackson was gorgeous in apparel, and seemed in tremendous spirits, very jocose—embarrassingly so—and quite the life of the company. But towards the end I missed her, and discovered her alone in the drawing-room crying quietly. I was so sorry for her—or was it only that I was sorry for myself?—that I sat down beside her and we mingled our tears!

We are settled in the Harbour House until August, when we go to Lochbervie, away up in the North, where Bice Dennis has a small place. It will be fun for the Bat to be with Arthur again, and there is a smaller boy, Barnabas, who will make an excellent companion for him. Alastair—he prefers to be called "The Bat" because it was your name for him—is really in great form. I think you would know a lot of difference in him. He has lost that repressed look (indeed he is getting quite upsetting!) but he still has the small concerned face and anxious blue eyes. He and I are reading just now all sorts of books on mountaineering, Whymper's *Ascent of the Matterhorn*, and Sir Martin Conway's books, trying to bring ourselves a step nearer to you! The Bat has almost decided to adopt mountaineering as his profession in life, but he is also allured by the thought of being a mole-catcher. Christina's "lad," he tells me, is a mole-catcher, and he regards it as an ideal life.

It is a queer Kirkmeikle now with Ravenscraig shut up, and no tall figure going in and out of Miss Jamieson's. Looking back on last winter it seems to me that I ought to have been ideally happy. You were here. I saw you nearly every day. You sat in this room and we talked. I can't think why I wasn't down on my knees, thanking Heaven fasting.

Do you remember that day we were in St. Andrews with the two boys? I think of that day so often. Why is it that some days shine out like gold among dross? The sea was grey, and the sky was grey, and we stood among grey ruins and looked at tombstones. Then we sat together in a cinema and laughed at the Bat. Not very much to remember perhaps, but I was happy, happy.

Your letter from Darjeeling cheered me a good deal. I had been dwelling too much on the grim side of the Expedition, on the danger, the hardships, and had forgotten how much fun there must be in it. All you tell me about the porters, and the humour and the cheerfulness of every one heartens me. It is a great adventure. I am counting that when this letter reaches you the attempt will have been made. Perhaps you will be in Darjeeling on your way home. . . .

It was an odd life Nicole lived at this time, filling in the hours with small domestic cares—she had taken on Barbara's housekeeping, visiting, helping Alastair with his lessons and playing with him, while all the time her mind was filled with thoughts of the Expedition that would now be wending its way towards the eternal ramparts of snow where Everest waited.

Barbara wrote very happily from Venice. They were having a leisurely trip and did not mean to be home before August.

Mrs. Jackson was having Rutherfurd swept and garnished preparatory to leaving it. The new villa which she had christened—surprisingly—"The Borders" was now ready for them. She wrote that it had every known comfort and labour-saving device, and was furnished straight out of Wylie and Lochhead's show-rooms. Everything was as new and as bright-coloured as possible. "Because," said Mrs. Jackson, "there is always Rutherfurd to show that we have taste; here we go in for pure comfort." She had renewed her interrupted friendship with Mrs. McArthur who, glad at signs of returning sanity, had been graciously pleased to hold out an olive branch in the shape of an invitation to stay with her while the furniture was being put in "The Borders."

"And I know now," Mrs. Jackson said to her husband, "what the Prodigal Son felt like, even to the veal, which we had three days running. And I never could abide veal—calves are such nice wee beasts."

The *Times* began to print despatches from the Everest Expedition. The sight of the large type heading brought Nicole's heart to her throat, and it was always some time before she could steady her voice to read them aloud to her mother and the Bat.

One morning a letter came from Simon describing the beginnings of the journey. It finished with: "I feel oddly happy, a care-free happiness that I haven't felt since I was a boy setting off with my father and brothers for a long day on the moors. Since the War I have felt so old, but I've suddenly been able to recapture if not the 'first fine careless rapture,' at least something remarkably like it. And this time I'm enjoying every bit of the way, savouring it, appreciating the beauty, and I feel confident as I never did before. Your face is with me always. I see it painted on the darkness as I lie in my tent at night, and in the day you seem to walk before me, just a little way before me, looking back and smiling, as you used to walk on the rocks at Kirkmeikle. God grant that we walk there again together."

That afternoon the *Times* was laid as usual on the oak chest in the hall. Nicole, coming in, carried it upstairs to read in the drawing-room, but her eagerness would not wait and she opened it as she went up the stairs. Yes, there was the large-type heading. She began to read and stopped. *Beckett* her eyes saw. Then—*Disaster —Beckett dead*.

She folded the paper carefully and laid it on the back of a sofa.

She was surprised to find herself standing upright for she felt bowed like an old woman. What had happened to her? Then the knowledge that Simon was gone pierced her heart like a sword, and in her pain she ran to the window for air. She looked down at her hands which unconsciously she had been twisting together and said to herself, "That must be what people do when they talk about wringing their hands. I'm wringing my hands for Simon." She felt numb now, with that merciful numbness which comes for a little after the first sword-thrust. Hardly knowing what she did she went downstairs and out of the house. The sea was lying blue and still. Over the rocks she went to the seat that was like a throne, where she and Simon had gone hand in hand. What had he said in his letter this morning. *God grant that we walk there again together.* Poor Simon. Poor Nicole. They would never walk anywhere together again. It was very sad, she knew, but it seemed far away from her as she sat idly picking up little stones and throwing them into the shining summer sea.

How long she sat there she did not know. A step behind her on the rocks made her leap to her feet, every pulse in her body bounding, a wild, unreasoning hope in her heart. She half-turned, and was confronted by Mr. Lambert.

"This is a good place to enjoy a perfect evening, Miss Rutherfurd," he said, seating himself beside her.

She looked at him in silence for a minute, and when she spoke he hardly knew her voice, so jangled and harsh were the sweet notes of it.

"I've just read in the papers that Simon Beckett is dead." The words as she said them seemed to chill her very soul, and she shivered violently.

"But—are you sure? It wasn't in the morning papers."

"It may have been in the late editions." The *Times* gets the news first. But what does that matter? She turned impatiently and looked at him. "It's true, I tell you."

Mr. Lambert was staring at her, his funny little puckered face quite white, tears in his eyes. Was *he* crying for Simon when she had not shed a tear?

"Dear me," he said. "Dear me."

Presently he began to speak, as much to himself as to his companion.

"I had a great liking for Beckett, and a great respect. I couldn't help envying him his chances. It's a great end. . . ."

"What was the use of it?" Nicole asked wearily.

Mr. Lambert shook his head. "I don't know. How can we judge with our small scale of values. I only know that high endeavour such as this keeps the ordinary man from feeling that life is nothing but a sordid struggle for bread and butter, a sort of game of Beggar my Neighbour. It makes one think better of oneself and every one else. Each one says in his heart, 'Perhaps it is in me to do this great thing, given the opportunity,' and the very hope that we might act greatly makes us not so small."

His voice died away thoughtfully and the two sat looking out to sea together.

The human, halting, little man vaguely comforted Nicole, his voice seemed to melt a little of the ice that was round her heart.

Suddenly she asked, "Do you suppose God means anything by it at all?"

The minister was silent for a minute, then he said:

"Some day you will answer that question yourself. I don't dare to try."

"Tell me one thing, do you honestly believe that there is another life, where we shall know each other again?"

"I can only give you Christ's own words, *I go to prepare a place for you.*"

"How glibly you say it! It's your job, of course, to preach that, but you're a good man and you wouldn't lie to me. Tell me, *Does Christ really mean anything to you?*"

The minister took off his shabby felt hat and held it in both hands as he said, "I am His joyful slave, and He is my Lord and my God."

Dusk was beginning to fall when Nicole stumbled into the Harbour House, into the arms of her mother.

"Simon is dead, mother. I loved him, but I didn't tell you . . ." Then the tears came.

And Lady Jane cried, "My dear, my dear, do you think your mother didn't know?"

CHAPTER XXXIV

"Nae living man I'll love again,
   Since that my comely knight is slain;
   Wi' ae lock of his yellow hair
   I'll chain ma hert for evermair."

The Border Widow's Lament.

It was October again in Kirkmeikle.

The ill-fated attempt on Everest was long since forgotten except by the few. For a day or two the papers had been full of it, and some people had preached the gospel of high endeavour, and the value such gallant attempts had in giving prestige to Britain among nations that did not hesitate to call us effete, others blaming such reckless throwing away of life. But it mattered little what anyone thought or said to Nicole as she battled among waves of despair that seemed as if they must overwhelm her. In time, because her heart was high, she won her way through to quiet waters and a measure of peace.

She and her mother, with the Bat, had been away for three months, first in Ross-shire, then in Surrey, and had just got back to the Harbour House.

On their way from the South they had spent a couple of nights at Rutherfurd, and found Barbara reigning there in great dignity, a most calm and confident young matron. Andrew made a rather subdued husband. Barbara knew so very well what was best for him and told him so with such firmness that, liking a quiet life, he nearly always acquiesced. It was odd to see her so entirely head of the house. She talked of "my" house, "my" car, "my" gardeners, until Nicole longed to make a face at her and beg her to desist.

They had two days at Rutherfurd, and every minute was planned out for them. Lady Jane, who would have enjoyed wandering about the place, and going quietly in and out among her old friends in the cottages, was told at breakfast:

"I knew, Aunt Jane, that you would want to go to Langlands, so I rang up and suggested ourselves for luncheon to-day. Then I thought we would go on to tea at the Kilpatricks, and it seemed such a good opportunity to work off some of the people I owe, so I've asked some people to dine. Andrew, you have a meeting at St. Boswells, you remember, at twelve o'clock. I think you'd better lunch there and come on to tea at the Kilpatricks."

"But must I go to Langlands?" Nicole asked rebelliously.

Barbara looked surprised and said in her cool, crisp voice, "Of course you must do just as you like, but it wouldn't be very polite to such old friends as the Langlands to disregard their invitation."

"But it wasn't so much an invitation on their part as a suggestion on yours—

however, perhaps I'd better go. To-morrow I'll visit my old haunts."

"Yes," Barbara said, as she helped herself to marmalade, "you will have time for a nice walk to-morrow morning. We're going to Kingshouse to luncheon, and—I do hope you won't mind, Aunt Jane—I promised to take you to tea with the people who have bought Greenshaw. They've heard so much about you and Nicole they begged me to bring you. They're really not bad sort of people, very new and terribly rich, but not too obtrusive, and frightfully appreciative of Rutherfurd—I suppose that is what softened my heart to them. *Must* you go on Thursday?"

"I'm afraid we must," said Lady Jane.

"But why? There is nothing to hurry you back, surely?"

"We've been wandering for quite a long time, and I confess I'm longing to get back to our own little house. It's odd with what affection I think of it."

Barbara turned to her husband. "Think of it, Andrew, hurrying back from this to a tar-smelling, east-windy Fife village! I feel rather aggrieved. I can't understand it."

"Oh, I can," said Andrew, who was helping himself at the sideboard. "Naturally Lady Jane longs for her own place, and all her own things round her, and I thought the Harbour House the jolliest place I'd seen for a long time."

"Ah, but you should see it in winter," said Nicole. "Then you would say it was jolly, when the waves come rolling in, and the spray dashes against the windows, and the wind howls round the steep roof and whistles down the chimneys, and the logs burn blue, and we are all so close together, the little houses and ourselves. Your mother is coming to see us some day. I think she'll like it."

"Oh yes," said Barbara; "looking back it seems quite nice, but of course it was cramped," and she looked round her own spacious dining-room and sighed contentedly.

Nicole had a few words alone with Andrew before dinner on the evening before they left. They were standing under the picture of the "Queen of Hearts," and Nicole looked up at it and smiled.

"My Lovely Lady! How long ago it seems since I was at Rutherfurd last. So much has happened—you and Barbara settled here. . . ."

Andrew took a step nearer her. "Perhaps you won't like me speaking of it, but I wanted to tell you how sorry I was when I saw . . ."

"Yes . . . Simon didn't come back."

"It's awful for you," Andrew said, and as he said it remembered Barbara's words when she saw the news in the papers. "*Poor Simon Beckett*," she had said. "*You knew he was a great friend of Nicole's? Yes, it is sad for her, but Nicole manages to take everything so lightly, she will soon forget.*"

"Oh, I'll get through somehow," Nicole said. Then she put out her hand and grasped his. "Thank you, Andy."

As they set off next morning in the train to Edinburgh Nicole looked across at her mother and said, "Matrimony doesn't always improve people, does it, Mums?"

"Not always," Lady Jane said, and they let the subject drop.

Nicole had both yearned for and dreaded the return to Kirkmeikle, but once back she wondered how she had been able to stay away so long. To her it was a place apart, this place that had known Simon. Here they had walked, and talked, and laughed; here they had loved and parted: to this little sea-looking town on the green brae had Simon's thoughts turned at the end.

And the Harbour House had lost nothing of its spell. Mrs. Martin, with Christina and Beenie, had on their return cleaned it from garret to basement so that it shone a welcome. And the Bat and Gentle Annie were glad to be back. Visiting was all very well, but this was home.

Mrs. Heggie had arrived almost at once to give them the news. She began before she was well into the room. "Ravenscraig's let—a family has taken it for a year. Sherwood is the name. Three servants, and nice-looking people; I'm longing to call and ask them to a meal, but Joan won't let me. She says I've got to give them time to settle down before I rush at them with invitations. Perfect nonsense I call it. It's always nice to give people a welcome early, don't you think so, Lady Jane?"

"I do indeed. And how is your daughter?"

"Quite well, thank you, but she's shingled her hair." Mrs. Heggie shook her head. "Not all I could say would prevent her, though her face isn't the right shape. A little round face with small features is all right shingled, rather pretty and boyish—but Joan's long chin and long nose, well, well—however, she's in great spirits. You knew, of course, that the Bucklers had some money left them—yes, isn't it nice?—and they're wintering in Italy! Well, they've had the good fortune to let Lucknow, a really good let Mrs. Buckler told me, to people called Beatson, a brother and sister, and the brother writes and the sister paints! You can imagine how pleased Joan is! She's just been panting for some one like that to be friends with. I think myself they're rather peculiar-looking, almost Jewish, and Joan says they're modern of the moderns, and I can't say that appeals to me either, but you can't have everything, and Joan thinks she's found kindred spirits and I'm glad to see her pleased. . . . Well, I needn't tell you I'm glad to see you back, and I'm not the only one; we've missed you terribly. Mrs. Lambert was just saying to me that she woke so cheery the other morning and couldn't think why till she remembered that you were expected back."

"How are the Lamberts?" Nicole asked. "I heard they were having a good holiday."

"Yes, and they're well, and settled down to their winter's work. Have you heard anything of Miss Symington—Mrs. Innes, I should say."

"I had one letter," said Nicole, "from North Berwick, where they had gone as a family."

"Ah, but I've seen her," said Mrs. Heggie triumphantly. "I met her in Princes Street one day last week. How she has changed."

"Changed?" said Lady Jane. "In looks or what?"

"Looks and everything. She's very well dressed now, and carries herself with such assurance. I used to try to be kind to her when she was Miss Symington and so dowdy and uninteresting, but I was quite amused at the way she condescended to me when I met her. Oh, Mrs. Innes is very well pleased with herself, I can tell you. And how is the other bride, Miss Barbara?"

"Most flourishing," said Nicole, and laughed, as if at something she had remembered. "We've just come from visiting her. Barbara had always a genius for managing a house, and she has everything perfect. I wish you had been with us, Mrs. Heggie, you are so appreciative about nicely-cooked food and pretty table appointments, and everything as it should be. And Andrew got her some lovely clothes in Paris, and she is looking so well, an absolute model of a young wife in every way. Isn't that so, Mother?"

"Quite so," said Lady Jane. "It is all most satisfactory."

"Well, I'm glad," Mrs. Heggie said, as she rose to go. "Here we are beginning another winter, and it seems no time since last October when we were all wondering about you. A lot has happened too. I don't mind pleasant changes like people getting married, but I'll always regret poor young Mr. Beckett, and you saw such a lot of him; it must be a sad loss to you. . . ."

It was a night or two later, about six in the evening.

Nicole was playing with the Bat, his good-night game. He had a regular performance which he went through every evening. He had tea in the drawing-room, after which he switched on the lights. Then came a story from Lady Jane either read or told, and a game with Nicole, a quiet game it was supposed to be, but even Halma or Tiddley-winks can be made quite exciting played with spirit.

"Now then," said Nicole, "you've beaten me fairly. Put away the table, Gentle Annie will be here in a minute."

Alastair groaned. "I wish it never came night. Why can't it always be morning?"

Nicole laughed. "Everybody hasn't your passion for early rising, my Bat-like one. In fact I think it would be rather a good plan in winter if we only rose twice a week."

"Now, that," said Lady Jane, looking up from the letter she was trying to write, "is a really attractive idea. Rise, say, on Mondays and Fridays."

"Yes," said Nicole, "and the rest of the time we would lie in bed and nourish ourselves with water-biscuits, because, of course, there would be nobody up to light fires or cook. What a lot we would save in coals and light and food and clothes!"

Her mother protested. "Look at the child's face! Don't send him to bed with such a nightmare thought. Here is Annie. Run along, darling, the sooner you fall asleep, the sooner morning will come."

"But it's so jolly here," Alastair sighed. "I've got six whole pennies in my pocket, Aunt Jane." He jingled them for her benefit, and added meditatively: "Jackie Coogan, poor fellow, is so rich that he can't carry his pennies in his trouser-pockets."

He looked seriously into Lady Jane's face, and she bent down and kissed him, saying, "Yes, but even boys with six whole pennies must go to bed. I'll be up to say good-night."

Alastair caught Nicole's hand. "Come and see me bathed."

"All right, but run now. I'll be up before your dressing-gown's on."

The bath over, and Alastair safely tucked up and kissed and blessed, Nicole said to her mother as they came downstairs together:

"Poor little Bat, though he sleeps like a top the night seems endless to him, dividing him from another happy day. I can remember too feeling that sleep was a terrible waste of time."

They entered the drawing-room and found that the careful Christina had tidied away all traces of Alastair's play, and made the fire bright, and laid the papers and the letters from the evening post on the bureau. The curtains were not drawn, for she knew Nicole's love for the lights on the sea-front. The two women sat down together by the fire still talking of the child that they had taken into their keeping.

"Arthur is keen that he should go to his own old school beside Barnabas," Nicole said. "He told me very seriously that he and Barnabas thought highly of the Bat, and believed that Evelyn's would be the very place for him. It's the child's courage that impresses them. They're afraid but make themselves do things, but the Bat doesn't seem to know what fear is. And no matter how much he has hurt himself he only grins, so Arthur tells me. Miss Symington had no good to tell of his parents, and it is difficult to understand how the unstable David Symington and his impudent war-flapper of a wife could have produced such a grave, fearless little spirit. He must be a hark-back to some remote ancestor, probably a Covenanter. Now that I think of it, the way the Bat has held on to the fact that he's a Liberal in the face of all the arguments and persuasions of Arthur and Barnabas, whom he so admires and desires to please, shows quite the covenanting spirit! 'If I had money,' I heard him say one day, 'I'd buy the House of Commons and fill it full of Liberals.' Arthur intimated rather coarsely that he was going to be sick. . . . Yes, the Bat's a big extra. Simon's little Bat."

"I've been wondering," said Lady Jane in a little, "what we ought to do this winter. Shall we go abroad after Christmas? The only thing is that neither of us care for the noisy, smart places, and the quiet places are so full of unattached women. It's quite all right for me, but not much fun for a girl like you."

"Oh, I don't know. At present I'm taking what almost amounts to a morbid interest in unattached women. I look at all the spinsters that I meet and wonder what story attaches to each. What a lot of different types there are! I like best the solid, quiet, dependable ones—those the world simply couldn't do without. The worst type is the persistently bright and vivacious, the arch old-young women who hint at many sighing lovers in the past. If ever you see me getting like that, Mother, for any favour stop me. But I've got about fifteen years to study the art of becoming the perfect spinster—you're not really a spinster till you're about forty in these days, are you? I may learn to wear my rue with a difference!"

"Ah, my darling, don't talk like that. Time heals. You can't tell now what you may feel later on. . . ."

Nicole shook her head. "It's not a thing to talk about, but one knows oneself. When I saw Simon's name, and '*dead*,' something seemed to snap. It's absurd, of course, to talk of broken hearts—perfectly healthy normal people's hearts don't break —but all the same something finishes. I don't believe that if you had been twenty-four instead of fifty-four when Father died that it would have made the slightest difference. We're born steadfast, you and I. It's not a thing to be either proud of or to

194

deplore. It just happens so. I'm not going to pose as any sort of a heroine. After all, the love between a man and a woman isn't the only thing in life by any means. I must fill my life with other things, that's all. What would you like best to do this winter?"

"I want to do just what you want."

"Mother, if it is ever my painful privilege to write your epitaph, d'you know what I'll put? *She never made a fuss.* And I can't imagine a nicer thing to have said about one."

Lady Jane smiled rather sadly as she picked up her work and said, "Ah, my dear, my life is finished, and it has been a very good one, but I can't bear to think that you . . ."

Nicole left the armchair in which she had been sitting, and curled up on the rug beside her mother.

"Honestly, Mother, I don't need pity. They were pretty bad, these endless summer days when beauty was everywhere and I walked alone in desolate places. I was bitter and broken, and there seemed nothing ahead but the same dry misery, but gradually I began to realise things a little. Simon has gone on ahead and I'm left, but he's still my Simon. Sometimes I feel rather like a sentry waiting for the dawn. It isn't, you know, as if we could give our souls their discharge. We've got to stand steady through the night, and fortunately, fortunately, Mums, the night is not without stars. It's a wonderful world for compensations. I couldn't live if I were always sad—*Werena ma hert licht I wad dee!* D'you remember how angry I used to make Barbara with my stupid gladness? Well, that sort of fizzy light-heartedness is gone, but I'm acquiring a sort of still happiness which is probably more enduring. I'd be the most ungrateful being on earth if I moped and whined when I've so much to be thankful for."

Lady Jane laid her hand on her daughter's head.

"My darling, you make me very thankful too. I never spoke, but I knew how hard these past months were for you, and now to hear you say that you can still be happy . . ." She stopped, and then said slowly, as if the words were coming back to her one by one. "*To the supremely happy man all times are times of thanksgiving, deep, tranquil and abundant for the delight, the majesty and the beauty of the fullness of this rolling world.*"

Nicole nodded. "Yes, all times are times of thanksgiving—and everything is in its proper place. And if the square peg is in a round hole it's for some good reason."

"And what is your proper place, my Nikky?"

Nicole looked up at her mother and smiled her impish smile.

"Where I am, of course," she said. "And very nice too!"

Printed in the USA
CPSIA information can be obtained
at www.ICGtesting.com
LVHW090044141123
763821LV00002B/354